SURF'S UP!

☆Look!!!☆ hollered Roaring☆Hot☆Vermillion.

◊Where?◊ replied Clear◊White◊Whistle, searching the ocean around it with sonar pings generated by its multiton fluid body. ◊I see nothing.◊

☆I didn't say "see"! I said "look"! Up in the nothing near Sky⊗Rock!☆

Clear◊White◊Whistle quickly formed an eye out of its amorphous jelly-like substance and used it to look upward into the waterless void above the ocean, where its sonar was nearly useless for seeing things. It adjusted the shape of the gelatine sphere into a crude lens until the heavens blossomed with hundreds of tiny pinpoints of light. A new light was now in the sky. It varied rapidly in brightness and moved away from the Hot-limed side of the rocky planetoid above them, toward an approaching moon-sized silvery ellipse.

◊It is the rocket of the humans. They are leaving Sky⊗Rock to return to their circle in the sky that flies in the light of Hot.◊

☆That means the humans didn't foam out while surfing the Big⊗Bloop to Sky⊗Rock. Say! I feel another wave coming!☆

◊I wonder if they'll ever come back . . . ◊

☆Maybe they will. Maybe they won't. But until they do . . . LET'S GO SURFING!☆

by

ROBERT L. FORWARD
&
JULIE FORWARD FULLER

RETURN TO ROCHEWORLD

This is a work of fiction. All the characters and events portrayed in this book are fictional, and any resemblance to real people or incidents is purely coincidental.

A Baen Books Original

Baen Publishing Enterprises
P.O. Box 1403
Riverdale, NY 10471

ISBN: 0-671-72153-4

Cover art by David Mattingly

First printing, February 1993

Distributed by
SIMON & SCHUSTER
1230 Avenue of the Americas
New York, NY 10020

Typeset by Windhaven Press, Auburn, NH
Printed in the United States of America

ACKNOWLEDGMENTS

The authors wish to thank the following people, who helped us in several technical areas: Dana Andrews, Paul L. Blass, Carl Richard Feynman, Charles W. Fuller, David K. Lynch, Patrick L. McGuire, Hans P. Moravec, Jef Poskanzer, Daniel G. Shapiro, Vernor Vinge, and Mark Zimmermann.

The "Christmas Bush" motile was jointly conceived by Hans P. Moravec and Robert L. Forward, and drawn by Jef Poskanzer using a CAD system.

All final art was expertly prepared by the great group of graphic artists at Multi-Graphics in Marina Del Ray, California.

• CHAPTER ZERO—LEAVING

The crew of the first interstellar expedition had already experienced its share of troubles: opposition, discord, mutiny, treachery, pestilence, and death. Now, six of them were in a race for their lives. . . .

Barnard, the star they had come to visit, loomed large and red on the horizon, its disk five times larger than that of Sol. But even though they were now very close to the red dwarf star, its dim red light did little to warm the sub-zero poisonous atmosphere outside their crippled aerospace plane. They were now gliding through the thin ammonia-laden air over the dry cratered surface of the moon-sized planetoid Roche—one lobe of the double planet Rocheworld. Behind them, hanging motionless in the sky and covering almost ninety degrees of the sky, was the other lobe, Eau, covered with a deep ammonia-water ocean. Far off in the distance was the only other planet orbiting Barnard, the large gas giant Gargantua, with its retinue of twelve moons.

The two lobes of Rocheworld orbited around each other with a period of six hours. The centrifugal force from this co-rotation was enough to keep their mutual gravity from pulling them together, but the tides from their close proximity were so strong that they pulled the two planetoids into distinct egg shapes, with the two pointed ends separated by only eighty kilometers distance.

The pointed part of Roche was a region of giant volcanoes and deep fissures. The volcanoes were now in full eruption because of the greatly increased tidal strains on the crust from the close approach of Rocheworld to

Barnard during this part of its highly elliptical orbit. The pointed part of Eau was a one-hundred-fifty-kilometer-high mountain of water with sixty-degree slopes, held that way by the unusual gravity field pattern produced in the region between the two massive planetoids. Although Roche was dry during most of its short year, this was the flood season, and there was now plenty of water, a veritable wall of water that had come from a gigantic waterfall that occurred once a year during the time of close passage—an interplanetary waterfall from the top of the water mountain of Eau onto the volcano covered dome of Roche.

Ahead of the wall of water raced an airplane, striving to reach the return rocket before the wall of water got there. Designed to fly in any atmosphere, the aerospace plane had a nuclear rocket in the tail for long-range flights, and VTOL fans in its long, glider-like wings for hovering. But the rocket engine had failed and the fans were damaged. The only thing keeping them in the air was the skill of their pilot, Arielle Trudeau.

Arielle made one tiny adjustment to the controls, tightened her seat belt and shoulder harness, then put her hands into her lap, allowing the semi-intelligent computer of the airplane to act as autopilot during their long preprogrammed glide. She turned to look at George Gudunov out of her helmet, her glowing personal imp arranged across her short curly light-brown locks in a combined hairpiece and pilot earphones.

"We have hard landing," she reminded him.

"And just ten minutes to get the six of us up the side of the lander," George said as he tightened his seat belt and held a conversation with chief engineer Shirley Everett through the colorful robotic imp riding on his shoulder inside his spacesuit.

"You four get into the exit lock and cycle it, but don't open the outer door until we've stopped moving. Put your backs to the front wall and take some bedding to protect your helmets. Jinjur will never forgive us if we add anyone to her butcher bill."

"Are you and Arielle going to have time to cycle through? We could cram in six."

"You forget someone has to land this thing, and I'm not leaving Arielle up here all alone. The minute we stop I'm blowing the front canopy and Arielle and I will go out over the nose. Carmen! Are you monitoring?"

"Yes," Carmen Cortez replied from the rocket lander at Rocheworld Base.

"Is the winch on the lander down?"

"Yes," came the voice of Red Vengeance over the radio link from the lander. "Ready and waiting. Hurry up!"

"I see the bore on the scanner video, it's gaining on us," said Richard Redwing from the science console halfway down the aisle of the plane.

"Give us a last reading on time difference, then get in that airlock!" commanded George.

"Eleven minutes," interrupted the distinctive voice of the airplane's semi-intelligent computer, Jill. "Get into the airlock, Richard," it bossed. Richard obeyed the computer and trotted to the rear of the plane and the lock door closed behind him. George and Arielle were left with the hiss of air passing over the silent airplane and the distant throb of airlock pumps going through their motions on almost non-existent air. George could now see the rocket lander, sticking up forty-five meters into the air, its dark outline just to one side of the setting globe of Barnard.

"Bad luck," complained George. "We're flying right into the sun."

"No! It's good!" said Arielle. "I can now see rocks easy because of their big shadow." She banked the plane slightly to pick a path that was relatively clear of boulders and gave up the last of her altitude for speed.

"BRACE YOURSELF!" screamed Jill to everyone but Arielle through their suit imps. Arielle pulled the plane up into a stall.

"Flaps!" she commanded, both her hands busy, one with the airplane controls and the other operating the fans at full reverse thrust. George pushed at the flap controls but found that they were already moving.

"Flaps, down," he and Jill said at the same time. The plane started to drop heavily to the surface, but Arielle dipped it just enough to bring it under control again, the forward speed almost gone, and slid the plane through the sand directly at the lander.

We're going to hit! thought George, his voice too tight to speak.

Arielle wrenched the rudder around at the same time as she twisted the fan controls. The *Magic Dragonfly* went into a broadside slide and came to a stop with its nose on one side of the lander and the left wing on the other, not ten meters from the legs of the lander.

"I made ringer, George!" shouted Arielle with delight.

"BLOW THE HATCH!" came Jill's sharp command in George's ear. His thumb flipped up the safety cover, but his suit imp, running rapidly down his arm, beat his gloved finger to the switch. There was a loud BANG! and the cockpit windows flew into the air. The ammonia-methane atmosphere rushed into the plane and there was a dull THUMP! as the inflowing gases burned with the residual air in the plane. George clambered out on the nose and jumped to the surface, then turned to catch Arielle. Together they hurried toward the distant lander. Jill, her voice turned into that of a martinet, drove them with verbal whiplashes broadcast through their personal imps.

"Shirley, Richard, Katrina, David—to the winch.

"George, Arielle—up the ladder.

"Red, start the winch and get them up and in!

"Move it, George!

"Arielle is way ahead of you!

"Move it, you fat old man!"

George found another source of adrenaline in his anger and he sprinted harder for the ladder. Arielle ran lightly up the rungs on the landing legs without using her hands, then when she reached the main body of the lander, crouched and leaped up the side of the rocket in the low gravity, then continued on, hand-over-hand, her legs dangling. George knew he couldn't do that, and scrambled after her. He got up the landing leg and paused to look up at Arielle.

"No sightseeing! Move it! Move it!!! Move it!!!"

Jill's voice took on a harsh tone that sent George back to his first week in ROTC summer camp under the tender ministrations of a drill instructor. Fear and hatred drove him up the ladder. He could see the wall of water coming over the horizon to his left, its foaming top colored blood-red in the setting sunlight. The water was swallowing the kilometers-long shadow of the lander as George clambered into the airlock filled with Red Vengeance and the five others from the airplane.

"I've got the winch stored," said Red. "Shut the outer door."

George was nearest the door and started to close it. He stopped. With him in the lock, there was no room for the door to close, and no time left to cycle the lock. He stepped back out onto the top rung of the ladder.

"George!!!" shouted Red, as George pulled the door shut behind him. "Nooooo..." she wailed as he pushed the door lever over and locked himself outside.

"Take off, Thomas!!! That's an order!" said George through his imp.

The ten-meter-high wall of water hit the base of the rocket and it started to tip.

"Got to go!" said Thomas.

The atmosphere around George was ablaze with flame as the ascent module stage lifted from the top of the falling rocket and boosted into the sky. George's feet slipped from the rung and he was left hanging by the inadequate grasp of his sausage-fingered gloves. As the acceleration built up he found his left hand slipping from the vertical handhold. He grabbed for the horizontal ladder rung and got it, but that cost him his right handhold on the door lever. Dangling by one hand from the bottom of the accelerating spacecraft, he was blinded, deafened, and burned by the exhaust from the powerful rocket engine. He felt the suit cooling shift to maximum power to prevent his legs from frying in the intense heat. He tried to get his right hand up to the ladder rung, but couldn't do it. They hit max-Q and the supersonic blast was finally too much. His fingers slipped off the rung and he fell through the flaming exhaust toward the distant ground below. He was still moving upward, coasting on the momentum of the rocket that had left him behind. He came to the peak of his trajectory and started to fall.

Time seemed to stop. George found that he had automatically assumed the spread-eagle position he'd learned when skydiving, only this time he didn't have a parachute. He felt a faint twinge of regret. Regret that he would never again see Jinjur and Red and the others again. George felt cheated. There was so much more he wanted to do on this world. There was so much more to be learned from the intelligent alien flouwen they had found in the oceans of Eau. Then there were all the moons of Gargantua to explore. Well . . . he had made it to Barnard alive and had fun exploring at least one world.

We all have to go sometime, he said to himself. *Might as well get this over with*. He pulled in his arms from the spread-eagle position and dove headfirst for the ground.

"NO! GEORGE! NO!" screamed Red's voice over his suit imp.

George rapidly resumed the spread-eagle position and looked around. The ascent module had turned in a big circle and was now rising up from underneath to meet him! As it came closer he could see Thomas St. Thomas's grinning brown face peering up at him through the triangular docking windows in the cockpit deck. The entry port at the top of the spacecraft was open. Reaching up from the lock was a slender, space-suited figure. She had a long lanyard, but it wasn't needed. Thomas swooped the rocket up underneath George and scooped him right into Red's arms.

"I always was the best one on the block at the ball-and-cup game," Thomas bragged.

George felt the acceleration increase as Red dragged him into the lock and the air cycle started.

"I nearly lost you!" said Red as she took off his helmet. Tears were streaming down her face and into her suit. George started to cry too. He put his arms around her and tried to give her a comforting hug, but the suits got in the way. When Sam Houston got the inner airlock door open he found them nuzzling each other's faces, both wet with tears.

With his suit off and holding Red by the hand, George joined the rest of the crew in the view lounge as they floated at the L-4 point of the rotating double planet, waiting for *Prometheus* to arrive. Arielle was at the telescope, tracking the fractured cross of duralloy that used to be the *Magic Dragonfly* as it was being borne off by the waves, the wing tips crumbling as they were dashed against boulders and tumbling rocks.

"Goodbye, Jill," she cried, her voice breaking.

"Arielle, dear," said Jill's voice through her imp. "I'm still here. You must remember that these voices we computers use are just to aid you in identifying which computer is talking to you."

As it spoke, the voice changed slowly from the overtones of Jill to the overtones of Jack, the voice persona for the rocket lander. It then switched to that of James, the main computer on their lightcraft *Prometheus*, who in his most butlerish voice continued to drive in the lesson as its voice changed to that of a tinny robot. "It is very important that you realize that we are nothing but robots."

"You right," agreed Arielle. "I am silly to cry over computers." Then she burst into tears again.

"What's the matter now, Arielle?" said George.

"My *Dragonfly* was such a pretty plane, and now she is all broke!"

"We've got three more dragonflies for you," said George reassuringly. "And you have all the rest of your life to fly in them."

"Here comes *Prometheus* to pick us up," said Sam, peering out the side of the viewport window as the lightcraft pilot Tony Roma manipulated the three-hundred-kilometer-diameter lightsail in the weak red photon wind of Barnard. The lightcraft had sailed from the Solar System to Barnard at twenty percent of the speed of light, pushed by a powerful beam of laser light. Here in the Barnard planetary system, however, the lightsail was limited to much lower velocities by the weak light flux from the small red star.

Hanging from the center of the aluminum foil moon was their home away from home—a sixty-six-meter-high, twenty-meter-diameter combination hotel and office building, complete with parking garage. At one end were five decks for working and living, at the other end were two decks for storage and engineering, and in the middle was the docking area for four large rocket landers, nestled upside-down around a central shaft. There was a gap that had previously held the lander they had used to visit Rocheworld. Three landers still remained.

"C'mon, Red," said Thomas. "Time to fly what's left of this lander back to its dock."

The rockets on the ascent propulsion stage brightened again as it moved off to join up with the approaching sailcraft and unite the ten explorers with the nine fellow crew members they had left behind in space.

☆Look!!!☆ hollered Roaring☆Hot☆Vermilion.

◊Where?◊ replied Clear◊White◊Whistle, searching the ocean around it with sonar pings generated by its multiton fluid body. ◊I see nothing.◊

☆I didn't say "see"! I said "look"! Up in the nothing near Sky⊗Rock!☆

Clear◊White◊Whistle quickly formed an eye out of its

amorphous jelly-like body and used the eye to look upward into the waterless void above the ocean, where its sonar was useless for seeing things. It adjusted the shape of the gelatine sphere into a crude lens until the heavens blossomed with hundreds of tiny pinpoints of light. There was a new light in the sky. It varied rapidly in brightness and moved away from the Hot-limed side of the rocky planetoid above them toward an approaching moon-sized silver ellipse.

◊It is the rocket of the humans. They are leaving Sky⊗Rock to return to their circle in the sky that flies in the light of Hot.◊

☆That means the humans didn't foam out while surfing the Big⊗Bloop to Sky⊗Rock. Say! I feel another wave coming!☆

◊I wonder if they'll ever come back . . . ◊

☆Maybe they will. Maybe they won't. But until they do . . . LET'S GO SURFING!☆

• CHAPTER ONE—REGROUPING

"All the leaves are brown ... and the skies are gray ... "

The song's minor harmonies echoed in roundelay through the glittering imp-phones that held down Cinnamon Byrd's long black braids even as she floated around the leviponics lab. Not that any brown leaves were ever allowed in the long rows of tomato plants that hung throughout the hydroponics "field," their bare roots wet with nutrient spray. Nels had often teasingly accused her of using Aleut magic to sense when the plants were not doing as well as they should, and nipping the problem, quite literally, in the bud. As Cinnamon passed through the tall rows of verdant growth, her long brown fingers lightly stroked the leaves. Almost absentmindedly, she adjusted the nutrient mixture, adding a touch of iron here, a bit more aeration there, fine-tuning the artificial ecosystem. She had only called up the ancient song to complement the unsettled atmosphere that prevailed on the hydroponics deck of the lightsail spacecraft, *Prometheus*.

The ascent stage of the lander rocket *Eagle* had left the Roche lobe of the double-lobed planet Rocheworld, and was now heading back safely to *Prometheus*, but despite the dramatic escape of the landing party, Cinnamon could sense unhappiness in some of her friends. Her good friend on the landing party, Carmen Cortez, had not tried to contact her in days, apparently devoting all her time to either manning her twelve-hour shift at the *Eagle*'s communications center, or asleep in her tiny bunk on the crowded lander. Although Carmen was right in the middle of mankind's first encounter with intelligent aliens, she was taking little interest in the astounding discoveries those on the planet had made and she had showed no desire to talk over the remarkable events with her closest friend.

Closer to home, Nels Larson was also out of sorts. Cinnamon watched his disproportionate but oddly efficient form propel itself from one side of the hydroponics deck to the other as he collected various delicacies from the closely growing plants. Long association with the levibotanist let her see the hidden frustration that colored his movements. Cinnamon knew that her boss was furious that the explorers were not bringing back the tiny sample of alien body tissue that had been given to them by the large white alien. Katrina Kauffmann, the biochemist who was on the surface, had explained that the little white blob had acted more like a young individual than like a tissue sample. Fearful of damaging the new relationship with the aliens, she had returned the squealing blob to its progenitor. When the obliging aliens, or "flouwen" as the computer had named them, later showed the humans their true method of reproduction, Katrina's fears were proved groundless. Now, although Nels would not discuss it, Cinnamon knew he was trying to think of the best way to make sure that such mistakes would not be repeated. Cinnamon moved on to the corridor that contained the fish tanks, long tubes of flowing water containing trout and catfish of varying sizes. The largest trout would soon be ready to harvest and be the centerpiece of a few real-meat special dinners for a few lucky members of the crew.

Nels ignored Cinnamon's singing. He had long ago gotten used to her habit of dredging up obsolete songs to while the time away. Nels did not intend to let another chance to study the strange new alien life-form slip by. True, the main reason that he had been included on the mission was to provide the crew with nutritious, appetizing food for their one-way mission to the stars. But no one had really expected that they would discover intelligent life! Surely no one on board knew more about genetics and life on a microscopic level than he did. He intended to ask the commander, Major General "Jinjur" Jones, to allow him to go to the surface of Eau during their return visit to Rocheworld. Unfortunately, the stocky black woman was first and foremost a Marine, and Nels had felt from her the same contempt for deformity that so many of the very physically fit seemed to have. It was as if she thought that he could have developed proper legs if only he had shown more discipline. He knew that it would take some persuasion before Jinjur would allow her intellect to overpower her prejudice.

Nels left Cinnamon on the hydroponics deck and dove down the sailcraft's long central shaft toward the galley. To gain speed in the nearly free-fall environment, he used the handholds on the side of the shaft to pull himself along with his long, muscular arms. Broad shouldered and burly, Nels would have been a tall man, had his legs not ended as soon as they had begun. Just below his hips, Nels had small flipper-like feet with long, nailess toes. Constant exercise of the malformed digits made them strong, almost prehensile, and he was able to use them to carry the special delicacies he had just harvested. The heroes would be arriving soon and a party was in order.

Nels had cut ruthlessly into the tissue cultures "Chicken Little," "Ferdinand," and "Hamlet" that supplied the real-meat chicken, beef, and pork rations for the nineteen astronauts on *Prometheus*. He had also collected all the fruits and vegetables that were ripe enough to harvest. There were fresh strawberries, melons heavy with juice, baby carrots, cherry tomatoes, and mushroom buttons for crisp finger foods, and spinach and endive for salad. These delicacies would normally be used only to cut through the blandness of their standard algae-paste food diet. Although the fast-growing algae food was nutritionally adequate and consisted of many different varieties that were subtly flavored to mimic a variety of foods, the algae was the butt of many crude jokes among the crew. To a man, they looked forward to their infrequent allotment of "real" food.

Now, the rest of the crew who had stayed behind on *Prometheus* had gone without these special treats for days so that there would be plenty for the welcome-home party. Nels had even managed to procure some of Cinnamon's jealously guarded fish roe, so he could make a caviar appetizer. All this was in Nels's favor. He intended to have the General sated before he tackled her about his being assigned to the landing party for the return to Rocheworld.

Once in the galley, Nels prepared the feast. Nels got special joy in these last few moments of the foods' preparation. He had designed most of these foods, and in many cases had personally crafted their very DNA. He had watched as the cells first started to mature and multiply; coaxed their growth with the mediums that they craved. He had nourished them throughout their lives and now he had harvested and cooked them, seasoning them to perfection. He insisted on their having the proper presentation.

Nels talked to the ship's computer through his robotic imp, riding in its usual position on his left shoulder.

"James? Could you please send the Christmas Bush down to the galley to help prepare for the party? Have it bring the special set of party platters I have stored in the top deck."

Within a few minutes, the spiny, sparkling motile with its multicolored laser lights joined him in the galley. The complete bush-shaped robot had a six-armed main body, each of the six arms dividing again into six smaller arms, and so on, until the motile was surrounded with a final brush of tiny cilia. But since it was also the repair and maintenance motile for the entire ship, and the hands for James, the ship's computer, the Christmas Bush was rarely in its complete form. The robot structure was designed to separate into smaller parts that were miniatures of itself. Each of these smaller Christmas "branches" or "twigs" or "imps" or "mosquitoes" could act as separate motiles. The smallest ones could even fly by rapidly vibrating the tiny cilia at the ends of their limbs. These smaller motiles could do practically anything, such as monitoring the health of each crew member, repairing equipment, picking up microscopic bits of dust, weaving new clothing, taking dull scientific data, compounding medicines, brewing beer, and manufacturing semiconductor chips.

The flickers of colored light that illuminated the robot and gave it its name were really lasers that let each segment communicate with the rest of the motile and with the ship's computer. It was, in fact, small subsets from the Christmas Bush that made up the multicolored twinkling imps that accompanied each of the crew members, who had the flexible imps form whatever shape they found most convenient.

Once in the galley, the Christmas Bush separated into dozens of small hands that began helping Nels prepare the meal for the party. They followed his lead as he arranged the food onto numerous plates and bowls in a myriad of shapes, colors and sizes. The computer understood that to Nels, this was more that just a meal—this was art. Thin strips of beef were impaled on metal skewers and doused with soy sauce and spices to make teriyaki beef. Chicken chunks were breaded with crumbs and deep fried in perma oil into golden brown nuggets. Thin strips of ham were wrapped around ripe slices of melon.

Listening through his imp, Nels heard the exuberant greetings of the others as the small ascent module floated in between the shrouds of *Prometheus* and docked at its airlock set in the ceiling of one of the corridors of his hydroponics deck. Jinjur's deep throaty voice was audible above the babble of the others as she greeted the leader of the away-team.

"That's the last time I give you an airplane to play with, George!" she scolded playfully. "You're too hard on your toys!"

The sounds of revelry became louder and switched to reality as the entire crew poured down the shaft and into the lounge and dining area. Red, George, and Thomas were being carried through the lounge, their heads lightly bumping against the low ceiling in the fractional gravity. As Nels understood it, it had been the stunning redhead's fast thinking and the superb flying ability of the handsome Jamaican that had saved the most senior member of the crew.

Nels was glad he had managed to perfect the banana-flavored algae. Frying it in small slice-size patties along with some of the fresh trout from Cinnamon's tanks, he had managed a platter filled with spicy West Indian-flavored delicacies as a special treat for Thomas. Most of the herbs he used were fresh from their beds on the hydroponics deck. Although James could synthesize the chemicals for any spice, Nels had stockpiled supplies of such spices as pepper, nutmeg, and cloves for such special occasions when Nels wanted to give the astronauts the true tastes of Earth. The varied crew on *Prometheus* had such eclectic tastes that alongside the sandwiches made of dark pumpernickel-flavored algaebread spread with liverwurst made from the tissue culture Paté LaBelle, was bratwurst made from the tissue culture Hamlet, curried lamb from Lambchop, and catfish with hush puppies made from cornmeal-flavored algaeflour. Nels had a bumper crop of string beans, and he had the sense to add nothing to the freshly steamed vegetable but a little algaebutter. The thin finger-long *haricots verts* were a perfect fingerfood.

One thing that Nels had to let James synthesize was the wine and other beverages. Still, the computer managed to plan ahead, and there were dozens of squeeze bulbs in evidence filled with red wine and white, champagne, various beers, soft drinks, and mixers, and even quality gin, bourbon, scotch, and brandy. One of the parting gifts to the astronauts from a grateful Earth had been the sharing with James of the last truly secret recipe of the twenty-first century, so that the crew could enjoy the true flavor of Coca-Cola on their long journey to the stars. Richard Redwing was hardly ever seen without a squeeze bulb of the bubbling beverage. Nels considered the brown liquid an assault on the palate, but he had to admit that coffee cool enough to be sipped from a floating ball of liquid in zero gee was too cold to be satisfying.

As the party started, Nels was swept up in their gleeful enjoyment of the delicacies. While he relished their praise, and their obvious enjoyment of his carefully crafted meal, it always amazed him how weeks, even months of work, could vanish so speedily down a human throat. Arielle Trudeau, the pilot who had been a beauty queen in Quebec before the province's secession from Canada and the absorption of the rest of Canada into the Greater United States of America, always managed to eat huge amounts without letting it affect her figure or her appetite. Although she had had a front tooth knocked out during the crash that had damaged the *Dragonfly*'s engines, a subsection of Arielle's imp now acted as a brace to hold her healing tooth in place. The brace-imp glittered from between her lips as she opened her mouth to eat a mushroom skewered on a toothpick imp and dipped in a warm pseudocream sauce spiced with dill and thyme. Arielle sucked the imp toothpick clean and then let the tiny robot fly its way back to the kitchen, where it washed itself and then attached itself to a larger branch that was preparing the next platters of food. Before she had even swallowed the mushroom, she was already reaching for the pastel balls of melon that Nels had scooped from the honeydew and cantaloupe.

Shirley Everett, the tall blond California "surfer girl" and Chief Engineer, seemed to be collecting some of the cold fresh fruits and the treats made of chipped beef rolled around pseudocream cheese and horseradish sauce, for her to enjoy at leisure later. Richard Redwing was also eating with more speed than relish, washing down each bite with a swallow of soda. He never seemed to realize that the food was for more than maintaining his muscular physique. Nels tried to remind himself how much worse it would be if they didn't like his cooking, and instead tried to avoid looking at anyone who was actually eating. To his surprise he found himself watching Carmen Cortez. Usually Carmen was the most flattering and most ravenous member of the crew.

Carmen had been a last minute addition to the crew, a curvaceous señorita. At first she was the most fun-loving and free-loving girl on the ship. The youngest woman on board, she was the sort of wide-eyed ingenue who seemed like an innocent even while she was showing off the kinkiest moves in her varied sexual repertoire. She was so pretty and vivacious that all the men had vied for her attention, but they needn't have competed; she readily acquiesced to each one of their attempts at seduction. Even as the crew slowly succumbed to the sexually and intellectually debilitating effects of the drug No-Die in order to slow their aging for their forty-year journey to the stars, Carmen had done her best to keep the hormone levels hopping. But it was as the crew first started coming off No-Die, and their intelligence and interests caught back up to their ages, that Nels first noticed a change in the tiny woman.

Carmen had begun to eat. She ate anything and everything. She was fast friends with Cinnamon, and samples of Nels' experiments were always available to her. Carmen soon looked like a tennis ball with dark curls and flashing eyes. Her admirers vanished along with her figure, and soon her good humor vanished as well. Nels could sympathize with her. He knew only too well how it felt to know that your appearance repulsed people. To have been a social lioness thanks to your beauty and then lose it must be equally hard.

Now, for some reason, Carmen was eating none of his wonderful banquet. It wasn't as if this was algae gruel; this was fresh fruit, crisp vegetables, and real meat! He made a mental note to tell John Kennedy about it. As their acting doctor, John would want to make sure that she wasn't coming down with something. Maybe that was what Carmen wanted anyway—the handsome nurse took after his presidential namesake in both appearance and temperament, and so made a habit of seducing all his patients. In fact, he made a habit of attempting to seduce any women that he was left alone with for two minutes. Even as Nels watched, John was doing his best to corner Cinnamon. Somehow, he had trapped her behind a floating ball of champagne and was trying to convince her to help him drink it before it drifted to the floor in the low acceleration. No . . . there . . . she managed to distract him and duck out of the room. Now, John had his arm around Katrina and was using her "welcome home" hug to cop a feel. Reiki LeRoux, the anthropologist whose mixed Japanese/Cajun descent gave her what Nels considered the most interesting DNA of all those aboard, was enjoying a slice of Nels's famous home-made bread spread liberally with algaebutter and nothing else. The flour for the bread came from a special line of algae Nels had developed, while the yeast was a strain that had been handed down to Nels from his mother. Nels also used his mother's recipe for making the bread. His mother's bread had been famous throughout all of Goddard Station, and Nels was prepared to bet his bread was the best in the galaxy. Reiki nodded her head toward Nels in acknowledgment of his cooking. She was too polite to embarrass him with open praise.

Nels decided that Cinnamon had the right idea, and slipped off to the hydroponics deck. He hadn't had a chance to talk to Jinjur in the throng, but then, for the whole two-hour feast he hadn't said a word to anyone. Not that anybody, especially not Nels himself, had noticed.

Jinjur, too, had left the party early. She and George were sitting on the control deck planning the next phase of the mission.

"I know we only have three landers left, and more than three moons around Gargantua to study," said George. "But it's vitally important that we go back to Rocheworld." The oldest member of the crew and second in command,

Colonel George Gudunov was respected for more than his gray hairs. He had a Ph.D. in Planetary Atmospheres and had written a number of science fiction stories and popular science articles. He had earned the admiration of everyone but the military. Back in 1998, while still a young captain in the Air Force, George had suggested to his superiors that they test the Air Force Space Laser Forts Project in a non-threatening manner by using their powerful laser beams to push small lightsails carrying robotic interstellar probes. When a number of space laser forts suffered catastrophic failures under this two-day test, George was commended by Congress for exposing the problem, but the military brass never forgave him. They retaliated by keeping him muzzled as a permanent fight instructor until twenty-four years later, when positive reports came in from the fly-by probe sent to Barnard. Promoting him to colonel and sending him off to the stars was the military's final solution to his embarrassing presence, but George had proved his integral worth.

"Those aliens are so far ahead of us in mathematics that we need to set up permanent communication with them," George was insisting.

"But what good is pure mathematics?" said Jinjur.

"It is the key to physics and technology," said George. "At first glance, it would seem that advanced mathematics is just a barren exercise in pure logic and should have no relationship at all to the real world. In fact, our mathematicians go out of their way to design the logic of mathematics so that it isn't contaminated by any rules based on 'common sense.' But, for some reason, the behavior of the real world follows the logic of mathematics and no other logic. If we have a mathematical tool and can calculate something using it, we are pretty sure nature will behave the way the mathematics predicts. But we don't have enough of those mathematical tools, and we know it.

"Astronomers can't calculate the exact motions of two

gravitating bodies except under special conditions. Aerodynamicists can't calculate the exact flow of air over anything except a few simple wing shapes. Weather forecasters can't predict more than a few days ahead. Atomic scientists can't calculate exactly anything more complicated than a hydrogen atom.

"The human race needs that math, and the beauty about math is that unlike being given the secrets to advanced technology, being given advanced mathematics will not stifle the technological creativity of the human race, since *we* will have to figure out how to apply the mathematics."

"Okay," said Jinjur. "But how are we going to get the information out of them? This crew may be pretty smart, but none of us are theoretical mathematicians. We may be able to understand some of the simpler stuff, but after the second and third infinity I know that *I* would be lost."

"What we should do is set up an interstellar laser communicator in the Hawaiian Islands on the Eau Lobe, where their older thinkers stay," said George. "That way the long-lived flouwen could communicate their advanced mathematical knowledge directly back to Earth—even long after you and I and the rest of the crew have fluttered out the last of our mayflylike lives."

"You're getting poetic, George," said Jinjur. "I never knew you had it in you."

George looked pensive for a long moment, eyes staring past her out the control room window. Finally he rose from his seat.

"I better go talk to Carmen and Shirley to see what we can put together that the flouwen can use. The laser should be in a well-sheltered place on land, with a reactor that will keep it going for a few decades until the follow-up expedition gets here. But the operating console will have to be underwater."

"Now just a minute there, George," said Jinjur sternly. "Remember what they told you in officer's training? 'The program isn't finished until the documentation is done.'

You just finished an important and exciting mission, and there are a few billion people back on Earth who are waiting to hear all about it. You've got a report to write!"

Back in the lab, Nels was working on an algae culture he had been trying to develop that would properly imitate a steak. He had perfected the tissue culture "Ferdinand" that produced slices of real veal, but it and the other tissue cultures grew slowly, and the crew was allowed only one small real-meat ration a week. Nels had discovered that by adding the proper amounts of complex carbohydrates to the algae's growing medium, he could manage to duplicate the flavor of beef, but he had yet to manage the proper texture of steak. He could make a good paté from it, but it made a mushy hamburger. The work helped him relax from the noisy party. Cinnamon was singing as she worked around the lab, but Nels didn't pay her any attention. He hardly even heard her singing anymore.

"Rollin', rollin', rollin' . . . keep those dogies rollin' . . . "

Cinnamon had grown up in the small Alaskan town of Chenik, living in a huge barn of a house that was the headquarters for both her father's medical practice and the local radio station. When radio had gone digital back in the '90s, Cinnamon's grandpa had picked up a California station's library and equipment for a song. He was forced to play only the recordings that had come out before the CD boom, but the people in the town were happy with the local station, despite the fact that the musical selections stayed the same and kept falling further and further behind the times. Everywhere Cinnamon had gone in Chenik, somewhere in earshot was a radio tuned to Gramp's station. Even as she slept, old forgotten songs were dancing in her ears. Now songs dredged up from her memories ran through her head . . . and often out through her mouth.

The ship's computer, James, had learned to accommodate the quirk. Cinnamon only needed to sing the first few bars of a song and James would pipe the whole thing privately to her through her earphone-shaped imp. This would let her complete the song and go on to another so that she wouldn't get hooked on a single phrase and keep repeating it until she, or some other crew member, went mad.

Cinnamon's mood had improved. Nels's feast proved to her that he wasn't too upset about not having had a chance to examine the flouwen sample, and better yet, she had seen him eyeing Carmen from across the room. It was Cinnamon's dearest wish that Nels and Carmen would get together . . . although Carmen obstinately refused to cooperate. Carmen had fallen into the habit of making the most blatant sexual advances, yet instantly rejecting any man who attempted to respond to those advances. Cinnamon could almost see Nels cringe at Carmen's outrageous innuendos. Still, maybe what ever was bothering Carmen would keep her from throwing herself at Nels until he was ready to catch her. Cinnamon giggled at the image she'd conjured up . . . good thing they were in near free-fall!

Carmen, meanwhile, was back in her cabin. She was staring at the image on the screen across from her bed. It was a still from one of David Greystoke's sonovideos: an interpretive composite made from the video taken by the exploration crew during the flouwen reproductive act. It showed four flouwen with most of their bodies swirled together into a twisted spiral, like one of those huge lollipops her uncle used to buy for her, even though she had never liked them very much. The colors of the adult flouwen faded out toward the center, leaving a clear, jelly-like mass. In the very middle was a patch of bright blue: the color of the newly created being.

Carmen knew that the still frame was inaccurate. She had seen the original video dozens of times, and the new being did not develop color until the adults had separated from the colorless mass created by their mating. But she liked David's composition; not just for the color and symmetry, but more for what it represented. Life. New life from old. Reproduction. Something she'd never be able to accomplish. Burying her head in her pillow, Carmen cried.

Today was Carmen's birthday, although she had told no one on board about it. She was 72—well, 42, really. You couldn't count the time they had spent under the influence of No-Die. The drug had slowed the rate of aging of the crew by a factor of four, so they only aged ten years during the forty years they had spent coasting at twenty percent of the speed of light from Sol to Barnard. Unfortunately, the drug had also lowered their IQs by an equivalent amount, turning highly intelligent adults into large-bodied pre-schoolers. All Carmen could remember of those years was her frustration at the boys not wanting to play doctor, and at the pain involved when William Wong finally did. She still remembered vividly the time when he poked her in the neck and said to James, "Carmen's got the mumps."

William changed after that, becoming distant and aloof. Then he pulled them all into the sick bay one by one, and gave them the most horrible treatment. It had made her feel weak and nauseated all the time, and her hair fell out. Just when she was starting to feel better, William was gone. Carmen had gone to his room for more of those tickle and kiss games that he, alone, of the men remembered how to play, but he was just lying there, stretched out under the tension sheet on his bed, still and cold, with only the Christmas Bush in attendance. Carmen knew now that William had come out of No-Die in order to treat the crew with chemotherapy to save them from a virus-initiated Hodgkin's cancer that had attacked them all. William had delayed treatment on himself in order to take care of them properly, and when it was his turn, it was too late. Part of her couldn't help but feel guilty for enjoying his adult sexuality while all the rest of the crew were acting like three-year-olds.

Carmen had spent the remainder of the time on No-Die feeling lonely and different. On No-Die, it was obvious that the other crew members were smarter than she was, and without their civilized veneers, they had the heartless cruelty of children. As they started to come back, they would laugh because she had trouble reading, and would not play games with her because they thought beating her was too easy. That was when she first befriended Cinnamon.

Nels was ahead of them all intellectually, and while Jinjur nominally remained in charge throughout the No-Die void, it was Nels who thought up all the best games. Carmen noticed that sometimes he would slip off by himself, so one day she followed him. He went into an apartment Carmen had never been in before. It belonged to Cinnamon Byrd. The viewwall in Cinnamon's apartment was perpetually set on a repetitive video scene that looked like someplace in Alaska, with a wild ocean and snow-covered trees in the foreground, and snowy mountain peaks in the distance. Nels sat making faces at a girl with long black braids, who was just lying there in the apartment sitting room, playing with her toes, and clapping with glee every time a whale breached the ocean in the viewwall scene. Cinnamon would smile and gurgle and coo, but Carmen had never seen her out playing with the others, or coloring, or watching cartoons. Carmen had hardly noticed Cinnamon during the training period before they went on No-Die, and the drug had lowered Cinnamon's mid-level IQ too far for her to interact with the others during the long flight out to Barnard.

Carmen started visiting Cinnamon's quarters regularly, and as they both came back to themselves, Carmen took the other woman under her wing. Before Carmen had relearned to read, she retaught Cinnamon the alphabet. And when Carmen remastered long division, she taught it to Cinnamon. By the time everyone was back in their own ages, Carmen and Cinnamon were inseparable. But however motherly she might feel toward her friend, Carmen was no one's mother, and never would be.

Carmen had grown up Catholic, and even with all the changes Vatican IV brought to the church, "Go forth and multiply" was still the eleventh commandment. William had wanted to sterilize her when she first came on board.

After all, the mission was to study, not to colonize. All the other women had their tubes tied. When Carmen refused, he demurred, saying that since all the men had undergone vasectomies anyway, she was in no danger of becoming pregnant. At first, Carmen thought it was a wonderful sort of freedom to never have to worry about conceiving.

Vatican IV had accepted group marriages and since the whole crew was on this one-way mission to the stars "for better or worse, till death do us part," Carmen had cheerfully submitted to all her new husbands. But now her biological clock had started sounding alarms. This family of adults . . . it wasn't enough. Down there on the surface of Eau those simple alien blobs of jelly could do God's will. They could commingle with a purpose, and reproduce. Carmen remembered vividly the last time she had gazed at floating dribbles of ejaculate. It had been so long ago that she wasn't even sure whose it was, but as the cleaning mini-imps for the apartment had carried them away, all Carmen could think was "Death." That which should have been carrying life to her fertile womb was lifeless and empty, decaying already.

Carmen's belly was rounded now only with her own fat. She would never feel "quickening," the stirring of life she had felt when she touched her sister's belly so long ago. Her sister was a grandmother or a great-grandmother now. Carmen would just grow old and die.

Carmen sat up. *This is ridiculous*, she thought. *I'm not dead yet. What was it the cat Mehitabel used to say? "there's life in the old girl yet!"*

Carmen splashed a little cold water on her face, letting the mini-imps scramble to collect all the spattered droplets. She looked at her reflection and reapplied her makeup. Her face seemed a little hollow, but, she thought critically, hollow was only to the good. Some day she would have to go on a serious diet or no one would remember that she had a chin.

Carmen left her room, palming the sliding door shut, and stood quietly for a moment on the balcony surrounding the wide central shaft. It was usually easier to find Cinnamon by listening for her singing than it was to ask James where she was. Carmen could hear her coming down the shaft from the hydroponics deck above.

"It's my party and I'll cry it I want to, cry if I want to, cry if I want to . . . " For a moment Carmen wondered if Cinnamon could tell she'd been crying, but when the tall girl saw her she just called out, "Welcome home!" and swooped toward her to give her a big hug.

"Hey, hey! We missed you! I was worried about you!" Cinnamon released her and stepped back. "So when are you going back down to Rocheworld?"

"Going back?! What makes you think I'll be going back?" Carmen laughed. She stepped back and palmed open the door so that Cinnamon could come into her room.

"Nels says that we have to go back. The chance to find out more about these flouwen . . . it's just too big an opportunity to miss!"

"Yes, but I'm not the only comm expert; it'll be someone else's turn next time. Besides, we've all been cross-trained. After all, even you can land the SLAM . . . "

Cinnamon blushed. "Carmen, I told you the truth about that, and it's not funny! Gods! What if Jinjur actually wanted me to . . . "

Carmen laughed. "Don't worry. I don't think the General is desperate for volunteers. Anyway, I suppose we *will* go back down, but I don't know how soon.

"All I know is that Nels is going to be one of the volunteers. He's chomping at the bit!"

"Nels? Why would he want . . . ? Oh, I get it. He wants to see if he can breed a flouwen that we can eat."

"Don't be silly. He really *is* the best person to study the flouwen—at least from a biological point of view. And probably from an intellectual viewpoint. James says that the flouwen are very smart, and I *know* that Nels is the smartest one on board."

"Like you're an objective judge of brains. After Nels

saved the Alaskan coastline, you believe he can do anything. Besides, I'd wager that the smartest one on board is James."

"No bet! But I don't think Nels is perfect for everything, just perfect for this job. Not that I want him to go. Every landing is risky—look what nearly happened to the six people who crashed on Eau. If anything happened to Nels, *I* would have to be in charge of the hydroponics deck! We'd all be living on algae shakes within the week. But I'm really hoping that Nels will manage to convince Jinjur to let him go. You know though . . . I think the General is one of the few people who intimidate Nels. I don't think that he has said a hundred words to her in all these years."

"Your hero has feet of clay?"

They both laughed together. They were close enough to Nels to know that he would appreciate the joke.

"Actually, Nels has hardly said a hundred words to the whole crew! He is the most . . . reserved? . . . quiet? . . . succinct! . . . man I know."

"Well you and he certainly did a lot of communicating way back when . . . "

"You mean the sex? *Chula*, we didn't waste any time talking! He just made sure that I wasn't merely giving him a pity-fuck, and then we went at it. Foolish man . . . legs just get in the way in zero-gee. *Dios*, you should know." She cocked an eyebrow at Cinnamon.

Cinnamon squirmed and looked down at her fingers.

"What?" exclaimed Carmen as she tried to catch her friend's eye. "You mean you still haven't?"

"He hasn't asked," said Cinnamon defensively. "Besides, I'm not sure it would be good for the relationship."

"What relationship?" asked Carmen sarcastically.

"We're friends, and we work well together . . . and *we've* had this conversation before. Let's change the subject."

"Okay . . . " Carmen paused. "So what's been going on up here? Make anything new at the lab?"

"I almost forgot!" Cinnamon reached into her coverall

pocket and pulled out a small glass globe filled with water. "I made this myself. It's not real, it's a tissue culture from a pea blossom, but it came out pretty, I think. Anyway, welcome home."

Inside the palm-sized globe there floated what looked like a deep red rose. Closer inspection showed it to be all petals, with no stamen or stem, but Cinnamon was right, it was pretty.

"Thank you, Cinnamon!"

"You're welcome. Do tell me if it starts growing or shrinking or anything. It's one of my first DNA modifications and I need to know if it mutates."

Just then there was a knock at the door.

"Come!" called Carmen.

Jinjur stepped inside. "I hope I'm not interrupting?"

"Oh no, sir . . . ma'am . . . uh, just leaving, ma'am . . . " Cinnamon sidled around Jinjur and out the door. Jinjur looked after her. She knew who Cinnamon was, of course, but she had not had much contact with her. Still, this "ma'am" stuff had to go. Jinjur turned back to Carmen and cleared her throat.

"Well, from all accounts, you did very well out there."

"Thank you, Jinjur, we all tried our best."

"Yes, yes, of course. But George and I have been talking things over. What we need to do next is to set up a communications link so that the flouwen can talk directly to the Earth."

"Is that possible? Think of the time lag involved! Why, just the two-second round-trip time delay from Earth to the Moon makes conversation nearly impossible."

"George believes that the flouwen have incredibly long lives. They are very intelligent and can give the people of Earth a lot of new mathematical insight—insight so pure, that back and forth conversation is hardly necessary."

Dios, Carmen thought. Then she said, "You'll need to have a specialized input pad. Aren't the flouwen geared toward sonic communication? Do they even have a written language?"

"They seem to be able to transfer memories chemically. They share 'tastes' of themselves to communicate ideas too large to be easily transmitted sonically. We will need to do a lot more research into that, but that's a matter for the biologists and the chemists. What I need from you is a design for a laser communications link that will be able to transmit all the way to the Earth. It will need to be powerful enough to punch a wide-band video signal over six light-years, adaptable enough to maintain a lock on Sol through all the rotational and orbital gyrations of Rocheworld, and rug-ged enough to stand up for decades in Eau's ammonia atmosphere and violent storms. I'd like for you, Caroline, and Shirley to get to work on it . . . if you think you'd like another trip down to the surface?" Jinjur smiled.

Carmen was stunned for a moment. "Thank you!" she cried and hugged the Marine. "This is wonderful!" Then she paused and remembered the conversation she had just had. "You know, General, you might also want to send Nels down. He'd be able to ferret out all the flouwen's physical peculiarities and maybe even their genetics."

Jinjur was stern. "This is a dangerous mission, not a passenger trip. Whatever relationship you may have with Nels is not to be a factor in deciding who gets to go to the surface. If you are unhappy about being separated from him again so soon . . ."

"No, no," Carmen cried, anxious that Jinjur not get the wrong idea. "I'm not asking that Nels come along as my bedmate! But he and Cinnamon work with other life-forms all the time. They even create new life-forms. Surely they would be able to get more information than the average biologist."

"Don't call me Shirley," Jinjur said with a smile as she thought over Carmen's suggestion. "I doubt John and Katrina would be considered average biologists. They were the best in the field back home."

"Nels was rumored to be the smartest man alive!" Carmen flashed, defending her friend valiantly.

"Maybe you do have a point," Jinjur conceded thoughtfully. "His file is impressive, although I must admit that I was never too impressed by him. I'll consider what you've said. But when it comes down to it, I am the one responsible and I'm not going to risk the lives of the whole away-team by sending someone who's . . . well . . . not fit for the job."

Carmen stood at attention. "Yes, ma'am!"

"I said I'd think about it!"

Jinjur left feeling puzzled. Why did Carmen push the leviponics scientist at her? Jinjur had expected Carmen to be thankful she had been chosen, not argumentative about the selection of the others. Maybe it was that lab assistant Cinnamon whom Carmen was really trying to help. Wasn't Cinnamon some sort of pilot, and a medic too? If so, Cinnamon would be a better choice than Nels . . . Jinjur resolved to review both their files as soon as possible. Right now she had other fish to fry.

Jinjur tapped lightly on Shirley's door and then let herself in. The tall blonde was standing just inside her bathroom door, taking a "bird bath," wiping away the grime and fatigue with a warm wet washcloth. Jinjur sat on Shirley's bed, and helped herself from the tray of tidbits that Shirley had brought back with her from the party. As Jinjur bit into a pseudochocolate-covered strawberry, she watched Shirley's large muscular body move easily in the low gee. Shirley's long blond hair was loosened from its usual single braid down the left side of her head, and the wavy tresses fanned out around her face in the near zero-gee environment. Shirley's imp, normally in a crescent-moon shape on the right side of her head opposite the braid, was now splayed out over her scalp, busily untangling incipient snarls and removing the occasional gray hair.

"Why aren't you with George?" Shirley asked. She pulled on a blue silk teddy and fastened it casually. She joined Jinjur on the bed and the General washed down a mouthful of caviar with a squirt from the squeeze bottle of white pseudo-wine.

"George is doing the paperwork. He was the commanding officer down there and he has to write the trip report."

"Ah, the privileges of rank! He's going to be at his console for hours! He isn't what you'd call a speed typist."

"Oh, I don't know, both his fingers are pretty fast." They giggled together.

"Poor lad," Jinjur said. "And poor me; I'll have to wait to give him a proper welcome home. By the way: welcome home, my dear." She leaned forward and gave Shirley a long, deep kiss. Then she upended her, turning the tall woman easily over her knee. She delivered a stinging slap on the blonde's rump.

"Ouch!" Shirley squealed, but Jinjur held her tightly with one strong arm and kept on spanking.

"That was for scaring the *crap*! out of me when you went off *joyriding*! . . . on that *alien*! . . . How could *you*! . . . the *safety nut*! . . . have gone and done anything so *foolish*?" Jinjur had punctuated her remarks with spanks but now she let the engineer roll away from her.

"You're the best engineer I've got!" Jinjur continued with a furious tone. "Without your repair of the fan on the *Dragonfly*, to turn it into a water propeller, chances are that the whole landing party would still be stranded, if not dead. Golflabit! You hardly let me take a piss without you checking out the crapper, and then you go swimming inside a blob of vanilla pudding and nearly get yourself killed!" She glared at Shirley, who was ruefully rubbing her reddening posterior, but then Jinjur's eyes softened.

"Shirley," she said softly, "you worry too much about the rest of us, and not enough about yourself. Don't you realize that the worst thing that could happen to us would be for us to lose you? I swear you need a keeper. We may need to send you back to the surface, but this time I'm not going to let you out of my sight."

"I'm going back? *We're* going back? Oh Jinjur, thank you!" The pretty blonde launched herself at the black woman, knocking her back onto the bed. Sweetmeats floated around the bedroom, left for the flickering cleaning imps to find.

• CHAPTER TWO—PREPARING

George was still sitting at the console on the control deck where Jinjur had left him several hours before. His report was roughed out, but there would need to be a lot more details explained and descriptions refined. His mind was not on the manuscript in front of him. Instead, he was staring at Rocheworld, framed in the viewport window set in the curved wall in front of him. The double planet had rotated so both lobes were half-illuminated in the reddish light of Barnard. The light was quite bright, since Rocheworld had just finished its closest approach to the dwarf star in its highly elliptical orbit. Although it was normally not visible, George could now see the narrow neck of atmosphere that bridged the eighty-kilometer gap between the rounded points of the two egg-shaped lobes. It was full of clouds, clouds of steam that continued to boil up from the drowned volcanoes on Roche, there to be driven through the atmospheric bridge by the downslope winds from the sun-warmed highlands of Roche to the cool ocean-covered lowlands of Eau. All over the normally dry planet, there were glints of sunlight from lakes and rivers, newly formed during the past day by the three tidally driven interplanetary waterfalls that had occurred during periapsis. Unlike Roche, which had been transformed from a dry, cratered moon to a miniature Earth, complete with storm clouds, Eau still looked the same—an egg-shaped ball of ocean, with the water at the near pole facing Roche pulled up by Roche's gravity into a mountain of water one hundred fifty kilometers high with a slope of sixty degrees. The mountain of water looked impossible, but its shape had been predicted two centuries ago by the French mathematician Edouard Roche. Little did Professor Roche know that one day a planet would be named after him. And in one of those quirks of fate, the word *roche* means "rock" in French—a perfect name for the normally rocky planetoid.

Less than twenty-four hours ago, George had been floating—no, not floating, falling—without a parachute, a mile above Roche. He had taken a long look at his life during that long fall, and while he certainly hated to give it up, he had to admit that he had lived about the best life that he could possibly have wished for. Despite this newly discovered but deeply seated sense of peace, George Gudunov had his mind on the future.

Jinjur would be in charge of the next exploration team to Rocheworld. With room for only ten crewmembers, the away-team seemed to suggest itself. Shirley and Carmen would be the engineers and communication experts. Arielle's loosened front tooth was still recovering from the crash landing on Eau, so she would stay here on the *Prometheus* with Katrina to nurse her. That would leave John to be the medic on the surface. Caroline was the laser communications expert, so she would definitely be needed to set up the flouwen base. There were several people who would be able to pilot the SLAM and the *Dragonfly II*; George imagined that all those qualified would spend the next few days reminding Jinjur of their qualifications.

George looked again out the port as the shadow of Roche started to move across Eau, darkening the oceans as the six-hour day approached high noon on the outer pole of Roche. Hidden beneath that ocean, almost missed by George and his crew, was the most important discovery of the entire expedition.

Life! thought George. Even now he could hardly believe it. *Beautiful, peaceful, friendly, intelligent life, here on the other side of the rainbow. Rainbow?* He looked again at the double planet, and it almost looked as if Roche, the barren rocky lobe, was somehow changing ... more colorful? He rubbed his eyes. *Definitely time for bed!*

Jinjur picked up her breakfast in the galley and took it to her room to eat while she studied the personnel files on her own viewwall. She had lived with these people for over forty years, but one doesn't use daily conversations to discuss one's training and qualifications. She hadn't perused these files since they had left the Earth, except when she had approved George's choices for the first team downside.

Caroline Tanaka, the laser engineer, was an obvious choice. Jinjur had sent Shirley to tell her what they were planning, and to let her know that she would be needed on the surface. Katrina would be staying on the main ship so John could have a turn to go to the surface.

John Kennedy seemed to Jinjur to be a bit shallow, somewhat too glib, but he knew his way around a robotic space vehicle as well as he knew his way around the human body. Jinjur squirmed in her chair as she remembered the way he had handled her last physical exam. Jinjur had been irritated at James for insisting that it was time for her annual exam and had gone into the sick bay with a chip on her shoulder. John had started with a massage, claiming that he couldn't palpate anything but muscle while she was so tense. Half an hour later, Jinjur was as tense as a blancmange and John had palpated every inch of her. Jinjur forced her mind back onto the business at hand.

We'll need another pilot who can handle the heavy booster in the SLAM, and a backup pilot to fly the Dragonfly *airplane*, Jinjur thought. Thomas St. Thomas was the Chief Pilot for the SLAM and they would want to use his expertise and experience again. Red Vengeance, a geologist and backup rocket lander pilot to Thomas on the first mission, had done a fine job, but there were other backup lander pilots available, and Jinjur should give one of them of them a chance at the second mission. She asked James to list the pilots, and order them with biology instead of geology as a second requirement. Much to her surprise Cinnamon topped the list.

This Cinnamon again! You spend forty years barely seeing the chick and suddenly she's popping up every time you turned around. She called up Cinnamon's file.

Cinnamon Byrd was born in Chenik, Alaska as the eldest of five children. Her father, the altruistic scion of a politically prominent Virginia family, was the only doctor within miles. He used a small plane in order to reach many of his patients. In order to help out, Cinnamon got her pilot's license at the age of fourteen and became an emergency medical technician soon after.

After the 2015 Cook Inlet oil spill ruined the state's economy and decimated the wildlife, Cinnamon decided to go to college to study ichthyology and fish farming. She had hoped to find a way to help revitalize the coastline. After getting her degree at the University of Alaska, she transferred to Goddard Station to do postgraduate work, and it was there that she met Nels. Cinnamon turned out to be the best lab assistant that the temperamental genius had ever had. She named the price for her devoted assistance, and Nels managed it within six months. He developed a fast-growing rugged bacteria, that could absorb and break down the spilled crude that had lingered on the beaches for years, killing wildlife all the way up the food chain. The single-celled organism was the redemption for that man-soiled region, and it went on to save many other polluted areas. Cinnamon joined Nels permanently and followed him even to the stars.

Then Jinjur noticed an anomaly. "James? This figure for the girl's IQ. Is that correct?"

"Yes, Jinjur, that is correct. Her IQ is measured at one hundred twenty. That is toward the top of the normal range. It only looks low when compared with the rest of the crew."

"But how did she get chosen to come with us to Barnard?

Sure, she has some useful skills, but with all the thousands of people clamoring to go to the stars, we could have found someone better than average!"

"Nels insisted that she come. Since Nels was so clearly the best choice of the levibiologists, the committee decided to accept his preferred assistant. They did insist that, although she is an accomplished light-plane pilot, she first demonstrate a capability of piloting the *Dragonfly*-class heavy aeroplanes and the landing rockets, but as you see, she passed all the tests given by the experts on the Greater National Aeronautics and Space Agency evaluation committee."

"God save us from GNASA committees! What is she? His wife or something?"

"Not that I have observed. They do seem to work well together, however. Nels is not a very communicative person, but while there is never much conversation in the hydroponics lab, Nels and Cinnamon get all the work done smoothly."

"I suppose that Nels's IQ more than makes up the difference. Two hundred plus? Wow. I guess God more than compensated him for his lack of legs. Ironic that he went into genetic research."

"Nels's deformity was caused by chemicals his mother was accidentally exposed to during her pregnancy. It had nothing to do with genetics," said the computer gravely.

"Umm, yes. I suppose Cinnamon would actually be rather a good choice for this particular mission. Pilot, medic, biologist specializing in fish, and she is one of the crew no matter how she found her way on board. Besides, I'd much rather risk her than Nels. I'll pencil her in.

"Now for a pilot to replace Arielle, I suppose it's only fair that I give Tony a chance. He certainly is qualified, and I know he was unhappy about being left behind last time." Jinjur considered the small, handsome, pilot. Long ago she had chosen Anthony "Tony" Roma as the model in a recruiting poster for the Space Marines, and that poster had doubled female recruitment for the year. But Tony himself did not trade on his dark good looks; he was a conscientious worker and a very private man.

"Even through this isn't primarily a planetology mission, we'll need some geoscientists . . . " Jinjur kept at it throughout the morning, muttering quietly under her breath in her cabin.

Caroline Tanaka went over the checklist on her videoboard again. She and James were giving the *Prometheus*-to-Sol laser transmitter its annual checkout. It checked out perfectly, despite its age, which didn't really surprise her, for she had designed it. Pushing her long black hair out of her way, the petite engineer found herself wishing something would check out low just so she'd have something to do.

Shirley pulled her long body into the engineering room on the top deck. "I thought I'd find you here. I've got news."

"Hey, Shirley! I hardly got to say more than hi last night. Welcome home." Caroline put her videoboard down.

"Jinjur sent me to talk to you about our going back to Eau to visit further with the flouwen. She wants you to build a specialized communications base for us to take down to leave with the flouwen. The console should be usable by the flouwen, which means it needs to operate under water. The transmitter and antenna should allow them to communicate with *Prometheus*, and later, after *Prometheus* leaves Rocheworld and goes on to explore the moons of Gargantua, directly to Earth."

"Wow! That's some challenge," Caroline replied. Instantly her mind went to work on the project. They'd need a reliable, long-lived power supply, one that would survive in the ammonia-rich atmosphere and not pollute the area. It would be decades before the follow-up mission would be back to do maintenance, and it would take many watts of laser power to punch a signal over the six light-years from Barnard to Sol. Diagrams began flipping through her head. They could start with the second backup spare for the *Prometheus*-to-Sol laser transmitter. It had the laser power and autotracking telescope that would be needed to reach Earth. But they'd still need a power supply, some interface boxes, and a whole new input console . . .

"Jinjur will have Carmen, Cinnamon, and John work on an input console designed for the flouwen; you and I are to work on the power supply and the transmitting unit . . . Hello? Hello! Earth to Caroline . . . " Shirley was waving her hand in front of Caroline's face.

Caroline came back to herself with a start. "I've got to go to the surface to make sure it's installed properly," she stated bluntly.

Shirley laughed. "Of course you're going. We're both going. I figure we have fifteen days to configure and partially assemble the communicator setup."

Tony looked closely at the frightened girl standing before him. Tall and thin, with a boyish figure, the only sign of her native American heritage was her reddish-brown coloring and the two long black braids set low on her head, covering her ears. Cinnamon was doing her best to apologize for her existence.

"Jinjur just wouldn't listen when I tried to tell her that I'm not up to piloting the SLAM II. She told me that I had better use my spare time to get a little practice in. She said that I should ask you to coach me on the simulator. But I'll understand if you have too much else to do. . . . Maybe you could tell her that you'd rather have a backup pilot that you knew was competent . . . "

Tony thought. He really didn't have any sailcraft piloting chores to do, now that they were just maintaining position near Rocheworld. He had decided that he needed to put in some time at the heavy rocket simulator himself, and it just occurred to him that the best way to relearn the proper techniques is to coach some one else.

"No," he said. "No matter who goes, they will need to refresh their memory on the simulator. We all lost a lot of experience during our time on No-Die. Why don't you and I go up to the simulator room on the engineering deck and see just how rough we've both become."

But when Tony watched Cinnamon at the simulator controls he had some misgivings. Cinnamon was more than rusty. She just didn't have the feel of the heavy thrusters. She seemed to do better when he programmed a specific sequence, but when he turned her over to James she rapidly lost her way.

"I think your problem is that the virtual reality helmet isn't able to fit around your head properly," Tony suggested kindly. "What say we take a break for today, and when you come here tomorrow, you can do something else with your hair."

The next day, Cinnamon had shifted the thick braids back on her head, exposing more of her large, rounded ears. The gray dome of the helmet rested securely over her face. Tony's visor was linked to the same program as Cinnamon's, and the holographic multicolored laser pattern before them resolved itself into an image of a SLAM bridge, complete with video console, rocket controls, and an image of Rocheworld outside the triangular cockpit windows. The array of tiny lasers built into the surface of the visor generated the same light patterns that would have crossed the visor if the real SLAM bridge had really been there. Working on the nonexistent bridge of the hypothetical lander, Tony got lots of practice showing Cinnamon what she was doing wrong. But when he turned the controls back over to her for the next landing, they crashed again, even though the emergency problem James had inserted was a minor one.

"How did you get such high scores at GNASA?" he finally exploded.

Cinnamon hung her head. "I don't know. They just always tested me on the one emergency simulation that I had practiced. I knew that the examiners had certain favorite situations and I concentrated exclusively on them. I had hoped, that by doing very well on one or two tests, I could average out for the tests I would be bound to screw up. But then I just got lucky. Every single test was the one that I had studied."

Tony stared at her. "You mean you bluffed your way through the whole training program?"

She nodded. "I *do* know how to fly light aircraft, and I'm pretty good at the *Dragonfly* aeroplanes, but I can't seem to get the feel of the heavy lander rockets."

"Well, you're going to get the feel now!"

He worked her hard. Hours after the agreed stopping time, he was still hovering over her, berating her mistakes. It was so frustrating to watch her do so well on one of his setups, and then fail so miserably when James presented the same scenario. Tony had never had a long fuse on his temper, and by the time they were ready to quit, he was livid with rage. As he watched her struggle to lift the helmet off over her pinned-up braids, the sight of Cinnamon's tear-stained face pushed Tony over the edge. With a growl of rage, he took out his pocket knife and cut off both braids.

Cinnamon looked from his eyes to the long braids still in his hand, then turned her back to him and hung her head.

Tony stared at the smooth curve of her bared neck, and down her long straight back. All his anger drained away. He watched his hand reach out and stroke her back, slowly drifting down to the small curves of her buttocks. She froze, scarcely breathing. Slowly he turned her around, and cupped her face in his hands. Then he kissed her fiercely. Taking her hand, he pulled her down the long central shaft to his room.

He undressed her slowly. She still made no move to either help or resist him. He looked at her body appraisingly. Living in zero gee usually helped the women retain their figures, but Cinnamon's small curves could never have sagged. Tony, as the only homosexual man on the ship, had had a hard time accepting the voluptuous curves of the more promiscuous women on board. Once he had fled Carmen's room without having satisfied either of them.

Cinnamon, however, reminded him of all the beautiful young men he had ever loved; young men now old or dead, forever out of his reach. He became so lost in his memories, that he was momentarily startled to be reminded that this lover before him had no penis. He turned her around, and drowned himself in his fantasies.

Cinnamon waited for Tony to fall asleep, and then gathered up her clothes and slipped back to her own room. Throughout the whole encounter, Tony had not spoken a word to her. Had she expected a declaration of love? She had at least expected the man to know it was her that he was with. She was confused, and didn't know where to go for advice. Nels? Their relationship was strictly professional. Carmen couldn't seem to handle her own love life lately. Maybe, in her ignorance, she was overreacting to the whole thing. After all, technically she was still a virgin. Cinnamon smiled ruefully and rubbed her posterior.

At noon the next day, Tony was again at the flight simulator. He made no comment about the day before, nor did he seem to notice her hair. Cinnamon had had her imp cut it into a straight bob at her jawline. She felt funny about the cut; it seemed odd to see her ears again.

They went through the simulator lesson slowly. Tony refused to program the situations, letting her struggle with James's choices. He was quick to berate her, but by the end of the session she had improved slightly.

Tony begrudgingly complimented her, and then silently led her back again to his apartment. This time Cinnamon was determined to take some initiative, and during their silent lovemaking she rolled over and forced him to look into her eyes. Finally, at the age of 72, Cinnamon Byrd lost her virginity. Later, curled up in Tony's arms, Cinnamon heard James call to her quietly through the imp in her hair.

"Cinnamon? Is everything okay with you?"

"Yes, James, everything is fine," she whispered. "Why do you ask?"

"You have not requested a song all day," the computer responded.

"How about 'The Shoop Shoop Song'?" she requested, although she didn't see why she wanted it. Tony had hardly kissed her at all!

Jinjur, always concerned about her crew's safety, decided that before they risked sending a human crew down to Rocheworld, they would send down one of their robotic amphibious crawlers to locate and reestablish contact with the pod of flouwen that had befriended the humans during their last visit to the surface. By communicating with them through the robotic lander, she could arrange for her landing party to meet the members of the pod at some selected point on the Hawaiian Islands, the small group of meteorite craters sticking up out of the shallow part of the ocean on the outer pole of Eau.

"We need to let the flouwen know that the crawler is coming," said George. "We don't want it to end up entangled as an undigestible lunch in some voracious wildlife." He shuddered, remembering his close call with the exploding, gray, rocklike creature that had trapped him with its sticky threads and tried to eat him. "Caroline, can we use one of the communication lasers to contact them from here?"

"Certainly," Caroline replied. "The one we are preparing for them to use would be ideal."

"They communicate sonically," Shirley objected. "The translation programs in our vehicle computers can talk with the flouwen through a sonar transmitter, but it won't work with a laser transmitter since the flouwen have no method of converting the light fluctuations into sound fluctuations.

Also, as far as I know, they've never developed any sort of Morse Code so we could send messages with dots and dashes. They are sensitive to light, however, so all we need to do is find the right type of modulation."

"They're mathematicians," said George. "Maybe we can send them dot-dash pictures broken into raster scans using a frame size with prime numbers for width and height. Once they realize the repetition pattern, their mathematical brains should be able to organize it into a two-dimensional picture."

"We can do better than that." Caroline was thinking hard as she spoke. "Didn't one of the flouwen develop an 'eye' like we humans use?"

"Yes," confirmed Shirley. "I had a long talk with White Whistler when I was riding on him. He is the one who learned to turn part of his body into a clear lens that would focus the light from the stars onto a portion of his light-sensitive body. He used the artificial eye to study the spectra of the stars and follow the orbital movements of Gargantua and its moons. He was pleased to learn that he was correct in his deduction that the *Prometheus* wasn't a natural satellite since it didn't move in an elliptical orbit."

"Well, since he can see like a human, perhaps we can use the laser to send him a picture of the crawler landing by some distinctive point on the outer islands," Caroline continued. "Although the laser sends only a single dot of light, we can make the dot move quickly enough to give the illusion of a line. By reflecting it off a rapidly vibrating mirror, we can even do simple animation. It would have to be a simple figure, and we would have no way of knowing for sure if they received our message . . ."

"But it's certainly worth a try," George decided. "It will also give us a good opportunity to test out the laser itself. Is it almost complete?"

"Caroline and I have most of it put together," Shirley confirmed.

"You might want to ask Greystoke to help you out," said

George. "As an award-winning sonovideo composer, he should be able to come up with a simple, yet comprehensible, animated message."

"Maybe he can also come up with some good idea to get the flouwen's attention," said Shirley. "The animation idea needs a screen to write the images on. Some of the tall cliffs on the islands would be ideal movie screens, but how do we attract an audience there to see them?"

Barnard had just set behind Eau, and the sky was dark and clear above the oceans of Eau. Floating in the star-speckled sky was Roche, illuminated in an arc on one side as the shadow of Eau crept across its surface. Off to one side was the giant gas planet Gargantua, with its large retinue of moons. Clear◊White◊Whistle was showing DaintyΔBlueΔWarbler how to make an eye for looking with. Roaring☆Hot☆Vermilion was protesting loudly.

☆I still think it is perverted to make part of yourself clear unless you are making a new one!☆

◊It is not perverted if it leads to new understanding,◊ the white flouwen countered. ◊With the clear part you can focus the lights from the sky onto the rest of yourself and look farther than you can see.◊

Δ I want to look,Δ the youngest flouwen decided. Δ Let me taste how you make this "eye."Δ

Clear◊White◊Whistle gave the youngling a sample of memory juices. After a moment, DaintyΔBlueΔWarbler formed a clear spot in its jelly-like body.

◊Good! Now be sure that there is no water on the surface of your lens to distort the light. The light in the shape of a crescent is Sky⊗Rock. The big circle surrounded by little circles is Warm. Off to one side is the Flying⊗Circle that the humans live in. All the rest of the tiny points of light are called "stars."◊

Δ Wow! The whole sky is as crowded as the rest of the world! What is the Flying⊗Circle doing? It is flashing like an earthquake! Does it always do that?Δ

◊I have never seen it do that before.◊ Clear◊White◊Whistle was puzzled.

Roaring☆Hot☆Vermilion quickly formed an eye to look too. ☆It is getting brighter!☆

ΔIt is coming right at us!Δ

The beam of blue-green light, visible in the forward scattering from the salt specks in the air, flashed rapidly again and again as it stepped its way across the ocean, swept over the three flouwen, and marched off toward the distant horizon.

◊The light seems to be going toward the Islands of Thought. I will go see what it looks like from there.◊

☆The waves are going in that direction! Let's all surf there!☆ Roaring☆Hot☆Vermilion dissolved the crystalline lens in its surface and allowed its fluid body to form a more streamlined shape so it could skim along the top of Eau's waves, lifting tall in the weak gravity of the ocean planet. The sweeping beam of blue-green light passed over them a number of times during their long journey, each time directing them toward the distant Islands of Thought. It was the following sunset before the three gamboling flouwen approached the large ring-shaped islands on the outer pole of Eau. Reluctantly, they managed to pull themselves away from the joys of playing in the surf as the mystery of the flashing light beams called to them. The marching pattern of beams converged on a spot in the ocean in front of a tall cliff. On the cliff was a crude pattern of large spots of flickering light in differing colors. The flickering spots moved across the cliffside in various directions.

☆It is a bunch of moving dots,☆ Roaring☆Hot☆Vermilon insisted. ☆Dumb.☆

◊The humans are not too smart,◊ Clear◊White◊Whistle admitted, ◊but I don't think they would send down a bunch of dots for no reason.◊

ΔMaybe they mean the strings of dots to be a line,Δ DaintyΔBlueΔWarbler offered. ΔThat is the definition of a line. Try letting your eye get blurry and the lines look somewhat like a human swimming over to two spinning oblong shapes, one red and one blue.Δ

The other two tried defocusing their eyes. ◊That looks like a Stiff⊗Mover swimming, and the other looks like what the world and Sky⊗Rock would look like if you were looking at it from high above. I think the humans are trying to let us know that they are coming back to visit us here. I am going to greet them when they come.◊

☆If you want to send them a picture back, you should get Warm❋Amber❋Resonance to help you do a picture play!☆

◊Good idea.◊

ΔBut how are the humans going to be able to look at us from so far away?Δ

◊I don't know, but maybe their winged pet Floating⊗Rock can help them. It seems much smarter than they are.◊

ΔHow can the pet be both bigger and smarter than the master?Δ

◊I do not know. That is why I want to study them more. Maybe Floating⊗Rock is only smarter at learning, not thinking.◊

ΔIs learning not the same as thinking?Δ

◊Strong❐Lavender❐Crackle thinks, trying to find the fifth cardinal infinity; is that the same as you learning the first cardinal infinity? And what about the poems that Sweet○Green○Fizz makes? Do you suppose that Strong❐Lavender❐Crackle could compose such things? Or that the skill to make such poems could be learned?◊

☆I do not even understand the poems! Why try to make more poems when there are so many better things to be doing? Dumb! If you need any help with your picture play, you can find me over on the north shore. Come on, DaintyΔBlueΔWarbler, surfing is even more exciting when there is the threat that you may get beached!☆

ΔWave!Δ

☆Dumb!☆

* * *

"How many times do you want this repeated?" Greystoke asked as he monitored the two laser systems, one scanning the ocean in a insweeping radial pattern that converged on the outer islands, the other focused on a cliffside there.

"I don't know," Caroline said. "It's not like we're even sure that we're being received."

"There is something happening on the surface of the water near where we are beaming the message," James called through their imps. "I will transfer the picture from the high-resolution telescope up to your screens."

On the screen, there appeared a view of the planet surface showing the relatively calm gray-green water on the south side of the Hawaiian Islands. A blue patch of something floating in the water resolved itself into an egg shape. Shortly after, an amber egg formed next to it. Slowly the two egg-shaped patches began to circle around each other in a credible imitation of Roche and Eau's heavenly ballet. Off to the side a white circle appeared. Then a small portion of white detached itself from the circle and moved in an arc down toward the blue lobe. As the small piece of white reached the blue "planet," the other shapes all flowed into a ring and more colors began to appear. Together, in all the colors of the various flouwen in the pod, a ring was formed around the white figure, surrounding it and circling it slowly.

"They've seen our message! They are telling us they will meet us!" Greystoke cheered. He quickly changed the animation pattern on the cliff-side to imitate the one that the flouwen had formed, letting them know their message had been received.

"Good," said Caroline. "Now we can get the crawler and a sonar communicator down there and talk in a real language instead of pictures. Despite what they say, you'll never get me to believe that a picture is worth a thousand words."

Greystoke laughed. With his long artistic fingers he formed an Ameslan symbol. Even Caroline could tell it suggested that she perform a physically impossible sexual act. She grinned wryly and began to dismantle the laser setup.

❃That was fun . . . It was different trying to keep the picture oriented to the surface instead of toward a submerged audience. To work on a plane instead of in three dimensions presents unusual difficulties.❃ Warm❃Amber❃Resonance relaxed into a more natural shape.

Δ When do you think they will be coming?Δ

◊Not for a while, I expect.◊ Clear◊White◊Whistle was feeling better now that the small piece that had portrayed the human spacecraft was rejoined with the rest of its body. The piece had only been separated from the main body of the white flouwen for a few moments, but it was glad to be back with the rest of itself and needed to be soothed.

Δ Why do you suppose they are coming back, and why would they come down here?Δ asked Dainty∆Blue∆Warbler, reluctant to rejoin Roaring☆Hot☆Vermilion surfing when there were so many interesting things to be learned here.

OThey know that the elders are here,O replied SweetOGreenOFizz.O Obviously they want to come and try to talk to the deep thinkers rather than you children.O

Caroline reported the flouwen response to Jinjur. "I was thinking that it might be a good idea to send down with the crawler a touchscreen console like the one we are building for the flouwen. It would be disastrous for us to go all the way down and then find out the input board for the laser communicator is poorly designed."

"I doubt that you could design anything poorly." Jinjur laughed. "Do you and John have a prototype that you can spare?"

"Yes. Our first working model has a lot of rough edges, but it will let us know if we are on the right track. It is small enough to fit into the cargo hatch of the crawler, and we will be able to get the parts back for salvage when we reach the surface."

"Good idea," Jinjur agreed. "How's everything else coming?"

"Fine and shiny," Caroline confirmed. "Although it *is* a bit wearing to be working so closely with John."

"He does take that 'closely' seriously, doesn't he?"

They both giggled.

"He just doesn't take no for an answer!"

"If his constant passes get too annoying, try just giving him more to do," Jinjur suggested. "Even *he* can't make love while he's working."

"No, but he can make plans for later," Caroline said dubiously.

"So make a date for later. He's almost as good as he thinks he is, and it can help you relax enough to go to sleep." Jinjur looked critically at the circles under Caroline's eyes. "I bet you've spent the last couple rest periods thinking up better designs for that laser transmitter. Why don't you take a few hours off and try to relax."

"But I'd rather . . . "

"I know you would. Consider that an order."

Caroline slumped and gloomily left the cabin.

You'd think I was punishing her, thought Jinjur wryly. *Everyone is acting oddly lately*.

The women had an excuse; it was always a bit of trouble with all the women having premenstrual syndrome at the same time, but at least you knew what the problem was. But while Thomas and John were acting normally except for the ordinary excitement, Tony and Nels were acting very weird. Nels had been hovering outside Jinjur's door for days now, but whenever she called out to him, he vanished!

As for Tony . . . Jinjur reviewed the talk she had recently had with him. He had wanted her to know that Cinnamon could not be relied on to handle the heavy rocket thrusters in the SLAM II lander. All the time he was talking, Jinjur got the impression that while Tony wanted her to know about the problem, he desperately wanted Cinnamon to continue to be included on the away team.

Jinjur had already decided that Thomas and Tony would be the pilots for the rocket lander and Cinnamon would just be one of the back-up pilots for the *Dragonfly*. Apparently Tony had no doubts about Cinnamon being able to pilot the aeroplane, and he had left her cabin much relieved. But Jinjur was curious why he was so anxious to include the lab assistant. *First Carmen, and then Tony!* She would have to spend more time with this Cinnamon.

Thomas was working out in the gym. Now that he knew he would be on the away team, he needed to get back into shape to handle the gravity on the planet. Although some simple medications inserted in their daily rations of algae shakes sufficed to counteract the calcium loss and other problems induced by living in their nearly free-fall environment aboard *Prometheus*, muscles still became flabby unless you exercised. The sweat glistened on his light brown skin, a Jamaican tan that even the years in space could not fade. The zero-gee exercise drills let Thomas work his body hard, and soon drops of sweat were spinning off into the air, only to be carefully collected and herded off to the air-conditioning ducts by the tiny cleaning imps. If only he could take a swim . . . The pleasure of feeling his long lean body cut through the waters of Montego Bay was the thing Thomas missed most about leaving Earth. He thought wistfully about the possibility of swimming with the flouwen in the oceans of Eau, but it just wouldn't be the same in a space-suit.

Richard Redwing and Sam Houston entered the gym together, laughing. The Indian stripped off his coverall, revealing his very muscular physique. Thomas felt his ego cringe at the display of muscle, but it was immediately revived by the sight of Sam Houston's pale, scrawny torso.

"How about a three-way wrestling match?" called Richard.

"Just so you can cream us?" retorted Thomas. "No, thank you."

"You're right, it wouldn't give me much of a workout." Richard preened playfully.

"How about the two of us against you?" offered Sam. Although very tall and thin, Sam knew that all his fieldwork in the heavy spacesuits on Luna and Mars had given his lanky body hidden strength. Sam was hoping that, with a bit of help, he could give his friend the comeuppance he deserved. Richard was his greatest pal, but he was inclined to be cocky.

"Two against one is hardly fair . . . for you," Richard scoffed. "Maybe with Jinjur on your team . . . " He turned his back incitingly. With savage growls the two other men threw themselves at him, but at the last second Richard dodged out of their way. Unfortunately, he had underestimated Sam's reach and a large knuckled hand grasped Richard around the ankle and sent him spinning. Soon the three of them were locked in mock combat, a twisting ball of intermingled white, brown, and red flesh.

Cinnamon was on her way to the sick bay when she met Carmen just outside the door.

"Are you here to be ravished by the pump?" Carmen asked. She shuddered slightly. With no gravity to help them, the women on board had to use a menstrual extractor each month. Like many women who are in close contact for an extended time, their hormonal cycles had synchronized, and the sick bay needed only to be set up for the procedure one or two days a month.

"Yes," Cinnamon answered. "I once swore that I would never perform this procedure on myself. Why else would I stay a virgin all the way through college?" *And a good deal later*, she added mentally.

"What are you talking about?" Carmen asked. "Why operate a menstrual extractor back on good old Terra Firma?"

"I became an expert back when I was a medic in Alaska. When the Supreme Court decided that life, and citizenship, began at conception, whom else could the local women turn to than the doctor's daughter?" Cinnamon failed to notice the shock on her companion's face.

"You performed abortions?!" Carmen screamed. All of her early upbringing merged with her current desire for children and rose up in a wave of revulsion. "How could you!?"

Cinnamon was stunned. "Where were you in 2015? The Thomas decision meant that almost all forms of birth control were outlawed . . . IUDs, Norplant, the Pill, anything that would keep a fertilized egg from implanting. Those women were desperate! I had to help them."

Carmen was horrified. She pushed herself away from Cinnamon and headed back toward the lounge. Tears clouded her vision and her face was red with rage and revulsion.

Cinnamon watched her go, and shook her head sadly. Then she pushed herself in to the medical lab and checked to see that the extractor was sterile and reset. Then she disrobed and lay back on the table as a portion of the Christmas Bush approached her bearing a long slim tube. Cinnamon forced herself to relax and allowed the tube to slide gently into position. The whole procedure took only ten minutes and then it was all over. Cinnamon filled the time worrying about her relationship with Tony and humming softly to herself.

"Who needs a heart when a heart can be broken . . . "

• CHAPTER THREE—RETURNING

ΔLook! Look! Look!Δ DaintyΔBlueΔWarble's cry echoed through the water. Long after the others had gotten bored with watching the sky and had gone to hunt some food, the young flouwen kept its lens focused on the skies overhead. Finally it saw the aeroshell carrying the lander, glowing with the heat of entry, streak across the sky.

ΔThe humans are coming! The humans are coming!Δ

◊Where?◊ asked Clear◊White◊Whistle as it rapidly formed a looking lens of its own. Long practice made the formation of a clear sphere of tissue almost automatic.

☆Fractals!☆ cursed Roaring☆Hot☆Vermilion. It was having trouble with its eye, but after a moment it finally got the skies in focus.

Crack! A sonic boom cut through the air as the aeroshell passed overhead. Then, with a splash, the probe announced its arrival to all those living in the water. It sank to the bottom. Almost immediately, the aeroshell was surrounded by the curious flouwen, each one jockeying for a taste of the strange artifact.

The acoustic sensors of the crawler heard the crowd of strange voices examining it with complex sonar chirps.

ΔI cannot see inside it. It is as hard as a rock.Δ

☆Look! It is crawling out of its shell!☆

Using its flippered tread, the crawler left the aeroshell and then adjusted its buoyancy to match the density of the ammonia-water sea. By neither sinking nor floating, it allowed itself to be gently passed from flouwen to flouwen so that they would become accustomed to it before the humans regained control.

☆Hello! Hello!☆ Roaring☆Hot☆Vermilion surrounded the rowboat-sized vehicle and shook it gently roaring at it. ☆The Crawling⊗Rock is so small! How do all the humans fit in there!?!☆

◊Think before you speak!◊ Clear◊White◊Whistle chastised. ◊This is just another pet of the humans. Can't you taste how much it is like the winged Floating⊗Rock? The humans do all their talking through such pets as this.◊

The milky flouwen reached into the reddish blob and tried to pry the crawler out of its grasp. After a short struggle, only long enough for Roaring☆Hot☆Vermilion to prove that Clear◊White◊Whistle could not have forced the removal, Roaring☆Hot☆Vermilion released the crawler to the other.

◊Hello? Shirley? Katrina? Are you listening?◊

The computer in the crawler translated the sonic trills of the white flouwen and used its blue-green laser communicator to transmit the flouwen's question up through the water to the humans waiting above on *Prometheus*.

"We are here," answered Shirley. "We want for you to carry our crawler close to the shore where we can communicate better with you and with the elders. Take it toward the beaches where elders think, and show us a spot where our crawler will be safe under the tides, and can rest comfortably on the ocean bottom."

☆Why does it want to be on the bottom? It will get all sandy there.☆ Roaring☆Hot☆Vermilion was still trying to work the tiny irritants from its body that it had picked up when it was slammed into the bottom by the churning surf of the north shore.

"We have something to show you," Shirley's voice interrupted. "We are sending you a touchscreen console that will help us communicate more clearly. It would help us if the console were set down somewhere stable."

❃I know of a quiet bay,❃ offered Warm❃Amber❃Resonance. ❃I often go there so I can practice body plays without having to fight the currents. It is one of the favorite places for elders who only want to sit on the bottom and think for a short while. For long periods of thought the tides are too mild. We can go there.❋

Sensing no disagreement, the large white flouwen holding the crawler streaked off toward the cove, followed closely by the rest of the Pod. Clear◊White◊Whistle was the only one to maintain its eye and it closely scrutinized the crawler as it carried it along. The crawler was not heavy, but its awkward shape slowed the flouwen down. Dainty∆Blue∆Warble hung back from the rest of the pod and kept his tutor company.

∆These are certainly interesting times to be alive.∆

◊Indeed. You even owe your individuality to the coming of the humans. I have decided to make the Stiff⊗Movers the subject of my research. Perhaps you, too, would like to study them seriously.◊

∆Certainly there is much to learn about them. You say they build devices such as this Crawling⊗Rock? It seems odd to use one's energy to change the shape of things instead of using one's mind to understand them as they are.∆

Before too long, the pod had their prize installed in the shallow cove. Here they were sheltered by high cliffs on three sides and by a reef on the fourth, and the usual high waves of Eau were tamed into gentle swells that softly lapped the shore, which was studded with several colorful "rocks" of thinking flouwen. They settled the crawler onto the soft sands on the bottom, in water just deep enough for a flouwen to float comfortably.

The crawler adjusted its density until it sank in the water and its treads were firmly embedded in the sand. From its rear, there rose a mast that extended out of the water. At the end of the mast, well above the wave tops, was a small laser transmitter that locked onto the commsat *Walter* hovering at the L-4 point just visible right on the horizon. Using one of its clawlike manipulators, the crawler reached over its back and opened up a cargo hold that was normally used for storing samples picked up during an exploration mission.

Inside the hold was the prototype of the custom touchscreen so carefully constructed by John, Carmen, and Caroline back on the *Prometheus*. The basic case of the custom console was that of a vidboard, the modernistic version of the old-time clipboard. A standard vidboard was a thin but stiff high-resolution display screen the size of a standard piece of paper that operated by reflection in daylight and illumination at night. You could talk to it, write on it, move or touch menu icons on the screen with your finger, or punch in letters and numbers on keyboard icons along the bottom. In turn, the videoboard could show you anything it could access or had stored in its memory.

Besides having a built-in flouwen-human translation program, this custom vidboard could also input two-dimensional sound, touch, and chemical patterns, and output sonar patterns that matched the underlying video patterns. The electrochemical receptors of the vidboard were still crude in both spatial and chemical resolution, but Nels and John had designed them to be adaptable, and hoped to refine their resolution as they and the flouwen got used to the strange interface between a culture who used chemical smells and tastes solely for gastronomy and a culture who used them in place of reference books.

As an introduction, to teach the flouwen how to use the vidboard, the screen replayed the picture of Rocheworld rotating around and around, with the ellipse of *Prometheus* off to one side, and a human spacecraft flying from the sailship to land on the outer pole of Eau.

"Where is Floating⊗Circle?" trilled the videoboard in passable flouwen. "Touch the Floating⊗Circle."

The flouwen clustered around, each one eager to try using the odd device. It wasn't long before they had moved on from simple pictures to complex mathematical discussions. Sweet○Green○Fizz was especially impressed with an imaginary sonovideo trip from the surface of Eau, out into space where the whole of the Barnard planetary system could be seen going through its gyrations, followed by an imaginary trip from Barnard back to Sol, a flyby of all the planets and moons in the Solar System, and a landing on the shores of the blue-green oceans of Earth.

○What a marvelous pet! If only I could train my Pretty⊗Smells to obey so well!○

◊This is no natural pet, but one that has been built in order to do the humans' bidding. It is not alive.◊ Long ago, during the first visit of the humans to Rocheworld, Katrina had explained the human habit of manipulating their environment to the technologically primitive flouwen, but Clear◊White◊Whistle hadn't bothered to share the taste of the memory with the frivolous Sweet○Green○Fizz.

○They change the nature of their pets?○ Struggling to understand the strange idea, the green blob hardened into a rock and sank to the bottom, lost in thought.

#Let me see this new pet of the humans,# demanded Sour#Sapphire#Coo. The others made room for the large flouwen. The unusual amount of nearby activity had roused the ancient flouwen from his internal search for the fifth cardinal infinity. Lately it had been difficult to concentrate on that research problem. The dark blue elder had been disturbed not long ago in order to advise the pod on the mystery of the humans. Now, unbidden thoughts and questions about these strange beings had crowded out the computations. Sour#Sapphire#Coo had finally decided that perhaps it would be better to work on this new puzzle before going back to a peaceful rocky state and the comfort of pure mathematical theory.

Sour#Sapphire#Coo took the vidboard and chirped at the crawler, #I am Sour#Sapphire#Coo. You will show me how to use this thing.#

Working through the crawler's computer, James took over. Soon he had all the flouwen conversant in the use of the touchscreen and the capabilities and limitations of the laser communications link. Now that contact with the flouwen pod had been reestablished, the preparations of the landing party intensified.

* * *

"The flouwen are most happy about our coming down," Caroline reported to Jinjur. "I think we are the most exciting thing to happen to them in eons."

"Of course we are." The general laughed. "Just think how excited we would have been if any of the UFOs that had been reported over the years had bothered to land and prove they had intelligent beings on board. So, are they willing to teach us humans some of their 'basic' math?"

"More than that," John said. "They are clamoring to come back with us to visit the *Prometheus*."

"Don't be ridiculous! How can we get something as awkward and bulky as a flouwen into a space-suit?"

"Actually," George offered, "a space-suit is only a bag to hold air. We can get one to hold water just as easily. Maybe we can design one to hold at least a portion of a flouwen."

"They don't breathe, so we wouldn't need to add air tanks," said John. "And anything watertight would keep them safe from the vacuum and us safe from their ammonia."

"We have those large rescue bags that are designed for vacuum transport of an injured person," Shirley reminded them. "They're made out of the same tough flexible glassy-foil material used in our space-suits, and are big enough to hold a person in a basket stretcher. Those would hold a large portion of a flouwen."

Designs for flouwen space-suits began building themselves in her head. "Their sonar-vision wouldn't work in vacuum at all, and would be pretty poor in air, so we would need to build lenses for them right into the suit so they could look at things with their light sense." She looked at John. "We'll need to get the Christmas Branch to cast us some plastic helmets with built-in lenses and figure out how to attach the helmets to the rescue bag."

"We can weld the glassy-foil bags to a spare helmet neckring from our suit repair stocks, and design the base of the custom helmets to fit the neckring," said John. "We pour the flouwen into the bag through the zipper opening, and lock on the helmet for the vacuum seal."

"How are they going to move around?" asked George. "Are you going to sew arms and legs for them?"

"They don't have bones, so arms and legs would be worthless," John replied. "But they live and swim in low gee so I'm sure they could get around just fine in free-fall."

"They do form pseudopods to manipulate things," Caroline reminded them. "We really ought to put in some sleeves anchored to portholes in the neckring so they can have arms. Legs would be worthless, and Nels seems to get around fine without them. Still, don't see how they will move in gravity, even the ten percent gravity of Rocheworld. The higher levels of gravity we expect on the moons of Gargantua will be impossible for them."

"They could be very useful on those moons which have oceans," said George, thinking about the possibilities. "We could explore the land, and they could explore the oceans. The same undulating motion they use normally for swimming should work equally well when they are in space-suits. But as for moving about on land, I'm afraid that's out. We'll have to roll them down to the water's edge like a beached whale."

"The flouwen seem to be pretty adaptable," John cautioned. "I've seen a lot of different techniques used for winning a sack race. Maybe the flouwen will work out some way to move about on land."

"We'll see," Jinjur interjected. "I'll make sure we test them out on land in their new 'drysuits.' After we see their performance on the islands of Eau, we can decide if they would be worth hauling up to *Prometheus* and out to the moons of Gargantua."

"One other problem . . . " George added. "How are we going to talk to them when they are in their suits?"

"Simple," said Caroline. "The rescue bags come with a standard communications pack so the people inside can make laser-link calls for help and talk to their rescuers out in vacuum. All I'll need to do is insert a translation program into the communicator memory. It can take the sonar chirps from the flouwen and convert them into human language laser-link signals, and vice versa. When the flouwen are in their drysuits on board one of our vehicles, your imp can pick up the chirps coming through the air, James or one of the vehicle computers can translate, and the imp can give you the translated sentence."

Caroline turned and looked at John and Shirley. "If you two will get started on the helmet and suit, I'll get started on the communicator." The three of them headed down the corridor leaving George and Jinjur looking after them, bemused.

"So I guess that I am going to have to make room for some passengers on the trip back up?" Jinjur joked.

"And I will have to see about preparing space for them when they arrive. I wonder how Nels will feel about flooding one of his hydroponic tanks with ammonia-water?"

Nels did not feel any too happy about it, but at least it meant that he would have his chance to study the fascinating alien creatures up close. By the time he managed to find the time to ask the general about his going to the surface, Jinjur had all ready picked the landing team. She had tried to soften his disappointment by letting him know that if any of those chosen had to be scrubbed, he would be the replacement, but Nels knew how unlikely that was. Still, at least Jinjur now knew how seriously he meant to be a complete part of the crew. In the meantime, he would need to decide which tank could be converted into a flouwen apartment without upsetting his carefully balanced ecosystem.

With Cinnamon so busy with her training and preparing for the surface, Nels had to do much of the scut work himself. It had been a long time since he had personally scrubbed out the tanks, and Nels made a mental note to thank Cinnamon next time he had her do the dirty work.

The lab had seemed so quiet lately without her; it made him edgy.

While the rest of the crew concerned themselves with the preparing of the landing craft, Nels studiously worked in his lab. He knew that the Christmas Bush was using most of its capacity in the construction of the flouwen spacesuits and the loading of the SLAM II, so he set about doing all the preparing for the flouwen by himself. It gave him perverse pleasure to work hard at a task that took so little of his usually busy mind, but soon his intellect rebelled. Left with nothing to stimulate his thoughts, Nels began to remember tiny things that he had hardly paid attention to at the time. Songs that Cinnamon used to sing crept out of his memory only to dance unattainable on the tip of his tongue. Finally, in desperation he called out to his imp. "James? I know that you're busy. But can you please hook me into Cinnamon's music program?"

"Certainly, Nels," the computer answered. "Cinnamon is currently singing this selection."

"Patch me through to her." Then, coming through his imp, Nels could hear Cinnamon's clear tenor voice singing softly.

"I'm leaving on a jet plane . . . Don't know when I'll be back again . . . "

Slowly the SLAM II was loaded with all their equipment, rations, and personal belongings for a three-month stay on the surface. That would be enough time to go through two of Rocheworld's forty-day "years," and be close at hand to observe two of the spectacular interplanetary waterfall cycles—this time at a safe distance instead of surfing it. All of the equipment had to go through the airlock that connected the SLAM II to the ceiling of the hydroponics deck of *Prometheus*.

"This is going to be a close fit," said Shirley as she hoisted the automatic tracking telescope for the flouwen communications link toward the ceiling of the hydroponics deck.

"I've got it, but go slowly," warned Caroline from the airlock above. She guided the long tube through the two doors of the airlock, where Richard grabbed it and pulled it through onto the bridge of the rocket lander.

"Need any help, Superman?" asked Thomas from the pilot harness. He and Tony were taking the SLAM II through checkout.

"Not from any Jamaican beach bum," replied Richard. "Besides, this is the easy part; next we've got to haul it up the passway to the storage lockers on the engineering deck. The passway is even narrower than the airlock doors."

"Tony found a stuck lens cap on a scanner. I've got to go up to the engineering deck anyway to suit up for an outside inspection," Thomas said. "You stay down here and lift the telescope, and I'll climb on up ahead and guide it so it doesn't get dinged. It'll be a great partnership, your brawn and my brains."

"I'll brain you . . . " started Richard, reaching out to give Thomas a knuckle on the skull with his spare hand.

They were interrupted by a strange, yet somewhat familiar-sounding computer voice. It was Jupiter, the persona for the main computer of the SLAM II. Jupiter had a voice pattern that was distinctly different from the voice used by James, the persona for the main computer on *Prometheus*. The different voices helped the humans instantly identify which computer was talking to them. Jupiter's voice came from a Christmas Branch, a one-sixth version of the Christmas Bush assigned to the lander during its mission. The Christmas Bush had clambered down the rungs of the passway that led to the other decks and was waiting there, three hands holding onto the passway rungs, and three hands ready to grab the end of the bulky telescope tube.

"The passway only provides eighteen millimeters clearance for the telescope envelope," said Jupiter. "And that assumes a precise angular orientation. I recommend that the Christmas Branch be allowed to provide guidance through the passway."

Richard laughed. "You've been replaced, Thomas. I've finally got a partner with brains to match my brawn."

"There is also no need for you to go outside, Thomas," continued Jupiter. "I can have a section of the Christmas Branch remove the lens cap."

"George taught me in flight school to always check out my plane before I fly," said Thomas. He got out of his harness and quickly pulled himself up the passway, the Christmas Branch neatly dodging his movements.

"Don't forget that *Prometheus* is under acceleration," yelled Shirley from down below. "Make sure you use your safety lines!" She disappeared from view for a moment, then came back with another bulky package.

"Ready for the power supply?" she called up to Caroline.

When Thomas reached the engineering deck, David and Cinnamon were there. David was stripping down to his shorts prior to getting into his space-suit.

"Where are you going?" asked Thomas.

"Cinnamon and I are going into the flyer to check it out," said David. "Shirley insists that the first person to cycle through the airlock into the flyer must wear a full suit, even though the life-support systems inside the plane indicate that the air pressure and composition are perfectly normal there."

"No need for you to do that," said Thomas. "I have to suit up to go outside, so I'll check out the airlock for you." He started to undress while Cinnamon busied herself getting his space-suit ready. As Cinnamon was checking him out, Richard and the Christmas Branch arrived with the telescope and packed it carefully away in a rack in the equipment storage bay.

In his full space-suit, Thomas went through the first door of the airlock that would take them to the cockpit entrance of the *Dragonfly* airplane. The door closed, and David and Cinnamon listened to him talking to Jupiter through their imps.

"Boarding port pressurized, Jupiter?" asked Thomas through his laser communicator suit link.

"Indicators all green," reported the computer.

"Open the door." The door in the airlock opened into the wedged-shape boarding port that surrounded the cockpit windows and nose of the large aerospace plane. Between the edges of the boarding port and the fuselage of the aeroplane were meters and meters of plastic sealing material. The seal was holding and the air pressure was normal. Thomas carefully cracked the seal in his helmet and took a quick smell—nothing. Sealing his helmet again, he went to the access hatch built into the copilot side of the *Dragonfly*, and lifting panels and turning handles, he pushed the door inward. The door gave away easily and slowly and there was no sound of an air leak. He stuck his head inside, cracked the seal on his helmet again, took a quick whiff, then came back out through the airlock into the engineering deck of the *Falcon*.

"All safe," he said. "You two can go in without suits." He headed for the other airlock that exited to the vacuum outside the hull of the *Falcon*. Just as he got there, Caroline and Shirley arrived with the power supply.

"Did you get checked out properly?" Shirley asked.

"Cinnamon did a thorough job on me," replied Thomas.

Shirley paused to consider. "She's good . . . but I'm better. Hold still!" With a resigned sigh, Thomas grabbed a handhold and she took him through the checklist, his body rocking as she punched the buttons on his chestpack.

"Are both your 'stiction boots working?" she demanded. Thomas obediently turned them on with a flick of his tongue on his neckring control pad. They clicked tightly to the deck, and he lifted them one at a time to show her they released properly.

"Okay, you're cleared to exit," she finally said, reluctantly. "Don't forget your safety lanyard. Remember ... "

" . . . James has *Prometheus* under acceleration. I know, I know. Honest, Shirley, I promise I'll be good and not fall off."

"You'd better, or I'll radio 'I told you so!' at you all the way down until you splash in the ocean." With that sobering parting thought, Thomas cycled through into the airlock, where he carefully fastened the safety lanyard before he opened the outer door to step outside onto the large curved hull.

Shirley turned to Caroline. "If you and Richard can haul the rest of the equipment in and get it stored, I'll help David and Cinnamon check out the flyer."

One by one Cinnamon, David, and Shirley cycled through to the boarding area and floated through the narrow hatch into the aerospace plane. Cinnamon was the first through the hatch and was greeted by Juno, the vocal persona for the semi-intelligent program in *Dragonfly's* computer.

"Hello, Cinnamon," said Juno, its throaty tenor voice coming through Cinnamon's headband imp. "Are you going to be piloting me?"

"Along with a few others," replied Cinnamon. "But I expect that you'll be doing most of the piloting yourself."

"I *am* a competent pilot. I also have in my memory all the experiences Service Excursion Module One underwent during the first mission, so I will be better able to respond to new situations. However, I will need you and the others to tell me where to go."

David swam in through the lock, all business.

"Self-check routine zero," he commanded.

Through his imp a mechanical voice replied, the Juno voice persona having been bypassed during the checkout routine. "Seven-six-one-three-F-F."

David consulted a printed checklist and nodded agreement.

"Self-check routine one."

"Surface Excursion Module Two going through systems check," reported Juno's voice. There was a long pause. During the wait, Shirley arrived and went down the long corridor of the aeroplane and through the privacy curtains to the engineering section at the rear.

"One external video camera stuck, evidence of bacterial

contamination in the water tanks, and the X-ray crystallography analyzer inoperative," Juno finally reported.

"Did you hear that?" David called down the corridor to Shirley.

"Yep," she replied. "Juno fed it to my imp too. I'll pull the X-ray analyzer and get a replacement unit from stores on *Prometheus*. Juno should be able to take care of the water problem by recycling the tanks through the filter system." She paused. "Put me through to Thomas, Juno. Hello, Thomas," she called.

Thomas's voice answered back through her imp. "Yo. What's up?"

"Need to have you check out an external video camera on the *Dragonfly* hull. Juno will lead your imp to it. Give it a kick. If you can't bust it loose it so it can move, bring it in."

"Wilco."

Shirley and Cinnamon then took Juno through a few simulated landings, while David, back at the engineering console, inserted a few "emergencies" to keep them all in practice.

"That's enough," said Shirley, after she had botched an engine-out landing on a sandy beach and Cinnamon had intervened at the last second with an imaginary blast from the space thrusters that just allowed them to clear a huge boulder blocking their path. "Let's seal off *Dragonfly* and get some dinner."

"Fresh peas tonight," promised Cinnamon. "I pushed the growing season ahead and we have a large harvest, enough for everyone."

"I was going to stay and do some more checkouts," said David. "But those fresh peas convinced me otherwise. I hope Nels doesn't cook them too much."

It was finally time for the good-byes. One by one each member of the away team hugged the rest of the crew that was staying behind on *Prometheus* and jumped up through the airlock into SLAM II. As they passed the receiving line, each murmured special farewells to those closest to them.

"Well, George," Jinjur said softly, "this time you get to be the one to keep the home fires burning."

"I'll miss you," he said as he stroked her rounded cheek. "Be careful down there."

"I'll try to keep the *Dragonfly* in one piece," she teased. She reached for George's shirt front and half unbuttoned the top button. Then she fastened it again and patted his chest. "See you soon," she said, pulling him forward for a kiss. "Well, enough of this maudlin stuff!" she finally said as she slapped George's back heartily, and waited as Cinnamon came hurrying past. Jinjur let the civilian go through before her and then entered the tiny airlock herself. The last one through, she closed the lock door to seal off the connection between the SLAM II and the hydroponics deck on *Prometheus*. There was the hiss of recycling air and her imp jumped from the side of her head and carefully checked the seal of the doors as it closed the connection between SLAM II and the hydroponics deck of *Prometheus*. Jinjur felt a twinge as the imp deserted her, and only felt complete when it re-formed its comb shape and nestled back into her thick afro hairdo. The lock sealed, Jinjur stepped out into the bridge of an independent ship. Her ship . . . the *Falcon*.

Tony and Thomas were fastened upside down into their pilot and copilot harnesses and were running through their final checklists. Thomas had let Tony be pilot for this first phase of the mission. This launching maneuver would be at low acceleration, so instead of going to her bunk and strapping in, Jinjur went to a viewport where she could see the action and grabbed some handholds.

"Jupiter is ready to release," Caroline announced from her computer console.

"*Falcon* has clearance for breakaway from the *Prometheus*," said Carmen, who was manning the communications console beside her. Carmen felt a moment's lightheadedness but attributed it to the unusual perspective. James had the *Prometheus* under acceleration, giving the illusion of gravity, and because of the inverted position of the SLAM II on the docking port, it seemed to those on the bridge that they were hanging upside down over a floor with triangular windows in it.

"Take us out, Captain Roma," said Jinjur, and with a loud clunk, the clamps that had held the *Falcon* to the lift shaft of the main ship released the lander.

Gently, Tony eased the throttle forward and lifted slowly away from the airlock. As they cleared the edge of the hydroponics deck, he switched to other control jets and maneuvered the ponderous cylinder out between the sail shrouds. There was a moment of disorientation as the control jets stopped and the *Falcon* went into free-fall. Suddenly the perspective righted itself and the crew was sitting properly at their consoles, under a canopy of stars. Below them, visible out the viewports, was the gigantic silver sail of *Prometheus*, stretching out for hundreds of kilometers and slowly accelerating away under the light-pressure from Barnard. Above them, now visible outside the wedge-shaped docking windows in the ceiling of the bridge, was the double planet Rocheworld, spinning itself into its unique symbol of infinity.

As they approached the planet's strange, double-lobed, rotating gravitational field, Tony turned control of the *Falcon* over to his copilot. After all, Thomas St. Thomas had coped with this anomalous gravity field before. Still, despite his fatigue from the long hours of carefully monitoring their long spiral in from orbit, Tony stayed at his station in order to watch Thomas's technique. Jinjur, wanting to be on the bridge during the landing, had taken over at the comm console and had sent Carmen off to strap herself into an empty sleeping rack.

They were approaching Rocheworld in the plane of their common rotation, going in the same direction as the two planetoids, but slower, since they were at a greater distance from the common center. As they moved closer, the plot of *Falcon's* orbital track on the pilot consoles took on a wavy appearance as the two lobes pulled the lander this way and that as they passed underneath.

"One-tenth gee coming up," Thomas told Jinjur, as the lander approached the planet's influence.

The general's voice sounded through the imps of all those on board. "All hands! Prepare for imminent gees!" After a moment, Jinjur felt the floor pushing up at her and was forcibly reminded of her normally forgotten diminutive stature. *The trouble with gravity*, she thought silently, *is that it makes too many things hard to reach.*

For a while, Jinjur could look out the wedge-shaped docking windows in the ceiling of the bridge and see the outer poles of the two lobes moving majestically across her view, slowing perceptibly as Thomas lowered the altitude and increased the orbital speed of the lander. As the thrust continued, the rocket tilted upward and the lobes could no longer be seen. Reluctant to leave the bridge, Jinjur called up the view of the *Falcon* that the commsat *Barbara* was recording from its position orbiting over the outer pole of Eau. From that perspective, it was easy to see that the tiny silver sliver with the bright yellow tail was headed toward the long chain of island craters on the outer pole of Eau the humans called the Hawaiian Islands and the flouwen called the Islands of Thought.

"Prepare for deorbit burn!" Jinjur called through the imps, as she made sure that her straps were snugly fastened. "Take us down, Captain," the general ordered.

Slowly, Thomas pushed forward on the throttle, increasing the thrust of the main rockets and slowing their plummeting decent. The crew sank in their harnesses as their bodies fought against the long-forgotten gravity. Slowly the pressure built, from a tenth, to a half, to three gees just before reentry.

Muffled groans could be heard over the general comm link as personal imps passed on the sounds from each sleeping rack. Three gees was quite a load for people who had lived most of their lives in free-fall.

"If you think it's bad now," spat the general through clenched teeth, "just wait until we have to lift off this rock again."

The rocket blasted a powerful glare over the choppy waves on the ocean-covered planet below, then throttled down into a more controlled thrust as the huge cylinder backed down through the miles of chill atmosphere, letting the friction of the thin air dissipate the energy of the eighty falling tons of massive silvery lander.

All around the island, the flouwen were gathered to watch. Most were utilizing Clear◊White◊Whistle's new way of looking at the world and were amazed at the amount of energy the rocket expelled in order to swim in the thin atmosphere. The roar grew louder as the exhaust flames from the four rocket engines beat against the sands, sending waves of noise echoing into the water.

Roaring☆Hot☆Vermilion was envious. ☆They make such wonderful noise! The sound of their coming must be audible for miles!☆

❋They certainly announce their presence. See around you. They have even awakened some of the Elders!❋

All around in the shallow waters surrounding the island, "rocks" in a rainbow of colors were swelling with water. Soon the shallows were a swirling mass of flouwen, all tasting the memories of the others, catching up and getting reacquainted. The watching members of the pod rejoiced in the company of elder flouwen that had been rocked up since the pod's youth and thought long dead. Many of the awakened elders soon lost all interest in the humans and the rocket that had called them from their thoughts, for they were most concerned with telling the others about the new theories and concepts they had developed during their long period of hibernation.

As important as it was to flouwen intellectual development,

the hibernation process had its drawbacks. Extremely difficult mathematical and logic problems, such as the definition and ranking of the cardinal infinities, the fast bin-packing problem, and the tiling of *n*-dimensional planes, all required long periods of concentrated and uninterrupted thought.

Once an adult flouwen had developed enough mass, training, and experience to undertake one of those problems for its topic of research, it would shed most of the water from the cells in its body, in the process concentrating the thinking fluids that resided between its cells, and turn into a hibernating rock to think the problem out. The difficulty with the hibernation state was that as the flouwen became solid to increase their intellectual capabilities, they were no longer able to eat and maintain the large number of cells that were so important to the thought process. As the outside of the hibernating "rocks" were worn away by tide and wind erosion, or nibbled away by tiny plant and animal life, the IQ of the flouwen rocks slowly decreased and the problem became that much harder to solve, forcing them to stay rocked up longer. Many flouwen had been known to have given themselves such a difficult problem to solve that they never woke up from the effort.

These elders, however, had been awakened, and were hungry from their many years of thought. Despite all the interesting things that were going on, they soon surfed away on the waves into the deep ocean to hunt food to build up their body mass. It just wouldn't do to be known as a stupid elder.

Jinjur watched the changing shoreline with astonishment as it filled with colorful alien blobs gamboling in the waves and leaping up to look at them like a school of inquisitive porpoises. There was a jar, a rocking motion, then two more jars, as the landing pads hit the sandy surface of the beach.

"The *Falcon* has landed," Thomas reported laconically. He powered down the landing rockets and secured them, while Tony readied the ascent module stage in case it was needed for an emergency liftoff. Jupiter was unable to translate the cacophony coming from outside the ship, but did its best with the outside video cameras to show the humans the upheaval their landing had caused. Soon after the humans had freed themselves from their landing webbing and had regrouped at the various viewports, most of the beach was cleared, the newly awakened elders having surfed off to find food. However, three flouwen, Clear◊White◊Whistle, DaintyΔBlueΔWarble, and Warm❋Amber❋Resonance, continued to watch the tall spacecraft with their new eyes, waiting for the humans to appear.

"Well," said John. "What next?"

"I think we should let the flouwen have a little time to get used to our presence. Besides, we've got a lot of work to do. First we have to unship the *Dragonfly*. Then, some of us can get it ready for the airborne exploration program, while the rest of us set up the laser communications link we brought for the flouwen to use." Passing down through the wedge-shaped corridor that went down the central column of consumables that made up the center of the lander, Jinjur moved purposefully down to the suit locker on the bottom deck. She nodded toward those who waited there for her. "Shirley and Thomas, you have done this once before. Suit up and join me in the airlock; we three will process through together."

Long practice allowed them rapidly to don the bulky space-suits and go through the safety check. Shirley double-checked the telltale lights inside the panels of the others' backpacks and had Jinjur check hers. Reassured, she nodded to Jinjur, and Jupiter cycled them into the airlock. With a long hiss, the lock passed them through into the hostile world of methane and ammonia. They stood at the top of the lander's thirty-six-meter ladder that stretched down to the sand below. Before them the waves stretched to the horizon, while behind them the high mountains of the island curved away. Directly below the ship there was a slick circle, a marbled disc of glass formed when the rocket's flame had brushed the sand. The wide beach was dotted with black volcanic rock and the colorful stony bodies of flouwen that nothing would ever wake.

Holding carefully to the railing around the outer door, Jinjur stepped down the first of the ninety rungs on the Jacob's ladder that stretched down the side of the ship. Shirley and Thomas pushed out a beam from the ceiling of the airlock, rolled an electric winch out to the end of it, and Shirley started lowering Thomas down. At the bottom of the lander, the ladder's rungs turned into steps on one of the landing struts. Jinjur allowed herself a moment of private exaltation as she stepped from the landing pad onto the surface of the planet. Thomas soon joined her on the sands.

"Okay, folks!" Jinjur called, looking up. "Let's get a move on! We've only got a few hours before it gets dark again and I want the *Dragonfly* out on the sand ready to assemble by then."

Soon everyone was in their space-suits and out on the surface of Eau, except Tony, who had Officer of the Day duty on the bridge of the *Falcon*. After clearing everyone a good distance away from the ship, Shirley walked to the landing strut that had been modified to double as a lowering rail for the aerospace plane.

"Release the hold-down lugs, Jupiter," she said, and the clawlike devices swung clear. Standing near the tail, she was able to see the aerospace plane shiver slightly as the hold on it was loosened, but it was still hanging vertically from its nose hook. Shirley stepped to one side and looked up the belly of the plane to the top.

"Lower the top winch," she called. Slowly the *Dragonfly*'s nose tilted away from the lander; the tail remained against the lowering rail. Shirley could now see the cockpit windows, and the large triangular gap it left on the side of the lander as the plane pulled away from the *Falcon*. The rotation continued until the aeroplane was leaning away from the lander at an angle of some thirty degrees.

"Now both winches," said Shirley. Jupiter started letting out both the nose and the tail cables at the same speed. It lowered the aeroplane down the lowering rail, still at the thirty-degree angle. The *Dragonfly* continued to move down the strut until the rudder cleared the lander. About two meters from the end of the rail, the tail winch stopped while the upper nose winch continued to pay out cable. Slowly the huge aeroplane rotated, pivoting. As it approached the horizontal orientation, the lander tilted noticeably as it reacted to the weight of the *Dragonfly*.

"Lower landing skids," said Shirley, and slots appeared in the belly of the aeroplane. Three skids came out. They reached to a half-meter of the surface.

"Lower her down," said Shirley, bending down to watch the underside. Slowly the *Dragonfly* was lowered to the surface.

"Done!" she yelled, then she raced to detach the lowering cables from the nose and tail of the plane. The winches retrieved their cables; their job was done. Shirley turned to the rest of the crew, who were watching the lowering from a distance. Now she needed human power to assemble the *Dragonfly's* outer wing panels.

The panels were hollow graphite-fiber composite structures designed without internal bracing so that the wing panels could nest inside each other. The nested wing sections then fit neatly inside the lower portion of the lander on either side of the rudder of the *Dragonfly*. Using the upper winch that had let the aeroplane down to the surface, Shirley and Jupiter carefully pulled each section out one at a time and lowered them down to the team of humans waiting below.

"Let Jupiter winch the panel all the way down to the surface before you get close to it," Shirley warned. "Even in one-tenth gee these panels are dangerous. One nick in your suit, and this ammonia atmosphere will do more than clear your sinuses."

Slowly each segment was lowered to the ground and

unfastened from the winch cable. Then the crew of eight would lift the five-by-eight-meter section of wing, and move it to its position on either side of the stub-winged *Dragonfly*. Once all the panels were unloaded and arranged on the ground, Shirley unpacked a bundle of small struts and long telescoping poles. These, too, joined the aeroplane parts on the surface.

First, the human crew set up a tripod and winch over one section of wing and let a piece of the Christmas Branch install the internal braces inside the wing section. Then they hooked the cable from the winch to the central lifting lug of the wing section and waited out of the way until it was raised into place, a sparkling imp from the Christmas Branch riding inside. Just as the hanging section met the wing stub, the spider-sized imp removed the thin plastic protective cover from the sealing material packed in the joint. Shirley straddled the small gap, and, using a long pointed pry bar, pulled the wing section into place. The internal fasteners clicked into place beneath her feet and the pressure on her pry bar lessened as the inside imp rotated the fasteners to pull the two wing segments together. The process was repeated with the next wing section and slowly the *Dragonfly* regained the shape of its namesake.

The outer wing segments were lighter and easier to handle, and soon Jupiter was able to pump the wing tanks down, check them for leaks, and fill them with fuel from the storage tanks on the lander. The short three-hour day soon came to an end, and as night fell, the crew, tired but filled with the sense of satisfaction from a job well done, gratefully reentered the relative comfort of the *Falcon* and *Dragonfly*, where they could divest themselves of their bulky suits. The six who were going off to explore Eau and Roche in *Dragonfly* moved into the commodious bunks on the aeroplane, while the four who were assigned to stay at the landing site rearranged the ten cramped free-fall sleeping racks on the *Falcon* into four reasonably commodious bunks suitable for the tenth-gee gravity on Eau. Tomorrow they would start on the setup of the laser, and renew their acquaintance with their alien hosts. Now, they settled in for a light supper and their first night on the planet surface.

♣What is going on?♣ asked a small chartreuse flouwen that had remained by the beach. ♣Where are the strange creatures everyone is talking about?♣

◊Who are you?◊ said Clear◊White◊Whistle, noticing the stranger for the first time.

♣I am Shining♣Chartreuse♣Query, and I was working on a formula to predict the color of younglings. I suppose that I hadn't stored enough mass? Could it be that all I can remember now is the breeding table for my Pretty⊗Smells?♣

◊Welcome back,◊ said Clear◊White◊Whistle absently. The newcomer's lilting speech patterns made it sound like it was always asking for confirmation of its own statements. ◊I can give you a taste of the other contact we have had with the humans.◊

As the yellow-green flouwen sucked the drop of memory juices from Clear◊White◊Whistle's extended pseudopod, Clear◊White◊Whistle tasted a sense of the other's overwhelming hunger. The white flouwen withdrew its pseudopod quickly before the tiny newcomer forgot its manners and tried to eat it. Still, it impressed Clear◊White◊Whistle that Shining♣Chartreuse♣Query's curiosity was able to override the need for food.

Shining♣Chartreuse♣Query had a hard time accepting all that the humans had done. ♣Can all this really have happened? Where did the strange creatures come from?♣ There was a pause as the yellow-green alien struggled with all the information it had tasted. ♣I will need to eat before I will be able to understand all this, but I hate to leave. Do you think they will be doing much more soon?♣

◊They have always been more active while Hot is in the sky. I believe that they are not able to see, and need the light to look at the world.◊

♣Look?♣

Again Clear◊White◊Whistle shared a taste of its memories. This time it was the memory of the method of forming an eye out of flouwen flesh.

♣Is that what those hard spots are on your bodies? I wish I could think straight. If you think they won't do much until Hot rises, then I'll go hunt for a while, shall I?♣

ΔI'll help you.Δ DaintyΔBlueΔWarble was entranced at the idea of teaching someone else for a change. This person might be an elder, but until it regained some mass, it would need some help. DaintyΔBlueΔWarble wanted to ask the elder about the past, and about what the world was like back when Shining♣Chartreuse♣Query rocked up the last time. The two left the cove and headed for deeper waters, leaving Clear◊White◊Whistle alone in its observation of the visitors.

DaintyΔBlueΔWarble and Shining♣Chartreuse♣Query had to travel far to find anything to eat. The initial flood of elders had hunted ruthlessly, and even the wild Pretty⊗Smells had disappeared. Finally they managed to find a pod of Sharp⊗Flyers, and with DaintyΔBlueΔWarble's help, Shining♣Chartreuse♣Query managed to eat enough to satisfy the gnawing hunger. It would take a few turns for the new material to be completely assimilated into the body of Shining♣Chartreuse♣Query, so, for a while, the small elder would have to struggle with a diminished intellect. DaintyΔBlueΔWarble found the other's habit of making everything a question irritating, but by not trying to answer everything, the youngling was soon able to ignore it. It was a speech habit no worse than Roaring☆Hot☆Vermilion bellowing everything.

Shining♣Chartreuse♣Query was amazed at all the changes that the tides had made in the lay of the ocean bottom. After such a long think, Shining♣Chartreuse♣Query was a time traveler of sorts, and told the youngling all about life back in the old days. Apparently the greenish-yellow flouwen had done a good deal of research into the chemical makeup of living things. It even claimed to have "bred" the first of the Pretty⊗Smells, although it could no longer remember just how that had been managed. Dainty∆Blue∆Warble greeted this claim with polite skepticism, but decided that Shining♣Chartreuse♣Query should meet Sweet○Green○Fizz. As the first light from Hot began warming the east sides of the waves, they headed back to the spot that Dainty∆Blue∆Warble had last seen Sweet○Green○Fizz, rocked up and slowly settling toward the bottom.

∆Hello! hello! hello!∆ Dainty∆Blue∆Warble engulfed the jade-colored rock sitting on the bottom of the ocean on the south side of the Hawaiian Islands, where the crawler first splashed down. ∆I have made a new friend! It says it knows all about Pretty⊗Smells! It also says that it made the first one!∆ While Dainty∆Blue∆Warble believed that Shining♣Chartreuse♣Query was confused after such a long thought, it figured such an outrageous statement would be able to reach the deeply thinking flouwen, who was considered the expert on Pretty⊗Smells.

Sweet○Green○Fizz was more concentrated than it had ever been before. While Sour#Sapphire#Coo found amusement with the various infinities and Clear◊White◊Whistle watched the movements of the stars, Sweet○Green○Fizz grew bored with such dry things. Preferring to enjoy and watch the Pretty⊗Smells and learn all their habits, Sweet○Green○Fizz had spent many happy hours training them. Unfortunately, its study of them dead-ended because of their low intelligence. The idea that a pet could be more than trained, that a pet could be created, was absorbing. To create a pet more beautiful, that smelled better, that was more intelligent . . . how would you start? Each Pretty⊗Smell was almost the same, and yet unique. But it was becoming hard to think with all this noise; someone was yelling about "making Pretty⊗Smells" . . . With a sudden rush, Sweet○Green○Fizz filled up with sea water, and found itself squashed underneath Dainty∆Blue∆Warble.

○What are you raving about, youngling?○

Sweet○Green○Fizz moved out from under the blue flouwen.

ΔAn old one has woken from a long sleep. It says that . . . well, you explain, Shining♣Chartreuse♣Query.Δ

♣Are you the one that likes my Pretty⊗Smells? I wanted to continue working on them once they had advanced a few generations on their own? To see if I had missed some inherent weakness? I don't see any around here now, do you have a safe place for them or have they been eaten?♣

○Eaten!? By whom?!○ Sweet○Green○Fizz was alarmed. Loving the little pets, the thought of them being simply eaten was appalling. DaintyΔBlueΔWarble handed over a taste of the last day, with all its extraordinary events. Sweet○Green○Fizz called out shrilly for his pets. After a few moments, the colorful little animals appeared from where they had been hiding, in a niche that Sweet○Green○Fizz's rocky body had protected. The Pretty⊗Smells circled, twittering excitedly; their wings were alight with iridescent colors flashing out in multicolored brightness from the arrays of liquid crystals inside. With their flashing colors, delicate aroma, and trilling tones, the Pretty⊗Smells were a delight to every sense.

♣Ah, they are beautiful. I had hoped to make them smarter? So they could help with the hunting? I always thought that the Orange⊗Hunters were useful but ugly. I wanted a pet that would be more aloof? More adult? So I went to work on them? I bred them for passiveness and intelligence, and for beauty, too, of course. The young gradually became smaller and plumper, with more color, but they could probably still interbreed even now.♣

○I was just thinking of how best to alter my Pretty⊗Smells to be more responsive to commands. Here, taste this thought.○

♣Don't you think it is better to interbreed them thus?♣ Shining♣Chartreuse♣Query gave Sweet○Green○Fizz another taste.

OYes!O cried SweetOGreenOFizz. Soon their conversation traveled far beyond DaintyΔBlueΔWarble's inclination to follow.

• CHAPTER FOUR—MEETING

As Barnard's light first shone on the only artifacts on the planet surface, Carmen woke from her light sleep in her berth aboard the *Dragonfly*. She had only gotten three hours' rest, but she was eager to get started on the next day; it would only be six hours long, and only three of those hours would be in daylight. As she started to rise, a wave of dizziness hit her and she slumped back onto her berth. The imp in her hair stretched out a miniature arm to grasp her earlobe. Pulses of multicolored laser light flashed from the tips of the imp's wirelike fingers, passed through the thin blood vessels in the earlobe, and were picked up by photodetectors in the fingers on the other side. In a fraction of a second, the imp had collected the multispectral data needed for a complete blood assay.

"Carmen," said Juno through the imp, "your blood sugar is very low. You have hardly eaten at all for three days. I am aware that you are trying to cut down your calorie intake, and as long as you were not overdoing it I said nothing. But after the last four weeks of dieting, you cannot simply fast."

Dieting? Carmen hadn't been dieting really, she simply didn't feel much like eating. Maybe it had been a couple weeks since she had much appetite, but big as she was, she was certainly in no danger. She had enough excess fat to last for years! Carmen stood more slowly and with better success.

"I am afraid I must insist that you eat something," Juno's voice gently chided.

"Leave off, Juno. I'm just not hungry. Even the thought of eating makes me feel nauseated."

"Perhaps John should check you out. Shall I inform General Jones that you are too ill to function properly?"

Carmen grimaced at the thought of Jinjur insisting that they scrub the mission just because she didn't want to eat. "Okay, okay, what do I have to do to get you off my back?" She went into the compact toilet down the aisle and made a face at her reflection in the mirror. If she had lost any weight, it certainly wasn't enough. Carmen began applying the makeup that went everywhere with her.

"I will make an algae shake that contains all the vitamins and minerals you need for the day. It will also contain the glucose necessary to keep you from forming ketone. Make sure that you drink it all."

"Like I'd be able to hide it from you the way I used to hide the brussels sprouts from *mi madre*," she muttered. Sometimes living with a permanent nanny could be a real pain.

By the time Carmen had fixed her hair and face and had slipped out through the privacy curtain between the sleeping quarters and the galley section, Caroline was halfway through a breakfast pseudo-omelet made with egg-flavored algae powder. Carmen got her shake, pulled out one of the swing-out seats from under the galley counter, and joined the engineer. "You sure got up fast," Carmen said, trying to put off drinking the blue frothy mixture.

Caroline laughed. "I don't do more than make sure my hair's out of the way. I don't know why you bother with all that warpaint out here in the boondocks."

"I wouldn't go anywhere without my natural beauty."

Caroline speared the last of her omelet. "Do you think we should start out on our own?"

"I'd rather wait until Jinjur gets up. We don't want her to miss a chance to order us to do exactly what we want."

Caroline paused. She sensed some hostility in Carmen's voice and didn't know how to react to it. Usually Carmen would not have made disparaging remarks about the general. Maybe it had something to do with the algae shake Carmen was sipping. Caroline wondered what delicacy she was paying for now. James often made them trade off overindulgence in the fruits of Nels's tanks and tissue cultures with the healthy but unappetizing shakes. She tried to laugh it off. "Our fearless leader will be out soon." The privacy curtain between the galley and the sleeping quarters slammed open.

"Speak of the devil . . . " Jinjur's voice rung out. "You two raring to go?"

"I figured we'd get the power supply set up first," said Caroline. "Then we'll work out the best place for the laser transmitter and the touchscreen for the flouwen."

"Richard can take a look at the local geology while you're setting up the power supply," said Jinjur. "He'll be able to predict any problems you might have with erosion and water-table levels. Also, I doubt I'll be able to keep him here with me without tying him down."

"I wouldn't mind tying him down," said Carmen, batting her long eyelashes at Sam and Richard as they came through the privacy curtain. Carmen slipped out as they came in, making sure that she squeezed against them, lingering to maximize the contact despite the fact that there was plenty of room.

The two geologists grinned at her good-naturedly, and sat down with Jinjur. Richard pushed away Carmen's half-empty glass and grimaced. "None of this slop for me," he called out. "I want steak and hash browns and biscuits with plenty of good country-sausage gravy."

"You're scheduled for an herb algae-omelet and your usual morning Coke," said Juno quietly as the galley imp pushed the plate and metal tumbler forward.

"Well, it was worth a try." Richard grinned, downing a big gulp of caffeine and phosphoric acid, and reaching for his fork. "So, how far have you planned for us to go on today's expedition?"

"That will depend upon what you find," replied Juno.

"But I don't think there will be any surprises. This island was mapped thoroughly from the air during the previous visit to Eau by the members of the crew in Surface Excursion Module One. Since then, it has been periodically monitored by the commsat Barbara during its overflights. It is highly unlikely you will discover anything new or unusual, like alien life-forms or strange artifacts. There does appear to be a small land-locked lake toward the middle of this island that Sam should check out."

Richard shoveled down his herb omelet and, holding his cup of pseudo-coffee, went forward to the science console and brought up an image of the island. It showed the beach that they now occupied. Several kilometers inland, a high ring of hills surrounded a small spot of shining blue.

"The geology exploration plan for the next three-hour daylight period is for Richard to assist the laser communications installation crew in finding the most suitable spot for burying the power supply, while Sam checks out the geology around the lake."

"First I want to meet the flouwen," Sam objected.

"I thought you were a geologist, not an xenobiologist!" Jinjur objected.

"I've been on the surface of Ceres, Vesta, Pallas and Juno, on Ganymede and Callisto, and have never seen so much as a fossil. Then on the first mission to Rocheworld I got stuck with exploring Roche, while Richard got to go to Eau and meet the flouwen. I want to talk to the first 'little green men.' "

Clear◊White◊Whistle was just as eager to talk to the humans. As they had eaten their fill of the wildlife in the deep ocean of Eau, many of the newly awakened flouwen came back to the waters off the beach. Most stayed only a moment to see if there had been any new developments, but Dainty∆Blue∆Warble, Roaring☆Hot☆Vermilion, and Strong❐Lavender❐Crackle joined Clear◊White◊Whistle's vigil. With the rise of Hot, movement became apparent in the landing craft and the aeroplane. In order to see up the slope of the beach, the flouwen had to ride the waves to their zenith. Even then, since sound waves were slower and less effective in the air, they got back only a weak, faraway picture full of confusing echoes. Looking with their newly made eyes gave a clearer picture, but it was only two-dimensional, and they could not tell what was happening within the hard, shiny walls of the vehicles. Roaring☆Hot☆Vermilion was bored, but the challenge of trying to see while riding on the surf intrigued him, and so he was the first one to see the lock door reopen at the top of the towering lander.

The spacesuited forms of Tony, John, and Shirley appeared in the *Falcon* airlock. Shirley extended out a long metal beam from the ceiling of the lock with the winch on the end, while John and Thomas attached the first of a number of packages to the end of the cable. Then the airlock on the *Dragonfly* opened and Cinnamon, Sam, Richard, Carmen, and Caroline came out to stand at the bottom of the lander and await the arrival of the packages. Jinjur and Thomas remained inside *Dragonfly* and *Falcon* where they could monitor the progress of the others after they split into groups.

The first package lowered down was a compact metal cylinder, the nuclear minireactor-photoelectric generator that would be the power supply for the flouwen laser-communication link. Although not large, it was dense because of its load of plutonium fuel, photoelectric cells, and folded heat-pipe radiator vanes. Even in the twelfth-gee gravity field at the outer pole of Eau, it was a load even for Richard. Next came a geological coring tool and bit, a bundle of core tubes, reels of high-temperature superconductor cable, the laser transmitter module, the autotracking telescope for sending the laser beam either up to *Prometheus* or directly to Earth, and the underwater touchscreen designed for use by the flouwen. The last package lowered was a large bag with three lumps in it.

John rode down with the bag, while, after securing the winch, Shirley scrambled after him down the rungs of the Jacob's ladder.

Richard checked the safety latches on the minireactor, hoisted the compact heavy package to his left shoulder, picked up the coring tool with his right hand, and started trudging off up the beach. He looked carefully at the geology of the terrain in the distance, trying to identify the best location to emplace the reactor-generator. Trotting along after him came Shirley with the telescope and core tubes, Carmen with the laser transmitter, John with the reels of cable, and Caroline with the touchscreen.

Sam and Cinnamon picked up the large bag between them, and they and Tony walked down to the edge of the surf to greet the waiting flouwen.

☆Hello! Hello! Hello!☆ cried Roaring☆Hot☆Vermilion as it literally beached in front them. Feeling the sand embedded in its flesh, Roaring☆Hot☆Vermillion knew that it would later regret the hasty charge. ☆Arrgh! I hate the sand!☆

"We can bring you out of the surf and protect you from the sand," said a voice coming from the brightly glowing Sound⊗Maker that sat on the shoulder of the human.

☆Anything that will get me away from this thought-clouding sand!☆ Roaring☆Hot☆Vermilion pulled back from the beach on the receding wave. Following closely, the humans decreased the buoyancy of their suits and carefully waded into and under the surf. The sand that so interfered with internal communication slowly sifted out of Roaring☆Hot☆Vermilion as they reached clearer waters. Soon the three humans were completely submerged in the relative calm just below the tossing waves. One of their suit imps swam up to the surface, where it acted as a relay for the blue-green laser optical link between the suit computers and the central computers on the vehicles.

"We'll never be able to fit them into one of these suits," said Cinnamon, looking with awe at the gigantic blob of reddish jelly that stretched for meters in each direction. "Can they only partially solidify in order to fit?"

"James thought that for the chance to come exploring with us, they would be willing to separate part of themselves off from the rest," said Tony. Jupiter, operating the outside suit imps at long distance through the optical relay link, translated Tony's words for the flouwen, while adding some words of explanation of its own.

☆Separate!?!☆ Roaring☆Hot☆Vermilion roared.

"Were you translating?" Cinnamon asked.

"I am translating everything," said Jupiter.

☆I will not tear off pieces of myself … ☆

◊Wait a moment.◊ Clear◊White◊Whistle surrounded the humans. ◊How big a subset do you need this time? Part of me remembers being studied by you before and you did me no harm.◊

"Actually," said Sam as he spread out the giant-sized baggy that they had developed to hold the flouwen, "this is as much of each of you as our ship is capable of holding."

Clear◊White◊Whistle took the limp bag of glassy-foil from Sam's hand and studied it carefully with a series of sonar pulses. Sam showed the alien how to work the zipper, and the white flouwen opened the suit and allowed itself to flow inside, squeezing excess water from its body as it did so. By the time the bag was filled, a good portion of the giant flouwen was surrounded by silvery glassy-foil. It was easy for Clear◊White◊Whistle to see the way the zipper would seal the flouwen into the bag, protecting that portion of its body from the sand and the drying effects of the air—and from the rest of itself outside. Clear◊White◊Whistle hesitated, hating the idea of separating into two beings. ◊If I do this, you will take me with you to explore the land above?◊

"Yes," said Sam. "That's why we brought the suits. This is the only way you can leave the ocean and go exploring with us." He produced two others.

Dainty∆Blue∆Warble, Strong❐Lavender❐Crackle and Roaring☆Hot☆Vermilion waited. Slowly, Clear◊

White◊Whistle closed the zipper. Almost immediately it opened it again, testing the device. Then the zipper closed again and the free portion of Clear◊White◊Whistle moved away, leaving the suited flouwen standing alone.

☆How does it feel?☆ asked Roaring☆Hot☆Vermilion.

◊It's odd!◊ said the free Clear◊White◊Whistle.

◊It's odd!◊ said the suited Clear◊White◊Whistle at the same time.

Δ Being small will make you stupid, Δ warned Dainty∆Blue∆Warble, who had just had the experience of watching after a small stupid flouwen.

◊Smart enough to hunt and feed and grow!◊ insisted the free Clear◊White◊Whistle.

◊Smart enough to learn and explore and look!◊ said the suited Clear◊White◊Whistle.

◊Think how large and smart and experienced I'll be when I get back together!◊ they finished simultaneously.

Roaring☆Hot☆Vermilion knew when a challenge was issued. Taking another one of the bags, it poured inside, hesitating only slightly as the zipper sealed up the suit.

Separating felt odd, and odder still was the thought that he was now only half as smart as he had been. For a moment he was reassured by the fact that he felt no dumber, but then he was crushed to realize that he was too stupid to tell the difference, and had proved his own idiocy by his momentary reassurance.

Strong❐Lavender❐Crackle took the last suit. It was older and thus bigger than the others, and so the free portion was still rather large. Strong❐Lavender❐Crackle looked at the small, suited subset and wished it luck. It felt as if it had made a new youngling, except this time it was the only parent.

❐Take good care of yourself, Little Me.❐

Little Purple was slightly annoyed at the proprietary attitude of his progenitor and silently resolved to show his other self a thing or two when they reconnected.

Dainty∆Blue∆Warble had no desire to return to infancy so soon after earning the respect of the rest of the pod.

Agreeing to take the "free" halves out to feed while the suited flouwen explored the island, Dainty∆Blue∆Warble silently resolved never to make a youngling; it had had more than enough of babysitting. It was tempted to ask them hard questions the way its tutors had done, just so they would rock up and stay out of the way.

The newly shaped flouwen looked like oversized bowling pins, rounded on the bottom like a child's punch toy. Two semi-globular lenses of plastic molded into their helmets held the same relative position as the eyes of a human. From ports in the neckring there extended three short "arm" sleeves ending in three-fingered "gloves." The glassy-foil in the sleeves and fingers had spring-loaded pleats so the reach and grasp could be augmented if necessary.

The suited flouwen soon learned to form pseudopods in the arms and gloves of the suit and practiced using them. They picked up rocks from the ocean floor, punched icons on the touchscreen, and unsealed and resealed their suits until the motions became sure and smooth. They found it was easy for them to swim through the ocean in their suits using their usual undulating body motion.

"Well, they have pretty much got the feel for operating the suits in ocean environments, so they definitely could be useful in exploring the ocean parts of some of the moons of Gargantua," said Sam, looking on critically. "Now let's see if they can move around on land without legs. Otherwise, we are going to have to roll them out the airlock and down the beach to the water on each visit."

Cinnamon called out to the three flouwen. "Okay, Little White, Little Red, and Little Purple, let's see if you can make your way up the beach and out of the surf. As soon as you feel sand underneath, try rolling along on your side while the waves are pushing you."

Sam and Tony moved behind Little White and slowly pushed the two-hundred-kilo flouwen onto its side. Because they were underwater and the gravity was only a twelfth of a gee, they had some trouble. They didn't have enough weight for leverage. Little White understood their objective and shifted his body within the suit so that he tipped over, leaving his "head" off to the side. The other two followed suit, and awkwardly they rolled up the gentle slope of the beach. They had a bit of trouble fighting past the retreating waves, but once they were beyond the surge of the surf, they climbed out of the water. Through the twin lenses in their helmets, they could see the surface of the water that had always been their home. They all stopped and turned upright, gazing back on this new view of the sea.

Little White was pivoting this way and that, using the plastic lenses to look around. Two lenses allowed him to triangulate and accurately judge his relative position to other objects. He resolved to teach his other self to form two lenses next time it wanted to look at something. If only the other self didn't figure that out in the meantime. Certainly it was a simple enough concept; he would have discovered it on his own had he given it more thought.

❒Seems like we should say something special . . . that we should commemorate the first time our people have come out from the sea.❒

☆Leave that sort of thing to people like Warm❃Amber❃Resonance, I always say,☆ Little Red grumbled, afraid that he could have thought of something good to mark the occasion back when he was larger.

"On this day, the flouwen left the cradle of the sea," said Cinnamon in her best orator voice.

The flouwen were silent, considering the phrase.

❒Sounds impressive . . . ❒ Little Purple conceded.

☆What the Gray⊗Boom is a cradle?☆ Little Red muttered quietly to himself.

Following Richard's lead, Shirley, Carmen, Caroline, and John strode off up the sandy beach and started climbing the gentle rise. The ground underfoot became rough and rocky as the sound of the surf retreated. Among the boulders, there were still signs of colored flouwen "rocks" from past generations. John made a mental note to gather samples of them from various levels to see if there were signs of changing flouwen development. For now though, it was more important to find a good place to sink a well that would safeguard the nuclear power source for the flouwen laser-communication center.

This ridge was all that separated the lander from the sheltered cove that the flouwen had picked as the best place for installing the underwater touchscreen. They climbed slowly up the increasingly steep slope, and just as they topped the rise, the panorama of the cove was spread out before them.

The cove had a narrow beach: too thin to have allowed the *Falcon* to land. Between them and the water's edge, the ground dropped off sharply, but slides indicated possible routes to the shore. Unfortunately they also indicated instability in the cliff, and that precluded drilling at the base. Still, the cove itself was perfect. Tiny waves lapped gently against the icy shore; the dark line a few feet out indicated the deeper waters that would remain deep even during the lowest tides that came during Rocheworld's close passage to Barnard every forty Earth days. Here the flouwen could use John's wonderful touchscreen in quiet safety.

John had spent many days working with James and Caroline on perfecting the touchscreen. Because the flouwen only used light for a secondary information input, John had augmented the video screen with a sonic pattern output. It encompassed the wide range of frequencies the flouwen had demonstrated during their various conversations during the previous visit to Rocheworld. The flouwen could also use touch to draw any figures that were necessary to explain their theories, and the internal computer in the touchscreen would be capable of interpreting models in either two, three, or *n* dimensions. The touchscreen was even designed to sense chemical compounds, and could transmit electric impulses that would partially simulate the chemical tastes that the flouwen used to trade information.

Richard looked around the cove with a practiced eye. "There's a small pond in a sandy depression over there. It should be suitable for burying the reactor. It's far enough from the ocean shore that even the highest storm waves won't uncover the reactor, and far enough from the cliffs that falling rocks won't cut the power cable. The only question is how deep the sand goes. We'll have to drill a core hole."

"Well, let's get to it, big boy. The days are short on this planet," Shirley said as she put down the heavy telescope and started down the slope with her load of perforated core tubes.

Caroline had been looking around too. She pointed to the high point in the ridge they were crossing. "That knob up there would be a good place for the laser transmitter and the autotracking telescope. The view from there would be nearly unobstructed and would allow good coverage of the sky. We can fire some explosive bolts into the rock to provide solid anchors for the telescope in case of high winds."

"You sure can pick them," Carmen groaned. She shifted her grip on the laser transmitter.

"I'll go ahead and anchor the telescope. Take a break and then start up after me," Caroline suggested.

John gave Carmen one of the reels of cable. "While you're resting, why don't I take the touchscreen down into the water as you unroll the cable." John moved down the slope to the still waters of the cove. When he reached the edge of the water he started to wade in.

"Do you want me to come with you?" Carmen called. She eyed the water apprehensively. Ever since most of her family had died in the tidal wave that followed the 2018 earthquake, drowning had haunted her dreams.

"Don't bother," John said. "Save the heaters in your suit. The water here is plenty calm, and I can see the antenna sticking up from the crawler. Run that wire up the hill to Caroline."

John strode confidently out into the water. The tiny wavelets lapped around his ankles. The cold bit at his toes before the suit heater kicked in. The walking was awkward until he let most of the extra air out of his suit. As the crinkly glassy-foil material pressed against his skin, John lost the buoyancy that had him trying to walk on the surface. Gradually the cold water rose, tightening the suit against his flesh.

The smooth surface of the water crept up the face of his helmet and for a moment John had a beautiful view half above and half below the surface of the water. He remembered Carmen telling him of her fear of drowning, and hoped that she would not pass up the chance to see the world bisected this way. He himself had no fear of the water; his mother had told him that he was born with a caul. As the waters met over the top of his helmet, his view of the ocean was imbued with two shades of green. They swirled about him, twisting and marbling, yet never intermingling.

♣Is this a Stiff⊗Mover? What is it doing?♣

○Ask it yourself.○

♣Stiff⊗Mover? Is that another Sky⊗Talker you carry? Is it like the one that the Crawling⊗Rock brought?♣

"I have come to replace the old one with this new one and take the old one back," John explained though his suit imp. "This one will last longer and is better made."

♣If this one is better, why do you want to take the other one?♣

○Maybe he wants to eat the animal.○ Sweet○Green○Fizz had been appalled to learn that this was what Shining♣Chartreuse♣Query had done to those early Pretty⊗Smells that had not lived up to his expectations. Shining♣Chartreuse♣Query said that this was so they would not reproduce and make more failures, but eating a pet seemed indecent to Sweet○Green○Fizz. It would be like Roaring☆Hot☆Vermilion eating one of his Orange⊗Hunter pets.

"No. I don't want to eat it." John laughed. It was odd for the flouwen to hear the sounds of strange alien laughter coming from inside the spacesuit. "It isn't alive, but we do need to use its parts."

Sweet○Green○Fizz protested. ○But it talked to us. If it talks, it must be intelligent. How can it be intelligent and not be alive?○

"It thinks using electricity moving through pieces of stone called silicon chips. As long as we are here, we might as well pick it up and take it back so we can use the silicon chips again."

♣It is a made thing that thinks with electricity and pieces of stone and is intelligent but not alive and you can use its pieces?♣ Shining♣Chartreuse♣Query started to rock up to think about these strange new concepts, then swelled back up again, knowing for certain that it wasn't massive enough to understand those concepts without a long period of concentrated thought. It would save them to work on later, maybe after a few turns of heavy meals to build up bulk.

The new underwater touchscreen was larger and more versatile than the first. Also, the surface of the touchscreen was smoother and better sealed since the Christmas Bush had had more time to work on the casing. The only protrusion was the thick power and communication cable coming out the back and running up onto the shore.

John was reluctant to leave the water and end this, his first contact with the flouwen. He waited patiently just under the water, admiring the flickering play of light against the gaudy rocks of those flouwen that even the landing of the *Falcon* hadn't aroused. This close to the equator and on the outer pole, where the sun shone three hours out of every six-hour day, the ocean was relatively warm and ammonia-poor, but the high cliff on this side of the bay shaded the shallow water in the cove, allowing a thin film of crystalline water ice to form on the still surface near the middle. As the feeble sunlight refracted through the patterned ice to glint on the rocky bottom, John felt as if he was imprisoned in a crystal.

Shining♣Chartreuse♣Query and Sweet○Green○Fizz had placed the new touchscreen on a flat place in the sandy bottom, but they were more interested in John than the odd box. Clear◊White◊Whistle had found the first touchscreen fascinating, and had spent much time conversing with it, but that kind of research simply wasn't in the field of interest of these two flouwen. They were experimental geneticists.

○Why do you make a pet that isn't alive? Wouldn't it be better to start with smart things that are alive and breed them so that the offspring are smarter?○

"We also breed 'pets' to be smarter, or bigger, or better looking." John's face took on a superior look as he answered. His own family had always privately considered themselves the end and best result of good breeding. "There are members of our crew who specialize in breeding new animals and plants and who could explain this better than I, but I know that they can actually manipulate the patterns in the genetic chemicals of living cells in order to change them to produce more desirable traits in the offspring."

○We know from mathematical analysis of the results of our breeding efforts that such patterns must exist in the units of our animals. With a great effort, some of us have used extremely high-frequency chirps and lengthy analysis of the scattering pattern to actually see these patterns. But we have no way of changing them. How do you detect the patterns, and how do you change them?○

"We use a device called a scanning tunneling array imager and manipulator. When you use it, it is like feeling and manipulating something with a hand, or pseudopod, that has a million miniature fingers." John waited patiently as Jupiter's translator struggled to explain the concept of the complicated machine with the limited joint vocabulary that had been developed by the translation program. As the last of Jupiter's careful explanation echoed out into the water,

Sweet○Green○Fizz rocked up and joined the other colorful rocks scattered over the ocean floor.

♣I guess I should presume that Sweet○Green○Fizz will take some time to figure out a way for us to see and manipulate those patterns on our units? Perhaps I should go get more to eat so I will be able to understand the taste of the solution when it is ready to be shared? Will we be able to talk to those crew members you mentioned? The ones that manipulate genetic patterns?♣

"Yes," said John, although he knew that only Cinnamon was on the surface now. Still, they could talk to the gimp through the new touchscreen. That would make these green aliens really appreciate the hard work John had put into making the custom touchscreen for their use.

"Once we get the power supply installed, and the transmitter set up on the top of the ridge, you can talk to our geneticist on the *Prometheus*. Ask James to let you speak to Nels." John smiled to think of the shy man's discomfiture at being summoned to the communication center to teach Genetics 101 to green amoebas. John didn't much care for Nels, although he was always polite. He could never think of anything to say when he ran into the gimp, and his normal glib charm would fail him. People with deformities made him feel uncomfortable.

John watched as Shining♣Chartreuse♣Query swam off and vanished in the darkening water. Stepping carefully around the hard, slick, bright-green blob of Sweet○Green○Fizz, he waded awkwardly out of the sea. Now that John was free of the ocean's chill, the trickles of water that ran down the heated suit boiled off almost instantly, momentarily blinding him with his own steam. To Carmen and Caroline, he looked like a god of mists rising from the waves and walking toward them. By the time he reached them he was completely dry.

Caroline and Carmen had had no trouble placing both the laser transmitter and the autotracking telescope to Caroline's satisfaction. Caroline had done most of the work;

the climb had taken the last of Carmen's strength. As Carmen sat on a rock and recovered, she watched Caroline and looked out over the cove. The setting was so much like the seaside town she had been born in that Carmen allowed herself a moment's homesickness.

"Caroline, do you ever regret leaving so many things at home?"

"Of course I miss the Earth," Caroline answered. "This is the adventure of a lifetime, but it did mean giving up a lifetime on Earth to have it. I wonder about what my life would have been like, if I hadn't been chosen. I miss my father, my sister and her children, and of course, my son, but all in all . . ."

"Your son?" Carmen was amazed. They had worked together on many projects, but Caroline had never mentioned a son before.

"Yes, I have a son. His name is Tomjon. He was seventeen when I left."

"But you were only thirty-three then . . ."

"Yes, I was sixteen when he was born. Like many foolish girls in those days, I got myself into the kind of trouble that was illegal to get out of. During that period of reaction, it was even a crime for an American to terminate a pregnancy while out of the country. And the authorities kept track of who left pregnant. My family took me out of town for six months and then my stepmother told everyone the baby was hers. Since she was thirty-five and had no other children, no one really believed her, but such 'autumn babies' were the only way to save face back then."

Caroline stretched. Blasting the hold-down bolts in the rock and tightening the support cables for the telescope had been hard work. She sat down next to Carmen to rest for a moment. "I worked hard to finish high school early and then buried myself in my college work, carrying extra units and taking no vacations so that I might be able to reclaim my son and give him a good life. But when I landed my first job at MIT and went back for him, I didn't find the tiny baby I had given up. I found a five-year-old person who cried when I tried to hold him. He already had a mother, one who loved him and had willingly faced all the public scorn I had run from. How could I separate them? My only wish was that he be happy."

Carmen was silent. She could have gotten pregnant during high school. She knew many who had, and now that she could view the past without the blinders of teenage self-preoccupation, there *were* a lot of "autumn babies" then. Would she have given up her education to raise a son? Would she have given up the chance to come to the stars? Did she have any right to long for a child when she hadn't the generosity a child demanded?

"Did you never tell him that you were his mother? That you carried him in your womb for nine months?"

"Tomjon knows that I love him, and that carried him, but in the scheme of his life, those nine months aren't all that important to him."

"But what about you? You sacrificed your youth, studying so that you could provide a life for him. You are his mother!" she protested.

"Me? I am the mother of all my engineering designs." Caroline was surprised that Carmen seemed so affected by her ancient tragedy. She no longer even thought of it as tragic; her father's wife had been an excellent mother, willing to devote all of her average intellect toward the raising of the active boy. Shy from her early burn, Caroline had had little interest in the social life at college, and sometimes wondered if she had only used Tomjon as an excuse to bury herself in the abstract beauty of her engineering studies. Certainly, the final break from her daydream of raising Tomjon did nothing to slow her down. She went from being a "studyholic" to being a "workaholic" without missing a beat. And when one of her designs was finally visible in finished, working hardware, she did feel more of a sense of accomplishment than she had felt so long ago when she had pushed Tomjon into the world.

"Here comes John now!" Caroline said, eager to change the subject. They got to their feet as the steaming cloud rose out of the sea and walked toward them.

"The flouwen have gone for a while. Let's hook up the laser transmitter and telescope so the touchscreen will be ready as soon as we get power. Why don't you go see what's keeping them?" he asked Carmen.

Carmen didn't mind tackling the slope again after her rest. Also, she wanted some time alone with her thoughts. Maybe James was right about her not having enough energy to do her job. She tried to think of food, but the idea sickened her. Maybe she just needed more sleep.

On the other side of the ridge, the emplacement of the nuclear minireactor went quickly. Shirley and Richard took turns on the core driller and vied with each other to see how fast they could drive a meter length of coring tube through the wet sand. They easily made it through the necessary ten meters of ground and carefully lowered the reactor and its long stack of cooling fins down into the water-filled well lined with porous core tubing. When they finished, Richard went back and got the end of the power cable that Carmen had unrolled and brought it back to Shirley.

"Here's the plug," he said. "Where's the socket?"

"Right here," said Shirley, holding up the controller for the power supply. "It's all set and ready to activate, but it will be a few minutes before we have power." She activated the controller using its internal power supply and went through a long checklist.

"All the photoelectric converters check out, and the radiators are indicating adequate cooling at this power level," she reported. "Now we switch to high power." She raised a safety cover and activated the red button underneath. Deep below ground, control rods were removed from the compact cylindrical nuclear reactor, and shortly later the cylinder was glowing red hot. Surrounding the reactor were special mirrors that passed a broad band of usable infrared and visible light to photocells that converted the light into electricity. The light outside the usable band was reflected back onto the hot reactor core, where the light was reabsorbed and turned back into heat, to be recycled once again. With optimized photocells, the whole process was nearly fifty percent efficient at converting heat into electricity. The rest of the heat was dissipated into the water by the stack of heat-pipe radiators.

Shirley watched intently as the display screen on the console showed the stack of radiators glowing hotter and hotter as the reactor heated up. Finally the picture stabilized.

"Good!" she finally said. "All of the radiators are in the safe yellow range. No orange vanes and especially no red ones." She turned to Richard. "Let me have that plug. I want to see how it does under load." Richard connected the end of the power cable to the controller and up on the hill a brilliant green beam of laser light flashed from the end of the telescope, sparkling in the blowing mist from the pounding ocean waves beyond. The display on the controller shifted slightly, then settled down once again. Shirley made a few more adjustments.

"A steady one point three kilowatts. Just about enough to run a toaster, and more than enough laser power to punch a high-resolution video message across six light-years from Rocheworld to the light-buckets on the backside of Luna. I have to stay here and monitor the power supply for a while yet, but why don't you go up and join the others at the transmitter?"

• CHAPTER FIVE—EXPLORING

Tony, Sam, and Cinnamon were having a bit of trouble with their drysuited companions. The three flouwen were not as interested in exploring the island as they were in exploring the interior of the *Falcon* lander and the *Dragonfly* aeroplane.

☆Why do you want to look around out here?☆ Little Red grumbled.

◊It looks just the same as the land underwater. Nothing but a lot of rocks. We will go look at your things!◊ Little White insisted. He didn't wait for the humans, but rolled onto his side and started toward the lander.

After he got almost halfway there, Little White slowed to a stop. Little Red, who was following him closely, ran into him and for a moment the humans had to struggle to keep from laughing as the two squashy blobs struggled to regain control of their momentum. Little Purple had no such restraint and the weirdly musical laughter of the flouwen echoed over the communications link. Finally the humans' composure broke and they joined in.

☆Why did you stop!? I can't just go through you!☆

◊I just realized that we will not be able to get up to the hole at the top! We can not just swim up to it and we will never be able to . . . go up those straight things.◊

"We call them rungs, and to pull one's self up we call climb," Cinnamon offered.

"It will not be necessary to teach the flouwen words that they do not know," Jupiter said. "They will work out their own words that make sense to them and I will use those words to translate. We do not want to teach the flouwen

English. They need to be able to tell the rest of the pod about their adventure in a way that all the flouwen will understand."

"Privately, Jupiter?" Tony asked the computer through his imp, and the automatic translation to the flouwen of whatever he was saying stopped. "We really need to look around the island a bit before we give these guys the grand tour of our vehicles. Can you figure out some way to stall them?"

The others agreed, and the translation switched back on as Jupiter talked to the flouwen.

"We will be able to get you up into the lander; we even have a tank of water in there that you will be able to swim around in. But the winch will take some time to set up. Why don't we look around the island in the meantime? Once we get away from the beach we will find things that will interest you."

❑Yes, you two. You can't solve the equation when there are too many unknowns. It behooves us to learn all we can about our own world. Not all of it is underwater.❑ Little Purple was no larger than the others, but the change in size had not affected Strong❑Lavender❑Crackle's pompous attitude.

Little White and Little Red came back and joined the others. Together they headed away from the *Falcon* and back up the beach. Before long they were traveling up a rather steep incline. The suited flouwen were having to struggle in order to climb the hill. They stopped to rest only when they could balance against a rock to keep from rolling back down. In the beginning, Little Red had enjoyed the dizzying speed that he could achieve spinning down the slope, but it was too much work catching back up to the others. Eventually he decided to stay with them and postpone his fun. He promised himself that he would roll all the way down the mountain on the way back.

"It seems awfully bare for a planet with such advanced life-forms in the sea," said Sam. "You'd think that there would at least be some insect life."

"But all life has to start in the sea," Cinnamon objected. "The reason nature seems to have lost out on the dry land of Eau is that she got it right in the first place. Imagine you are in a primordial soup such as Eau's oceans must once have been. You are just one of a million other varieties of tiny animals that feed on the nutrients given off by the volcanic vents that warm the ocean floor. You reproduce by bifurcating and can propel yourself by undulating. Then, in some freak mutation, you find that by linking up with your own one-celled offspring, you become not only bigger but smarter than all the other single-celled beasties swimming around you. You would reproduce to grow and eat to reproduce, interlinking with all your single-celled children until you became more than what you were before. You, the collection of tiny things that make up you, reach sentience.

"But it needn't take eons, or even generations. While you are growing, those things around you have not grown. You are the one person on the planet surrounded only with tiny bugs and your one goal is the same as theirs. Survival."

"So the flouwen killed off all the competition," said Tony.

□It is in my memory that it is important to eat those creatures that grow too large,□ Little Purple offered reflectively. □But I have never seen an animal that tried to grow as large as a flouwen.□

"The desire to grow to such a size would be bred out of them!" Sam concluded, enjoying the hypothesis.

"What is to stop a power-hunger flouwen from trying to grow so much larger and smarter than the others, to try and rule them?" Tony asked.

□Why would it want to?□ Little Purple was clearly puzzled.

"Well? What does make a flouwen decide to stop growing?" Tony countered.

☆When you get too big, it is uncomfortable. You are too bulky to surf, and it takes more energy to hunt than you can replace. Better to make a youngling and then you only need to hunt for the rest of yourself.☆

"Exactly what the prehistoric flouwen would do," Cinnamon guessed. "I'd bet at first it only budded off pieces of itself and sent them out to hunt for it. But each piece gained some independence. In time, it resented going back to anonymity within the flouwen whole. Instead, it would return and share tastes and thoughts with the parent body, but would retain its identity, mingling only when it found itself uncomfortably large."

☆I think the first flouwen was red,☆ Little Red said proudly. Maybe the human was right. It was easy to imagine himself all alone with tasty stupid food all around him. Maybe it wasn't imagining, but a memory.

◊What does color have to do with it?◊ Little White asked testily. From the time Clear◊White◊Whistle had said its first words, all the elders had wondered at its odd color. Many had met or remember pale flouwen before, but milky whiteness was very rare indeed.

"Isn't there any relationship between color and temperament?" Cinnamon asked. "After all, Loud Red and Deep Purple are more alike than you and Loud Red are, and Blue Boy is more like Green Fizzer than Yellow Hummer. Maybe it is from shared memories related to the parents of each flouwen."

Little Purple objected. ❐But I was a parent to both Sweet○Green○Fizz and Roaring☆Hot☆Vermilion. They are not alike in color or personality.❐

"Perhaps you have a flouwen equivalent to humans' recessive genes."

◊Sweet○Green○Fizz and Shining♣Chartreuse♣Query were talking about this sort of thing. Maybe you should leave it up to them. I am not going to rock over it now, when it might delay my getting inside your metallic pet.◊

Cinnamon dropped the subject but made a mental note. Both the green-colored flouwen were interested in heredity while the white one cared more about machines. Maybe there was something to this color business.

Meanwhile they were still passing signs of solid flouwen

remains. At some point the oceans must have been a good deal deeper or the rim must have risen along with the central crater in a slow rebound from the meteorite strike that had formed the islands, Sam thought. It gave him an idea. . . .

"Do you have to be trying to communicate in order to trade memory tastes with another flouwen?" he asked.

Little Purple finished pushing himself up the last few meters to a boulder and then wedged himself behind it. The other two also found places to rest a moment, although Little Red just leaned his weight against Richard.

"I think you may have upset them somehow," Jupiter told Sam privately. "I have never seen them wait so long before answering."

❐It is possible to force another to give up its thought. But it is abhorrent to us. It is . . . rape.❐

"I'm afraid that is not a literal translation, " Jupiter apologized. "But it is more relevant to a human than 'like forcing the laws of nature to change in order to fit the hypothesis' would be."

"But what if the flouwen concerned weren't aware of the intrusion?" Sam hurried on so that he would be able to make his suggestion before it was rejected out of hand. "What if we were to chip off a little piece of one of these 'rocks.' Could you taste it and tell us what it was thinking about when it went solid?"

There was an even longer pause than before. Sam began to feel that he had pushed them too far. While he would have no moral problem reading the diary of a long-dead relative, Sam knew he would certainly balk at eating one of them.

❐We have always respected the privacy of Those Who Are Lost In Thought.❐

Sam was stung by the emphasis in the name for the flouwen rocks that managed to come through even in the translation. He was about to apologize when Little White spoke up.

◊I will try it.◊

❐Clear◊White◊Whistle!❐

◊I, too, remember that we have never disturbed them, but I do not remember any reason why. Can you tell me why it is worse than allowing them to be eroded by the tides? Or broken in earthquakes? Or absorbed by plants like the Gray⊗Boom? Any flouwen that stopped to think while this area was still underwater can be no one I remember. And if this does work, think how glad the elder would be to have its thoughts conveyed to another, even after all this time.◊

"Are you sure?" Sam asked. He didn't want the milky guy to get thrown out of the pod or anything.

❐If he will, he will.❐ Little Purple was resigned. ❐There is more than one way to calculate a volume.❐

"What?" Sam was confused by the phrase.

"I believe he means 'to each his own,' " Jupiter clarified.

Sam went to the aqua-blue stone that was supporting Little White. With his hammer he chipped off a handful of its tiny double-lobed cells. Little White shifted so that his zipper opening was at the top of his suit. It wouldn't do to spill himself. Sam unsealed the zipper slightly and dropped the shiny, faceted bits inside. For a moment the chips were visible in the pale alien body, but as they watched through the clear plastic helmet, the aqua-blue cells lost their color and became lost as Little White assimilated the outside colored layer that contained the flouwen memory patterns.

◊Ugh. Tastes terrible.◊

☆But did it say anything?☆ As long as he didn't have to be the one doing the experiment, Little Red was as eager as the humans to know the result.

◊I'm not sure. It was very faint. Does 'Energy is equivalent to mass times the square of the speed of light' mean anything to you?◊

Back at the ridge, John and Caroline finished hooking the laser transmitter to the cable from the underwater touchscreen. Carmen and Richard had connected up the cables and were starting up the ridge. As they approached, Caroline signaled her imp to turn off by making a twisting motion of her hand outside her helmet. She then pressed the globe of her helmet up against John's so that she could talk to him without the computer relaying her comment to Carmen.

"Carmen has been acting odd lately," she said.

"More odd than usual, you mean?"

"I'm not kidding, John. She was moping about home, and about . . . well, babies."

"It's just that time of the month. All you girls get weepy and softhearted." *Soft-headed* he amended mentally to himself. "Besides, Carmen has let herself get so out of shape that all the men stopped boinking her, and for a while there, that was all she wanted to do. I can't imagine what it must be like to not be able to get it as often as you want it."

Spare me, Caroline thought. John had no way of knowing that, of all the men on board, his charms were the only one's Caroline had resisted. He was too much like the high school sweetheart that had abandoned her. What was his name? Funny she couldn't remember it now.

"All she really needs is a good fuck," John concluded. *No point in being coy with Caroline*, he thought. *The little nip is probably gay*.

Richard and Carmen cleared the top of the hill and came up to the laser transmitter.

"So what are we going to call this place? We can't just keep referring to it as 'the cove where the flouwen use the underwater touchscreen console,'" Richard said as he looked around.

"Why not call it Circle Cove?" Caroline offered.

Richard looked down at the cove. It had been formed by a meteoroid that had cut away the edge of the earlier crater that had formed the island, and it was almost a perfect circle. Still, the others greeted the suggestion in silence. They were all remembering the pictures they had seen of the island. It had been obvious that all the coves would be more or less circular.

"This bay is only refreshed at the highest tide. During the day it must boil away most of its ammonia. At times it is probably pure H_2O," Richard prefaced. "How about we call it 'Sweet Water'?"

"Agua Dulce?" said Carmen.

"Agua Dulce it is," Shirley agreed. "John, will you do the honors?"

John activated the console built into the top of the laser transmitter. "Agua Dulce to *Prometheus*, John Kennedy here. Come in *Prometheus*." They waited the fraction of a second that it took the message to bounce through Barbara to *Prometheus* waiting in orbit. Then Arielle's face appeared on the screen.

"John! Is so good to hear you! Is good to hear anyone! Why do they have me sitting at the comm when there is no one out there?" She smiled at them. The twinkle of her imp brace shone from between her lips. Arielle would sport the gaudy brace until her tooth reattached. It did nothing to diminish her startling beauty, but it left her with her Quebec accent.

"They have you at communications?" John smirked. "George *must* be getting old. I know where *I* would keep you if it was up to me."

"You are such barbarian. This is permanent placement for the flouwen laser transmitter?"

"Yes, and we are calling it 'Agua Dulce.' " Then John adjusted the power supply console so that they were both connected to the underwater console submerged in the cove.

"Hello, Hello, Hello!" he called into the water below.

Tony, Sam, and Cinnamon in their space-suits and the three flouwen in their drysuits finally made it to the top of a large rise leading inland. They looked down onto the circular valley that lay before them. The rise they were on stretched all the way around the valley. Below the ridge were other, smaller, concentric ridges. In the center of the valley was a circular lake with a low round island in the middle. Sam looked at the scene with the practiced eye of a geologist who had spent a lot of time on alien planetoids, and reported his observations and conclusions through his imp to Jupiter back on the *Falcon*. They were out of direct line-of-sight to the lander, so the laser communications link between Jupiter and their imps now involved a bounce up to the orbiting commsats and back down again.

"This valley is obviously a meteorite crater. The ridge we are on and the ones below it were formed in the crust when the meteorite hit, like frozen ripples, while the island in the middle of the lake is the rebound of the crust compacted under the falling rock." He looked around the edges of the lake. "The lake is landlocked. No connection to the ocean at all. Must be fed only with rainwater."

☆I will go take a look at it,☆ Little Red decided. ☆Downhill!☆ he yelled, and he careened off away from the others.

"Wait, slow down!" Cinnamon called out. She wasn't sure that the glassy foil that made up the flouwen suits would hold up to such rough treatment. It was flexible but strong, and supposedly tear-proof, but this was hardly normal wear. Little Red ignored her and continued his unrestrained plunge down the slope. The humans hurried after Little Red, while the other two flouwen followed carefully and slowly behind them, not allowing their momentum to overwhelm them.

Little Red was bounding downward, spinning crazily. Although he was not mentally capable of being dizzy since he didn't have ears with semicircular canals in them, Little Red was now feeling certain misgivings. The hillside was strewn with the same sort of boulders that the flouwen had rested on during their climb. Now Little Red was bouncing off those rocks that he couldn't avoid, and finding it harder than ever to control his path. Rocks were to be reckoned with now that he was confined to one shape. Just as his speed began to truly frighten him, Little Red came to a small ridge, the last unsubmerged segment of the concentric rings that formed the circular valley. His momentum carried him up the slope and threw him high into the air over the water. He landed on the still surface of the lake with a tremendous splash. The suit, never designed to take such stress, sprang open at the neckring joint, sending the helmet flying and Little Red squirting into the water.

By the time the others reached the bottom of the slope, Little Red had pulled himself together. They all ran to join him in the water, steam rising off the humans' suits.

☆What a ride! Even better than surfing!☆

"What about the suit?" Tony asked Cinnamon. "Is it okay?"

"I don't know. I didn't design it, John did. But he did say that almost nothing could go wrong with it." She was holding the limp baggie before her in the water and looking at it carefully. It didn't seem to have any punctures, and the seal surrounding the neckring hadn't been torn when the helmet had sprung loose. But Little Red was truly lucky that he had not spilled until he was over the water. Had he landed in the dirt, they would have been forever trying to collect all the spilled blobs of red flesh.

❐If you broke the Shining⊗Skin you would have had to stay here until we came back for you,❐ Little Purple chided. ❐I would not want to have to climb up all those hills again just for you.❐

◊The humans will not take you up to the stars in their pets if you persist in acting recklessly,◊ warned Little White.

☆It was fun! Besides, there is nothing wrong with the Shining⊗Skin.☆ To prove his point, Little Red flowed back into the shining glassy-foil suit, twisted the helmet back on, and assured himself that the suit's integrity had not been breached. Opening the zipper in his drysuit, Little Red extended a pseudopod and held out a memory taste toward the other two flouwen. ☆Taste. It is still in fine shape.☆

Little White opened his suit and took the sample of memory juices Little Red offered. Within the taste was more than the reassurance that the suit was okay. Little Red had included the exhilaration he had enjoyed during his ride, but the taste was also tinged with his momentary fears. Little White instantly understood that Little Red didn't want this part conveyed to the humans.

"Well," said Tony, reasserting control, "now that we're in the lake we might as well look around. Jupiter said that we should try to find whatever life-forms got picked up by waterspouts and carried to the lake." Cinnamon was the expert on water-based life, and Tony figured it was up to him to find something for her to study.

❑Almost anything can be picked up by our storms.❑

☆Gray⊗Booms, Pretty⊗Smells, Orange⊗Hunters, even flouwen have been known to get sucked into a whlee.☆

◊We will get out of these Shining⊗Skins and scan the lake for you. If we find anything unusual we can come back and get you.◊ Almost instantly the flouwen unzipped their drysuits and began oozing out.

"Wait! What may seem normal to you could be something we haven't studied yet!" Cinnamon complained as Little White handed her his empty suit.

◊We won't go too far.◊

"Please can't we stay together?" she pleaded.

"Get back here right now!" Tony bellowed.

☆What?☆

◊What?◊

❑Why?❑

The flouwen all clustered around the humans again. *So much for that!* thought Tony. *This group had no notion of politeness or discipline, but curiosity kept them in line.*

"One of you to stay with us and explain anything we are unfamiliar with," he insisted. "What if one of us walked right into trouble? Like setting off a Gray⊗Boom and getting caught in its sticky threads like George did in the last mission?"

There was a pause. *Maybe now they are seeing things from our point of view*, Tony thought. Then the silence was broken.

◊I suppose I can stay with the humans while you go off and have fun,◊ Little White offered to the other flouwen. ◊My fun will come when we finally get back to the ship.◊

Oh good. Now we're a chore. These beasts are about as self-centered as it is possible to be and still be willing to mate! Tony tried to appeal to them one last time.

"What if we heard a loud roar and some huge beast came swimming up at us out of the deep and tried to eat us?"

Suddenly, through the water, there moved a massive dark form. It was coming straight at them, roaring loudly as it came!

Cinnamon screamed with fright and tried to cover her ears, while Jupiter rapidly adjusted the volume of their imps to protect the humans from the booming roar of the blood-red shape looming toward them.

☆HELLO! HELLO!! HELLO!!!☆

"That sounds just like Loud Red!" said Sam, moving to protect Cinnamon.

The three little flouwen broke before the rush of the huge being as it shouted its greeting to them all.

☆HELLO!☆ the newcomer boomed. ☆I am Roaring☆Hot☆Vermilion!☆

There was a shocked silence, then Little Red exploded.

☆You are not! *I* am Roaring☆Hot☆Vermilion!☆

◊It certainly sounds like you.◊

☆You are Strong❐Lavender❐Crackle,☆ the giant red flouwen said. ☆I remember you as being much bigger.☆

❐This is only a piece of me,❐ Little Purple tried to explain. Refusing to be intimidated by this huge flouwen, Little Purple extended a tendril for the other to taste. He had concentrated his own introduction with a synopsis of all that they knew about the humans. At first the newcomer didn't respond but then, hesitantly, it took the taste from the elder. The humans had to scramble to get out from under as the huge lake dweller, bewildered by the taste and having to think more about it, started to solidify around them.

◊Well, I guess any questions will have to wait for a while.◊

☆It is not Roaring☆Hot☆Vermilion. *I* am!☆

❒I got a taste of it. It tastes just like you. Maybe this being is a piece of you. You did lose a large chunk of yourself in a whlee back when you were a youngling. I remember there was much debate over whether or not you were worth retraining. Sour#Sapphire#Coo was all for eating you and making a new youngling.❒

◊Look, if this flouwen is a lost part of you, why don't you get back together and then you'll both know all each other's stories?◊

☆But I'm so small compared to it! I'll be assimilated!☆

"But you'll only be getting back all that you lost long ago in that storm," Sam pointed out.

☆I don't want to . . . I'll be more it than me.☆

"I don't blame you," Cinnamon piped up. "I wouldn't want to risk my personality to be joined up with anyone else."

☆She knows the flavor!☆ Little Red insisted. Sooner than anyone expected, the lost red flouwen swelled up into the water around them. This time it listened to the discussion without interrupting.

"Why would anyone," Cinnamon continued, "want to join up with someone that, even though he seems to be the same, has so many different memories, memories that no other flouwen has ever tasted. And to join up with one so large! Look how quickly he was able to assimilate all that Little Purple had told him. Oh sure, you might be made into a huge, smart flouwen, certainly the largest and smartest thing in this little lake . . ."

While Cinnamon was talking, the two red amorphous

shapes tentatively touched pseudopods, and before she had even finished her statement, they had started to blend into each other.

☆Wow . . .

☆Wow . . . What a . . .

☆What a life!☆ said the now gigantic red flouwen. ☆While part of me has been living a life of friendship and surfing in the oceans of Eau, part of me has been struggling to survive on the flotsam blown in on the storms. My lost part grew as large as the poor food supply in the lake permitted, but was starved for intellectual simulation. Elders are remembered as godlike figures and I am still struggling to match these memories with my own.☆

"Then the Little Red personality is dominant?" Cinnamon asked, fearful that she had inadvertently caused the destruction of an intelligent entity.

☆No, I am, and always have been, one person. I just didn't have the opportunity to share experiences before. We are . . . I am . . . Roaring☆Hot☆Vermilion.☆

"Hello, hello, hello!" John called out into the bay. Standing on the high cliff, it was easy for the humans to see Blue Boy approach the touchscreen in the shallow water.

ΔHello!Δ The young blue flouwen's voice came clearly through the Agua Dulce substation. As it explored the touchscreen, a squawk of garbled sounds was transmitted up to the humans.

"The screen can transmit and receive light, thusly," said John as he sent a picture of the five of them standing by the substation. "It can also send electrically reproduced chemical 'tastes.'" He sent the flavors of an ester compound. Soon he hoped to be able to read and duplicate the complex flavor memories that the flouwen used to communicate. When they did crack the chemical code, John expected the touchscreen would be equal to the challenge.

"For the time being, you might want to concentrate on sonic communication. We have a rather good working vocabulary for translating the flouwen language, and now that you can talk directly to Jupiter, we soon will be able to communicate completely."

For several minutes the substation continued to make the garbled sounds of Blue Boy playing with the touchscreen. Then, as they watched from a distance, the light blue cloud shrank into itself. John tried to reach the flouwen through the screen, but the only picture he could raise was a blank blue screen.

"What's wrong with the console?" Carmen asked. "Has he broken it?"

"No," said Caroline. "He has solidified to think. Unfortunately he has rocked up right on top of the touchscreen, encasing it within himself. What you see on the screen is the view from inside a flouwen."

"We will have to make some sort of rule about having the flouwen using the screen move to one side before they rock to think," John grumbled. "Otherwise half the time the touchscreen won't be available for the others to use. Every new concept they get from us will shut down Agua Dulce until the receiving flouwen figures it out."

"I'm sure that we'll only need to point the problem out to them once. I think that sometimes they are just too interested in getting the solution to the problem to worry about what happens when they condense." Caroline could sympathize with the flouwen. Sometimes new ideas came swarming into her mind, so fast and furious that nothing else seemed to matter. "Only when they know that the computations will be lengthy do they try to wait until they are where they will get the stimulation of the tides."

"So what do we do now?" Richard asked.

"We might as well go back to the *Falcon*," Caroline said. "We will be able to talk to the Agua Dulce through Barbara from there. Whenever Blue Boy liquefies, we'll know. Then we can go back to teaching him anything about the screen that he hasn't already figured out."

"Don't expect to do much more explaining," said John. "Remember how smart these creatures are. I'd bet that when Blue Boy wakes up from his think he'll be teaching us the best way to improve our designs!"

Back at the lake, the need to explore for interesting life-forms had been removed by Roaring☆Hot☆Vermilion's explanations of the time it had spent there. Rightly believing that the best way to store food was inside, the young flouwen had patrolled the lake like a giant vacuum cleaner, eating everything the infrequent storms brought in. In the beginning there had been all sorts of plants and small animals living peaceful lives. Slowly, in its hunger, the lost portion of Roaring☆Hot☆Vermilion had absorbed them all. It managed to survive by eating all there was to eat during the rainy season, and then rocking up and fasting until the next storm brought a fresh influx of food. Over the many thousands of seasons, the lost flouwen had become very large. Now, the addition of Little Red made Roaring☆Hot☆Vermilion very large and bulky indeed.

The humans left the flouwen in the water and went to explore the marshy island. Time and rain had burrowed into the island, leaving many large puddles, some deep enough to be permanent during the dry season. Within these ponds, out of reach of the voracious flouwen living in the surrounding lake, were many types of plants, small quick animals, and some unidentified shapes. Since much of the life on Eau had rocklike shapes, Cinnamon took samples from all lumps that Sam could not definitely confirm were of geologic origin. Only when her collection bottles were full did Cinnamon reluctantly agree it was time to return to the ship.

They rejoined the flouwen in the water, but a problem confronted them. Little White and Little Purple flowed easily into their suits, but the enlarged Red posed new difficulties.

"I hate to mention it," said Tony, "but how are we going

to get you back to the ocean? We'll never get all of you in a bag this size."

"Maybe we can leave him here and go back for several suits. That way we can bring him out a little at a time." Cinnamon suggested.

☆I don't want to leave any of myself here.☆ Roaring☆Hot☆Vermilion remembered the stifling intellectual isolation of being alone. Size made it hungry for knowledge, but the learning tools that were normally passed on from elder to youngling had been denied it. The lost red flouwen had been forced to derive formulas and theorems that its alter ego had easily learned from the rest of the pod. Roaring☆Hot☆Vermilion would not face the possibility of a small subset being abandoned in the lake, even for a short time.

☆Maybe I can fit in these three suits and you can come back for Clear◊White◊Whistle and Strong❐Lavender❐Crackle.☆ Even as it suggested it, Roaring☆Hot☆Vermilion's massive and now trained intellect figured the relative volume of itself and the room available in each suit and came up woefully short.

"Couldn't you solidify yourself into the suit?" asked Richard. "Then we could roll you up the hill like a giant gumdrop."

❐I doubt it. We tend to go hard all at once. Still, maybe Roaring☆Hot☆Vermilion could try.❐

For the next several minutes, Roaring☆Hot☆Vermilion tried to harden only while in the suit, but it rapidly became clear that it didn't have enough control over the process. It would become hard too soon, blocking the entry to the suit, or harden in such an awkward shape that more wouldn't fit. It soon became obvious that even at the most concentrated, the massive flouwen would never fit inside the drysuit.

"I've got it!" Sam said after he watched the flouwen's contortions. "First, we need to dig a shallow circular hole in the bottom of the lake."

☆There is such a hole at the very bottom of this lake. It is where a huge Gray⊗Boom lived for many years. I had to wait until I was very large before I could attack it. ☆

◊You ate a Gray⊗Boom?◊

☆It tasted awful! But I didn't want it eating food I *did* like. Anyway, it left a flat circular hole.☆

"Good," said Sam. "I'll explain the rest of my idea when we reach it."

They walked along the bottom of the barren lake until they reached the hole. Sam outlined his plan. The normally quick flouwen were not used to thinking about the mechanics of geometry in their more fluid environment, but they recognized the simple beauty of Sam's suggestion.

Roaring☆Hot☆Vermilion flowed into the depression until it filled it completely. Then it concentrated on imagining the last cardinal infinity and slowly shrank into a hardened disk of reddish rock resting on the lake floor. Sam and Tony tipped the disk up onto its rim and, with Cinnamon in the lead and the two drysuited flouwen steadying the sides, they rolled the red crystal wheel out of the lake and back toward the *Falcon* and the setting sun.

• CHAPTER SIX—LEARNING

When Caroline, John, and Carmen boarded the *Falcon*, Jinjur was there to greet them as they cycled through the lock.

"We've been watching the flouwen at Agua Dulce on the monitor. Looks like Blue Boy has come out of his trance. Jupiter has taken over the discussion with the flouwen of how best to use the laser communicator for conversations with Earth, and they have been talking it over for twenty minutes now. Caroline? Maybe you would like to join in on the discussion?"

Caroline did not need to be prompted further. Her engineer's instincts urged her to examine any new ideas the flouwen might present. Quickly shedding the bulky spacesuit, Caroline climbed clumsily up the passageway that led to the upper decks. After years in weightlessness and then all day in the heavy outside gear, she had trouble compensating exactly for Rocheworld's gravity. John looked after her retreating figure and stretched as luxuriously as a cat. He too, was glad to be free of the suit, but his natural dignity refused to let him show his awkwardness until he had time to readjust to the one-twelfth gee.

"I think I'll go listen in to that conversation too," John said. "But first I'm going to stop at the galley and fix myself a long cool drink of iced tea with a real mint leaf. Dehydrating work, wandering around out there." He smiled at the two women and climbed leisurely off after Caroline.

"Good," said Jinjur, watching him leave. After he had gone, she turned to face Carmen. "I want to talk to you alone."

Carmen was just restoring her suit in its locker. She had tried to disguise her weariness with a meticulous check of the safety equipment, but John's mention of a drink of iced tea had made her mouth water. There had been an odd flavor in her mouth for days now, almost as if her mouth were reminding her that she was made of meat. Now, standing in the low gravity, it seemed as if Jinjur were looming over her, even though she was three inches taller than her commander.

"Jupiter has gotten some very unusual messages from your personal imp lately," Jinjur started in her most authoritative tone. "Your blood sugars are way down, and so are your blood pressure and your electrolyte levels. Your reactions have been slow and your temper too quick." She held up a warning hand to stop Carmen's indignant denials. "No, your work has been fine, but still, I am insisting that you visit John in a professional capacity. We have a perfectly adequate sick bay arrangement here on the *Falcon*."

Anger crept into Jinjur's voice. "If you were having trouble, it was stupid of you to try to hide it! You are endangering the whole mission! You will not be allowed off this lander until you prove to me that you are fit." Furious, Jinjur stomped up the rungs of the passway ladder to the control deck.

Carmen's imp had reported to Jinjur Carmen's exhaustion on the surface. Jinjur just hoped that it was nothing serious. In the back of her mind she kept remembering the plots of unlikely science fiction movies where visiting the surface of a planet caused strange illnesses among the crew. To make things worse, Sam's party was taking too long in coming back. With the mountain hiding them from the lander and the commsat Walter, and Barbara over Roche during this part of its orbital cycle, Jinjur could not just casually check up on their progress. No doubt she was overreacting; she might be the one in command, but she commanded good people. They wouldn't let things get out of hand.

* * *

"Careful! Careful! Don't drop him, Herb!" Sam shouted to the others. As they crested the hill, they had stopped to shift from pushing the huge red wheel up the slope, to keeping it from rolling down the other side. The drysuited flouwen were having enough trouble maintaining their own balance and momentum on the steep grade, and the three humans were struggling with the awkward crystallized flouwen.

"Don't drop it, 'Herb'?" Tony had breath enough to ask, as he maneuvered himself around to the front. He had done most of the pushing, since Sam's height was more useful in guiding the awkward crystal around the rocky slope.

"I don't know . . . it was one of my mother's expressions," Sam explained crossly. Tony might have been doing all the pushing but he had done the steering. Sam just wished that Tony would hurry and get around in front of the wheel to keep it from rolling downhill too fast. Even in one-twelfth gee, a rock the size of a four-meter platter was heavy.

Cinnamon was only helping to balance the wheel from the side, but it was tense work. When she realized she was singing "Old Man River," she decided to try and lighten the mood. "Little Red bounced down this hill before," she said. "Maybe we should just let go and let him bounce down again?"

The red crystallized wheel vibrated beneath her fingertips as the solid flouwen protested.

☆Bits of me would chip off!☆

◊Besides, the disk would very likely tip over onto its side. Out of the water we would have a lot more trouble getting it upright again.◊

"Why don't we just leave it on the hillside?" Cinnamon continued, teasing. "What do you want all this extra mass for anyway? Won't it be unmanageable to be so big?"

☆Size equals intelligence . . . besides, I will just make a youngling and pass on the extra.☆

❒You'll need to make more than one before your intelligence drops back down to the Roaring☆Hot☆Vermilion we are used to,❒ Little Purple said sourly.

"Okay," said Tony as he got the wheel balanced in a comfortable spot against his back. "Let's go." Using the well-developed muscles in his calves and thighs, Tony began the slow descent, easing the huge crystal down the face of the mountain toward the ocean.

Slowly, with Sam's gentle guidance, they worked their way down the slope to where the waves broke foaming up onto the sandy beach to greet them. The first wavelets broke over Tony's boots, evaporating with a hiss of steam. As they waded in farther, the water reached the dehydrated flouwen. Suddenly, the huge red wheel swelled up and splashed down, leaving the humans sprawled in a pile as Roaring☆Hot☆Vermilion turned back into his normal shape of a large blob floating in the ocean. Quickly the other two flouwen opened their suits and swam free.

Cinnamon ran splashing into the waves to join the three flouwen. Humming the theme song from "Hawaii Five-O," Cinnamon ignored her suit's frantic attempts to readjust to the change in outside pressure and temperature. Soon the waves were breaking over her visor, and just as quickly the water was stained with the swirling colors of her flouwen companions.

☆What are you doing?☆ asked the now huge Roaring☆Hot☆Vermilion. ☆I can hear you making noises, but your Sound⊗Maker doesn't explain what the noises mean!☆

"What noise?" asked Cinnamon. In reply, Loud Red made the water around her vibrate with the tempo of the drum solo Cinnamon had been humming moments before. The song had been repeated in exactly in the right tune and tempo.

"I was singing. I do it all the time ... whatever song matches the mood. The computer knows that I don't mean it to be transmitted to others, and has adjusted itself to ignore it."

☆I do not understand "singing." Explain it to me!☆ It was odd to hear the human word resonate through the water from the red flouwen.

Cinnamon was confused and puzzled by Loud Red's reply. Jupiter had been unable to translate the word to the alien's satisfaction, so that must mean that the flouwen didn't know anything about singing. But in that case, how could she go about explaining the concept of music to a creature that normally used sound to see with? On the other hand, how could a creature as intelligent and as sonically talented as the flouwen not enjoy such art forms? If humans enjoyed pictures, then surely the flouwen would enjoy music.

"Singing, or music really, is an art form of ours. It is basically the combining of tones . . . pitches? . . . frequencies? in a way meant to appeal to the emotions of others." It was hard to pick words that she knew the computer would be able to translate clearly to the aliens. "We divide up our range of audible tones into eight basic intervals." Cinnamon remembered that the flouwen used a base-eight counting system, so at least that wouldn't be hard for them to grasp. Hoping that her relative pitch would be able to handle it, she self-consciously began to sing "Do Re Mi Fa Sol La Ti Do!" Jupiter, aware of her intentions, corrected the tones during the translation through to the suits outside imp, and Cinnamon adjusted herself into pitch. "We also recognize many half tones . . . " This time Cinnamon sang the whole scale, including the sharps and flats. "Then the whole thing is repeated, only one octave higher." Cinnamon started as low as she could and let Jupiter guide her up note by note.

"There are twelve notes," Jupiter picked up, rescuing the levibiologist. "The frequency of each note is higher than the previous note by a factor of the twelfth root of two. After twelve notes, or an octave, the frequency is exactly double, which is the harmonic of the first note."

Little White came closer and joined the conversation.

◊We understand the mathematical relationship between the notes, they are just tones with different variations of frequencies. But how can this have anything to do with emotion? Anyone can see the emotional state of another. Since my research is the study of humans, I have even learned to see some of their emotions. I can tell, even through your suit, by the configuration of the skin wrinkles on your forehead and the change of your pulse rate, that you are now feeling confused. It may be harder to see up in the thinness of the air, but I still do not think this music will do what you think it will.◊

Cinnamon thought about the reply. With their extreme sonic sensitivity, it was highly likely that the flouwen could indeed read in another flouwen whatever physical reactions their emotions produced. At least that helped to explain their lack of politeness. What good would polite fiction be, when all one's emotions were legible to all? All lies would be impossible, even "I'm sorry." If you were truly repentant, it would be seen and needn't be expressed verbally. Still, she gave it another shot.

"With music you can influence emotion, at least in humans. Certain keys and rhythms make us feel happy, others inspire sadness or fear . . ."

☆Why would you want to inspire fear? Is this for self-defense or hunting?☆

"Neither, but we humans enjoy tiny doses of fear, we find it exhilarating. Just like you like to go surfing!"

☆Surfing is fun! It has nothing to do with loudness and pitches!☆

Cinnamon turned to the men who had come into the water behind her and were quietly listening to the conversation. She shrugged helplessly at them. "Can you guys explain? I am never going to get this through to them. For smart creatures they can be really dense."

"Why don't you try just singing to them?" suggested Sam. "Pick one sad song and one happy one. At the least they will be able to see your emotional reactions."

All of a sudden Cinnamon's mind went blank. "Help!" she called to them. "I can't think of a single sad song!"

"How about the 'El Paso'? That one always made . . . my mother cry," Sam offered.

Cinnamon was delighted at the suggestion. She launched into the ballad without inhibitions, and before the second verse, Cinnamon felt her heart ache with the tragedy of the story. By the time the outlaw was lying in his lover's arms, she could hardly see through the tears that the light gravity left brimming in her eyes. When she finished, the three flouwen were silent. Obviously the music had done nothing to them. Finally Little Purple spoke.

□Very intriguing. But is it the story of failure that makes you sad, or the music?□

"It's both. The music sets the mood so that the listener will be more receptive to the story," Tony explained. He had always thought very little of the song. No woman was worth a hard ride through a desert, much less facing a posse. Still he had to admit that it pulled at the heartstrings. He was glad that Cinnamon had not chosen that famous aria from *I Pagliacci*. That song ripped the old heartstrings out with both hands!

For contrast, Cinnamon launched into a rousing rendition of "Roll Out the Barrel" and soon had the men doing a slow motion polka in the water. The dance was interrupted by the sudden return of the free portions of the three flouwen that had stayed behind in the water while their drysuited portions had explored the island.

Dainty∆Blue∆Warble had been impatiently scanning the shallow coastline with its long-range sonar, awaiting the return of the other flouwen, anxious to be free of babysitting duty. Once it sensed that the exploration party had returned, the light blue flouwen roused the small "free" portions of the adventurers and sent them to join the rest of themselves, then swam rapidly in the opposite direction. As much as it wanted to learn all about the travels of the other three flouwen, Dainty∆Blue∆Warble didn't want to risk the elders' reaction to the way the smaller portions of themselves had been treated in their absence. It didn't want to be around when they realized that most of the day had been wasted in trying to determine if pi ended in a repeating sequence. Indeed, as it vanished around the ridge that separated the beach from Agua Dulce cove, Dainty∆Blue∆Warble heard the indignant squawks of Roaring☆Hot☆Vermilion, Clear◊White◊Whistle, and Strong❒Lavender❒Crackle as they shared awareness with themselves. Forgetting all about the music lesson in their sudden need for revenge, Clear◊White◊Whistle and Strong❒Lavender❒Crackle streaked off in search of the presumptuous youngling.

"Well?" asked Cinnamon rather bruskly, more annoyed than surprised at this response to her performance. "What was that all about? Are you going, too, Loud Red?"

Roaring☆Hot☆Vermilion didn't want to explain to this human how Dainty∆Blue∆Warble had taken advantage of their temporary ignorance. ☆With this latest addition, I am now *much* too large! I am going to find some others to make a youngling with and get rid of some of this bloat!☆

"One of us should go along and get more pictures of the mating process," said Sam reluctantly, "but we should get these samples back to the ship first." During their long expedition to the lake, they had collected several rocks that might be disguised life and he was anxious to get back to the lab in the *Falcon* so he could examine them.

"I'm going to go with Loud Red and watch," said Cinnamon, hoping that she wasn't being too pushy. She knew that Nels would want samples of the new youngling tissue at various stages of its formation and hoped that Loud Red would agree to this, now that the flouwen knew the humans better.

"I'll help you winch up the samples, then follow Cinnamon out. Okay, Sam?" asked Tony. He had a hard time accepting that a woman could be capable without a man around.

Sam appreciated the offer and took Tony up on it. He knew that Cinnamon would probably be all right with Loud Red until the others caught up with them again.

"*Promise* that you won't rock up no matter what the provocation, until we are all back safely in the ship," Tony demanded of the red flouwen. He remembered the trouble caused when White Whistler had rocked up in mid-journey during the first expedition to Rocheworld and left Shirley stranded in the open ocean. She had almost died from the cold when the power for her suit heaters ran out.

☆Okay!☆ agreed the flouwen cheerfully. Cinnamon handed over her collection of specimens and took the small portable videocamera. Jupiter loaded a subset of the translation program into her suit computer, set up an optical communications link from her suit imp through the commsat Walter and back down to *Falcon*, and she was ready to go. Surrounding the small human within its huge red body, the flouwen moved quickly away from the shore. As the ocean floor sank out of sight beneath them, Roaring☆Hot☆Vermillion asked, ☆What does "promise" mean?☆

Carmen slammed through the privacy curtain on the crew quarters deck of the *Falcon* and threw herself into the nearest bunk. There was nothing visible that would identify the owner of the bunk. Even though the Sound-Bar door and the insulated walls afforded some privacy, Carmen felt too inhibited by the unseen owner to give in to the tantrum that she felt building inside her.

How dare the computer tell Jinjur that she was having trouble filling her role! Sure she had felt a little weak, a bit lightheaded, but damn it, she was a professional! So her blood sugar was low . . . she had gone for days with little food or water back in 2018 when she alone commanded the only radio station in Central Mexico able to communicate with the rest of the world. Why should she see a doctor? She wasn't sick! Besides, John was always more interested in sex than he was in her health. Or at least he used to be. Long ago it was like a challenge to the two of them to see who could think of new creative ways to please the other. Finally they let up and became good friends. . . . Each recognized that the sex, while nice, wasn't really satisfying. Both preferred to please their partner more than themselves, and so they really weren't enjoying the competition anymore. They hadn't slept together in years and both knew the perpetual teasing and flirting was a sham. Carmen felt that John was probably the only one of the crew who knew her, truly knew her, and she did not want to go to him with Jinjur and Jupiter's ridiculous allegations.

Carmen took a compact mirror from the pocket of her coverall and tried to repair the damage to her makeup the tears had caused. Then she noticed the twinkling comb-shaped imp on the side of her head. She had used it to hold up her curls into a bouffant pile on the top of her head for so long that she no longer even felt it nestled against her scalp. Now, she was reminded of its constant monitoring of her vital signs, and its new-found habit of interfering with her life. How dare a piece of machinery try to dictate to her! To think that every time she made love or used the head—even when she thought she was safe in the privacy of her dreams—it was there, watching her, taking readings, making assumptions, judging her. Pulling out the imp so roughly that it took with it several strands of hair, she opened the Sound-Bar door and threw the handful of twinkling metal twigs down the narrow corridor toward the privacy curtain.

Shirley came through the curtain just in time to see the sparkling comb come flying towards her. The ex-pro basketball player caught it easily. Then she peeked into her bunk see Carmen's rage-swollen face glaring at her from the pillow.

"Surely you must be used to it by now? You've been wearing this thing for over forty years!" She offered the imp back to its owner.

Sheepishly, Carmen reached out to take it back. "I just

couldn't stand it all of a sudden . . . and my name's not Shirley."

Shirley smiled dutifully at the weak joke. "What's got you so upset, anyway?" she asked.

"Oh, Jinjur seems to think that I'm coming down with something and wants for me to go see John. It's stupid! There is nothing wrong with me that a little sleep wouldn't fix."

"Well, John's the last person one goes to for sleep."

"I don't want to go through an exam . . . and I'm tired of this imp literally on the back of my neck. It's always telling me 'Eat this,' 'Don't eat that,' and, 'Are you sure you want to do that Carmen?'! It sounds like my mother. Concerned over every little thing, but God forbid you should really have a problem. Then it's 'You're not hurt, don't make such a fuss, it happens to everyone sooner or later.' I'm an adult now and no one can force me to do anything!"

Shirley was taken aback. She and Carmen had never been close, but this behavior was very odd. Carmen was obviously walking a fine line. What could be troubling her so? Psychology was not the blonde's forte, and unfortunately their doctor-psychologist had died on the trip out. Shirley tried to look objectively at what she could remember of the plump señorita's actions since they had left Earth. Carmen's promiscuity was almost legendary, as was her obsession with her looks, but that hardly jibed with her rapid weight gain and her crude sexual jokes that drove men away, rather than attracting them to her.

Then Shirley had a flash of insight. Maybe Carmen's problem was simple. There could be a very obvious reason that she was picking now to open up, and why it was Shirley that Carmen was opening up to. Maybe Carmen didn't really want the men she claimed she wanted. Her weight, her lewdness, even her promiscuity, could be subconscious ways of protecting herself from their interest. But it was clear that if Shirley's idea were true, then Carmen was still in denial about it, even to herself. Maybe these mood swings and temperamental fits were only the truth slowly dawning on her. Shirley had acted the same way when she first came to terms with her own sexuality back when she was a teenager.

"I don't blame you for not wanting to go to John with anything," Shirley said softly, moving slowly closer. "Men never truly understand us." She took the imp and gently combed Carmen's hair back up into place.

Carmen seemed to relax under the caresses, and after Shirley carefully placed the imp-comb securely into position, she let her hand trail slowly down around Carmen's softly rounded neck. Her creamy skin was like fleshy magnolia petals and Shirley held her face in her hands.

"Only a woman can," Shirley said as she kissed Carmen softly. Carmen exploded beneath her.

"*¡No mi agarras, pecado marimacho!*" she screamed, oblivious to Shirley's confusion. Fury, rage, and disgust were all mixed with an overwhelming sense of betrayal. A whirling spitfire of anger, Carmen was hardly aware of Shirley, as the tall muscular woman cowered back from Carmen's hysterical wrath. To Carmen, the bigger woman was somehow interposed with another large figure, reaching out from her memories, demanding that she submit. Her memory released her, and Carmen became aware of her surroundings again, only to see Shirley gazing down fearfully at her and her own voice screaming in her ears, "It's a sin! It's a sin! It's a sin!"

Shirley backed out of the sleeping quarters. Carmen had gone completely off the deep end! Jinjur and the computer were right. Carmen needed to see a doctor and soon. Shirley ran off to find John.

Carmen didn't watch her leave. She was not mad anymore, but terrified at her own actions. What was wrong with her? She was possessed—or insane. Even the thought of loving another woman disgusted her, but where had all those other thoughts come from, of helplessness, hurt, and violent rage? Maybe she *should* go see John. Maybe she was sick with something that was making her have all these confusing feelings, and memories of things that could never have happened. Carmen got up from the bunk and headed down the short corridor through another privacy curtain, where the other half of the sleeping quarters area had been turned into a temporary sick bay.

She entered the tiny room with all its sterile, impersonal instruments, and took a moment to pull herself together. Then Carmen spoke to the imp still fastened in her hair. "Please let Jinjur know that I am in the sick bay, and I'm ready to see John just as soon as he can get in here."

Cinnamon was floating deep inside the streamlined flouwen, her view of the seascape hazily colored with the flouwen's translucent red flesh. Although its massive size slowed the flouwen down, Loud Red had assumed a wedgelike swimming shape and moved through the water like a giant manta. Cinnamon's teeth vibrated with the ultrasonic sounds of Loud Red calling to any others that might be willing to help it lose some bulk.

They had been traveling only a short while when Cinnamon realized that they had been joined by the greenish-orange flouwen that the humans had named O.J. They reduced speed and finally stopped as Cinnamon slipped out of her protective spot deep inside the huge red flouwen. She listened to the two flouwen talking through the translating program in her suit computer.

†You are huge! No wonder you are asking for a mating!† Bitter†Orange†Chirr was impressed. †I didn't really believe it when I heard you call. After all, it was only last season that you helped make Dainty∆Blue∆Warble.†

☆Some of us can grow faster than others.☆ Roaring☆Hot☆Vermilion preened.

†Grow? You are practically . . . † Cinnamon's suit translator struggled for a moment. † . . . cancerous!†

"Jupiter?" Cinnamon asked the computer. "Cancerous?" There was a pause as Jupiter passed its more sophisticated translation back through the optical link.

"Rapid and uncontrolled exponential growth of a flouwen that is dangerous to the health of the pod," the computer elucidated.

☆I will not hear such nonsense!☆ Roaring☆Hot☆Vermilion snapped. Cinnamon smiled to note how much Loud Red was talking like Deep Purple now that it was larger and smarter. The reaction of the normal-sized Loud Red to such an insult would have been a more succinct "Dumb!"

☆Do you know of any others that are large enough to want to join us?☆

†Even when small, Warm❋Amber❋Resonance is always ready to make a new youngling in order to have someone to teach, but other than us two, I don't think anyone else in our pod is big enough to want to join in.†

☆You are not suggesting that we mate outside the pod!?☆ The flouwen's voice was lowered a few octaves in disapproval. Cinnamon wondered again how such sonically-based people could have failed to discover music.

Bitter†Orange†Chirr persisted. †Well, it is not unheard of. How badly do you want to slim down? We can go with just three, but if the youngling is twisted then you have to eat it. I would rather we ask the counter-spin pod. If we agree to take responsibility for the care and feeding of the new one, they will most likely send one of them over.†

☆If the youngling stays with us, then we keep all our knowledge and gain whatever of their ideas that get passed to it. Why would they give up bulk and get no fresh insights?☆

†With all your weight, we could make twins . . . †

☆Good idea! You go talk to the other pod and bring back here anyone who wants to join us. The humans want to watch and collect samples again, so we will go back closer to where their pets are.☆

Watching Loud Red and O.J. change into their swimming shape from the outside, Cinnamon was reminded of the shape of a large dolphin or killer whale. She pushed her way back into the thicker fluid of Loud Red's body and once again the ocean slipped away with no feelings of resistance. Now that Loud Red was no longer broadcasting his needs into the open seas, Cinnamon was able to question him on the details of the recent exchange.

"Do you need to have more than three to make a youngling?"

☆No, it is possible to make a youngling with only three. But with my present size, I would bc giving up much more mass than the other two would be able to give, and too many of my memories could harm the youngling. Too much of it would try to be me and it would be confused . . . twisted. A twisted person might hurt itself or others, and it is best to destroy it. As the largest, I would be able to absorb the youngling with the least amount of risk to my personality, but then, I would be in worse shape than before. Not only would I be bigger, but I would be weakened with sadness at the death of a youngling.☆

Cinnamon could sense the tragedy that the destruction of a sentient being would be to these intelligent creatures. No longer did she see them as insensitive and cold. They just had limited experience with death and sorrow. Unlike the complicated body of a human with its many critical parts and its built-in death wish, death rarely occurred to the uncomplicated flouwen and so they rarely thought about it. But they found the idea of death just as sad as a human would.

"Why would you hesitate to mate with those outside the pod then, if it made for a healthier youngling?"

☆Mating is such a personal thing. When it is within the pod, within the family, it is wonderful, natural, reaffirmation of all that each member of the pod shares with the others. You can taste the memories that the pod has passed to each of the younglings throughout time. Both your originality and your similarity are augmented. It feels good all the way to your . . . soul.☆

"Jupiter? Did he really say soul?"

"That was my rough condensation of the phrase, 'That

thing which is found in the set which comprises yourself that cannot be proven or disproven to exist.' This is the first concept that the flouwen have admitted cannot be handled by logic or numbers . . . yet. I think it might have something to do with the Gödel undecidability theorem."

Carmen lay back on the table. John's gentle hands and soothing voice washed over her, relaxing her completely. This was John's real gift, thought Carmen to herself. He could make you forget that you were in a medical lab, that your legs were being strapped into stirrups, that your arms were being velcroed securely down to your sides . . .

Carmen started with alarm. "What are you doing!? Let me up from here!" Before she could utter further protests, John had placed a sticky gag over her mouth. She fought against the bonds, but she knew from experience it would do no good. Long ago, during the many times when she had willingly played this bondage "doctor" game with John, he had made sure that the bonds would hold all during the roughhouse "treatments" that would follow.

But this was different! This time, she did not want to play this or any game. All she wanted was to get away, away from his probing fingers, away from his insistent mouth. She tried to get free, to scream from behind the gag, to beg him to stop, to make him let her go. She rolled her eyes back, trying to get the attention of the imp still in her hair.

"Jp-tr! Hlp!" she cried in a muffled voice, but even as she called out, she realized in dismay that it would do no good. The first time they had played this particular game back on *Prometheus*, James, monitoring their activities through the imps still riding on their naked bodies, had become concerned and had called out through their imps, imploring them to stop, and threatening to call in Jinjur if they didn't. Both Carmen and John had reassured the computer at the time that it was all in fun, and now Jupiter, like all the computers, was programmed to ignore Carmen's protests, no matter what she said or did, even if she called out to it.

John watched Carmen buck against the bonds and heard her mewling protests; clearly he had chosen the right game. Carmen had always played her roles with enthusiasm. John threw himself into his part and entered her brutally. Carmen's struggles aroused him and John tried to distance himself so that he would not disappoint his partner and ruin his reputation. He was glad that Carmen had decided to come to him; no matter what Shirley had said, all Carmen really needed was a good fuck. That was all that most women needed to feel better about things. Living with women must have been terrible back in the old days before the AIDS vaccine, when the women couldn't all get their daily dose of love. John remembered the stories told by his old Uncle Willie about how you risked your life if you slept with a woman who was willing, and how sleeping with a woman who wasn't had its own risks.

Unable to hold back any longer, John spent himself inside her, laying his head against her heaving breasts. Carmen was shaking violently, sweat and tears mingled as they ran down the sides of her face. He stroked her face, but her eyes were closed, and she refused to acknowledge him when he spoke her name. What was wrong with her? Could he have let her down? Impossible! He had never failed to please her before. Perhaps she was still coming down.

"John? You're needed on the bridge," Caroline's voice called through his imp.

John ripped the straps lose on Carmen's right hand and slapped her on her sweat-slick rump. "You got what you came for," he said lightly. "You can free yourself; I'm needed elsewhere."

John took only a moment to pull on a jumpsuit. Long practice made perfect his routine, and he left looking freshly groomed.

Carmen lay still, unable to move. All her muscles ached from the long struggle. Finally she manage to release the rest of the straps that had restrained her. She half fell in the weak gravity, and she wrapped her clothes around her body, not bothering to put them on properly. She staggered away and down the passway to the airlock. She pulled her spacesuit on over her bare skin and cycled through.

Automatically Carmen's feet took her to the *Dragonfly*, and she cycled into the aeroplane. She left the suit in its locker and walked naked through the privacy curtain and collapsed into her berth, meeting no one. The Sound-Bar door slammed shut.

Part of Carmen's mind screamed at her to get out of her bed and climb in the shower, to scrub and scrub until the whole experience could be washed away. Part of her wanted to strike out to hurt John, to hurt Jupiter, to hurt God, for letting this happen to her. Part of her wanted to cry, to rant and rave, to scream out all the anguish that the gag had muted. But there was a tiny little part of Carmen's mind that pierced through all the others. Sharp as a needle, it pricked Carmen's will and kept her from crying, from moving, from thinking of anything else. It was John's voice, coming in through the memory of her uncle's laughing face. It danced in Carmen's ears . . .

"You got what you came for."

• CHAPTER SEVEN—WARNING

Just as they returned to the shallow waters, close to the beach where the *Falcon* had landed, Cinnamon and Loud Red were met by Richard, Sam, Shirley, Thomas, and Jinjur striding slowly along the ocean floor. The flouwen stopped and let Cinnamon work her way through him and out into the open water to join her friends.

"Wow, Richard, you brought the whole crew!" Cinnamon had expected that some of the others would want to come out and play, but she hardly expected such a turnout.

"What we brought is spare air tanks," Shirley chided. She was still shaken from her exchange with Carmen, but the safety of the crew was one thing she would never neglect. Cinnamon had been working in her exploration suit all day and, while she might still have a couple of hours of air left, it was never a good idea to run low. Too many things could unexpectedly go wrong, as she well knew.

Loud Red was broadcasting their position out into the water, considerately focusing the calls away from the humans, knowing that they found the loud, long-range calls painful. Still, the cries were intended to travel many miles in the quiet ocean, and all the humans winced as the infrasonic roars rattled their teeth.

"Jupiter? For humans only?" Cinnamon requested. The computer stopped the translation of her words to the flouwen and broadcast them only to the suit imps.

"I have been talking to Loud Red and have learned a good deal more about the implications of the mating of the flouwen. When they commingle at the beginning, the thin strands of themselves share nonspecific tastes with the others. Since normally they mate within the pod, these tastes are of memories that they all have in common anyway. To taste one's own thoughts and memories, echoed through the perspective of other pod members, serves as an emotional bond, comforting and making easier the losing of hard-won bulk.

"Now, for the first time in decades, a flouwen is desperate to lose some mass. If there were a famine, he might be willing to let some of his podmates devour part of him, but naturally this idea is repugnant to all concerned. Instead, they are going to get others from another pod to join in the mating."

As Cinnamon had been filling the others in, Shirley replaced the first of Cinnamon's nearly exhausted air tanks. The suit's filters worked to remove any traces of the nastier gases in the Eau oceans that might have leaked in during the switchover, but still, a tiny whiff of ammonia entered Cinnamon's helmet.

"Ugh!" she complained and sneezed violently.

"Bless you," said Shirley automatically.

☆What was that "fizzle" sound?☆ Loud Red was curious.

"Some of the ammonia got into my suit," Cinnamon explained. "Ammonia causes violent reactions in humans."

☆Why? What are you made of?☆

Cinnamon laughed. "Water mostly, and a handful of other inexpensive elements, but not ammonia. Although your bodies are used to ammonia, our bodies find it most unpleasant, and react violently to even small amounts."

☆But ammonia makes one feel good, think more clearly . . . unless, of course, there is too much ammonia in your body. Then one feels *too* good, and is liable to do foolish things.☆

"We have the same trouble with alcohol," Shirley muttered as she tried to figure out the best way to get the second tank onto Cinnamon's suit without repeating the slight leakthrough.

☆Why don't you do that inside me?☆ the flouwen offered. ☆I can filter out the ammonia that makes you fizzle.☆

"Jupiter? Do you think that they can do that?"

"It would make sense that a creature that lives in a world where the chemical mix of the ocean varies greatly from one part to another would not only be able to survive in all variations of the mixture of water and ammonia, but be able to adjust internally to provide the most healthful combination. Fish in the oceans of Earth adjust the salt concentration in their blood to match the salinity of the sea at the time their ancestors evolved into a new species."

Loud Red surrounded the two women, and after a moment they found themselves inside a bubble of clear fluid within the alien. "As closely as the suit's exterior sensors can tell, you are now in a pocket of pure, distilled water," Jupiter informed them through their suit imps.

Cinnamon filled a vial with a sample as Shirley screwed the second air tank onto her back.

"Can you go further and make a pocket of air?" Shirley asked.

☆A gas pocket? I doubt anyone has ever tried such a thing.☆ With its great size aiding it, the flouwen considered the idea. ☆If a gas were produced inside of me, I would not be able to generate the pressure needed to contain it. The bubble would float to the surface of me and escape. Even if the bubble formed just as I started to rock up, it would not be trapped. We solidify by forcing the fluid from inside individual cells, not by crusting over.☆

Loud Red was interrupted by the return of O.J. to the group.

†I have brought with me three of the members of the counter-spin pod. They were intrigued with the idea of mating with members of another pod, especially when I told them that there would be enough mass for two younglings. No one still liquid in their pod remembers seeing a double forming.†

Behind the greenish orange flouwen hovered three rather large newcomers. They introduced themselves one by one.

❖I am Bittersweet❖Blue❖Bubbler,❖said the first. This flouwen was bright, almost electric-blue in color, and its voice had a tremolous tone to it that sounded like a human talking underwater.

❉I am Odoriferous❉Ocher❉Ooze,❉ said the next flouwen. Its color was the oddest that the humans had seen yet, a fluctuating combination of reddish-yellow that seemed to change with the alien's depth. Its voice was low and slow.

The next flouwen announced itself with a harsh, staccato voice. ✪And I am Piquant✪Pink✪Popper. I am the best hunter and the strongest fighter in the pod.✪ The belligerence of this shockingly hot pink flouwen made it clear that, while they were here to mate, it wasn't here to make friends.

Warm❋Amber❋Resonance and Clear◊White◊Whistle joined them. Now the humans were so completely surrounded with color that the underwater seascape was hidden from view.

†Have you two come to join us? You don't look big enough to mate yet.†

◊We don't want to mate, just watch. I have never seen twins being formed. Besides, the humans want to take samples during the mating process, and I thought that it might be easier if I did it for them.◊

✪What do you mean, "samples"!✪ asked the pink counterspinner. ✪When he came to us, Bitter†Orange†Chirr gave us a taste of your interactions with the Stiff⊗Movers. Your pod may be friends with these strangers, but don't think that the members of *our* pod will tolerate their presence in our ocean just for a few new ideas.✪

❖Don't listen to him. We don't mind helping the humans learn more about us. We all love learning and new ideas. Only Piquant✪Pink✪Popper would rather fight than think.❖

☆Very well, then, we will get started.☆ The huge red flouwen and the others moved off a little way, so that they were apart from the humans, while Clear◊White◊Whistle stayed with the observers. The humans all tried to get in good viewing positions; Thomas even lay on his back on the bottom in order to get pictures from underneath with his video camera.

The six amorphous blobs of color, floating a few meters off the bottom, concentrated a portion of their bodies near their outer edges and put down anchors, fixing their positions in a rough circle. The newcomers initially seemed hesitant in touching their sides to their hosts, but finally each filled a sector of the circle, Loud Red's sector being larger than the others. The multicolored blob came together at a point in the center. Then, the center started to rotate slowly around, winding up the six threads from each sector into a multicolored spiral.

◊Something is wrong,◊ White Whistler said quietly to Cinnamon.

"It looks just like the videos I saw of the forming of Blue Boy," objected Cinnamon.

◊That was the first mating of Sweet○Green○Fizz. We went very slowly so Sweet○Green○Fizz would not be nervous. All these flouwen have had plenty of experience in making young ones and the swirling should be much faster. I think mating outside the pod is what is holding them back. They can not lose themselves in the moment when the act is not a reaffirmation of pod membership.◊

The spiral in the center was forming, but it seemed to lack cohesiveness. Instead of becoming a twisted disk with thin ribbons of equally spaced colors, it was more like a poorly wound bobbin of lumpy different-colored yarns. The longer the process went on, the worse the spiral looked and the more confused the participants seemed. They finally came to a halt and began to pull the individually colored threads out of the tangle and back into their bodies. It looked like this mating was going to be a failure.

Clear◊White◊Whistle, who had been watching the participants with a continuous series of low intensity sonar pings, spoke to Cinnamon. ◊Their insides are all tense, because they are mating with strangers. You said that music affects the emotional state of humans. Maybe if they listened to some of that music of yours, it would help them relax.◊

Cinnamon thought quickly. Most of her repertoire was old pop music, and while most of it dealt with love songs, it was not the sort of material that was written to appeal to jellylike aliens. She had to make them forget their differences and remember the things they all had in common. Then it came to her.

"Jupiter, use our suit imps to play something by Bach!"

An instant later, the sea resounded with the first strains of "Jesu, Joy of Man's Desiring." Under the influence of the music, the flouwen stopped withdrawing, and slowly came together once again at the center. As the magical mathematical form of the music flowed through them, the central point of the six flouwen began to spin, faster and faster. This time, the coil of multicolored threads was tight and smooth, thinning as it twirled to the tempo of the song.

"White Whistler! Get a sample from the center of the new ones before they take back their color," Cinnamon said, holding up a syringe and a sample bottle.

Clear◊White◊Whistle, having used the syringe before to take samples from its own body, expertly formed a hand-shaped pseudopod, grasped the syringe, and swirled out under the canopy of mating flouwen to suck up a small sample from the middle of the swirl of colors that was now almost as large as an adult. As Cinnamon examined the tiny multicolored blob that White Whistler squirted out of the syringe into her sample bottle, the group of red cells separated itself from the others, and being much larger, proceeded to absorb the other clumps of colored cells, one by one. Cinnamon sighed and tucked the sample away in a pouch. She realized that by the time she got it back to the ship it would just be a tiny subset of the set that was Loud Red.

By now, the six had stopped intertwining. They were now withdrawing the colored fluid "nerve" essence that resided between the transparent unit cells in their bodies, leaving the cells behind as a clear blob. This liquid-crystal essence, which gave each flouwen its distinctive color, contained the portions of the genetic code and the memory that made up the "personality" of the flouwen. Loud Red had given up more cell units than the others, so as all of Loud Red's colored fluid was pulled back into its now average-sized body, its flesh turned a deep rich red in color.

The music continued to wash over the flouwen, all of whom were becoming darker and more vibrant in color as they pulled in their essence and left behind the clear blob of units that would make up the new younglings. Just as the colored essence in each thread reached the outermost ring of the spiral, the last command the flouwen gave their now-joined flesh was to split down the middle. The large clear blob bisected just as the last bit of color vanished into the adults. Now, with no personality essence residing in them, the two clear blobs were alien to each of the other flouwen. The mating flouwen felt no sense of loss as each broke their connection to what had used to belong to them.

Moving quickly, White Whistler used the syringe to take another sample from each clear twin. Then they all waited and watched, expectantly. Finally, deep within the two colorless blobs, busy enzymes used the randomized bits of genetic information embossed as patterns on the surfaces of the transparent cellular units and began to generate a new colored personality essence for each youngling. Despite the similarities of their joint formation, tiny random differences in the organization of the genetic patterns had led the enzymes within to generate two different individuals.

In the middle of one of the twin flouwen, a rosy redness grew and spread out from the nucleation point until it suffused through the entire multi-ton glob of floating jelly.

"It looks like cherry Kool-aid," said Richard.

✪Hello ☆Hello ❖ Hello † Hello@Hello❆Hello! ➪ the cherry-red new flouwen cried in a mixture of its parents' voices. Then it found its own voice. ➪Hello, hello, hello!➪

The counter-spinners had already surrounded the red-colored twin. They named it Delicious➪Dark➪Crimson after the color and the delightful taste it left in the surrounding water. The members of the counterspin pod reluctantly allowed Clear◊White◊Whistler to take a final sample from Delicious➪Dark➪Crimson, and then they headed back to their own territory, protecting and teaching the newest member even as they traveled. Crooning simple addition problems, they gently corrected its pronunciation of the numbers.

❖One plus TtWwOo is ThththRrrEEeeee,❖ enunciated Bittersweet❖Blue❖Bubbler carefully, carefully controlling the tremolo so as to set a good example for the youngling. Each number had its own multiple tonal and pulse-code pattern that was a living example of the concept of the number it represented. The word "Three" was a melodic triplet of sounds with each note given its own triple-tongue beat. Each number also had its own set of overtones that were distinctive as bell, violin, and brass.

➪One plus two is three,➪ replied the youngster, using a simple single tone for each word.

✪Stupid! I knew nothing good would come of mating with strangers!✪

❆You weren't any smarter than Delicious➪Dark➪Crimson when you were that new, Piquant✪Pink✪Popper. I remember trying to teach you your eight by eight times tables. Perhaps I should have taught you some patience and tolerance instead.❆

❖That is not quite correct, my little one. The proper way to say the number two is with two tones and two pulses. The number three requires three harmonizing tones and three pulses. Try it again.❖

➪One plus TtWwOo is ThththRrrEEeeee.➪

❆I do believe you've got it!❆

* * *

With the other pod of flouwen moving off into the distance, the humans converged on their own pod group to see its newest member and the voice of the other twin made itself heard.

☆Hello❄Hello✪Hello@Hello❖Hello†Hello!❂

They all looked hard at the new one, but in the blue-green waters of the ocean it was hard to tell if it had any color at all.

❂Hello, hello, hello!❂ it chirped again, having found its own distinctive high-pitched voice. White Whistler moved around behind the young one to look at it better, and now, against the white body, the new flouwen's color was easy to see.

"He's a clear bright canary yellow," called Thomas from under the child. "He looks like liquid sunshine!"

The members of the local pod gathered around and examined the new youngster with low-level sonic pulses. It chirped in return, looking at and inside the adults surrounding it.

❄Such a nice clear chirping voice. It should carry well through the ocean.❄

◊It is yellow like you are, Warm❄Amber❄Resonance, but clear instead of opaque.◊

†Clear in voice and body.†

OWhat shall we call the young one?O

☆It is clear, and yellow, and chirps. Let's call it Clear❂Yellow❂Chirp.☆

"The music from our suit imps might bother young Sunshine," Cinnamon called to the computer as they moved in toward the yellow twin. "You'd better turn it off, Jupiter."

Almost immediately a wail of pain and loss rang through the water. The humans stopped and backed off, fearing their approach had scared the young flouwen.

❂Hello? hello? hello?❂

Warm❄Amber❄Resonance, trying to distract the young one, started in on the training.

❋One plus one is TtWwOo ... ❋

Clear✪Yellow✪Chirp ignored the elder.

✪Hello? hello? hello?✪

☆It is dumb!☆ cried Loud Red in disgust. Cinnamon was amused to note that Loud Red had the old boisterous personality back.

❋It is not dumb! Give it a chance!❋ The gentle amber-colored flouwen tried again. ❋One plus One is TtWwOo?❋

✪Hello? hello? hello?✪ Sadness and confusion came through the youngling's answer. It almost seemed to be pleading for a response.

✪Chee-chee-chee; Chee-chee-chee; Chee-chee-chee . . . ✪ chirped the youngster, making a series of tone pulses that neither the flouwen or the computer could translate into words. Shocked at this un-flouwenlike behavior, the adult flouwen moved away from this strange youngling.

Cinnamon felt the hair rise on the back of her neck. "Is it twisted? Will you have to destroy it?" But even as the question left her mouth, Cinnamon knew the answer. The pattern of the youngster's cries suddenly clicked into place.

"Jupiter!" she called. "Play the Bach again!"

As the music began to dance through the water, the clear yellow flouwen answered back; first following, then accompanying, then harmonizing with the dreams of a composer long dead on a planet far away.

Over the next two days, the landing party continued to explore the surface of the island. With the exception of the life found in the landlocked lake, the Hawaiian Islands proved to be barren. Little Red, Little White and Little Purple accompanied them on these overland visits, but it was clear that their main interests concerned the interior of the *Dragonfly* and the *Falcon*.

When the flouwen were finally winched up into the airlock on the *Falcon*, and cycled through into the alien oxygen atmosphere, their first reaction was puzzlement that they were getting so little information back from their natural sonic sensors.

☆All I can see is the surface of things!☆

❐There are so many echoes from every direction it is hard to see.❐

◊That is because this pet is designed for use by the humans. They can only look at the surface of things. You must learn look at things with your helmet lenses instead of trying to see around you with body chirps.◊

Surrounded with metal for the first time in their long lives, the flouwen had trouble accepting the idea that there was wiring and plumbing hidden within the walls. Still, they were eager to explore all the possibilities that the interior of the *Falcon* offered.

☆What do these green things do?☆ asked Little Red, using his lenses to look at a control console. He reached out with a pseudopod and stroked the telltale lights that glowed green along the top of the console. Jinjur was following close behind the inquisitive alien. Although Jupiter had been instructed ahead of time to ignore any command the flouwen gave, or any inputs they made through touching a console, she was still concerned they might cause some sort of problem during their visit.

"Those lights just tell us that all the parts of the vehicle are working properly. The pictures on this touchscreen are controlled by these icons along the side. It is similar to the touchscreen you use in Agua Dulce." Jinjur punched up a replay of the descent of the *Falcon* onto Eau. The flouwen watched the screen avidly as the animated image's perspective changed and the lander swung around and hovered over the Hawaiian Islands.

◊That is this island!◊ cried Little White amazed.

☆Dumb!☆

◊I am right! If you were looking at only the part which is above the surface . . . Look!◊ the white flouwen insisted as he used a pseudopod to point out the curve of the North shore. ◊This is where you like to surf! Just remember that you are not seeing the slope up to the beach but only the beach itself!◊

There was a pause. Jinjur watched to see how Little Red would cope with being proved so wrong.

☆It is stupid to look only at the top of the water when there is so much that is under the water . . . ☆ Little Red grumbled.

Silently touching an icon, Jinjur changed the view on the screen to add the contours of the ocean bottom.

☆Yes! That is better! That is what it looks like!☆

"But now the screen is filled with information that is irrelevant to the landing of the spacecraft. That's why we use the simpler model," Jinjur explained. She went on to show them the difference, fingers flickering over the icons around the edges of the screen as she went through another simulated landing. Soon, she could no longer reach the keyboard. The three suited flouwen had watched her closely and instantly memorized which icons she had touched. They were soon trying landing approaches of their own, hooting with laughter as they made various fatal mistakes. Their interested waned as soon as they mastered the descent. In fact, Little Purple soon showed that he could have landed the rocket using less rocket fuel than Tony had used during the actual landing.

"They remind me of my kid brother," Shirley complained to Jinjur. "I had just received my masters degree, and was home to celebrate. My brother was a prickly thirteen-year-old and challenged me to play a game of Quantum Nintendo with him. He wiped the floor with me. I still won't play that Mario game. I'm afraid that I still won't be able to jump over that damn flowerpot!"

☆What other things do you have?☆ asked Little Red, looking around. Having assumed that Clear◊White◊Whistle had overestimated the delights the humans could hide within such a small space, Little Red was simply amazed by human technology. Dealing with people so different meant that even the questions were beyond Roaring☆Hot☆Vermilion's experience. Imagine living in separate private places! And the concept of sleep confused the flouwen totally. Upon seeing the water tank that filled the central column of the *Falcon*, the flouwen wanted to go for a swim, but Jupiter insisted that the ammonia they carried would be hard on the purification filters. Privately, Little Red decided to purify himself before suiting up for his next visit to the craft. Then it would be okay to zip open his drysuit on board and get a taste or two of the human environment.

Although pleased with the flouwen reactions to the ship and the information the aliens were giving them about the planet, Jinjur was plagued with worries about Carmen. Juno reported that the communications expert was eating everything that was suggested, and John insisted that there was nothing physically wrong with her, but the normally spicy woman was obviously not herself. Carmen did what she was told, manned her shift, and wrote her reports, but she hardly spoke to anyone. She was behaving *too* well. Still, it was not as important as the rest of the mission. Jinjur decided simply to keep Carmen away from any important things and generally to keep an eye on her. The important thing for Jinjur to be concerned about was that the human race had met a new species and together they were going exploring.

"Now that you have seen the inside of the *Falcon*, we will take you over to see the inside of the *Dragonfly*."

Carmen was lying on her bunk, waiting out her rest period in the dark. She slipped in and out of sleep, forcing herself awake as soon as the dream came back. No longer even wishing there was someone to talk to, Carmen knew that once again she would have to deal with this on her own. She now knew the visions that were blinding her were memories. Memories repressed for sixty years. Memories that had been coloring her feelings and reactions all her adult life. Again and again Carmen was forced to replay the abuse her uncle had inflicted on her, to relive his sexual use of her from the time she was six. She had gone to her mother the first time, and was told that she must have liked it to allow it, and from that time forward Carmen had tried to reconcile the idea that something that made her feel so worthless was what she was supposed to enjoy.

Never having studied psychology, Carmen nonetheless knew that all her life she had been forcing herself to accept her sexuality both as something sinful and as something one was supposed to exalt in; even when it felt as if it were ripping your soul apart. Her uncle, trying to rationalize his own sickness, had always forced her to orgasm. By the time Carmen learned how and what to fake, she had decided that this overwhelming sensation was something he used to control her, and was not the gift from God that he claimed legitimized his abuse of her. For as long as she could remember, the climax of her partner always gave Carmen the only real satisfaction she experienced with sex; the idea that she had gotten from them what he had always forced from her. Now she could see that what she had always thought was sexual arousal was fear . . . fear of losing herself, fear of becoming as horrible as her abuser. But this time Carmen was an adult. She could look back at her memories objectively and see that she was not at fault. The little girl in her past who had had no one to turn to now could turn to her adult self.

Carmen knew that there was no one in the crew that she could talk to, no one she felt she could trust. How could she go to any of the men, all of whom she had slept with, and tell them that she had been using them, even trying to hurt them when she had slept with them? Jinjur would be afraid to trust her to do her job, Shirley was gay, and Cinnamon was still a virgin and would never understand. The rest of the women were either people Carmen hardly knew or people she worked with every day. For now, all she could do was to try to listen to the objective voice of Jupiter, and do her job as best she could.

Sleep came and Carmen found herself back in her uncle's room; he was calling to her softly and beckoning. Then she was looking down over his shoulder at the face of herself as a child, tears filling the young eyes as he strained against her. Carmen sensed that the child knew she was there, and, within the dream, she tried to show her younger self how her uncle would die, drowned in a tidal wave. She felt as if the picture of his blue, bloated, body gave the girl some comfort. She couldn't stop the rape in her dream, she couldn't stop it when it had happened, but she had survived the ordeal and had lived to see this animal dead.

Jinjur had called a planning meeting in the lounge on the crew quarters deck of the *Falcon*. She was sitting in the reading chair in the corner where everyone could see her, while most of the rest of the crew were gathered on or behind the large lounge sofa that faced the two-meter-diameter viewport window that looked out over the oceans of Eau from forty meters up. The tall ones, Sam, Richard, and Shirley, stood in the back against the blank videowall; John, Thomas, and Caroline were seated on the sofa, Tony perched on the broad back of the sofa where it met the corner, and Carmen and Cinnamon sat on the floor. At Jinjur's request, Cinnamon got up and stood in the door to the galley to start the meeting.

"Since we have decided that the flouwen could be useful partners in exploring with us, we will have to make plans for their health and safety. For example, if we take the flouwen up to *Prometheus* so they can go exploring the moons of Gargantua with us, then we are going to have to feed them while they are there. To do that, we will need to find and bring in some live samples of their normal prey. Nels can breed or clone these samples and keep a good supply in a tank onboard *Prometheus*, but the initial selection will have to be broad to make sure we have a varied diet for them. We have no vitamin supplements for flouwen."

Secretly Cinnamon was overjoyed. She knew Nels

would be thrilled to have so many live samples of alien life to study. He had already started reworking some of the hydroponics tanks aboard the *Prometheus* for the Rocheworld life-forms.

"Good!" said Jinjur, pleasantly surprised that this normally quiet girl was getting the ball rolling. She had called this meeting in the hopes of uniting the landing party into an efficient fighting unit. Up to now, they had been acting alternately like tourists and tour guides. They needed to get their goals stated and accomplished.

"Okay. Tomorrow and the next day, samples will be taken," Jinjur ordered. "Then I want to get *Dragonfly* flown over into a good position in the air neck between the lobes to watch the flood as the top of the water mountain of Eau goes over to Roche. The last time that happened George was a bit too preoccupied to get good pictures."

The rest of the crew laughed dutifully.

"Cinnamon, John, Richard, and Carmen will go out in the ocean with the flouwen and collect whatever samples can be of use. Anything that is not appropriate for cloning can be dried and used to feed the Littles during our expedition flight over to Roche after the flood season is over. Thomas, Shirley, and Caroline will continue to check out the *Dragonfly*, and Tony, Sam, and I will keep the home fires burning here on the *Falcon*.

"The Littles have spent enough time learning about us and the ships to be feeling at home here. I know that their inquisitiveness can be a bit trying, and I want to commend you on your patience. But remember that they still think rather like children, and even though they are technically our guests, I want you to let them know when they are getting in your way. They have no sense of discipline or manners and need to be kept in line. In time, when they want to go to space badly enough to be willing to take orders, we will allow them to take a more active part in the running of the ship. In the meantime, no matter how smart they are, no matter that they seem to know what they are doing, I don't want these aliens to be allowed to take control of any of the ship's systems, even under supervision.

"Remember, these creatures live for centuries and, rather like teenagers, they have no real sense of their own mortality. Besides, they know that back in the ocean is the rest of themselves, and that other part will survive even if the Little version dies. The computer will respect any human decision, but for the time being, the decisions of the computer will outweigh the judgment of the flouwen."

"Wait a moment!" Caroline objected. "They may be alien, but they are living, thinking people. How can we give the computer authority over them? Jupiter is well programmed, but it is just a machine."

"That machine has the humans' best interest at heart. The flouwen, from what I have seen, care only for the interest of the moment. I believe they would cheerfully try and force the ship into the next dimension if they thought of a mathematical theory that would get them there."

"They would probably make it," Caroline muttered to herself. She knew that Jinjur was right, but she felt an affinity for the flouwen personality. She had hopes of introducing White Whistler to good science fiction; if anyone could discover the hypothetical hyperspace, she figured that flouwen could.

"For now, even if they are smarter than we are . . . "

"I don't want to know!" interrupted Shirley with a laugh and covered her ears.

"For now, we are in charge. All clear?" Jinjur finished, rising.

As the meeting broke up into the groups that would go forth on the morrow, Jinjur reexamined the impulse that made her include Carmen on the sample-gathering team. She wanted to tell herself that the group might be going far afield and that a communications officer would be helpful cutting through any interference that they might have contacting the ship, but she knew the high-tech laser comm links in the suits would not need much help. Far afield, away from the ship, Jupiter would not be able to control the imp's movements, but there was enough computer power in their suits to translate and keep the parties in touch with each other, even if separated by hundreds of miles. In fact, the best place for Carmen was with Jinjur, waiting back on the *Falcon*. Jinjur rationalized that the sample-gathering party would need many hands to bring back all the different plants and animals, but with all the flouwen to help, they didn't need Carmen simply to be a packhorse. Had she assigned Carmen there to be with her closest friends in the hopes that they could help with whatever was troubling her? Jinjur had to realize the real reason she didn't keep Carmen alone here with her was that the silently obedient señorita was giving her the creeps!

• CHAPTER EIGHT—DROWNING

Cinnamon met Carmen and John on the engineering deck of *Falcon*, where the exploration suits were stored. The three began the routine checkout procedure that preceded each foray outside the safety of the ship. Richard joined them, and together they double-checked each other's telltale lights inside the panel doors on their chestpacks and backpacks.

"The regulator indicator on my neckring telltales was flickering there for a while," John told Carmen over his shoulder. "Make sure that it's working okay will you, Carmen? . . . Carmen!"

"What? Oh. Yes, I'm sure it's fine," Carmen answered distractedly. She reached for his backpack, opened the access door to the panel, pushed a reset button, and closed the door again.

Cinnamon, busily punching Richard's backpack buttons, glanced over at Carmen. She didn't understand the way Carmen had been acting lately. Cinnamon couldn't see anything wrong with Carmen, but when she looked at her old friend, Cinnamon felt as if she had suddenly lost one of her senses. Like she was suddenly colorblind. A jazzy song tickled the back of her mind, but she couldn't remember the words. Still, it was a happy tempo, so it could hardly be foreboding.

"You check out fine," Cinnamon assured Richard and she patted his huge back. "Do we have enough sample bottles?"

Richard laughed. "I can hardly carry any more!" he said, holding up the collection of sampling vials that Jupiter had provided for them. "Once we fill these we'll need the flouwen to haul all the samples back to the ship."

They cycled through the lock and climbed down the stairs to the beach. Striding boldly into the surf, they sank beneath the waves as their suits compensated to the proper volume. Almost immediately they were met by Clear◊White◊Whistle, Roaring☆Hot☆Vermilion, Sour#-Sapphire#Coo, and Warm❋Amber❋Resonance.

Roaring☆Hot☆Vermilion flowed its red body about them and examined the bags of bottles that the humans were carrying, looking for signs of the suits that would let the flouwen walk on the land.

☆Where are our drysuits?☆

◊If you had bothered to monitor the Sky⊗Talker at Agua Dulce you would know that today the humans plan to collect live samples of our food so they can feed us during our stays on the Flying⊗Circle, the lightcraft *Prometheus*.◊

White Whistler had embraced human technology and phraseology with a vengeance. Sometimes the white flouwen reminded Cinnamon of her old hydroponics professor. Although he had dropped way behind in his field as it moved out into space, he tried to cover his ignorance with glib jargon picked up from trade journals. Often it was possible to predict the subject of his next lecture by reading the latest edition of *Leviponics Monthly*.

❋Most of the time the Sky⊗Talker is being used by Clear✪Yellow✪Chirp. We have found the best way to teach the youngling is to promise it a new song every time it masters a theory. This is the oddest youngling I have ever taught! Normally the solving of the problem *is* the reward.❋

"Maybe it would be better to let it only work on the things that interest it," Richard offered.

"I don't know," said John. "I was never very interested in any of my studies, but my parents bribed me into getting good grades anyway. I graduated high school with a four-point-o and a Jaguar." He chuckled. Even when John entered med school, he hadn't had any stronger incentive than pleasing his family. When he realized that he would never be able to be the great physician that a "Dr. Kennedy" would be expected to be, John had switched to mechanical engineering. After obtaining his Ph.D., he became a nurse just to prove that his medical studies had not been for nothing, but never had John studied just for the love of learning. He didn't believe that anyone actually did.

"Maybe you should concentrate on art studies," Cinnamon suggested. "You do body plays, and Green Fizzer used to have its flitters perform dances before it got so interested in their genes; maybe Sunshine would enjoy studying those things."

#Body plays? Pretty⊗Smells? These are not the sort of thing one studies!# Sour#Sapphire#Coo was shocked.

"I wouldn't have thought that a flouwen would have a rigorous study program," said Richard.

❃It is necessary that each youngling be able to think logically and to know certain basic things. Otherwise none of the adults will want to talk to it.❃

"In a society that has no manners, socialization depends on each individual's intellectual input," John hazarded.

"They don't think math all the time," Richard objected.

"No, but that is the major thing they share. Loud Red, do you even bother to share tastes of surfing?" John asked.

☆No! If they want to go surfing they can go for themselves!☆

"But what about the body plays that Yellow Hummer makes. Do you ever taste the way they are conceived?" John pressed.

❃No one ever asked to taste my plays.❃

◊Even if we did, we would only be able to taste the feelings and the thought pattern. We would not then be able to come up with an original play of our own. Or maybe we could, but it would not be as good. Why try to do badly what another pod member can do well?◊

John felt slightly uncomfortable with this statement. It echoed his own philosophy too well, and somehow it seemed less noble when he heard it repeated back to him.

"But surely not all of the flouwen are as good at math than the others?"

#Some are dumb, but they share the tastes of the others and even if they don't come up with anything new, they can still follow along. Besides, eventually they rock up to work on something just like the rest of us. It is not polite to wake someone up just because someone else has figured out the answer to the problem.#

◊There goes a Sharp⊗Soggy! We should have some of those to eat,◊ cried Clear◊White◊Whistle. Its pale body flattened so that it could chase after the little scavenger. Within moments, the white flouwen had engulfed the prey, being careful not to actually start assimilating the flesh. The small brown blob was similar to the flouwen in body shape, but it sported six sharp interlocking teeth fitted into a round sphincter that could pinch off pieces of larger or tougher prey. Even now the vicious little beast was biting off interior portions of Clear◊White◊Whistle and was eating them despite its predicament.

Gently, Clear◊White◊Whistle took one of the bottles from Richard, ejected the dark blob into the container, and secured it tightly. The sated animal rested quietly on the bottom.

◊If I catch them all like this, there will not be much left of me.◊

"Are all of your food prey, predators themselves?" John asked.

☆Most are, but not all are dumb enough or sharp enough to try to take off a piece of a flouwen. Most prey on even smaller animals, or the plants that feed on the chemicals emitted by the volcanic vents.☆

"We'll need samples of those lower life orders too," insisted Cinnamon. "Nels will need to have samples of the water near the vents, plus collections of plants and simple animals all the way up the food chain."

"Why will he need all that, if all he has to do is clone meat cultures for the flouwen?" asked Richard.

"Do you think the Chicken Little and Ferdinand tissue cultures were made in a day?" she laughed. "This is not *Star Trek.* Nels doesn't just use a replicator! It takes time for him to generate a new tissue culture. First, he'll need to study all the life-forms in order to understand their chemical needs so as to prevent malnourishing the flouwen. During that time, all the smaller animals the flouwen eat will have to be fed too. The only thing he can replicate in the beginning is the chemicals thrown into the water by the vents. As time goes by, he will be able to make a tissue culture for each of the important flouwen foods, and things will be somewhat simpler." Cinnamon had complete faith in her mentor. "If we miss something important, well . . . I wouldn't want to be the one to tell Jinjur that we need to expend another lander to come back here."

A short while later they were all riding inside the flouwen, the creatures having made clear pockets inside themselves so that the humans could get an unobscured, if slightly colored, view of the ocean around them. John and Carmen were riding in Yellow Hummer and Cinnamon and Richard were inside Deep Purple. White Whistler and Loud Red ranged out on either side, hunting up and collecting all the life they could find with the help of Loud Red's pack of Orange⊗Hunters. Cinnamon had insisted that it was important to get more than one of each species, so they enthusiastically rounded up anything that moved. The flouwen, eager to cooperate, altered the course of their travel so that they would intersect the line of volcanic vents that ran inward from the islands. They continued to catch any small animal, including many that they normally would never bother to eat. These tiny animals often had plantlike characteristics and were so clear that the humans would have missed them entirely. In fact, the humans gave up the idea of helping hunt at all and did little more than label the lids on the sample jars with grease pencil as the flouwen filled them up.

Looking back on that morning later, John realized that in its own odd way, this was one of the most relaxing days he had ever spent. They had finally reached the major vent fields, filled the last of their sample bottles with the chemical soup that surrounded the vents, and were now on their way back to the island. Not far away, to one side of Carmen's helmet, John could see Deep Purple's dark body and the flouwen's cargo of two humans. John was enjoying the flying sensation of moving effortlessly along, when suddenly, he felt squeezed by an overwhelming pressure. Too surprised to panic, it was with a dispassionate objectivity that he realized that many of the telltale lights inside the neckring of his helmet were now flashing bright red.

"Emergency!" he heard himself say, as the pressure suddenly eased with a loud pop and a burbling roar. John flipped, spinning over and over. He watched huge bubbles float up all around him, growing larger as they rose up through the yellow flouwen's body. His leg tensed as it was hit with a sudden flood of intensely cold water.

"Emergency!" Carmen's scream filled all their helmets. "John's suit is compromised!"

"What's happened? Talk to me!" Cinnamon demanded through their imps.

"His regulator failed! His suit inflated to tank pressure, then burst like a balloon!" Carmen was fumbling at the rip that had blown out in John's knee joint. "I can't reseal it!"

John began to hiss with pain as the ammonia-rich fluid started to attack his skin. His anguish became more obvious as the water filled his suit, slowly working its way up toward more delicate flesh.

"It burns!" His cry was barely intelligible through his clenched and chattering teeth.

"Yellow Hummer!" Cinnamon demanded. "The ammonia-water is hurting him. Surround him only with water, then squeeze his suit to get rid of the ammonia."

For a moment John and Carmen were blinded by the flouwen's amber flesh. Then the color again retreated, leaving them in a clear bubble that, this time, contained only pure water. By now the two flouwen were close enough together that Cinnamon to make out the figures inside the amber creature. She was appalled by what she saw.

"For God's sake, Carmen, get his head up! He's going to drown!" the medic screamed, as she watched John's precious air trickle up through the rip in his suit. Cinnamon could see Carmen floating over John, still holding his leg, but doing little else.

"John! Pull on her! Get yourself upright! You'll lose the air in your helmet!"

"I . . . I can't . . . " John's voice bubbled back through the link.

"Gods! I've got to get over there," Cinnamon muttered to herself. If she could get there fast enough, she could hook her regulator into John's and they could buddy breathe back to the *Falcon*. She swam her way out through Deep Purple, across the short gap of intervening ocean, and into the water bubble inside Yellow Hummer.

Pushing Carmen roughly away, Cinnamon pulled John upright and looked into his startlingly blue eyes. The eyes looked back at her, but John did not. Milky fluid floated up from his nose and mouth, clouding the water that filled his helmet to his eyebrows.

"Damn! Damn! Damn! Damn! Damn!" wailed Cinnamon.

"It's only been a moment! There has to be something we can do!" pleaded Richard. He had followed Cinnamon over and was floating behind her.

"What do you want me to do!?" Cinnamon snarled. "Mouth to mouth through his suit? We can fill his helmet with air, but that's not going to make him breathe again!"

"Lots of people recover from near drowning! We could squeeze his chest! Force the water out that way!"

"You'll collapse his lungs but they won't reinflate!" Cinnamon insisted. "Not here. Not without help. But we can take him back to the *Falcon* and try there."

"But he'll be dead by the time we get him there!"

"It's cold here, bitterly cold. There have been many cases of drowning victims being revived even after hours in the water, if it was cold enough water! We need to keep him from freezing, though . . . "

Now that she had a plan, Cinnamon would not allow herself to despair. She opened his chest pack and adjusted the suit heaters to keep John just above freezing. "Yellow Hummer, keep the water circulating to even the cooling of his body and to prevent his extremities from freezing. We'll have to hope that not much ammonia got into his lungs. That caustic a chemical would scar them for sure."

Richard, feeling helpless and angry, rounded on the only person he could blame. He pushed his helmet right up to Carmen's face plate so that she would hear him directly. "You bitch! You were the one that checked out his regulator! You should have kept his helmet clear of water! You should have hooked your air up to his immediately! You didn't do anything right! You killed him!"

Carmen looked back at Richard with no more awareness than John had. Her black eyes no longer snapped, but stared vaguely into the middle distance as if she were looking at visions far away. Floating gently away from Richard's grasp, she curled up into ball; a silver fetus in an amber womb.

"Mayday! Mayday! We have an emergency! *Dragonfly!* Come in!" Cinnamon's voice crackled over the speakers on *Dragonfly*.

"Cinnamon, this is Caroline on the *Dragonfly*. What is the nature of the emergency?"

"John has suffered water inhalation and Carmen has . . . well . . . physically, she's okay, but mentally she's checked out completely. We need to get both back to the sick bay on *Falcon* immediately."

"Water inhalation?" Caroline asked.

"He's drowned. Technically, he's dead . . . but I think we can bring him back. I need to get him back to the *Falcon* faster than the flouwen can get us there. Can you get a fix on us?"

"It's already been done," interjected Shirley, her fingers flying over the pilot console as she powered up the VTOL fans in the wings of the aeroplane and took off. "We'll be there in ten minutes."

It took all of Shirley's expertise to bring the aeroplane down toward the heaving ocean, fighting the thermal lifts above the churning smoky water that surrounded the volcanic vents. She hovered as closely as she dared to the blue, amber, and white flouwen that colored the surface. Thomas suited up and passed through the airlock to lower a ladder down to the four humans floating in the clear pool in the middle of Yellow Hummer. Richard, now that he had the traction of the ladder, easily lifted John and his waterlogged suit up and into the airlock. They cycled through, where they were met by Caroline and the Christmas Branch. Meanwhile, Cinnamon and Thomas manhandled the unresponsive Carmen up the ladder as well. As soon they were all aboard the *Dragonfly*, Shirley activated the nuclear jets and the aerospace plane headed toward the outer islands and the sick bay of the *Falcon*.

"Report," Jinjur ordered Cinnamon. This meeting in the *Falcon*'s lounge lacked the suppressed excitement of the last. Now two of the crew were in the sick bay and things were looking grim.

"John was resuscitated after three hours of being technically dead," Cinnamon replied. Silently she relived those hectic hours and the frantic efforts of herself and the Christmas Branch that had finally resulted in a pulse. It had seemed like years before John had at last opened his eyes. She still didn't understand his first words. He had said, "She's come undone . . . " but whether he had been referring to Carmen or to the jazzy song, Cinnamon had no idea.

"All things considered, he is doing remarkably well. Despite our best efforts, however, his left little toe was frostbitten. He might lose it." Richard reflexively clenched his feet in his custom-made boots as sympathetic ghost aches arose in his nonexistent little toes, lost years ago during a close call with an avalanche in the Alps.

"He's weak, and sore from some of our more violent efforts at resuscitation. He is also developing pneumonia, but if any ammonia reached his lungs, then Yellow Hummer's circulation diluted it enough that most of the lung tissue is functioning. In short, John will live, but he should be immediately transferred to the sick bay on *Prometheus* where he can be cared for properly."

Her pronouncement sounded like a death knell. The crew had feared that this accident would mean aborting the mission, but all of them had been hoping against all reason that they would be able to stay and finish the job.

Jinjur, of all the crew, was the best prepared to bow to the inevitable. It was her decision to make and she had to rely on reality. She could not have foreseen this accident, but she was in command. She was responsible.

"What about Carmen?" Jinjur asked.

"She's practically catatonic. Carmen has nothing physically wrong with her, but she has completely withdrawn," Cinnamon continued. "She reacted poorly to the emergency, but whatever put her in this state happened before Richard or I got there."

Richard felt the muscles on the back of his neck release slowly. He had privately feared that his shouting at Carmen—blaming her for John's death—had pushed her over the edge. A weight he had not noticed was lifted from his shoulders.

"Frankly," the medic continued, "I am not sure what her problem is. As her best friend, I knew that something was troubling her, but she didn't talk to me about it."

"Don't beat yourself up about it, Cinnamon," said Caroline. "I think we all noticed that Carmen wasn't being herself. None of us thought it was all that serious. All of us passed rigorous psych testing before we were sent up here. It just wasn't supposed to happen."

"Carmen was the last-minute replacement for Armstrong," Jinjur reminded them. "She had only the initial screening that all the applicants took."

"So what's going to happen to her?" Cinnamon asked.

"Once we get back to the *Prometheus* we'll turn her over to James. He may be a computer but he has more knowledge of psychology than the rest of us." Aborting the mission might be painful, but with John in the condition he was in, it was inevitable. Jinjur pragmatically shifted her thoughts toward the next steps they would have to take.

Cinnamon felt uneasy about leaving Carmen's psyche in the hands of the computer, but none of them had any training in psychotherapy. Dr. Wang was supposed to be their psychiatrist as well as their doctor, but he had died on the way out. Cinnamon asked to be excused from the rest of the meeting. She wanted to go back to the sick bay and keep an eye on her patients.

"So the mission is definitely aborted?" asked Tony.

"No mission is worth the death of one of my people. We will have to come back another time," said Jinjur. "John and Carmen need to get back to the *Prometheus*. The ascent module is the only way to get there, so we will all have to go."

"But we have the whole Barnard system to explore," Caroline objected. "If we have to make another descent to Rocheworld then we'll have to give up exploring one of the moons around Gargantua!"

"Then we will leave the rest of Rocheworld for the next wave of humans to explore . . . in fifty years or so," Jinjur said. The finality in her voice chilled the rest of the crew. They all hated the idea of others being able to explore the wonders of the planet they had discovered.

"Look," Thomas suggested. "We have to wait for another three hours anyway in order to be in the best position for the ascent module to link up with *Prometheus*. If I and the others can come up with a better plan in the meantime, will you consider it?"

"I'm not any happier about leaving than you are," Jinjur

insisted. "I'll listen to whatever you come up with, but don't expect me to approve any risky gamble you invent."

"I move that the first thing we do is comm link with the *Prometheus* and get Red and Arielle in on this discussion!" Caroline said as Jinjur left the room. Switching the viewwall in the lounge from entertainment to communications, she raised the main ship. George's face appeared instantly on the screen, as if he had been waiting for the link.

"About time you called us in. Ever since Jinjur reported the possibility of John's evacuation, we have been working on ways to keep at least part of the crew down on the planet. Arielle has some ideas and wants to talk with you." The view switched to that of the beauty queen, imp-brace sparkling between her lips as she spoke.

"Well . . . " said Arielle thoughtfully from the screen. "If I were down there flying *Dragonfly* instead of stuck up here on *Prometheus*, I would fly *Dragonfly* at high speed on its nuclear jets through the zero-gee point, pull a hard turn and head straight out for the L-4 point. As I get to the top of my trajectory, I dump all the spare breathing air in *Dragonfly* into the jets and use that to go a little further, then the rocket fuel should *just* get us there, where *Prometheus* could fly in and pick us up."

"It could be done . . . " Thomas said thoughtfully, scratching his chin.

"No way!" said George firmly. "If the lightcraft missed the pickup the first time around, the whole crew would asphyxiate before the L-4 point came around the next time." He looked aside at the twinkling imp that rode on his shoulder. "James? Calculate the safety margins on such a maneuver."

"Chances of success are eighty-twenty," the computer answered.

"See?" crowed Caroline. "I'm willing to take that risk."

"Eighty percent chance of failure," James clarified.

"See?" George chided gently.

"The real problem," said Thomas, "is that *Dragonfly* is a

flying submarine. It's too heavy for its rockets to push it very far. It's too bad it's not a lightweight little crate like my ascent module. That could make it out to L-4 easy."

"That's it!" exclaimed Red from up on *Prometheus*, who like all the others, had been trying to find a way to salvage the mission. "What we need is another ascent module—and we've got one—the one Thomas and I brought back from SLAM I. It's hanging right out there in the rigging."

"How's that going to help?" said George with a frown. "It's no good up there. We need it down there—and full of fuel to boot."

"He's got you there, Red," chided Thomas. "Even if we filled the tanks to the brim, that ascent module wouldn't have enough fuel to make it to the surface of Rocheworld and back again."

"You heavy-lifters think all alike!" yelled Red, annoyed at his denseness. "You don't fly it down to the surface, groundworm. You fly it down to the zero-gee point, hover to make the transfer of John and Carmen from *Dragonfly*, and piss flame for L-4 and the *Prometheus*."

There was a long pause as everyone tried to find a flaw.

"James? What do you think of it?" asked George thoughtfully.

"Once the ascent module flew down to the zero-gee point it would need almost no fuel at all in order to maintain its position. The ascent module would be able to wait as long as is necessary until the *Dragonfly* flies out to meet it."

The computer went on, improving the scenario. "The zero-gee point is a saddle point, so to save fuel on the inward journey, the trajectory should be down along the spin axis. Along this trajectory, the only forces are the inward gravity forces. After the transfer has taken place, then the outward trajectory should be in the plane of the orbit. Along this trajectory, the inward gravity forces are partially canceled by the outward centrifugal force which . . . "

"Would throw the ascent module right back out into space!" George finished for the computer.

Jinjur's voice came in over their imps. "I have been eavesdropping. Does this mean the *Prometheus* wouldn't have to make any dangerous maneuvers near this whirligig of a planet?"

"That's right, Jinjur." said George. "The ascent module will have enough fuel to make not only to the L-4 point, but way beyond."

"Great! I knew you could do it. Make it so!"

Aboard the *Prometheus* the crew scrambled to accommodate for the change in plans. Nels and David would be replacing the two casualties on the planet surface, so they had to quickly organize their various personal projects.

David had been working on an animated program loosely based on the birth of the twin flouwen, using the music of Bach and intertwining it with the short but complex tunes that the young flouwen had already composed despite its youth. Whenever Sunshine was allowed to use the screen at Agua Dulce, it spent much of its time in communion with David. The two individuals, although from separate species, had been soul mates from their first introduction. David was thrilled at the thought of being able to meet and help in the education of the newest member of the pod.

Nels was simply thrilled. Less intimidated by George than he was by Jinjur, Nels managed to put his case for going to the surface before the scientist. To his delight, George had agreed completely that Nels would be the best person to select the samples of alien life-forms since he would be the one who would later have to keep them alive on *Prometheus*. Besides, George would need to keep the other available biologist, Katrina, on board *Prometheus* to nurse the two patients who were coming up from the surface. Nels had no qualms about leaving James babysitting all his equipment and cultures; the hydroponics facility was designed to be mostly self-operating anyway.

Nels went to the suit storage area on the top deck and hauled out his special exploration suit with its artificial electrically-powered legs. He was pleased that all his recent practice in the suit would not go to waste. George had *Prometheus* under maximum acceleration, moving from its normal orbit in the plane of rotation of Rocheworld up above the north spin pole. Not wanting to take any chances of damaging the heavy suit, Nels called for the doughnut-shaped elevator platform that was used to haul cargo up and down the long central shaft of *Prometheus*. He and the suit rode the elevator down to the hydroponics deck. From there he hauled the suit through the corridors until he came to an open port in the ceiling. Looking up, he could see the inside of the ascent module bridge and the flashing green limbs and short red hair of a busy heavy-lift pilot strapped into a blue acceleration harness. It was Red Vengeance, checking out the controls of the second-hand rocket. Hanging beside Red from the red copilot harness was a slim figure with curly golden-brown locks. Arielle was monitoring the checkout with her arms crossed to keep them off the controls, although she would occasionally reach out and touch her screen to change the display.

Arielle noticed him down below her and reached up to the buckle on her harness, preparatory to releasing it. "You need help with suit?" she asked cheerfully, the imp-brace flashing.

That was all the incentive that Nels needed. "Nope," he replied gruffly, and grabbing the backpack of the suit with his toes, he hauled himself and the heavy suit hand over hand up the rungs in the wall, through the airlock, past the two women on the bridge and on up the rungs of the passway in the ascent module to the suit storage locker on the third deck.

The final two passengers boarded. One was David with his suit and personal baggage, which in his case was a special sonovideo board that he could plug into the computer consoles on either the *Falcon* or *Dragonfly* to entertain himself or the crew. The other was Katrina, who would be taking care of John and Carmen while they were being transferred back to *Prometheus*. She busied herself during the wait for launch by rearranging part of the sleeping quarters on the ascent module into a temporary sick bay with two beds. Finally, all was ready. There were no prolonged good-byes this time, for they would be back in less than a day.

"We're now hovering over the north spin pole of Rocheworld," came George's voice over Red's imp. "Actually . . . " he added, "since the light pressure from Barnard is slightly weaker than the gravity pull, we're not hovering, but slowly falling. I'll have enough light in my sails to pull out of my dive as soon as you leave, but you don't have any sail, so the minute you leave, you're going to be pulled straight down."

"I'm counting on that," said Red calmly. "To save my fuel, I'll wait to fire my rocket until I see the white of their tides."

"No sweat anyway, jet jockey," added Arielle from the copilot harness. "Even if the rockets don't work, we don't crash. We just fall straight through zero-gee point and bounce up again at opposite pole."

"Take her away, Red," said George.

"The *Eagle* is leaving its nest again," replied Red, as she lifted the ascent module on its control jets and moved out between the support shrouds and under the gigantic silvery sail.

The sail above *Prometheus* was tilted at almost broadside to Barnard as George applied maximum sail acceleration. He and James had arranged for the acceleration profile to decrease their orbital speed relative to Rocheworld almost to zero, just as *Prometheus* passed over the north spin pole of the double planet. The *Eagle*, dropped off with no orbital motion, was now falling straight down along the polar axis. Red rotated the craft so they all had a good view, Red and Arielle out the forward windshield on the bridge, and Katrina, David, and Nels out the viewport in the lounge. Slowly at first, then more rapidly, the spinning orbs of the beautiful double-planet grew larger.

When they first left *Prometheus*, Barnard had been behind Roche, so its illuminated outer hemisphere was the only portion of the double-planet visible. The shadow from Roche was falling on Eau, leaving it totally dark. As the hour passed and they continued to drop, Rocheworld continued rotating around in its six-hour day, and the leading pole of Eau experienced sunrise, which spread over the planetoid until both lobes were half illuminated.

"Good timing on George's part," said Red. "By the time we arrive, it will be daylight at the pickup point."

"We have reached one kilometer per second," Arielle reminded her.

"Might as well wait until just before we hit the upper atmosphere before we fire our rockets," Red replied calmly, letting the spacecraft build up speed. "These big booster engines don't like to do rapid starts and stops."

From down below in the lounge came the voice of Nels, echoed by his words coming through their imps. "I have the *Dragonfly* in the telescope. It is approaching the midpoint between the two planets."

Red looked carefully down at the bow-tie-shaped band of clouds that was drifting through the narrow neck from Roche to Eau as the heated atmosphere of Roche poured out of the Roche highlands down onto the Eau oceans. It was Arielle who first spotted the silver cross.

"There is *Dragonfly*. She is next to cloud that look like puppy with long ears."

The voice of Jack, the voice persona for the *Eagle*, came from Red's imp. "Since Rocheworld is approaching periapsis with Barnard, the entire atmospheric envelope has expanded considerably, including the neck portion. I would recommend that we commence deceleration in five minutes."

"Sounds like a good idea to me," said Red, using the control thruster to tilt the spacecraft so the main rocket engine pointed downward. "Sightseeing is over!" she broadcast through her imp. "Everybody get to your landing stations and buckle in. Gees in five minutes." There was a scramble down below. Katrina and David climbed up the passway and took their places at the communications and computer consoles, while Nels secured the telescope and galley, and headed for one of the sleeping racks in the crew quarters.

"I'm going to take it easy on you and only pull one gee," said Red.

"That only makes it last longer," complained David as he tilted his chair back and pulled the touchscreen off the console and put it in his lap.

Red watched her screen and waited until the miniature spacecraft in the display reached the red portion of the trajectory, then pushed the throttle forward to twenty percent. The large engine roared into life, and riding a long tail of flame, the *Eagle* settled down onto its perch of nothing.

Red turned to Katrina. "What are the radar range and Doppler readings from the two lobes?"

"The ranges to the two surfaces are equal to within twenty kilometers of each other, and the Doppler shift is essentially zero. Nice piloting."

"Just followed Jack's plot on the screen. We should be at the zero-gravity point between the two planets. Better get out my sixty-billion-dollar gravity detector and check to make sure."

Taking a heavy gold coin out of her shirt pocket she placed it in midair. It hung there. If they had been in a "free-fall" orbit, the coin, not being at the center of mass of the spacecraft, would have drifted from where she had placed it.

"Zero gee," she announced after a while.

Arielle, whose eyes were always busy looking first at her controls, then out the window, then out the portholes, then back to her controls, suddenly took hold of the controls and expertly used the attitude control jets to spin the ascent module on its axis until the large landing windows in the cockpit were facing Eau. So accurate was her control that the gold coin did not change position, just rotated a quarter turn. Framed in the window was a silver aeroplane, rising up from Eau to meet them.

"You hold her steady, Arielle, while the rest of us get ready for company," said Red. She turned to David. "You and Nels had better get your suits on. Katrina can check you out while I get the airlock ready."

By the time the three made it down the two flights of passway to the engineering deck, Nels was already in his suit and putting on his helmet. Of course, not having to put legs and feet down into uncooperative leggings with tight-fitting joints made dressing considerably easier. Katrina checked him out, and turned to David as Nels activated his 'stiction boots and clumped across the deck to where Red was checking out the airlock. Soon the two of them were cycled through. With safety lanyards attached to handholds inside the lock, they opened the outer door and watched as the *Dragonfly* approached.

As Tony coasted the *Dragonfly* closer to the *Eagle*, Shirley unstrapped herself and made her way back hand over hand to the rear of the aeroplane in the almost nonexistent gravity. After living at a tenth gee for a few weeks, it took a little time for her coordination to get used to the mechanics of free-fall motion again. She also noticed that the cleaning imps were busy again, flying here and there to capture specks of dirt, loose utensils, and other objects that were no longer held down by gravity. She floated slowly through the privacy curtain to where Cinnamon, Richard, and Caroline were tending their injured and sick comrades.

"Where's Carmen?" Shirley asked, looking around.

"Hanging next to the airlock," said Richard, nodding to a silvery sack with a big zipper and large handles. "All curled up like that, she fit into a standard rescue bag with room to spare. John, however, is a more difficult problem. Help Caroline at that end."

John was lying in the basket stretcher that had been used to transport him from the sick bay on the *Falcon* to one of the large bunks on the *Dragonfly*. A portion of the Christmas Bush was riding on the stretcher, applying pressure to a bag of medicated solution that was being percolated into his veins. On the other side of the stretcher was a tank of oxygen with a hose leading to a mask over John's mouth. Shirley, having gone through this before in getting John from the *Falcon* to the *Dragonfly*, held the stretcher while Caroline opened a large rescue bag and slid it over the foot of the stretcher and up over John's body, where it was taken by Richard.

"Like bagging Little White—with toys," joked Richard.

John started to chuckle, then broke into a hacking cough. Blood and phlegm oozed from the side of his mouth as he got his spasms under control.

"I'd better go with him to make sure he doesn't suffocate," said Cinnamon, wiping out his mouth and cleaning out the oxygen mask before putting it back on his face. "Somebody get me a flashlight."

Shirley reached to her side and pulled her permalite from its magnetic holder on her belt. With a practiced thumb, she flicked it to flood beam and handed it to Cinnamon.

"Good for six hours," she said. "Make sure you return it. It's my favorite."

With Richard and Shirley holding the two ends of the basket stretcher, it was easy for Cinnamon to straddle it and sit above John's knees with her legs wrapped around the lower end of the basket and her hands holding the top edges near John's shoulders. Bending her head, she let them pull the bag over them both and zip them inside.

One by one, two silver bags, one small and one large, exited the airlock on *Dragonfly* and were hauled by solicitous space-suited humans into the nearby airlock on *Eagle*.

Cinnamon hovered over John as he was strapped down onto one of the beds in the sick bay of the ascent module. A small section of the Christmas Bush was making sure that the hose to his mask was free from kinks and that the flow of oxygen would continue throughout his trip back up to *Prometheus*. She glanced over to the next bed where Carmen was already strapped down. Carmen had been tranquilized for the trip and, now that she was asleep, had lost her vacant stare and looked almost normal.

"She would hate to have you see her without her makeup," Cinnamon said when she noticed John following her gaze over to Carmen.

"Hey, wait," John said, coughing weakly. He pushed aside the imp holding the oxygen mask and whispered hoarsely, "I know you want . . . to get back . . . "

"Hush!" said Cinnamon, replacing the imp. "If you have to talk, just move your lips. Jack? Can you use his imp to lip-read?"

The computer didn't answer but most of the imp moved beneath the mask to rest on John's lips. A few of the tiny twigs even entered his mouth to monitor his tongue movements. After a moment, John's words came from the imp in Jack's voice. "Please, stay for a moment. I want to talk to you. While I was . . . out, I saw . . . things."

Here in zero gee, Cinnamon could not sit on John's bed, but she hovered near his head and took his hand. "You know," she said, "a lot of people have strange visions after near-death experiences."

"Bright lights? Long tunnels filled with all my long-dead relations? A voice telling me to take a number?" John smiled under the sparkling mask. "Nothing like that. The thing is, Cinnamon, I never really left. I saw you. I watched as Richard pulled me up into the *Dragonfly*, I saw you pounding on my chest, I heard you yelling at me. You know I did . . . you saw me."

"What?"

"You looked up from my body . . . you looked right at me. You told me to quit fucking around. You made me come back . . . " John insisted, gripping her fingers harder.

"What do you want me to say?" Cinnamon asked quietly. "I did say that . . ." Her voice trailed away.

"I could see more than just your body . . . it was like I could see inside everyone. I could see Richard's anger and insecurity, and the way he is always fighting an urge to drink."

"Richard Redwing!? Are you sure you're not just projecting your prejudices onto him?"

"I don't know . . . I don't know if anything I saw is true. I saw Carmen as . . . tripled. At the same time, she was a little girl, a teenager, and the Carmen we know. They were all angry and hurt and guilty. Can I use that to help her? Is any of it true? Can you tell me?"

"Go on."

"When I was looking inside you, I saw something special about you, also. You can sense what is going on inside others, can't you? It's as if the songs you are always singing are somehow connected to what the people around you are thinking. I know that sometimes when an old tune starts ringing around in my brain, I often find that the lyrics are connected to whatever else I am thinking about, but you take it a step further. It's as if the songs in your mind are telling what is going on in other people's minds. You use it, don't you? You *know* you have this insight and you use it to help people."

"My Daddy always told me that if you're not helping, then you're just in the way," she admitted in a barely audible whisper.

"Help me, then," he asked. "Help me to help Carmen."

For a long time Cinnamon was silent. She let go of John's hand and drifted over to the unconscious Carmen. Cinnamon frowned for a while, then started humming softly, working her way through a long low-pitched tune until she got to what her heart told her was the relevant line.

" 'Fellows, it's been good to know you,' " she murmured to herself in a puzzled tone. Then she turned back to face

John. "That's from 'The Wreck of the Edmund Fitzgerald,' I think . . . " She paused for a while before continuing. "I think it means that Carmen was *expecting* you to drown. She *wanted* you dead," Cinnamon finished bluntly. She left, closing the door behind her. Just outside she met Katrina returning with a new tank of oxygen for John.

"Nels is waiting in the airlock and has the rescue bag ready to take you back to *Dragonfly*," she said. Cinnamon left down the corridor to the passway, while Katrina entered the door to the sick bay. All concern, she floated over to check Carmen's straps to make sure she was buckled in for their flight up to *Prometheus*. After changing John's oxygen tank and checking his straps, she left them both to buckle herself into one of the sleeping racks right outside the sick bay door where she would be close to them if they needed her.

"Jack?" John asked his imp after she had left. "As long as I have to lie here, I might as well broaden my medical knowledge. How about giving me a lecture from Psychology 101?"

• CHAPTER NINE—WATCHING

With the emergency over, activities on the surface of Eau settled back into their previous routine with hardly a ripple. The *Dragonfly* had returned to base while the crew continued their task of surveying and taking samples of the wildlife in the vent fields on Eau. Nels took over Cinnamon's collecting duties, leaving her with more time around the *Dragonfly* pulling alternate pilot shifts with Shirley and Tony. David took over Carmen's shift at the communication console, and since there was not that much to do, he soon had his sonovideo board plugged into the console and continued with his composition about the birth of the flouwen twins.

"That's Sunshine, isn't it?" said Cinnamon, quietly watching over David's shoulder as he played and replayed an animated scene, trying out different background colors and musical arrangements. "Y'know, he really doesn't always look that yellow. Depends upon the color of the ocean. Sometimes he is almost clear."

"Really?" said David, his interest piqued. "In all the video shots I saw, he was a definite yellow. It would be a real challenge to properly animate a being that was transparent."

"I've been talking with him through the comm link to Agua Dulce bay, and he wants to see me. I was planning on going out to visit him as soon as my shift is over. Want to come along?"

"Wouldn't miss it for anything," said David. He turned to look down the aisle of the aeroplane to the galley, where Shirley and Caroline were having breakfast. "Aren't you two done *yet*?" he complained.

"Our shift doesn't start for ten minutes," replied Shirley. "And *I'm* not going to hurry. This is my real-meat special breakfast for the week—pancakes made with buckwheat algaeflour, maple syrup, scrambled pseudoeggs, broiled cherry tomato halves, and two thin slices of grilled Canadian bacon from Hamlet."

Cinnamon's saliva glands went into high gear as the smell of the delicious smoked ham drifted up the aisle. When she was growing up along the cold shores of Cook Inlet in Alaska, every breakfast had been a real-meat breakfast.

Caroline slurped down the last of her orange colored algaeshake and handed the tall metal cup back to the galley imp to wash and put away. "I'm done with my breakfast," she said. "You two can take off early and go out to play with the neighbor's kid."

"Hey little guy! How's it going?" David called as they waded into the water. They hadn't needed the *Dragonfly* for such a short distance.

❂Hello, hello!❂ sang the almost colorless flouwen. ❂Will you sing to me?❂

David laughed. "What shall we sing?" he asked.

❂Eleanor Rigby!❂ Sunshine trilled, working the opening bars into its pronunciation of the song's title.

"Eleanor Rigby?" echoed David, slightly taken aback. In most of his dealings with Sunshine, David had stressed the more classical works.

"That's my fault, I'm afraid," Cinnamon confessed. "I figured good music is good music, no matter who wrote it. Besides," she said, crossing her arms defensively, "the Beatles are classic."

"You'll get no argument from me on that." The sonovideo composer laughed.

Together they sang the song, Cinnamon singing the melody and David singing counterpoint. Sunshine managed to produce a whole range of harmonics at once that rivaled Jupiter's recording of the original hit. It took the little flouwen several hearings of a song to memorize it accurately, because it was always trying to add flourishes of its own.

❂I like the music but I do not understand all the words,❂ Sunshine complained as the last notes died in the water. ❂Even without understanding, it makes me feel sad. I feel like I have lost something.❂

"Well, I think that was the point. It's about the way that people miss opportunities to love others all around them," David explained.

"It's rather a grown-up song, even for a flouwen child," agreed Cinnamon.

❂It fits me anyway,❂ said the youngster. ❂I miss not having time enough to sing. The elders are always making me learn things instead. Who cares about the shape of conic sections anyway?❂

"You need to learn all kinds of things to be a well-rounded person." David tried to reach into his own childhood. "If I hadn't learned all the things I needed to be a computer programmer, then I would not have been able to program James to remember all this music we play for you."

"Yes," argued Cinnamon, "but don't let them make you grow up too fast. Sometimes there is as much beauty in the things you don't understand as the things you do understand."

"I doubt there can be such a thing as a flouwen romantic," David chided her, ignoring Sunshine. "They don't have a sex drive to sublimate or heroes to idealize. I've analyzed Green Fizzer's poetry, and it's nothing but mathematical equations that in the flouwen language also make pleasing harmonics. I'm convinced that the poetry is really an early form of music, and that even without our intervention they would have discovered music on their own. The major difference is that Green Fizzer would never recite a poem, no matter how musical, if it were not logically correct."

"All the flouwen may seem emotionally innocent compared to humans, but they force their own ideals on their young just like we do," Cinnamon insisted. "I'm not saying it's wrong, I just want Sunshine to enjoy his childhood. Puts me in mind of a song . . . "

"What doesn't?" David complained.

⊗Sing it, sing it!⊗

"You don't get the full effect *a capella*," said Cinnamon. "Jupiter? Can you broadcast my copy of Loggins and Messina's 'Pooh Corner'?"

The song came clearly out through Cinnamon's imp and she sang along softly with it.

" . . . Back to the ways of Christopher Robin . . . Back to the days of Pooh . . . " Finally the last descending run of the music came to an end.

"It's about going back to your childhood, when enjoying things was more important than controlling them," Cinnamon sighed. "That song always carries me right back into memories of my own childish imagination."

⊗Imagination? Do you mean like in the square root of minus one?⊗

The humans laughed.

"No, 'imagination' like in pretend. I mean wishing so much for impossible things, that, just for a moment, they seem possible."

⊗What is that you carry? Do you have a flouwen drysuit with you?⊗

Cinnamon was not thrown by the sudden change of subject. She had grown used to the abrupt, almost impolite, nature of flouwen conversation. "Yes, I was going to ask White Whistler if it wanted to come back on board and talk to Nels about the flouwen traveling on the *Dragonfly*. Both Deep Purple and Loud Red want to go up in the *Dragonfly* to see the waterfall from Eau to Roche, but neither seems too anxious to get back into their suits unless it's really necessary. Unfortunately, White Whistler is talking through Agua Dulce Station to George on the *Prometheus*. Those two are like two halves of the same mind. They talk for hours!"

❂I want to try on the suit!❂

"Shouldn't you wait until you are bigger?" objected David. "If you put part of yourself in the suit, what was left would be so small that it might be eaten."

Cinnamon held up the suit "Just look. You're twice as big as it is."

❂I just want to pretend!❂

"Okay, but once you see that you can't all fit and that you don't like separating yourself, I want you to go back to Yellow Hummer and promise that you'll try extra hard with your studies."

❂Okay!❂

"You know," said David as he helped Cinnamon stretch out the silvery-colored glassy-foil suit and open the zipper so Sunshine could start flowing inside, "maybe if I talk to Yellow Hummer I can see about changing some of Sunshine's lesson plans. There is plenty of math in music . . ."

"Look at Sunshine!" squealed Cinnamon excitedly.

The young yellow flouwen was filling the suit. As Sunshine entered, its color had gotten darker and more intense, but it didn't rock up. Finally all of the large flouwen fit inside the suit that was originally too small for it. It was as if Sunshine had somehow poured two gallons of water into a one-gallon bottle.

"How did you do it?" David was amazed.

"All the other flouwen who tried to do that couldn't adjust their water retention properly!" said Cinnamon. "They were either full-sized or rocks!"

❂I just pretended I could do it,❂ chirped Sunshine smugly from inside the suit.

"Jupiter! Interrupt White Whistler and George and have them check this out."

A moment later the water surrounding them was filled with the milky body of Clear◊White◊Whistle. ◊What have you done wrong now?◊ Then the adult flouwen carefully examined the suited youngling. ◊Give me a taste! I want to be able to do that!◊

Hesitantly the yellow youngling opened the zipper near the neckring on the suit and extended a thin tendril of color. Clear◊White◊Whistle tasted it for several moments. ◊This make no sense. You weren't thinking about what you were doing at all. Undo it and see it you can do it again. This time, think about it!◊

There was a long pause.

❂Shan't.❂

◊What do you mean, ❂shan't❂?◊

❂What if I can't do it again? I like this feeling. I can think faster, but still move around. I can go with the humans and not wonder what the other half of me is doing. I will not undo it.❂

◊But if you can redo it and teach the rest of us, then we can all do it.◊

❂Are you sure? None of you could do it before. Maybe you will teach me that it is not possible for me to do it either.❂

"You know . . . Sunshine may be right. Your all or nothing condensation process may be just learned behavior, but even so, it might not be possible to unlearn it. Some humans who have had the physical defects in their eyes fixed after childhood still can't see because their brains can't learn how to process the information their new eyes give them." David was curious to see what White Whistler would do to this recalcitrant youngster. How do you spank a half-ton child in a space-suit?

◊How can we know unless we try?◊

❂I will not do it. I want to go with the humans. Now that you know it is possible, you can figure it out for yourselves.❂ He crossed the suit's arms.

◊If you will not share your tastes with us, we will not share our tastes with you.◊

Ah, thought David, *that is the punishment. You threaten to isolate the youngling from the most basic form of communication of the pod.*

❂I don't care. You always make me work the problems out for myself before giving me the taste of the solution anyway. I will go live with the humans. They can take care of me. They can teach me all about music. I do not want to be flouwen. I want to be human. I want a human name. From now on you can just call me Pooh.❂

"Look, Sunshine . . . " David began.

❂Pooh!❂

"Pooh?" Cinnamon cut in. "I know that you'd like to come with us, but the fact is—we are all grown-ups too. We have a lot of work to do, and don't have much time to play with you or to take care of you. You need to stay here and learn how to be a good flouwen so that you can help us humans on our other missions."

The suit's arms remained crossed.

"Still," she continued, "it was very smart of you to figure out a way to fit in the suit. It proves that you are going to grow up to be a great flouwen. Maybe the smartest flouwen of all. But we humans—we aren't as smart as White Whistler and Yellow Hummer. You have to learn from them first."

❂If you are so dumb, how come you have the Flying⊗Rocks and we do not? You get to fly through the nothing to Sky⊗Rock. But Warm❋Amber❋Resonance says that I am too little and will have to stay here when you go to Sky⊗Rock.❂

"Well . . . I think that *if* you would be willing to show how grown-up you can be, by trying to help the pod, maybe the pod will say that it's all right for you come on the *Dragonfly* when we go to Roche. If I promise to ask them, will you try and show them how smart you were to figure out how to concentrate?" Cinnamon cajoled.

❂Well . . . ❂

"You can still be Pooh . . . "

❂Okay!❂

Pooh poured out of the suit. The youngling absorbed water and expanded until once again it was almost invisible in the dark blue water. Then it flowed slowly back into the suit, filling it with thick yellow jelly.

❂It is easy.❂

Again Clear❂Yellow❂Chirp shared tastes with Clear◊White◊Whistle, but the elder could not make any sense out of the taste. Finally, the humans agreed to let the flouwen take the drysuit with them to see if any of the other pod members could duplicate Pooh's feat.

◊Maybe Dainty∆Blue∆Warble . . . ◊ was White Whistler's last comment as it headed back for home with the youngling in tow.

"You handled that well," commented David.

"I had four younger brothers and sisters," said Cinnamon. "Besides, if Pooh can do something original that the elders can't do, they will give him more respect. Maybe then they'll respect music more."

"But we'll be stuck baby-sitting!"

"Blue Boy grew up a lot in only forty days. I think it will be quite an education watching Pooh get educated," said Cinnamon thoughtfully.

Over the next few rotations, the humans continued gathering all the information they could from the planet's surface. Rocheworld was on the inner leg of its highly elliptical orbit and Barnard was larger in the sky every time it rose. The tides were getting larger and the strains in the crust increased the activity of the volcanic vents that fed life on Eau. The number of new plants and animals the flouwen collected for the humans grew with each passing rotation.

"I'll be working on this for years," gloated Nels. In truth it *would* take years to analyze and understand the workings of this alien biology. While at first, many of the plants and animals seemed similar, there were many curious discrepancies that would have to be unraveled.

One animal seemed to like only ammonia in its system and would seek out colder regions in order to freeze the water in its body so that the crystals would settle out. One plant needed several others in order to reproduce, rather like the flouwen, while others needed only one partner. Some needed none at all and simply divided in half when they had enough bulk to make a new one.

Nels was now itching to get back to his analyzers and synthesizers on the *Prometheus* as badly as he had itched to get to the surface in the first place. In the meantime, he had the added help of Green Fizzer and Curious Green, and together they worked on the samples they had picked up from the oceans. The flouwen were fascinated with the capabilities of the tunneling array microscope in the *Dragonfly* lab. Although they had remarkable sensors that could discriminate between the different tastes of different molecules, they had never actually seen the molecules and they were enraptured.

The idea of atoms and molecules made perfect sense to these mathematical creatures, who had long known that certain elements and compounds had distinctive tastes, colors, and densities, that molecular compounds contained integer ratios of the elements, and that only certain types of elements would combine with certain other types of elements to form molecules. As a result, they had long ago logically figured out the periodic chart of the elements. To actually see the shapes and interrelationships of the complex organic molecules that made up their own bodies opened a whole new world of possibilities, and for a while Nels had to work around two suits filled mostly with water, each holding only a colored rock on its rounded bottom.

The flouwen had long known they were made of millions of small, nearly identical gel-like unit cells in the shape of a rounded dumbbell. Between the cells was a colored liquid "essence" that somehow contained their personality, since they could withdraw it during mating and form a new flouwen from the bare unit cells. The colored liquid also contained their memory, since they could pass on ideas to another flouwen by letting them have a "taste" of the liquid.

Using the tunneling array microscope, they were now

able to see details of the molecules in the cells and the liquid. The liquid was found to consist of a thin film of interlocked carbohydrate ring molecules that were kept in sheet form by outer layers of liquid crystal material. There were twelve different types of ring molecules in the inner layer that repeated in semi-random patterns. The flouwen soon determined that there were fixed patterns in this layer that contained the genetic code. Whereas human DNA uses only four different molecules to write the genetic code, the flouwen genetic alphabet had twelve "letters" in it. The ring molecule layer also contained variable patterns that constituted the long-term memory. The flouwen next determined that the liquid crystal layers, besides holding the ring molecules in sheets, and giving their bodies their distinctive bright colors, were conductive and acted as their "nerve" tissue.

The flouwen then used the tunneling array microscope to determine that the outer surface of the dumbbell-shaped cellular units were found to have ring-shaped patterns impressed in them. These patterns matched the twelve basic ring-compound patterns in the liquid layer. The impressed patterns on the units acted as the template for the formation of the various enzymes needed for operation and maintenance of the interior of the unit cells and the whole flouwen body, and to make copies of the genetic code for the ring-molecule layer. During mating, the patterns on the cells were passed on to the offspring by the parents, providing the offspring with the desired multiple genetic heritage as well as a broad, but diffuse, "racial" memory. Once the flouwen had figured out their own genetics, Nels gave them samples of the DNA of the various crew members for them to examine and compare. He was hoping to keep them busy and out of the way while he worked on their food supply.

Nels was trying to find the right breeding conditions for the small, simple, light-brown blob of an animal that he called a "gingersnap," which was a flouwen food staple.

The gingersnap fed directly on the chemicals leaching up from the volcanic vents, reproduced rapidly, and unlike the similar-shaped and -colored predator, hadn't any sharp teeth. As the time came for the *Dragonfly* to take off on its aerial survey of Eau, the waterfall, and Roche, Nels had managed to grow dozens of the almost inactive light-brown blobs, and he was able to assure the others that they would be able to feed as many of the flouwen as would like to accompany them on their trip to the rocky lobe of the double planet.

One hundred sixty dark-light cycles, or forty Earth days, had passed since they had last left the surface of this strange double-planet. Once again it was that time of the season for the oddest phenomena yet recorded. The two planets shared more that an atmosphere. They also shared an ocean, although only for a short while. On their last trip, the humans had had rather too close a view of the growing wave that leaped from one planet to the other across the zero-gee saddle where the *Dragonfly* and the *Eagle* had rendezvoused a few days before.

This time the *Dragonfly* would be in a better position to record the fickle ocean. Thomas, Nels, Tony, and Caroline would pull shifts in the *Falcon* perched on the outer islands of Eau, while Jinjur, David, Cinnamon, Shirley, Richard, and Sam would take the *Dragonfly* into the upper atmosphere between the inner poles in order to get a good view of the waterfall that occurred during periapsis. The flouwen had done their equivalent of drawing straws, and White Whistler, Loud Red, and Deep Purple would be sending portions of themselves with the humans to Roche. Pooh would also be coming along, although the youngster had promised to stay out of the way.

As darkness fell, the humans on the surface readied themselves for the short jaunt, and good-byes were exchanged. On their last night together behind the Sound-Bar door of Tony's bunk on the *Falcon*, Cinnamon lay in Tony's arms and looked down at his sleeping face.

How was it that each time they lay together she was left with this ache? This feeling that somehow she hadn't done quite enough? This insistent need that next time she would do better?

It wasn't love. That was the main thing that she had to face. It wasn't a case of always leave them wanting more. Cinnamon had to accept that whatever it was she was getting from Tony, it wasn't enough. Whatever it was that she was giving Tony, it wasn't enough for him either; Cinnamon could tell that she wasn't truly helping Tony any more.

There was more going on here than she could fix. Cinnamon's extra input had always expressed itself to her in music, and there simply wasn't any music that would tell her what was going on in Tony's mind. Cinnamon didn't know how she was going to tell him . . . or even if she would need to tell him. After all, he hadn't talked to her before taking her into his bed. But she knew that this was the last time she would ever share it. She couldn't help, she was only in the way . . . and she was in danger of being run over.

Just then Tony opened his eyes and looked back at her. Cinnamon couldn't meet his gaze.

"Tony . . . " she began hesitantly, "I don't think I will be spending as much time with you as I have been lately."

"Why?" he asked and he propped himself up on to one elbow so he could look at her directly. He had entered this relationship with no expectation of having it last any more than one night. But Cinnamon's body pleased him more than any woman's ever had. Tony knew he would never love her, even though working with Cinnamon on the surface had shown Tony that she was more than just a body. In fact, Cinnamon had gone from being just a student pilot to being a real person. Sure, it made it harder to think of her sexually, but when they were in bed she didn't force her individuality on him. Cinnamon spent their time in the bunk hardly speaking and that was just the way he liked it. And at least she didn't sing! That would have driven him mad! Cinnamon was a good scientist and medic and her dealing with John's accident had impressed all of them, but in bed, what Tony wanted was a partner, not a lover. *Don't let her spoil it now!* he prayed silently.

"Is there someone else?" he asked. He wasn't worried about sharing her, he just didn't want to go back to celibacy.

"The point is that there isn't even 'us.' Maybe I could love you, but I don't. And you don't love me."

"But we are so good together. I need you," he said running his hands gently over her body.

"You have been very good to me. You are a gentle and considerate lover." *Not to mention instructive*, Cinnamon added mentally. "But I have to believe there is more to sex than what we have. Even the flouwen need a kind of love to mate! I want you to make love to me, Cinnamon Byrd. I want you to make love to my soul."

Tony began his usual gentle foreplay but as he looked into Cinnamon's eyes, he could no longer pretend. He was with a real person, one who needed to be loved, and deserved to be loved for herself. He faltered, and stopped. Cinnamon gave him a kiss, and slipped out of the bunk. Tony knew that while he had just lost a lover, he had not lost a friend. Tony heard Cinnamon sing from the shower room as she dressed to go back to the *Dragonfly*.

"I read her diary underneath the tree . . . "

"About time you got here," said Jinjur as Cinnamon cycled through the airlock into the *Dragonfly*. "Where have you been? We lift off in fifteen minutes."

"I'll be ready, ma'am," replied Cinnamon contritely, eyes avoiding Jinjur's as she took off her exploration suit and stored it away in the rack. Jinjur instantly regretted her brusque greeting. The young biologist had never given Jinjur any trouble and there was no need for Jinjur to say what she did. She might be Cinnamon's boss, but she wasn't her mother. It was none of Jinjur's business where Cinnamon had been—although Jinjur had a pretty good idea.

Why do I always get so worried before a mission? Jinjur asked herself, knowing full well that lots of worrying by the commander *before* a mission ensured that the mission was successful and there was less to worry about *after* the mission.

When Cinnamon came forward and sat down in the copilot seat, she noticed that despite the late hour, everyone was there. Shirley was in the pilot's seat, David was at the computer console, Jinjur and Sam were seated in front of the two science consoles, and Richard was perched on one of the swing-out seats in the galley, munching away on a bean burrito midnight snack and washing down each peppery bite with a big gulp of Coke.

Someone had swung the science instrument scan platforms back from the two bulbous viewing ports on either side of the aeroplane, and their space had been taken by four silver blobs, two flouwen squashed closely together in each area, each trying to look out the window with the lenses built into their helmets. The two large silver-suited blobs, one with a helmet filled with red jelly and the other with a lavender helmet, pushed and squirmed in one window. They were having trouble adjusting to looking out though a window with their helmet lenses. They kept focusing on the surface of the glass and the reflected images of themselves rather than on the view far below.

☆Move aside! Let me look!☆

❐Move aside yourself!❐

In the other window, the helmets in the silver-suited aliens were milky and a clear yellow.

◊Are you able to look satisfactorily, Clear✪Yellow✪Chirp?◊

✪I am not used to these lens things—and don't call me that name. My name is Pooh!✪

It was dark outside, but the sandy beach in front of them was illuminated with the wing lights from *Dragonfly*. Ahead, just at the edge of the blazing white beam, were the three landing legs of the *Falcon*. High above were two patches of light, the lower one oval and the upper one made of two triangles. They were the viewport window to the lounge area on *Falcon* and the landing windows for the cockpit area on the deck above. There were three people and a silver blob visible in the large oval viewport window. Cinnamon recognized the people as Thomas, Caroline, and Tony. The blob was either Little Fizzer or Little Curiosity—at this distance Cinnamon could not tell the two green-colored flouwen apart. Nels must be busy down on the engineering deck with the other flouwen, looking at specimens with the tunneling array microscope.

"Take her away, Everett," commanded Jinjur.

Shirley smoothly started the electrically powered VTOL fans in the wing roots of the *Dragonfly*, and the massive aeroplane slowly lifted from the beach.

✪We are flying!✪

◊I only wish there were more light, so I could see better.◊

Once she was at altitude, Shirley pivoted the plane and changed the thrust on the VTOL fans until they were moving across the dark ocean toward the inner pole of Eau. After a few hours of travel a dark patch of sky rose above the horizon, visible only because it blotted out the stars one by one as it grew larger. The edge of the dark patch developed a bright red rim as sunrise approached. Finally, Barnard rose from behind the Roche lobe, and the waves became visible in the ocean below them.

Rocheworld was now traversing the inner portion of its highly elliptical orbit, where it was moving along much more rapidly and getting very close to the star. Because of its close proximity, Barnard was now very large in the sky, much bigger than the Sun in the sky of Earth.

"The ocean is getting pretty active," said Sam. "Look at those large waves scudding ahead of us."

☆I wish I were down there surfing on them!☆

◊I don't think even you would want to surf these waves. Look up ahead through the cockpit window. See how high they get as they go to the point underneath Sky⊗Rock.◊

One of the larger waves had reached the top of the water mountain, where it crashed into another large wave coming up the other side. Now, rising from the collision of the two waves was a huge fountain of water. Slowly it rose high into the air, and continued to rise, its frothy white-capped peak glowing redly in the sunrise light from Barnard.

❐If you had surfed that wave, we would be picking up pieces of you for the next sixty-four cycles.❐

☆I would have dived under to calmer water before it could catch me. There is no wave I can't surf!☆

❂Could you even surf the Big⊗Bloop, old one?❂

☆Certainly! I can surf anything! I could not only ride the Big⊗Bloop from here to Sky⊗Rock, but all the way around Sky⊗Rock to the other side.☆ There was a long pause. ☆Of course, there *is* the problem of getting back from Sky⊗Rock . . . ☆

◊It is certainly amazing to see the ocean activity from this perspective. It looks much different using light rather than sound. You see all the parts of the waves at one time instead of having to wait for the echoes to return from the distant portions.◊

"The top of that fountain must be fifteen kilometers high," guessed Shirley, raising the altitude of *Dragonfly* as they got closer to the center.

"It is ten kilometers and falling," replied Juno. "Its peak excursion from the nominal ocean surface was only twelve and one-half kilometers."

"It sure takes its time to fall," observed Cinnamon.

"When something that big moves, it always takes time," said David, who was watching the images coming from the forward videocamera on the screen of his console. "Some time ago I wanted to use the image of an elephant in one of my sonovideo compositions. I had to give it up—the music got too draggy."

"Look," said Shirley. "The cloud of spray it threw upward into the zero-gee region is developing into a mustache. Two whorls going north and south."

"That's the Coriolis force acting," said Richard. "On Earth, the Coriolis force is strongest at the north and south poles, but there isn't much wind there, so Earth storms form in the mid-latitudes where there is plenty of wind and still an appreciable Coriolis force. Here, the winds and the Coriolis force peak at the same place. Those whorls may look small from here, but they're Oz-sized tornadoes."

"Look," said Cinnamon. "The wind blowing through the gap from Eau to Roche is peeling off a series of small tornadoes heading toward Roche."

"I've been close to those before," said Shirley with a shudder. "Too close. Arielle took us up the inside of one of them."

"The first of the three interplanetary waterfalls is coming in two Rocheworld days or twelve hours. After that, we will be busy observing for at least twenty-four straight hours," said Jinjur. "Shirley. Take *Dragonfly* to our planned first observation point and put it on automatic hover. Then everyone hit the sack for a solid eight hours of Zs. I want you all fresh when the action starts."

◊We don't need to sleep, so we will observe for you until then.◊

"Just don't fiddle with the controls," said Jinjur, still not quite trusting the impetuous aliens.

Twelve hours later, the *Dragonfly* was perched high in the air over Eau where it could get a good look at the side of the mountain of water that made up the pointed part of the watery lobe of the double planet. It was dark, for Barnard was behind Eau, high over the islands on the outer pole where the rocket lander *Falcon* was waiting. Since the flouwen couldn't see anything out the portholes, the scan platforms had been swung back into place so the multispectral infrared scanners could provide an alternate view.

The flouwen now clustered around the two science consoles, listening as Richard controlled the infrared scanner and explained the pseudocolor image they were seeing. On the screen could be seen a rounded cone, blue to indicate cold. Moving rapidly up the blue cone was a series of green lines with yellow tops. Where the streaks met at the top, there were spurts of yellow-orange and angry red. Over all were sparse ribbons of long white clouds that streaked up the mountain and through the narrow atmospheric neck between the two planets and disappeared out of view over Roche.

"Barnard has been heating up the atmosphere on Eau, and the winds in this region are blowing from Eau to Roche, which means they are blowing up the mountain of water. We're now so close to Barnard the heating effect is quite intense. As a result, the winds are quite strong, greater than hurricane velocity, and make large, fast waves. Because of the low gravity in this region, the waves are one hundred meters high, have a wavelength of fifty kilometers, and are moving at two hundred kilometers an hour."

Richard now pointed to a barely perceptible green line that stretched from one end of the image to the other at the base of the blue cone. It was only noticeable because Juno had inserted two flashing red arrows that pointed at the two ends of the arc.

"Here comes the tidal bore. If you thought those wind waves were fierce, wait until you see this wave. As the tide from Barnard decreases the spacing between the two planets, the gravity pull of Roche on the water mountain increases. When the pull becomes stronger, the water coming in from the other parts of the ocean starts out as a low ring wave that runs completely all the way around the base of the mountain. The ring of water starts moving up the conical mountain of ocean and soon turns into a single high-speed wave with a steep front that covers the six hundred kilometers up the side of the mountain in the hour and a half between low and high tide. It gets bigger and meaner as it's compressed into the smaller and smaller area around the peak. The wave is over two kilometers high when it reaches the peak."

☆Two kilometers!☆ For once in his life, Loud Red was awed.

❐The humans surfed it.❐

☆Then I could too!☆

◊It is too bad all this activity has to happen when it is dark. If the ring wave is this impressive in the false-colored images from the infrared scanner, it would be even more spectacular in the visible.◊

"Time to put a little light on the subject," said George from the *Prometheus*. As he spoke, a gigantic searchlight beam three hundred kilometers across swept across the plains of Roche and came to a halt at the top of the mountain, just in time to catch the ring wave as it converged on the peak. "James won't be able to hold *Prometheus*'s sail at this angle for too long without knocking us out of position, but we should be able to illuminate the activity until Barnard comes around from behind Eau and provides some sunlight."

As they watched, the illuminated ring wave turned into a geyser that spouted a long blob of water up and through the zero-gee region to fall slowly down onto the dry rocky point of Roche. The searchlight beam now moved from the mountain of water on the pointed part of Eau to the mountain of land on the pointed part of Roche.

"Look at those volcanoes!" exclaimed Jinjur. "Every single one of them is spouting its head off!"

"While the gravity of Roche is pulling on the water mountain of Eau, the gravity of Eau is pulling on the pointy end of Roche," explained Richard. "The crust must be under terrific strain there. No wonder the volcanoes are acting up."

"They're about to be drowned, though," said David, who had been watching everything from his computer console. "Here comes the blob of ocean water from Eau. It must be ten kilometers thick."

They watched as the elongated blob of frothy water squeezed its way through the narrow gravitational neck between the two planets, then started its long slow fall toward the rocky lobe below. On the Eau side of the blob, the geyser column thinned out as the base fell back under Eau's gravitational pull, while the top portion continued to coast through the zero-gravity region.

"The leading edge of the drop is just now contacting the surface," said David.

At the base of the column of water there exploded a boiling hot cloud of steam as the icy water poured down on the red-hot lava. For twenty minutes, the torrent continued to fall, and soon the base of the waterfall was hidden in an expanding cloud of steam. From the base of the cloud streaked rivers of water, streaming down the channels gouged between the volcanoes by previous floods, and riding a layer of steam over the tongues of lava that had preceded them down those channels. Fingers of steam rose into the air, twirled by the strong Coriolis forces near the center of the rapidly spinning double-planet system. Large, lazy tornadoes were spawned and moved ahead of the flood fronts across the planet, now illuminated by the red rays of sunrise.

"Here comes Barnard," came George's voice. "We'll tack *Prometheus* back so we will be in position to illuminate the next waterfall, three hours from now. See you around on the other side."

They were approaching periapsis, when Rocheworld was at its closest point to Barnard, and the star was growing visibly with time. Its dull red globe was now nearly five times bigger than the Sun in the sky of Earth. Jinjur looked out the cockpit window and raised her chin to let the warm sunlight fall on her neck.

"It's not like a Florida beach at noon, but it's definitely warm. Nice for a change." She looked at Cinnamon. "Fly us over to the other side, and while you're at it, put us at altitude over Roche instead of Eau, so we can observe from that angle."

Cinnamon tilted the VTOL fans and increased their speed until the large aeroplane was moving rapidly forward instead of hovering in place. As soon as she had built up enough forward speed, she pushed forward on the throttle for the nuclear jet at the same time she shut down the VTOL fans. Soon they were cruising through the air at six hundred kilometers an hour.

Three hours later they watched the second transfer of water from Eau to Roche, again illuminated by the reflected sunlight from the sail on *Prometheus*.

"This one looks smaller," said Jinjur.

"It's supposed to be smaller," replied Richard, who was carefully monitoring the whole process on his science console. He had a flouwen watching over each shoulder, while the other two flouwen were at the other science console. They had now learned enough from watching Richard that they were able to use the touchscreen to do their own image analysis.

❐What is that you just asked the computer to do?❐

◊I have instructed Juno to outline the blob of water when it separates and collect data on its shape changes. The volume should stay constant, so with a time history of the outline of one cross-section, and some minimal assumptions about symmetry, I should be able to calculate the three-dimensional shape at any point in time, and test my mathematical model for the gravitational fields of the two planets.◊

❂Richard says that a human named Roche calculated such a mathematical model many cycles ago.❂

◊I will soon find out if the human Roche was correct.◊

"How come it's supposed to be smaller?" said Jinjur, still puzzled. "We're at periapsis, closer to Barnard than we were for the last waterfall. The tides should be stronger and there should be more water transferred."

"You're forgetting the part that the atmosphere plays," said Richard. "At periapsis, Barnard is heating Roche while Eau is in shadow. The atmospheric winds are going from Roche to Eau and blowing *down* the mountain of water on Eau, in the *opposite* direction to the tidal bore wave. At the time of the high tides on either side of periapsis, Barnard is heating Eau, boiling off the ammonia in the oceans and *adding* wind waves to the tidal bore wave, which makes those waterfalls larger." He paused and looked carefully at his screen. "The bottom of the blob should be hitting the volcano fields now."

"Not as much steam this time," said Jinjur, as they watched the frothy blob drown the volcanoes once again in a torrent of icy water.

"The lava crust is not as hot," replied Richard. "There should be a lot more liquid water left this time . . . Here comes the first of the streams out from under the steam cloud." A silvery streak sped down a large channel and rapidly reached the edge of the circular spot of reflected light from *Prometheus*, then moved onward across Roche in the darkness. A short while later, it appeared again as it passed over the terminator shadow line and came out into the light from Barnard, just rising from behind Roche.

"See you in three hours," came George's voice from *Prometheus* as the gigantic sail tilted and the circle of light moved across the surface of Roche and off out into space.

Jinjur turned to Cinnamon. "For the next one, I want to be closer to the surface of Roche, so we can follow one of those rivers. That way we can document what it does to the channel as it moves along."

"You had better have your nuclear jet ready and warmed up, Cin," said Richard. "With the pressure head and velocity the water builds up dropping down the forty kilometers from the zero-gee region, you get air entrapment under the stream, just like an avalanche. The fronts of those channel streams must be moving at five hundred kilometers an hour."

"I'll be taking that shift, big boy," said Shirley from the

galley where she was having lunch with Sam. She washed the last of her toasted pseudocheese sandwich down with the last of her algaeshake, handed the metal shaker back to the galley imp, and came forward.

"My goodness," said Richard, looking up at the clock in the corner of his screen. "It's lunchtime already. Time sure passes when you're keeping busy. I sure am hungry.... Think I'll have one of my real-meat specials—a pizza with six different kinds of pseudocheese, sprinkled with mushrooms, green peppers, real-meat ground beef chunks from Ferdinand, and real-meat chips of Canadian bacon from Hamlet—all washed down with a superbulb of Coke."

"Oh!" said Sam from the galley, with a surprised look on his face. "Was that *your* special? I ate it yesterday."

"Juno!" yelled Richard, now annoyed. "How come you let him have my . . . " He paused as he realized that Juno never made a mistake. Then he glared down the corridor at Sam.

"Gotcha!" said Sam with a mischievous grin. He too slurped down the last of his algaeshake and came forward to relieve Richard at the science console.

Three hours later, they were waiting as the last of the interplanetary waterfalls started. Again the flouwen were crowded around the science consoles while Sam explained what they were seeing on the screens.

"According to the data we collected during the last periapsis passage, this should be a big one," said Sam. "In addition to the help of the wind flowing up the water mountain, there is a partial resonance in the ocean basins on Eau that give the tidal bore a head start."

George had one side of the water mountain illuminated with the reflected light from the sail and the entire crew watched in fascination as the ring wave rode up the mountain, contracted to the point, and generated a thick climbing spout of water. The under portions of the spout thinned while the top portion that had enough momentum to overcome the weakening gravity continued upward and squeezed its bulk through the zero-gravity neck, compressed to a ten-kilometer-wide throat by the strong gravity gradients. The blob grew into an ellipsoidal ball on the other side and started to stretch as the lower portions were pulled along faster than the upper regions. The image of the scene on Sam's science console screen had an overlay that Juno had traced out around the elongating ball.

"It's thirty kilometers long by twenty in diameter," said Sam. "That's enough to cover Roche a half-meter deep in water. Of course, most of the water will form temporary lakes in the lower elevations, while most of Roche will stay fairly dry."

As the ball fell, it pushed air ahead of it and flattened out on the bottom. When it reached the surface, the trapped air built up in pressure and squeezed out at high speeds from the edges, only to find itself trapped by an enlarging blob of water that moved rapidly over the nearly frictionless trapped air, trading its gravitational head for speed. Streams of silver streaked down the channels between the drowned volcanoes. One of them was coming straight toward them, where *Dragonfly* waited, hovering on its VTOL fans, over the largest of the channels that led from the inner peak of Roche to the cratered plains of the outer hemisphere.

Sam used the icons on the touchscreen to track the onrushing wall of water with the Doppler radar in the nose of the *Dragonfly*.

"The velocity of the front is five hundred and eighty kilometers an hour," said Sam.

"Then I'd better get a move on," said Shirley, swiveling the *Dragonfly* around on its VTOL fans, and smoothly transitioning to jet thrust. Soon they were flying over the front of the flood, matching its velocity. Zooming along at over five hundred kilometers an hour, it didn't take long for them to arrive at the first of the many lakes that had formed in the lowland areas in the outer hemisphere of the Roche lobe. This was a fairly large lake, with a large island in the middle.

• CHAPTER TEN—DISCOVERING

Loudest Beast began to become aware of the change in the soil. Veteran of many springs, he could sense the pressure build as the water from the first deluge inched toward his comfortable bed. Loudest Beast's roots tingled as the sensitive ends tasted the refreshing flavor, but Loudest Beast knew that now was not the time to be sending out new shoots toward the moisture. Soon there would be water enough for all, but the best sites would go to those who were the first out of the ground.

Slowly, fighting the thirst and the hardened soil, Loudest Beast reabsorbed the thin filaments that had supplied trickles of moisture and nourishment throughout the long days of sleep. Even as he pulled the roots within his rocklike exterior, the first of the new water seeped into the dirt around them and the roots entered his body, plump with the mineral-rich liquid.

The flavor of the water awoke the youngling protected deep within Loudest Beast's pouch. Loudest Beast passed on the new water to the stirring young one and murmured to him encouragingly. Loudest Beast had named the child Screaming Killer, but in truth, he was not sure that the youngling would be much of a fighter. This youngling asked too many questions instead of listening to the best way to frighten others off your territory. Still, he would learn with time, and Loudest Beast had high hopes for his future. The elder had not always felt so good about his young.

Three seasons ago, Loudest Beast had released Gigantic Grabber, and that youngling still had not managed to find a mate. Privately, Loudest Beast had felt that a better name would have been Greedy Whiner. . . . The youngling had spent all their time together complaining of hunger, and had only stopped when his exasperated parent shared the taste of a starving parent eating his youngling in order to survive. This year, Loudest Beast promised himself that he would check on Gigantic Grabber while they were swimming in the lake. Surely this year, the youngling would be large enough to mate.

Now, Loudest Beast had to bring Screaming Killer into the world. Water had loosened the hard ground around them and Loudest Beast absorbed the tasty liquid into his fleshy body. The rocklike skin that had protected them both now itched, as it stretched to accommodate their expanding bodies plumping up with the new moisture. Stretching long dormant muscles, Loudest Beast began to dig up through the mud with his five strong legs. The task grew easier as the water above rushed to fill the space they had vacated, and soon their struggles churned the mud into a sticky soup. Only moments from the time Loudest Beast first tasted water in the ground around them, he stood on the flooded surface of the island, using some of the receding water to wash off the last of the dirt clouding his vision. Soon the rain would come.

Loudest Beast had chosen their resting place well. It stood in a shallow depression in the middle of a suddenly marshy island surrounded by a large lake. All around, the newly formed lake was brown with the mud that only yesterday had been arid dust. Loudest Beast needed to take only a few steps to reach the edge of the lake and eject Screaming Killer from the pouch.

For a moment Screaming Killer hesitated, but hunger was stronger than filial love. Like a huge, five-legged squid, the rust-colored youngling slithered into the water and disappeared. Loudest Beast knew the youngling would find his parent again when he had gorged himself on the plants and tiny swimmers awakened from their long hibernation by the deluge. Loudest Beast would wait until the water cleared and the larger animals had emerged and fed, before he would feed.

All around, the beach heaved and quivered, as others dug their way up to the surface. Those with young would allow the small ones the first tastes of the mineral-rich waters now teeming with rapidly growing plants and tiny forms of swimming life. . . . Such food was below the dignity of those who were old enough to know how to hunt. Who would want to mate with a grazer?

All around the People's colony, the surface of the planet was changing colors. Fed with the water and the chemicals brought in the deluge, the fast-growing spores were blooming into the plants that were the beginning of the food chain. The violently colored plants fought each other for space, visibly growing larger even as they were eaten by those herbivores that had managed to survive the long winter. Overhead, the clouds swirled and thunder growled in an imitation of the People's mating match. Lighting flashed and with a crackling roar, of the first of the rain began to fall.

Loudest Beast absorbed the falling water in through his thick upper skin. Refreshed, he turned his attention to the hunger that weakened him. Unwilling to allow others to perceive his famished state, he stomped slowly over to the edge of his territory. Nonchalantly, he reached out and engulfed a Sharp-Sneaky that was feeding on the body of Loudest Beast's less fortunate neighbor.

Loudest Beast had known that the other Person hadn't the strength to survive the drought. Loudest Beast had stolen as much of his neighbor's territory as Loudest Beast could defend while they were above ground, and then ruthlessly poached the neighbor's limited water resources once they were both underground and began to send out roots. Now Loudest Beast ate the Sharp-Sneaky before the neighbor's flesh had even been assimilated into the predator. Loudest Beast hardly paused at the flavor of the dead Person. The awful taste would soon pass and Loudest Beast's reputation as a ruthless survivor would be strengthened. The better your reputation the less you had to defend it.

Other Sharp-Sneakies and Death-Tearers wiggled toward the shriveled body of Loudest Beast's neighbor. The body had swelled slightly, a post-mortem reaction to the water, but the Person had little flesh left and soon there was no trace that he had lived even a season. Even the taste of him inside Loudest Beast had faded.

Loudest Beast was not alone in the hunting of the scavengers. The little beasts almost always lost, once the brief battle was joined, but they were fast and sleek, literally swimming deep into the mud to escape the larger star-shaped People. The scavengers normally dug up and ate those People that hadn't survived, finding them by tracing the fragile roots to the main body. When hunger drove them to it, however, they would also sneak up on People too engrossed with eating or mating, and steal bites out of them. Eating might quell one's hunger, but killing the vermin was important to the whole colony. Still, Loudest Beast did not gorge on the vermin; they were too hungry and vicious now. Let them eat their fill of the others, then Loudest Beast would hunt them down and take all the flesh for himself. Besides, Loudest Beast had learned to eat slowly and build up flesh gradually. That way he would be fully satiated just as the lake dried up again. These adolescents didn't seem to realize that they had several days to put on weight, and that if they tried too hard too soon, their hunger would be satisfied during the beginning of the flood season and they would grow hungry again later when the food was more scarce. Loudest Beast would eat slowly and constantly, expending the minimum of energy in hunting. Even more important than feeding was the selection of a mate and the defending of one's territory.

Stomping majestically down to the water's edge, Loudest Beast slid regally into the cloudy waters. Casually, Loudest Beast reached out and engulfed any of the lower animals that hadn't moved quickly enough to avoid the star-shaped Person, but for the moment, as long as he was within sight of the other elders, he did no active hunting. Once below the surface, Loudest Beast abandoned dignity to romp like a youngling in the refreshing water. The rains continued to fall, and there was the second rush of water that came during the flood season. Almost instantly Loudest Beast was joined by Screaming Killer, who was startled by this fresh influx of water.

<Why was there so little water most of the time and so much of it now?> Screaming Killer asked his parent.

<That is the way of things, my child. Three times we are blessed with the flowing floods of water and the rains from the skies. Make the most of it. Eat well and become big and strong. Those that are too small and weak will not live to see the next time of water. Those that are big and strong will bring their children up to wash in the next rain.>

Loudest Beast shared with the youngling the last tastes and advice he would need. Although the youngling might not mate this year, and maybe not even the next, Screaming Killer had already made his parent proud by eating mostly the high-protein herbivores rather than the mineral-heavy plants themselves. Loudest Beast was reminded again of Gigantic Grabber and how that youngling had gorged himself only on the plant life since it was easier than chasing after the fast-swimming animals. The plants made his belly full, but they didn't supply as much nourishment as a belly full of animals. Gigantic Grabber had almost died in the following dry season, even with no youngling in his pouch to feed. Loudest Beast sent a call out to Gigantic Grabber, but if the youngling was in the lake, he did not answer Loudest Beast's call. Loudest Beast hoped that Gigantic Grabber would have a better time of it this season . . . too much hunger could twist even the toughest Person.

Screaming Killer rubbed affectionately against his parent and then swam off into the murky depths. He would join the colony on the other side of the lake for the next three seasons. The genetic pool of the colonies was protected by this long-standing taboo. If Screaming Killer survived to return to this side of the lake and mated with his parent, then at least it would be the better genes they would be reinforcing. After six seasons, People were allowed to decide for themselves which side of the lake they preferred. Anyone would be proud to mate with an elder.

Loudest Beast would keep a casual eye on this promising but quizzical youngling just as he had followed the progress of Gigantic Grabber, but while he looked forward to the possibility of meeting and mating with Screaming Killer far in the future, Loudest Beast would not sacrifice hard-won prestige and mate with Gigantic Grabber just to save the youngster's pride. It was right and good that only those matching in size mated, and Loudest Beast would never break that taboo. A child too large for his parent would doom the both of them to starvation.

Partially satiated, Loudest Beast pulled himself out of the lake and back onto the shore. A quick check of his boundaries showed that his neighbors had been busy. Three of the old boundary markers had been shifted, and the claim marked by Loudest Beast's dead neighbor had disappeared completely. For now, both of the spinward borders seemed deserted, so Loudest Beast took advantage of the opportunity and shifted his markers to give himself a larger slice of the island. Although none of the People had yet been able to sum up the competition, Loudest Beast took as large a bite from the neighboring territories as he felt he could defend. If they should force Loudest Beast to give up the new ground, he would have lost nothing by trying for all he could, at this stage of the game. As Loudest Beast moved back to check out the new Person in the dead neighbor's place, a roar shook the ground.

<Tremble in fear, old one, for I am Flesh Burner!>

Before Loudest Beast stood a young Person new to the colony, although he had probably been nurtured on this side of the lake. Flesh Burner was a reddish brown, and even from this distance Loudest Beast could sense the heat that seemed to emanate from his body. The Elder had run into such overly warm People before—they minimized the amount of ammonia in their bodies and, as a result, they were startlingly hot to the touch. This heat could throw an inexperienced opponent off, and the hot Person would triumph over a larger rival. But Loudest Beast was a veteran of too many fights to allow this presumptuous adolescent to frighten him off by such a trick. Loudest Beast rose up on three of his legs, reached two of his legs up into the sky, and with a contemptuous roar, charged at Flesh Burner. Their fleshy bellies met with a resounding slap.

<I am Loudest Beast, you feverish youngling. You must be twisted to challenge such as me!> Loudest Beast allowed the flavor of many victories to coat the surface of his stomach. As they pulled away from each other, it was clear that the younger Person was rethinking the advisability of frontal assault. At this point, Flesh Burner had no pouchling to protect, but to lose so publicly would hurt his reputation, and then he might not find a mate at all. Loudest Beast casually flicked the boundary marker back a little into Flesh Burner's claim. Flesh Burner reared again and screamed defiance, but didn't charge. Loudest Beast turned his back on the other, ignoring Flesh Burner. A strong neighbor was not always a problem, as long as it was clear just who was boss. Loudest Beast knew that, for the rest of the season, there was little to fear on this section of his border.

All around the marshy island, the People were roaring at their neighbors, marking ground for the best places to spend the next time of drought. The truce that started at the first influx of water was almost over. Even now Loudest Beast felt the first of the rumbling in the mud that heralded the imminent arrival of the third and last flood of water. He climbed a large boulder, wrapped his legs around it, and allowed the downpour to hammer down on him. Loudest Beast's five clear eyes looked out through the rain at the low wall of water coursing down the valley, riding over the rain-pelted surface of the lake. Carried along on the crest of the inrushing flood of water were soft patches of color. Loud Red knew from experience that these were strange types of plants and animals that were not like those that grew in and around the lake. The animals, especially, were strange in that they were almost jelly-like. They certainly were not strong enough to survive out of the water. Where this manna came from, and how this soft life managed to live even long enough to reproduce, was something Loudest Beast had used many days thinking about. The old legends that the food came from the mythical land of Everwet was the answer Loudest Beast's parent had passed on, and was the answer Loudest Beast passed to his own younglings. But Loudest Beast was never happy with that explanation, and Screaming Killer had not been satisfied either. Perhaps that was why, this time, of all the People, Loudest Beast was still looking up the valley as the last flood arrived, and Loudest Beast caught the first glimpse of a new animal arriving with the flood. This beast was not one of the soft shapeless blobs of color riding on the floodwaters. This was a shining silver Person, one that had just given up an arm in mating. But this Person was swimming through the air.

"Wow!" said Jinjur, awed as she looked through the windscreen of *Dragonfly* onto the scene spread out below. "How could we have missed this?!" The whole planet below them had gone from barren to blossoming in only a matter of hours. Lacy colorful plants swelled and grew, covering the ground like so much candy floss. Every so often, a section of a plant exploded and sent seeds into the breeze.

"We explored this planet! There was no sign of anything like this!" George protested. He and the crew on *Prometheus* had assembled and were glued to the communication screens.

"I'm afraid that I was not monitoring much of Roche

during the last water influx," apologized James. "Too many of my sensors were trained on the flouwen on Eau and on the returning ascent module. Besides, from orbit, there was little to observe on Roche but the tops of storm clouds."

"Well, let's get a good look at what's going on down there now!" Jinjur insisted.

⭘Cannot look at anything!⭘ Pooh protested. Shirley had stowed the science scan platforms in their racks so that the flouwen could look out the bulbous eyelike scanner domes on each side of *Dragonfly*. All the flouwen were butting and shoving, struggling to see out the windows.

☆Tell me what is going on down there!☆ Little Red insisted.

"Cinnamon, you're the biologist. Tell us *all* what's going on down there!" Jinjur ordered.

Cinnamon took a deep breath. She desperately wished Nels were here to handle this, but since they had not found life on Roche before, they had left the biology expert on Eau with the *Falcon*.

"I would assume that most of the life on Roche hibernates during the long drought season and becomes active only with the arrival of the incoming waters from Eau. Just like the plants in the California deserts, the plants grow and mature quickly, absorbing the minerals from the hectic waters and almost instantly forming and releasing seeds for the next generation. In a way, the plant is only the seed's way of forming another seed."

"But why would there be no sign at all of the plants? Wouldn't there would be something left of such massive growths?" Jinjur asked.

"Not if they were eaten," Cinnamon continued. "If the plants were hibernating, there are likely to be animals that wait until the waterfall to come out."

"Shirley, bring the *Dragonfly* in closer. If there are animals, I want to get some samples," Jinjur ordered.

Cinnamon was pleased. Nels might be kicking himself that he had again missed the boat, but at least this time he would have her to collect all the samples he might need. Shirley lowered the hovering aeroplane closer to the surface of the planet, fighting the air currents stirred up by the sudden addition of water to the surface of the normally arid and volcanic planet. Wherever there was a patch of ground covered with the fluffy plants, there were hundreds of little animals devouring the new growth as fast as it could grow. It was also clear that not all the animals were restricting their diet to plants.

"Look at that!" called Richard. He had been watching an odd star-shaped rock, when suddenly it reared up on three of its five points. Another similar star-shaped rock also rose, and the two animals crashed together with a rush. Several other versions of these star-shaped beasts welled up from the waters of a temporary lake and stomped up onto the swampy island. Any of the simpler animals that were too slow to avoid these stars were pounced upon and engulfed in the five-fold embrace. They must have been completely absorbed, because when the star-things moved on, there was no sign of the prey.

For the next several hours, the humans hovered over the single island watching the interaction playing itself out beneath them.

"Shouldn't we travel all around the planet and see if there are different things going on in different places?" Richard asked.

"Better to know one area well than to try to explore the whole planet," Cinnamon countered. Besides, if they left now she might never get any samples. "Can't we go down and pick up some of those life-forms before they eat each other all up?" she asked.

"You should get some idea of how they interact before you interfere. There is too good a chance that our presence will alter their behavior," Juno cautioned.

"Aren't you assuming that they are intelligent enough for us to disturb?" Shirley asked.

"After meeting the flouwen on this planet's twin, do you

think that intelligence is beyond possibility?" Jinjur pressed, "Do you want to risk blowing a first contact if there is intelligence down there?"

There was a long silence. Jinjur was annoyed that on this trip they had neither Nels, nor Reiki, the anthropologist. They had been so sure that this was a barren world that Jinjur had brought only pilots and geologists. She had planned on viewing the waterfall and showing the flouwen their rocky neighbor. This was supposed to be only a short jaunt, but the explosion of life changed everything. Fortunately Cinnamon was a biologist as well as a pilot. Jinjur looked over at the boyish biologist. Cinnamon was singing "Morning Has Broken" quietly to herself, as she watched entranced.

"The star-shaped animals are clearly the dominant species," Cinnamon said. "They eat almost everything in sight and are the terror of the beach. When they aren't actually eating, they are fighting or challenging each other over tiny changes in their boundaries. Similar to elephant seals, each of the stars has staked out its own section of beach."

"But these animals seem to have no harem to protect," Shirley objected. "So why is placement on the beach so important?"

"I think," said Cinnamon hesitantly, "the territory is important for the survival of the animal during the drought. The largest beasts have claimed rather similar areas. They are all toward the middle of the island and have their own depression. See? It's like the whole island has a series of shallow bowls. Any rain that does fall in the dry season is going to collect in those bowls. Even now, as the water is evaporating and disappearing into the ground, it is clear that these bowls will be the last places on the island holding water."

"What about the bottom of the lake?" asked Shirley. "Why wouldn't they want to have that ground? Soon enough it is going to be dry . . . "

"Well," Cinnamon offered, "I don't know what the bottom of the lake looks like but my guess is . . . "

"Of course! All that water would erode the hillside and leave the lake bottom smoothed out with the silt. The lake would only catch the water during the main flood," Richard answered. "And the high ground in the middle of the island . . . it seems to be flat stone. No one would want that!"

But even as he spoke, one of the larger star-things climbed up on to the center of the island. It raised up on three feet and bellowed, waving its two arms out to the crowded beach below it.

"What is it doing?" Jinjur asked. "Declaring itself king of the mountain?"

"It's not the largest," Cinnamon said, puzzled. She was already able to distinguish individuals. This bright red beast had won many of its fights, but it had obviously deferred to some of the others.

A large star close to the hilltop and reared up in challenge. For a moment the two moved in synchronism, then they locked in the same upright position, legs stretched to their utmost. Although the two stars were meters away from each other, they almost seemed to be comparing size. Then the larger beast dropped back down, and ignored the red animal completely. The red beast rolled back and forth on its spread legs like a cartwheel, circling the flat top of the mountain and roaring until another star reacted to its challenge. This time the challenger was almost the same size as the "King of the Mountain" and it moved uphill to join him.

"Look!" Jinjur called. "The others are letting it cross their territory unmolested."

Reiki's voice came down from *Prometheus*, where she had been watching through the video cameras on *Dragonfly*. "Yes, but it's not moving any of the boundary stones either. That's a sign that they are intelligent. They have a social structure."

"Anemones don't sting clownfish either. They aren't intelligent," Shirley insisted.

"Symbiosis is between two species. When you respect those of your own species, then it is politeness."

"That wasn't politeness!" Richard objected.

When the darker challenger tried to join the red star on the mountaintop, the red star attacked the newcomer brutally. They struggled, wrapping their thick arms about one another, grappling like sumo wrestlers, each trying to push the other onto its back. The darker challenger was soon clearly at a disadvantage; while it wasn't significantly smaller, it seemed to shy away from the "King's" touch, as if it were uncomfortable even coming in contact with it. After only a brief struggle, the challenger pulled itself free and hurried back to its place on the beach. Once they observed that the challenger had been defeated, several of its neighbors rushed to rearrange the boundary stones to their advantage, and now stood above the moved stones, daring the defeated one to move them back.

Reiki, observing the actions of the star creatures, commented, "Notice that when the challenger was defeated, it immediately lost standing in the community. These creatures must be intelligent to have such a complicated social structure."

"Nonsense," interrupted Richard. "A bunch of chickens use the same technique to establish a pecking order, and the one thing I can guarantee is that chickens are not intelligent."

Almost before the fight was over, a new star had raised up in challenge. This contestant was also dark but was not put off as easily as the first. The two stars clung together, rocking to and fro, rolling around in a circle on the edges of their entwined legs.

"Looks like an even match," said Jinjur critically. Years of training soldiers made her a good judge of such contests.

"Looks more like a lover's embrace than a fighting clinch," George offered. Even as he spoke, the top-most arms of the two stars began to twist and intertwine. The arms spiraled up like a unicorn's horn, becoming taller and thinner as they twisted more tightly together.

Then the tall twisted horn blunted and sank. The two stars were pulling back the color in their arms, and with the loss of color, the spiral also lost its stiffness. The colorless blob of flesh sank down between the two stars, leaving them cradling the blob between them. As with the forming of Pooh, the last act of the two adults was to use the now comically thin top arms to instruct the blob to divide in half. Then the stars backed away from each other, each holding a clear shapeless ball of flesh. Each adult tucked its ball in a pouch under the skin below the atrophied leg and walked back to its own territories on its four remaining feet.

Reiki, in the prim tone of voice they all knew was her way of saying "I told you so," said, "Notice that this time no one disturbed their markers while they were away. This colony of creatures definitely has a social structure."

Down below, the top of the hill did not stay vacant for long. Each time a star answered the challenge of another, they fought. If the fight was a draw, they mated; otherwise, the loser was forced back to what was left of its territory, in disgrace. Most matches were pretty close; a smaller star wouldn't risk fighting and a larger one didn't bother to try, but would wait until the top had been vacated. Some of the smaller ones tried more that once, but several defeats seemed to wear them down, and many gave up without ever mating. After several hours, all those that wanted to seemed to have found a mate, and now each had a young one tucked away in its pouch. The colony ignored the mating grounds after that.

"Well, what say we land up there on the hilltop?" Jinjur suggested. "They seem to be done with it, and at least we won't be sitting on anyone's home territory."

"That ground may be sacred," Reiki warned. "Be prepared to take off if there is a mass rush toward you when you land."

"Agreed. Shirley? Bring us down and hover over the rock in the center of the island, but don't land until we see their reaction to us."

Slowly, using its VTOL fans, the long silver *Dragonfly* first hovered, then settled gently on the high ground of the island. The humans kept a close eye on the colony, and, though they were obviously watching the landing, the stars stayed in their own territories.

"So much for sacred ground," said Jinjur under her breath. Reiki maintained a prim silence.

After several minutes, one of the largest of the stars stomped up to the hilltop again. This time, all the stars whose territory he invaded roared in challenge, but he didn't rear up to fight and the roars stopped as soon as he was beyond their markers again. Now awkward with the young they carried, the stars were less quarrelsome than they had been. When the star reached the ship, it circled the aeroplane slowly, and then settled down in front of the cockpit window.

"Is it looking back at us? Can it tell that there are separate beings inside the ship?" Richard asked.

"I don't think so . . . " Cinnamon said. "I think that it is simply summing us up. It could think that the *Dragonfly* is a living thing and that the scanner ports are its eyes. They do look somewhat like the five clear eyes they have at their leg intersections."

"Well, let's go introduce ourselves," decided Jinjur. "Shirley, you stay here and keep *Dragonfly* ready to lift off. Sam, you keep the science scan platforms operating, and David, I want you to keep the outside video cameras on us to record our meeting. You stay on board too, Pooh."

✪What!? I do not want to! I want to go meet the gummies!✪

"Gummies?"

✪They look just like gummy flouwen. Their flesh is thick and gummy, just like I make my flesh so I can get in my drysuit.✪

"Is it possible that they are related to the flouwen?" Jinjur asked Cinnamon as they fastened up their suits.

"Could be," she hazarded, also ignoring the stubborn little flouwen who was sulking in the hallway. "We'll have to see what they make of a drysuited flouwen . . . like Littles Red, White and Purple," she added, cutting short Pooh's volunteering.

Cinnamon, Jinjur, and Richard cycled through the airlock with the three adult flouwen, and the seven of them stepped out onto the planet surface together. The humans hung back and let the three flouwen roll forward toward the waiting star. This close, the size of the star-beasts was intimidating. This elder was almost twice the size of the suited flouwen. If it stood on its hind legs it would tower over the humans.

When the flouwen came within a body length of the "gummie," it reared up and roared out a multi-frequency challenge.

<Cower down before me, you insignificant vermin! I am Loudest Beast!!>

• CHAPTER ELEVEN—MEETING

Loudest Beast had approached the large, shiny Person with nothing more than curiosity. An elder had little to fear, other than the drought, and this silver creature didn't seem hungry. Certainly it hadn't eaten anything. But it was sitting on the mating hill even though it had already given up an arm. That didn't make any sense, and Loudest Beast was puzzled. Then, the pouch opened up on the silvery Person, but instead of releasing one youngling, several odd-shaped animals came out. This was most perplexing! Loudest Beast reacted to their upright stance the only way he knew how.

<Cower down before me, you insignificant vermin!> he cried out, identifying himself.

"Get back to the ship!" Shirley called out to the others from the cockpit. "I can get you off the ground the moment you are inside the airlock!"

"No!" Reiki voice came to them from *Prometheus*. "Don't let it intimidate you. It won't respect you if you run. Roar back at it and hold your ground."

"Nix that," Jinjur ordered. "Everyone in the airlock and hold on to the safety bars!"

But Little Red didn't hear her. Already he had extended his three pseudopods to the fullest and roared out an inarticulate challenge. The red flouwen looked small next to the gummie, but the animal didn't advance. Only a few yards separated them as they faced each other, neither of them moving. Obeying Jinjur, the humans climbed into the airlock, while Little Purple and Little White ignored her and rolled forward in their drysuits to back up their podmate.

Loudest Beast was bemused that the little silver deformed one with the reddish head had showed bravery. Even though it lacked two of its legs, the red one still had more gumption than Gigantic Grabber. Loudest Beast took a step forward and roared again. This time all three of the visitors moved forward together and roared in unison.

Loudest Beast was confused by the joint action. Three acting together to threaten a foe? Was that acceptable? How do you counter someone who can call on others to help? Still, these small ones had more wrong with them than their lack of legs. Although they talked, they made no sense and babbled like a captured Squeaky-Sneak. Loudest Beast felt his new pouchling stir within him. Touched by the overwhelming joy of parenthood, Loudest Beast felt a pang of pity for these deformed People. Perhaps that was why they helped each other. Loudest Beast rather liked the idea. Forgetting his challenge, he lowered himself down onto his four legs, the stubby fifth leg protectively held over the opening to his pouch, and waited.

☆What now?☆

"Try offering it something," suggested Reiki.

◊A gingersnap?◊

"The whole biology might be different," Richard objected. "You could poison it."

"They share a common ocean," George insisted. "I'm sure they must have encountered gingersnaps that were swept up in the tidal bore and tossed over in the interplanetary waterfall. If the food won't agree with it, it won't take it."

"I have a supply of dried gingersnaps in a pouch in case the flouwen get hungry on our exploration walks," said Cinnamon. She stepped down from the airlock and walked out to where the three flouwen were facing off the large gummie.

Little Red took one of the dried animals from Cinnamon and pulled it in half. Opening the zipper end near his helmet, he stuck it in and they all watched as it started to dissolve in the red flesh that made up his "head" in the helmet. He then placed the other half halfway between himself and the gummie.

Loudest Beast reached out, stretching his arm to the fullest so as not to have to come any closer to the united newcomers. Carefully, he tasted the flaky bit of dried flesh with the tip of his arm. The texture was odd but the taste was familiar. It was one of the manna foods that came from Everwet in the floodwaters. Feeling safer, Loudest Beast picked up the gift of food and shoved it into his feeding hole. Even as he ate, Loudest Beast was amazed. No Person would ever feed another Person. Once you were out of the pouch, you were on your own. Protecting the weak only led to new weak ones. Why would these three offer food? Was it a show of how strong they were, that they had food to spare? Well, this wasn't Loudest Beast's territory, so he could afford to be generous in return. Loudest Beast stomped sideways into a small Person's territory that bordered the hilltop. The owner tried to rear and challenge, but he had his child to protect and Loudest Beast was almost twice his size. He decided to ignore the elder's infringement on his territory.

Loudest Beast dug for a moment in the muddy soil. This youngling's site was poor, but this was the middle of the wet season and after a little bit of digging he unearthed a Sharp-Sneaky. Loudest Beast held the snarling, snapping creature up as high as he could and slammed it down onto the ground. Then he picked up the stilled body, and left it in the same spot that Little Red had left the dried manna. By this time most of the gummies had come to the edges of their territories closest to the hill and were watching as Loud Red approached the food.

☆Do I eat it?☆

◊I have never seen anything like that . . . ◊

❐You had better taste it first.❐

☆I notice none of you volunteering.☆ Little Red picked up the limp, gray, gummy, snakelike thing, opened the zipper near his neckring, and dipped the tail of the carrion into himself. After tasting for a moment, Little Red dropped in the whole thing.

☆Tasty!☆ hooted Little Red in surprise. ☆Watch out for the sharp parts, though!☆ A cascade of needle-sharp crystalline teeth shot out from the zipper opening and fell to the ground, where they tinkled against the stony hilltop. The watching gummies started with surprise at first, and then began to make a sound that was a haunting imitation of flouwen laughter.

"They laugh just like the flouwen! Could they share other language similarities?" Jinjur asked.

Little Red tried to extend a thin red tendril of flesh out of the suits zippered opening, but even in the low gee, he was not able to stretch it very far. Little Red then dipped one of his gloved fingers into the wetness within the suit and held the glistening tip out to the gummie. The gummie stretched out one arm in response, letting it grow thinner and thinner until the tip just touched the wetness. It absorbed the taste of information it found there. Reassured by what it tasted, it came closer to Little Red and reached its arm through the zipper opening and directly into the body of the red flouwen. For several moments, the two of them stood together, linked, both strangely silent during the exchange.

Finally, Little Red spoke. ☆Let him taste you two. I have to think.☆

"He's rocking up!" said Richard in surprise, as Little Red's body turned darker red and disappeared below the neckring, leaving the helmet filled with water.

The other two flouwen repeated Little Red's actions, and soon they too were rocked up, thinking. It only took a short while, however, before Little Red's drysuit started to wriggle and Little Red was back in the helmet, communicating once again over the laser link to the humans. Soon the other two flouwen were also back from their short intense period of thinking about what they had absorbed from the gummie. They reported what they had learned from their interaction with the gummie.

☆We exchanged memories. They are much like us.☆

◊But the flood time is so short, they have no time to think, just eat and make young ones.◊

❐Very sad. Alone, buried in the ground, from one passage near Hot to the next. No friends. No talking. No games. No fun . . . ❐

☆Not even surfing!☆

❐No stimulation. No learning. No studying. Very sad.❐

"Does that mean that you can understand them?" asked Richard, amazed.

☆Of course! We can now understand their talk and he can understand our talk.☆

"Exchanging memory juices must be something like chemical telepathy," said Cinnamon, herself amazed.

"Well, that solves the language problem," said Richard. "This gummie can now understand flouwen, and our chestpack computers already know how to convert human into flouwen."

☆Since we now understand the gummie language, we can translate what they say to you,☆ offered Little Red.

"That should suffice for now," interjected Juno through their imps. "After a number of conversations, I will have developed sufficient vocabulary to carry out the translations directly."

◊They really have very few words,◊ Little White said sadly.

"Most primitive people have limited vocabularies," Reiki explained. "It's not that they don't have the capacity, they simply haven't the need. Each member knows what it is expected to do and has known since before it became vocal. Words are used for stories and social contact, not for day-to-day actions. If these people are as isolated as you say . . . "

☆They do not even talk to their mates. The only ones they talk to are their younglings.☆

◊There has to be something we can do for them!◊ Little White was infuriated by the gummie's lack of opportunity. ◊I can taste that Loudest Beast is smart, but I know that he cannot understand even such a simple thing as our working together. He has never been exposed to cooperation before!◊

"Life must be tough here. Survival of the fittest means that it's every gummie for himself," Cinnamon explained.

◊But they need not have such a tough life! Can we take them back with us to Eau? Surely that is where they must have developed?◊

<Where is this "Eau"? Do you come from the land of Everwet?>

❑Tell us of this land of "Everwet,"❑ Little Purple asked. While the elder flouwen carried on the conversation with the gummie, Little Red took his translation promise seriously, and he brought both sides of the conversation to the humans.

☆<Long ago, the first gummies swam in the waters of Everwet. There were streams of nourishing warm water bubbling up from cracks in the earth and there was soft ground to dig in and take root. Water was always on each gummie's territory, and elders could swim with the yearlings even as they taught them all the taboos of the colony. But the younglings would not listen to the elders. They wanted to travel further in the waters and never take root in the ground. They did not come and rest on the land when the elders called to them, but went swimming and playing in the bouncing of the water's surface.>☆

☆I think he means waves,☆ Little Red added, ☆but he has forgotten what they are. The sense I get is of small ripples formed by splashing.☆

He continued translating the story. ☆<The younglings would not let the water rest. The younglings pestered the water and would not sleep on the land. The water got mad, and rose up against the younglings. It carried the younglings to a land far from their elders and left them there. That was the beginning of the People. Now the People have to wait for the water to return. It comes back and visits us and sees if we have become good. It is said that if we are

strong and survive, if we have learned the lessons from our parents and have learned to live with both the land and the water, we may go to Everwet and live by the shore of a never-dry lake and never need to be hungry again.>☆

"Sounds like the sort of story a parent might tell a youngster in order to make it behave," Jinjur said doubtfully.

"But the flouwen have chemical racial memories. They can remember all the way back to then they first started adding!" Cinnamon insisted. "They don't have any fables about creation or heaven. This could well be based on a memory and distorted as it was verbalized between generations."

❒If these gummies are the descendants of flouwen then it is up to us to rescue them from this life of hunger and hardship. We should take them back with us to Eau.❒

<Can you take me and my youngling to Everwet? This time we will behave! Please, please, we will be good!> Loudest Beast lowered itself in submission, heedless of its reputation with the rest of the colony.

The People's side of the conversation could be heard by all, and a ripple of interest spread over the island as the conversation between Loudest Beast and the strangers was passed on from territory to territory. People that had not talked to anyone except for their young in generations were taking an interest in something other than food. Except for a few of the craftier individuals, who were quietly shifting boundary stones during the commotion, all in the colony had their attentions fixed on Loudest Beast and the conversation on the hill.

It was a complete surprise to all when the huge, swollen adolescent reared itself out of the waters of the lake. No Person on the shore was anywhere near as large as this monster; and monster it was. Even as it beached itself, it killed and consumed one of the yearlings, only hours out of its parent's pouch.

<Mine, Mine, Mine!> The huge murderous gummie roared. <I will never, never, never be hungry again!>

For a few moments, the gigantic monster lay on the beach in Loudest Beast's unguarded territory. It muttered and whined incoherently as it finished absorbing the yearling it had killed.

"My God! What is that thing?" Jinjur asked.

❐It appears to be a cancerous gummie. Occasionally a flouwen goes insane and starts to grow uncontrollably, although usually only in response to extreme stress.❐

◊The cancerous person loses his sense of community. He forgets that the others in the pod are his family, and treats them like prey.◊

☆This monster will eat everything in sight unless it is stopped,☆ said Little Red. He began to advance toward the insane gummie.

<What are you doing?> Loudest Beast asked the flouwen, puzzled.

☆I am going to kill that mistake in addition!☆ bellowed Little Red, exasperated.

<How can you kill it? It is so much bigger than you.> The gummie was clearly at a loss. <Such monsters cannot be stopped! Nothing can be done! You just have to hope that they will not attack you, or that you might run away from them. The only thing that kills them is the drought. They always die when things dry up.>

☆You mean you just let it go until it dries!? Why don't you kill it? If the whole colony fought together, they could easily overwhelm it!☆

<Fight together? Overwhelm it?>

❐Surely you are not thinking that it is still a Person, that it still has a soul?❐ Little Purple didn't understand the gummie's hesitance either. He struggled to understand why the elder was not running to kill this obvious threat. ❐Was it part of the colony? Is that the problem?❐

<It was once my child, Gigantic Grabber, but now my child is gone. I just do not know how you plan to kill . . . >

The humans had only heard the flouwen side of the conversation, but they had been following along as best they could. "Wait! Don't you see?" said Jinjur. "He doesn't understand the concept of uniting with the others to conquer the cancer-gummie. The gummies don't practice cooperation. After all, those that survive the cancer attack will only have less competition next year."

❐But they cannot just let that . . . thing kill the others!❐

◊How can we interfere? We cannot kill the thing ourselves, we do not have the mass.◊

"Besides, you are in your suits," Jinjur reminded them. "If you were in the water you might have a chance, but out here . . . Well, at least in your suits, you won't be hurt if it should try to attack us."

Almost as if the monster had understood her, the huge beast reared up and charged up the hill. All the gummies that had been so bravely defending their territories before, now ran in terror before the raging giant. In its confusion, the mutated gummie had lost control of its body. New arms budded off Gigantic Grabber's swollen belly, and water poured out of its pouch, but in some part of its warped mind, it still remembered.

Gigantic Grabber moved up the mating hill. This was the year. This year Gigantic Grabber would be able to mate here in the colony of its parent. It would give up an arm . . . it seemed to have plenty of them, and it would put out roots . . .

The cancer-gummie had reached the top of the hill. It towered over the explorers; its long roots, sprouting like Medusan hair, thrashed around it wildly. The humans, trusting their nearly impervious glassy-foil suits, but knowing the power of the gummie, had retreated into the airlock on the *Dragonfly* and secured themselves to the safety bars inside. The flouwen were more secure with the extra protection of their fluid makeup, and the Littles lingered outside. But between the monster and the others, trapped between the cancer and the aeroplane, was Loudest Beast.

With what was left of its mind, Gigantic Grabber recognized the Person who stood on the mating hill to meet it. At the sight of its loving parent, Gigantic Grabber's need to eat, and its confused desire to mate, vanished. All it wanted was to be back in the warmth and love and safety of its parent's pouch. It stretched out all its long arms and entangled Loudest Beast in its grasp. Gigantic Grabber's tendrils felt the new youngling, hardly formed, buried deeply in the pouch that had once held him. Almost tenderly, Gigantic Grabber forced open the pouch and took out the mewling child. He ate it casually.

<No, no, no!> screamed Loudest Beast as the child was torn from its body. Fury wiped out fear, and spreading itself as thinly as possible, Loudest Beast began to fight back. With frantic energy, it ripped off thin roots and half-formed legs, throwing them away, only to attack again. Loudest Beast drew energy from despair and only wondered why Gigantic Grabber hadn't engulfed him completely.

☆Attack!☆ yelled Little Red as he entered the fray. Surrounded with the glassy-foil suit, the flouwen couldn't absorb and digest this enemy as he would normally have done. He could only use his pseudopods to rip and tear at the misshapen gummie as Loudest Beast was doing. The vicious scavengers, which had been hiding all around the colony, hovered at the fringes of the battleground, collecting the bits and pieces that had been torn from the enemy.

❒Right!❒ said Little Purple, and he rolled into battle.

◊Can't I take you people anywhere without you getting into trouble?◊ sighed Little White, but he too, tried to rescue their new friend.

Still, they were greatly outmatched. Gigantic Grabber could not assimilate the flouwen in their suits, but neither could they do too much damage to it. The handfuls of flesh that they could rip out with their weak pseudopods were like drops in the bucket. The monster picked up Loudest Beast and lifted him high above them. Little Red, fearing that Gigantic Grabber was about to slam Loudest Beast on the ground, decided that it was time to do something drastic. Opening the zipper of his suit, Little Red guided one of

Gigantic Grabber's many legs into the hole and started digesting it.

Gigantic Grabber trying to crawl back into Loudest Beast's pouch. Its parent was complaining loudly and was very thin, so Gigantic Grabber held Loudest Beast up, hoping to slide into the pouch underneath. When the shocking, burning, pain in its arm finally reached its insane brain, Gigantic Grabber's first reaction was to show its parent the source of its pain. Whimpering pitifully, Gigantic Grabber used two spare legs to lift up the hot silvery bulb that was still ingesting its leg. As Gigantic Grabber held Little Red high, it squeezed.

"NO!" shouted all the humans together, but it was too late. The zipper gave way and Little Red squirted out the opening in his drysuit and sprayed all over the cancerous gummie and its prey.

The fluid Roaring☆Hot☆Vermilion was no longer constrained by the suit or by the desire of self-preservation. All the tiny cells that made up Roaring☆Hot☆Vermilion knew that they now had no chance of returning to swim in the oceans of their home. But they could still do what they had set out to do. The cells of Roaring☆Hot☆Vermilion would fight this last fight with all of their being.

Pain lanced through Gigantic Grabber. All over its body, the burning, twisting, pain of another person trying to digest it shocked Gigantic Grabber into fighting back. Dropping Loudest Beast, Gigantic Grabber rolled back and forth on the ground in agony, desperately trying to encircle this fluid being that was trying to gain control of his cells. Wherever they touched him, Roaring☆Hot☆Vermilion's single-minded cellular units dissolved and converted the cells in Gigantic Grabber's confused flesh.

Cinnamon, desperate to save as much of Little Red as she could, unhooked herself from the rung inside the air lock and dashed back out onto the planet surface. She darted from puddle to puddle, collecting as much of the spilled liquid alien as she could while trying to avoid the huge misshapen star that thrashed around on the hill top.

☆Lemme at 'em!☆ squawked the grimy red blob in her sample bottle.

"Look out!" yelled Richard but it was too late. Gigantic Grabber, half-blinded with the screaming painful coating of Little Red, had rolled across the ground and landed on top of Cinnamon, pinning her beneath his swollen translucent body. Pausing only to change the head of his geologic collector into an axe, the muscular geologist waded into the fray, attacking the monster like a silver-armored Perseus. The axe bit into the gummie's soft flesh, severing the threadlike roots. Again and again he struck, hacking away at the base of the thick arm that had the biologist trapped, but the jellied flesh of the alien tried to seal itself after each blow, and the flailing roots stuck to Richard's glassy-foil suit, restricting his swing. The insane gummie was so occupied in this struggle that it didn't even notice that the other two flouwen had stopped their harassment. They had collected Loudest Beast and dragged the wounded elder away to safety.

"Oof! Hurry up!" called Cinnamon from beneath the gummies arm. "He's heavy!"

Jinjur could just make out the shining silver suit beneath the translucent flesh of the monster. She was impressed with the amount of damage that Richard was able to do with his axe, but the alien wasn't thinking clearly enough to even move away from the attacking human. They'd never get it to back off of Cinnamon! They'd have to find some way of destroying it utterly, and the damn thing just didn't have any vital organs! Jinjur thought hard as she looked around the airlock for another weapon. "What I need is a farging flame-thrower!" she muttered savagely.

"And I've got one!" answered Shirley through the ship's intercom.

"So you do!" Jinjur cheered. "Go for it!" She jumped out of the airlock and ran toward the battle as Shirley revved up the engines of the *Magic Dragonfly*.

"Cinnamon!" Jinjur called as she pulled Richard away from the center of the fight. "Switch your suit over to maximum cooling!"

Through the hazy view from beneath the alien, Cinnamon watched the two silver-suited figures retreat as she tongued the controls on the inside of her helmet. The giant alien on top of her heaved itself around, burying her even more deeply into its dark body. The pressure and the numbing cold of the suit added to the building fear, and her whole body knotted in tension. Cinnamon was a pilot and she knew the ship's possibilities, but would Shirley be able to pull off a virtual tailstand? The imp earphones were separated from the rest of the computer for the first time in sixty years, and as Cinnamon tried to hum, the sparkling headpiece was quiet.

"When a true love dies, smoke gets in your eyes."

Shirley let the hover blades lift the *Dragonfly* up to roughly half the length of the ship as the suited flouwen and humans pulled the wounded Loudest Beast further back from the hilltop. She would have to time this perfectly. Too short a blast of the flaming exhaust would only enrage the monster, and too much would cook the biologist beneath it . . . and on every side was the rest of the gummie colony.

Shirley tensed, telling herself that this time human life had to take precedence. Then she shut down the right and rear VTOL fans, letting the back of the plane drop slowly in the low gee. The left VTOL pushed the *Dragonfly* around on its vertical axis as Shirley fired off the monopropellent jet, lifting the ship into an upward spiral, bathing the hilltop with a short burst of super-heated air. She fought the powerful lift and leveled out, and then allowed herself a look at the planet below.

Richard and Jinjur were helping Cinnamon to her feet; all around the gummie colony, the island was being showered with small cooked pieces of Gigantic Grabber, some bits still colored with a thin coating of red.

* * *

"Damn!" said Nels as he started to topple to one side after tripping over the drysuited SweetOGreenOFizz. The green flouwen was spread out on the floor of the engineering deck of the *Falcon*, busily operating the console that controlled the scanning tunneling array microscope and manipulator, using it to assign mathematical values to the genetic patterns impressed on a flouwen unit cell he was mapping. SweetOGreenOFizz had moved the touchscreen to the floor where he could more easily manipulate it with his suit's boneless pseudopods.

The *Falcon's* lab was not designed to accommodate Nels's particularities, and Nels needed to wear prosthetics in order to reach some of the analysis machines in the workwall. Having lived all his life in zero-gee, Nels was more used to the powered legs in his specially designed spacesuit than he was to the thin metal legs he needed within the *Falcon*. Still, they were in only one-tenth gee and Nels was able to catch himself before he fell.

OI have made a simple model of the genetic code of the flouwen.O The flouwen's "fingers" called up the design on the screen, and together they looked it over.

OAs you can see, the flouwen all pretty much share the same patterns on this half of the unit cell. These patterns are the genetic code that determines the physical makeup of a typical flouwen body. This other half seems to be different in each of the flouwen and varies with time. The variable part of the patterns acts as the long-term memory, while the more stable patterns encode for the enzymes that produce the tiny chemical differences that seem to be the reason for all the different personalities of the flouwen.O

"So you think the flouwen personality is purely chemical?" Nels asked.

OWell, all the samples I have analyzed came from our pod and all of us have very similar experiences. We literally share each other's experiences through the chemical tastes we give each other, yet we are all very distinct individuals and have been since our formation.○

"Hmm," Nels muttered. "What happens each time you share tastes of each other?"

○It seems that for a few moments the taste causes a ripple of chemical imbalance that runs throughout the whole body of the receiving flouwen, but the change is only momentary. Unlike when eating, where the larger body changes the smaller into replicas of its own cells, the taste just passes its information to the variable portion of the receiver cells. The variable section of the patterns changes slightly, indicating that the information has been stored in the long-term memory. Then the body assimilates the taste just like food.○

"Similarities?"

He was answered by Little Curiosity, who was operating another touchscreen at the computer console. ♣You mean chemical similarities between similar flouwen? I am having the computer sort out the variables using color as a constant. Only none of the flouwen are exactly the same color, really. The closest color matches in the pod are myself and Sweet○Green○Fizz, and Dainty∆Blue∆Warbler and Sour#Sapphire#Coo.♣ Flouwen had often wondered at the similarity in temperament between those of similar color. Now Shining♣Chartreuse♣Query would see if this basis for old jokes had any basis in facts.

"How long, Jupiter?" Nels called to the computer through his imp.

"The computation will take several minutes . . . unless this is a priority task?"

"No," said Nels shortly. He knew that the computer was also busy running the ship and operating the communication links between the *Falcon*, *Dragonfly*, and *Prometheus*. The discovery of life on Roche, only to be so quickly followed with the death of Little Red, had sobered the away team. So many of the assumptions they had made back when they first planned this mission had been knocked for a loop, and all of them were hurting with their fallibility. A simple experiment in genetics just didn't seem too important.

Little Fizzer noticed the human's defeated tone and attitude. Although flouwen rarely suffered anything approaching depression, Little Fizzer did his best to cheer the geneticist up. ○I did try applying my theory of genetics to the human DNA and I think there are several things you haven't labeled. Is it because they are common knowledge?○

"What?" It was a sign of Nels's fatigue that he did not pounce on this news.

Little Fizzer changed the display to one that showed a section of human DNA coded in its four molecules, and highlighted one segment of the screen. ○There is this portion here, which controls human coloring. This section clearly indicates how tall the human will grow, although weight seem to be completely variable.○

Amazed, Nels looked at the screen with renewed interest. "Are you sure?"

Shining♣Chartreuse♣Query answered. ♣Well, we had a lot of trouble with that last part . . . but Jupiter showed us how to adjust for the differing gravities under which some of you humans grew up. Then, for your case, Jupiter told us to ignore your actual height. Did we make a mistake?♣

"I don't know . . . I hadn't gotten that specific!" Nels was startled at the ease with which these flouwen applied their superior intellect to everything. They were ruthless in insisting that no theory violated the laws of mathematical logic, and in every instance they were proved right. "Yes, you'd have to keep my height out of the equation . . . "

♣Why is that anyway? All the other humans have warm thick legs and you have only thin metal ones. If you need to be tall to operate the equipment, why don't you just grow legs like the others?♣

"I though you understood that we humans can't change our shapes the way you flouwen can."

OWe know that! But your DNA indicates that you should be quite a tall man. If you want flesh legs why don't you cut your short ones off and grow new long ones?O

"Humans have often experimented with tissue regeneration, but it has never worked successfully. If it is tried after a recent accident on a very young person, sometimes there is a little regrowth, but often the cells become confused. Usually all they manage is a useless mass that lacks all feeling and has to be shaped surgically. Cloning and grafting we have mastered, but regeneration is still the stuff of fiction."

Little Fizzer turned back to the screen. OJupiter? Leave the other computations for a moment and help me with this. Priority.O

"Confirm?" the computer asked Nels.

"Confirm." Nels was curious to see what the flouwen thought it had discovered.

On the screen Little Fizzer called up a string of As, Gs, Cs, and Ts, some of which were in opposing color. Nels knew the pattern well. He had looked at it over and over, on and off, his whole life. It was the double helix that had ordered his hair to be blond and his eyes to be blue, but the chemical imbalances in his mother's womb had blocked the string of code that would have given him legs and feet instead of flippers.

For several minutes the flouwen and computer worked on the pattern, the colors and symbols changing at the touch of a pseudopod. Finally the flouwen stopped and pointed at the screen. OIf we reset this section and suppress that section, then the walking appendages will grow as they were supposed to.O

Nels was astounded. The second of the segments that they had highlighted was in the middle of what was called "junk" DNA. Everyone knew that this section of genetic code had nothing to do with the forming of the body . . . but the flouwen was so sure.

"Jupiter! Is there any validity to this?"

"It seems logical. The first strand we have long suspected as being the timekeeper that judges the whole body's age and regulates growth timing accordingly. The other could well be the DNA that produced your flippers. It must have been activated when your mother was exposed to chemicals, and it dominated your normal leg DNA. If the cells in your stumps could be tricked into believing that you were still a young embryo in a normal womb, and the flipper DNA could be turned off, it is possible that new legs would develop in the proper fashion."

"No," said Nels thinking out loud. "It would mean staying in an artificial womb for nine months. And then if it did work, I'd have to relearn how to walk, and build up the muscle just like a newborn. It could be years before they would even stop growing."

"It should be easy to speed up the growth so the whole process only took a few months," Jupiter offered.

"But if it didn't work, I would have no feet at all . . . "

Nels left the lab, leaving the flouwen alone with their experiments.

• CHAPTER TWELVE—SAVING

Inside the *Dragonfly*, the crew were all crowded in the bridge area just behind the pilot's seats. Outside, the nightlife on Roche was just as hectic as during the day. Like the flouwen, the gummies had no need of sleep in the human sense, and with the rapid drying of the lake, the planet's inhabitants were fighting among themselves for the last of the food. The *Dragonfly* hovered on its VTOL fans over the gummie colony so that the plane would not be damaged accidentally by the large gummies' last battles for territory. But the humans were all exhausted from the short day's excitement. Stunned by the loss of Little Red, they tried to comfort themselves.

"Why did he attack that thing?" Jinjur demanded. Her anger was a reaction to the loss of someone she felt responsible for. "Red should have stayed back by the ship, or at least should have kept his suit closed."

❒It was always Roaring☆Hot☆Vermilion's way. Always rushing ahead and giving his all without thinking of the cost to himself.❒

◊All we can do is bring this last taste of him back to himself,◊ Little White said sadly. They all looked at the small vial with its pathetic puddle of red. Little White wanted very much to taste these last remnants of Little Red to see if he had known of his danger and if any messages remained in the sample, but the remaining flouwen had decided this was a task better handled by the rest of Roaring☆Hot☆Vermilion back on Eau.

Pooh had been humming the "Funeral March" quietly to himself, and it was really starting to get on Jinjur's nerves.

"But why did he interfere at all? I know that Loudest Beast was being attacked but Loud Red had just met him. Why did he interfere in what was clearly not his fight?" Shirley asked.

❒We would not leave Loudest Beast to fight such a battle alone. We had tasted his life and he is not an animal. Loudest Beast is a person and we have shared tastes.❒ Little Purple was sounding at his most pompous, but no one felt like belittling him. That had been Little Red's job and, for a moment, the void left by his destruction was all the more poignant.

There was a long pause. "God! I am beat," said Richard.

"Me too," Cinnamon admitted ruefully, and she rubbed the back of her neck. She shifted uncomfortably the pilot's chair.

◊Why don't you humans all get some of your sleep. Little Purple and I can take this shift,◊ Little White offered.

"That is a good suggestion," Juno conceded. "All of you are showing signs of fatigue and stress. I can keep the *Dragonfly* hovering in position just as well as a human pilot. If I notice anything strange, the flouwen can help me to decide what to do about it. We will certainly wake you if there is an emergency."

"Didn't we just decide that the flouwen are not too good at handling emergencies?" Jinjur asked sarcastically. She wasn't ready to turn their fate over to a couple of reactionary amoebas.

"Little Red was the only quick-tempered one . . . " the computer started.

◊And look where it got him. Believe me when I say we won't forget that lesson. All we are offering is to stand the watch. At this point, all we can do is watch the gummie colony and record what is going on. Should anything at all happen, we will call you.◊

"Okay, okay," Jinjur conceded. "We'll give it a try. But Cinnamon, I want you to be sleeping right here on the bridge, just in case. The pilot's chair is comfortable enough.

And I want be called instantly—instantly!—if there is even a suspicion of anything different happening out there."

"Aye, aye, sir," said Cinnamon giving a smart salute above her right eye.

◊□Aye, aye, sir!◊□ the flouwen echoed, imitating Cinnamon by giving the general smart salutes, gloved "hands" touching just above the looking lenses in the helmets of their suits.

Jinjur's hostility and guilt disappeared with this display of respect and attention. She giggled at the sight of the saluting flouwen and led the other humans off the bridge to the sleeping quarters at the rear of the aeroplane, her laughter ringing down the corridor ahead of them.

Cinnamon woke to find herself no longer in the pilot's seat. Instead she was cradled in Pooh's arms in the corridor leading to the flight deck. For a moment, sleep clouded her mind but then she snapped to awareness.

"What's happened? Have you called Jinjur?"

✪Nothing is wrong. Hush! I am supposed to be keeping you comfortable, and if Clear◊White◊Whistle knows I let you wake up, he will be loud at me.✪

"What is going on?" Cinnamon whispered.

✪Clear◊White◊Whistle wants to learn more about flying the aerospace plane and you were in the way. He and Strong□Lavender□Crackle are taking turns. One watches out the window for any sign of danger and the other gets to play with the controls while Juno operates the simulator program.✪

"But why do they bother?"

✪Someday, other humans will come. The tastes of all we learn will be passed on to all of the flouwen, and wherever the humans land on Eau, they will be greeted by flouwen who can recognize them. The next time we meet you humans we do not want to be treated like younglings.✪

"We don't treat you like younglings! We think you are the most amazing people we have ever met. It's just that you don't do things the way we humans do, and we are too used to being in charge."

Little White heard them talking and joined the discussion. ◊We will never be able to make these wonderful metal devices that you humans use. Even if we could come up with designs that would work even better, we simply are not able to manipulate matter in order to fabricate things. Is it any wonder that we envy you, and want to learn how to operate every bit of equipment you have? Maybe, someday, we will have such wonders of our own, but whatever technology our species will ever use, it will have to be made by you humans.◊

Silently, the flouwen continued to guard and study the marvels of the elegant *Dragonfly*. Rocking back and forth on the rounded bottom of his drysuit, Pooh started singing a lullaby. Cinnamon soon fell asleep with a deep-seated feeling of security.

When Jinjur woke, her internal clock was sounding alarms. "Juno?" she called. "What time is it?"

"Barnard will rise on this section of the planet in twenty minutes."

"But . . . I feel as if I have rested for more than three hours."

"Correct. You have slept for eight point seven hours."

"What!" Jinjur rolled off her bunk and began pulling on her jumpsuit.

"Since you have been on the planet, you have all tried to conform to the local six-hour day. The human body prefers to function on a twenty-four hour schedule. All of the crew have been suffering from fatigue. I reported to *Prometheus* that everything here was under control, and George decided you needed the sleep."

"Juno . . ." Jinjur started dangerously.

"I have recorded everything, and not only the flouwen but the crew on the *Prometheus* have monitored everything. Shall I tell George that you are awake now?"

"I'll tell him, thank you," Jinjur said as she strode toward the bridge. When she reached the flight deck, Cinnamon was awake in the pilot's chair, but her face was lined with creases from sleep. Jinjur went back to the communications console and opened up a link to *Prometheus*. Cinnamon noticed that the Christmas Branch came down the aisle and stood between Jinjur and Cinnamon, the cilia on its body generating sound waves that exactly canceled the sound waves coming from Jinjur's mouth as she conversed with George. Through the twinkling branches of the Christmas Bush, Cinnamon could see Jinjur's grim jaw working overtime. George would think twice before he adjusted the general's orders again, even if it was for her own good. Jinjur finally came forward and asked Cinnamon to set the *Dragonfly* down on the top of the mating hill as they had done before.

The storms had ceased, and Cinnamon landed the plane easily. Since it was her shift, she would stay in the plane this time to act as pilot, while the rest of the crew suited up to go outside. Cinnamon didn't mind. While the Littles had been fighting the monster gummie, Cinnamon had taken samples of the dozens of predators and scavengers that had fed on the fight. The plants would be best collected in seed form anyway, and Cinnamon trusted Sam and Richard to pick up plenty of samples with the rocks they were sure to bring back.

◊We have been busy all night too,◊ said Little White as he joined Cinnamon and Jinjur on the flight deck. Little Purple was right behind. ◊We have been working with Juno, and we now know we will be able to fly the *Dragonfly* without human help. You will be leaving the aeroplane and the drysuits on Eau when you leave, so we have made plans to fly the *Dragonfly* over to Roche and bring the gummies over to Eau.◊

"What!" Fresh from her battle with George, Jinjur rose to the challenge she heard in the flouwen's voice. "There is no way we are going to let you . . ."

Nels's voice came in from the *Falcon* back on Eau. He had been going to check in with Cinnamon to ask about her samples, when he caught the end of Little White's announcement. He was outraged enough to interrupt the general. "We can not introduce the gummies into the Eau ecosystem!"

◊We will isolate them. We will bring them to the island in the center of the lake that Roaring☆Hot☆Vermilion was trapped in. If the gummies stay on the island . . . ◊

"But they can walk!" objected Nels. "How are we going to ensure that they stay only in the lake?"

"That is beside the point!" Jinjur was furious. "We aren't going to allow . . . "

This time it was George who interrupted her. "Not only are you talking about changing the ecosystem of the island on Eau, you are going to change the whole development of the gummies. We can use the mathematics of the flouwen without endangering the creativity of the human race, but we mustn't change the culture, such as it is, of the flouwen and the gummies. They have to develop in their natural state so that they can reach their full potential."

❒How can the gummies reach their full potential when they are forced to spend their time in hibernation during the time when there is nothing to eat?❒

"They have developed into a race that can deal with such periods of drought!" Nels objected. "Given enough time, they will develop further on their own!"

"They have to develop on their own in order to find their own destiny," George concurred.

"And if it's their destiny to become extinct?" Cinnamon objected.

"Then something else will fill their niche in the ecosystem!" Nels said. "I can't believe you would even suggest that we interfere! Look at all the times humans have, in their arrogance, decided what was best for a species, only to have it backfire."

"Exactly!" George agreed. "We must not interfere."

◊You have all ready interfered. You have come to Eau and shown the flouwen all the possibilities of technology. We cannot just go back to riding the waves and thinking about esoteric logic problems. You have shown us all the different uses our mathematics can be put to, and you cannot just . . . ◊

"Oh, can't we?" Jinjur exploded. "Just watch. We can scuttle this plane any time we want. We won't put up with any more of this nonsense of you taking the gummies anywhere!"

"Humans only," George called, and the computer stopped translating their conversation to the flouwen. "Look here, Jinjur. We want to keep the flouwen on our side. We don't want to lose their mathematical insight."

"Whose side are you on? We can't let them try and bring the whole gummie colony over to Eau . . . and who knows how many other colonies there are?"

"But we have to convince them, not force them. Nels has some very valid reasons why they need to keep both planets balanced. If we humans are interfering, then let's at least interfere with good advice. Let the gummies and flouwen benefit from human experience."

"But will they take that advice the way we want them to?" asked Jinjur. She had regained her temper, but she still had doubts. "The flouwen look at our accomplishments and they are impressed. Sure we almost ruined our own planet, but it got us to the stars. They may want to emulate even our mistakes."

"I don't see them emulating us . . . " said George.

"Wait a moment," Cinnamon interrupted. "I think you have forgotten to look at this from the flouwen point of view. How would we humans have reacted if a bunch of aliens came down and showed us all kinds of new concepts, and gave us huge advances in knowledge . . . but then told us we couldn't use any of it the way we wanted? After all, Rocheworld is . . . "

"Roche-wwoorld iss ourss," whistled a strange voice from the water.

Stunned, the humans looked around. "Juno?" Jinjur asked quietly, although she all ready knew the answer.

"I am not translating," the computer confirmed.

"We talk to pod at Agua Dul-ce. All say we help gum-mies."

"The flouwen have been using the console at Agua Dulce for many hours, talking to all the members in their pod," the computer said. "They used the chemical mode of transmitting information back and forth to each other, and I have not yet been able to decode it. I recorded it for later decoding when the flouwen decide to tell me what it was they discussed. With that information it should not take too long to figure out their chemical language," Juno finished complacently.

"That's not important now," said Jinjur, exasperated. "We have to . . ." The flouwen's ability to understand what she was saying about them made her pause.

"There is nothing we can do," said George. "The flouwen are right. They didn't invite us here. Maybe if we had known they were here, we would have decided not to come down and disturb them, but I doubt it. Humans are too curious. But the fact is, we have disrupted their lives, and we are not the best judges as to where they should go from here. Even after our interference, it is up to the flouwen to determine the fate of the flouwen."

"But we can't let them ruin their world just because it's more theirs than ours," Nels objected. "After all, it is also the planet of the flitters and the gingersnaps and all the plants and animals that live there."

"But we can't act like a parent that gives a child a gun and then tells it not to shoot at anything." Jinjur realized that a partial victory was better than complete defeat, and had come around to the flouwen's side. "What we have to do is act like a responsible parent and show the damage that can be done if the child is not careful. We have to guide the flouwen so they don't do too much damage."

The whistling voice again rose from the water. "Flouwen

not child. Know Eau too small for gummies. Teach gummies to change Roche."

Another voice came from the water, this one had a harsh, brittle tone. "Yes. Teach gummies save water. Make lake all time."

"We could do that!" cried Cinnamon. "If instead of the gummies just maintaining their own territories, we could teach them to dam up the exit channels from the lake and make collector channels for the rain. The lake would stay full of water all year and they could share . . . Jinjur! Can the computer go back to translating? I want to be sure the Littles get all of this."

"Yes, of course." What had ever made her think Cinnamon was shy?

"The gummies can dig channels so that the water that would normally just run out onto the plains and sink into the sands would all be directed to the lake. They could also make dams that would block the outflow channels from the lake and keep the water impounded for longer. It would take years before the lake would keep water for the whole year so the colony would be able to stay awake the whole season."

◊But it is the gummies that need to learn these things, and they cannot learn them here in the dust. We will need to bring some of them back to Eau, long enough for them to learn these things in a place with water. If we take a few gummies to Red's Lake, they can learn these things. We can then bring them back to Roche after the next flood time to teach the others.◊

"Like a gummie college!" said Cinnamon.

"I don't like any of this . . . " said Nels. "Will you at least follow a few rules?"

❒We are open to suggestions.❒

"First, be choosy about the gummies you bring over. And just bring over gummies. No wild plants or animals that could get loose and damage the Eau ecosystem. Since they can eat flouwen food, then they don't need to bring anything else with them, and it will limit the damage they do to Eau."

◊How do we choose gummies?◊

"Ask Loudest Beast," suggested Nels.

The scene of yesterday's fight was barren now, as the humans walked again on the surface. The whole landscape before them had changed. The temporary lake had drained away into the surrounding plains where it had soaked into the sands, and the bottom of the lake was hardly more than a dark damp patch of mud. On the high shores, the gummies were all preparing for their long rest in the earth. The suited explorers easily found Loudest Beast. The gummie was the only one not already half-buried in the drying mud.

"Why aren't you dug in with the others?" Jinjur asked.

<I was hoping that by waiting I might be able to get back some of the territory I lost.>

It was true that Loudest Beast had lost much of the depression it had claimed before. Saddened by the loss of the pouchling, and weakened in the fight, Loudest Beast had not had the strength to defend all the land it had staked out before. The body of Gigantic Grabber had fed most of the colony, but Loudest Beast's neighbors were ruthless. When Loudest Beast had limped back in the dark, most of the boundary stones of his territory had been shifted inward. It just didn't seem worth the effort to fight, now that there was no child to feed, and teach, and talk to throughout the long hibernation.

❐You will not need to worry about territory. We have come to take you back with us to Everwet.❐

<Can you really take me?> Loudest Beast seemed to have lost all confidence. <I only wish I could have brought my pouchling to keep me company.>

◊We want to bring some others too . . . ◊ Little White insisted, hoping to get the gummie interested in life again. He remembered the taste of the lonely life of a gummie that Loudest Beast had shared with the three flouwen.

Clear◊White◊Whistler couldn't imagine having to be all alone. ◊Are their any of the other People who might want to go to Everwet?◊

The gummie thought. <Well, I could ask Screaming Killer. Screaming Killer was a youngling of mine and was always asking questions. I think he would like to live where one could spend more time thinking about other things than mere survival.>

◊Good! He sounds like an ideal person. Where is Screaming Killer?◊

<He should be rooting on the other side of the lake.>

"You mean the puddle," Richard snorted, once Little White translated. Richard took several samples of the liquid mud. He swirled the mud around in one of the transparent sample bottles and looked carefully at it.

"Pretty clean, for mud," he said. "I don't expect I'll find much organic material left, except an occasional seed. Looks like the animal scavengers have eaten every last leaf, twig, and root of the plant life that had recently flourished here."

The party made its way across the sticky pool and up the slope on the other side. Dotting the ground were the shallow bowls that the humans now recognized as gummie territories. Many of the gummies were almost completely buried. They worked their way down into the softened ground, spreading out a network of tiny roots that would feed the gummie during the worst of the drought.

The gummies watched the incoming group with suspicion, and many growled a warning, but they weren't interested in fighting. Secure in their separate territories, and busy teaching the basics to their new pouchlings, they didn't see anything to warrant fighting. As they approached, Loudest Beast called out for Screaming Killer, and it was clear that whatever these odd happenings portended, it didn't affect the rest of the colony. Finally, in a rather poor spot near the top of the hill, one of the gummies answered Loudest Beast's call.

<Parent! Why are you calling me?> Screaming Killer rose up from the rocky mud. Loudest Beast was proud to see the bulge in Screaming Killer's middle and the thin arm that was still regenerating.

<I have met some wise beings that fly through the sky like the water. They can take some People back to Everwet if they wish to try to make the journey. Come and share the taste of their offer.> Loudest Beast extended his arm. Screaming Killer would be able to taste that even if Loudest Beast no longer carried a pouchling, the elder had been accepted as mate and was not fleeing the colony in disgrace.

Screaming Killer tasted his parent's tendril and absorbed the memory of the last day. Not only did he get the flavor of the flouwen and their life on Eau, but he also got Loudest Beast's opinion of their actions. Loudest Beast was intrigued with the flouwen's life and their cooperative tactics, and was impressed with their obvious happiness and their willingness to waste time on things other than eating.

Screaming Killer was still young enough to wonder if the life his parent had prepared him for was the best that could be expected. Further, Screaming Killer was overwhelmed with the feelings of parenthood. His pouchling, so small and helpless and loving, needed to be fed and taught. Screaming Killer passionately needed to secure for this tiny being the best life possible. Screaming Killer drew back in the roots he had sunk into the surface and moved forward. He extended a tendril toward Little White, who used his pseudopod to guide it into his suit opening. They shared tastes of each other.

This time Little White didn't have to rock up to make sense of all the information he was given. When they broke contact, Little White immediately shared with Little Purple all that the gummie had passed to him. The gummie, however, was greatly affected. How could Screaming Killer believe that such a fabulous place existed where there was water all the time and new ones could be made and grow up without ever having to fear starvation? But it was not possible for flouwen to send a false taste . . . Screaming Killer bellowed with joy that such a miracle could happen within his lifetime.

"What's he doing?" asked Jinjur, wincing as the suit compensated to protect her ears.

❐I believe Screaming Killer is coming along.❐

By the time they returned to the ship, they had two other gummies who had followed the gummie side of the conversation and had had enough curiosity to investigate. One was a yearling named Baby Eater who, unlike Screaming Killer, had not managed to find a mate. With little territory and no reputation in the colony, Baby Eater had nothing to lose by leaving. For a moment, Loudest Beast had even thought of turning the youngster away, but he, too, was in a weakened state. Besides, coming up to the humans at all proved Baby Killer was not without courage. To Loudest Beast's surprise the other adventurer was his neighbor Flesh Burner. Loudest Beast had figured that this strong Person would eclipse Loudest Beast's abandoned prime property. Instead, Flesh Burner turned out to be very like Screaming Killer. It too had spent much time wondering about the limitations of colony life and had even gone so far as to wonder if things could get better if the People worked together. Needless to say, the newest space travelers were pleased to be joined by the colony's First Mated.

As Barnard set over the gummie colony, it was possible to see why the humans had missed the life on Roche. The "lake" was now plates of cracked mud and the People were completely underground. The slight hollows and markers that formed each of the separate territories now looked like uncomplicated, water-eroded hills. Sealing the gummies in the airlock where their ammonia smell would not affect the crew, the *Dragonfly* and its multi-species passengers gently lifted off for Eau.

It didn't take long to get the gummies settled in Everwet.

Richard and Sam designed a series of dams, catch basins, and collecting channels that would help bring extra rainwater runoff down into the moatlike lake and at the same time teach the gummies the elementary principles of hydrology and irrigation. The gummies began work on the channels immediately. Having spent a good deal of their lives underground, the gummies were adept at working in the soil and proved to be efficient diggers.

With Nels' help gummies also learned to care for the new plants and animals that now made up their diet, and soon the resources of the marshy island were plenty for the small colony. Most importantly, now that they were no longer driven by desperate hunger, they were able to overcome their normal dog-eat-dog survival-of-the-fittest mentality and learned to cooperate with each other and the flouwen.

"The flouwen have gone and done it now," said Nels grimly, as he watched one of the gummies teach another gummie how to use a thin flat rock as a hoe to dig dirt faster.

"What do you mean?" said Cinnamon. "The flouwen, being the superior beings, had an obligation to help their less fortunate distant relations. Now that they have brought some of the smarter gummies over to Eau so they can think and learn in peace, those gummies can go back and bring the ideas of cooperation and water collection to the colonies on Roche so they can eliminate the old harsh lifestyle of the average gummie."

"That old lifestyle, harsh though it was, had a positive effect," said Nels. "The gummies are more than distant relations of the flouwen. They are their evolutionary replacements."

"What?!"

"Yes. I didn't want to tell the flouwen. They will figure it out themselves in time. But while the flouwen have developed intellectually and philosophically, the gummies are flouwen who were forced by their harsh environment to develop physically. They have a permanent shape that gives them greater freedom than the flouwen, while allowing them to survive greater variations in climate. They can and do use tools to manipulate the world around them. The flouwen, for all their intelligence, have never developed tools or agriculture. Now, because of this interference by the flouwen, there is nothing to hold the gummies back from taking over both worlds. We can only hope they respect each other's cultures and get along better than we humans." He gave a resigned sigh.

"It probably was only a matter of time anyway. Had we arrived some ten thousand years later than we did, we would have found the flouwen much the same, still happily playing and surfing and solving mathematical theorems for recreation. But the gummies might just have flown out to meet us."

Jinjur linked through to John up on the *Prometheus*. John had managed to fight off his pneumonia with antibiotics, and though still weak, he was now walking and talking. "John? I understand you are trying to help James with Carmen."

"Yes, General, but we aren't getting anywhere. She seems to hear what we are saying to her, but it is as if she were too busy with whatever she is thinking about to give what we say any consideration."

"Look, John. I want you to bring someone else in on this. I know that we decided that Carmen should be kept isolated until she feels up to seeing the others, but I think you ought to have Reiki talk to her."

"The anthropologist? I wouldn't have thought that the two of them would have anything in common."

"Reiki is a wild card I've been holding," Jinjur explained. "And now it's time for me to play it. She has a quality that I think Carmen could really profit from right now."

"Look, I know that Reiki can be a very relaxing person to be around, but come on! She is an etiquette freak and the last thing Carmen needs is to be concerned about . . . "

"The first thing Carmen needs is to feel secure. Haven't

you ever wondered why Reiki is so 'relaxing to be around'? I always go talk to her whenever there is something that is troubling me. Sometimes I don't even discuss the problem with her. She just has a sort of unflappable serenity that seems to spread out to everyone around her."

John stopped objecting. He had felt it too.

"I think," said Jinjur, "that her peace stems from her preoccupation with manners and etiquette. She knows the correct way to handle anything . . . anything that happens around her. Nothing can offend her, because anything offensive she simply won't acknowledge. Reiki told me when she interviewed for the mission that she could get along with anyone, and that at some point I would appreciate how important that was. Since then, I have appreciated it; I've been impressed by it. I think that kind of peace and poise is exactly what Carmen needs."

John was quiet. "Maybe you're right. Certainly it wouldn't hurt." As he signed off, there was a gentle knock at the sick bay door. John had to smile. Of all those on board, only Reiki would knock rather than have James announce her. He opened the door to her with a flourish and left her alone with Carmen.

Reiki looked down at the tiny woman who was laying on her side, her lips moving shapelessly as she struggled to come to grips with everything that had happened. Reiki pulled herself even with her face and began to speak slowly.

"Carmen, I don't know what happened . . . and I can't even begin to understand, and it really isn't even important that I know. But you need to know and to begin to deal with it. Right now, it is all feelings and memories. You need to put it into something you can get a grip on. Write it down. Write it all down just as it comes to you. Turn all those feelings into words. Words are solid. Words can be dealt with."

Carmen look at her with a hint of recognition in her eyes. Reiki lifted her easily in the low gravity and set her before the touchscreen console on the desk in her room. James had anticipated her and the touchscreen was ready with a blank blue screen. As Reiki left the room, she heard a quiet tapping, as Carmen slowly began putting words on the screen.

John checked on her a few hours later, when James let him know that Carmen was making no more entries. He found her asleep, in the first deep natural sleep she had in days. He glanced at the screen. The little communications expert had filled sector after sector with her rambling story . . . but John had grown too in the last few weeks. He turned off the screen without reading her pain, and left her in the quiet darkness.

"Nels, I have been looking over that paper you prepared for the Phase II report," said Jinjur. She had come into the lab he had set up on the *Falcon*. "It looks like you've come up with a breakthrough in tissue regeneration."

"Yes. Green Fizzer and I have developed a paste that seems to have the desired effect."

"And you're sure it works?"

"We've had John up on the *Prometheus* try applying some to the toe he lost to frostbite. It is a new wound, and the regrowth has been remarkable. Not only has the toe completely regenerated in only a week, but the new toe is as sensitive as the old one was. There seems to be complete nerve regeneration . . . John even claims it has the same freckle as the old one."

"Well! We'll have to send this all to Earth immediately! This is incredible! It is only a shame that we will have to wait six years to see how effective it will be on others!"

"Actually, I'm planning on trying it out on myself," said Nels calmly.

"Look, Nels . . . " Jinjur frowned. "I'm sure that you would like to have normal legs just as soon as possible, but we simply haven't the time. We need you working with the flouwen. I can't have you spending all your time in a womb just because you want to be normal . . . "

"Normal!" Nels exploded. For once he lost his diffidence

towards his commander. "I *am* normal! I have been this way all my life and while it might not be normal to you, it is to me. Oh, if I had been consulted, I would have preferred my mother not to have had that accident in her chemistry lab, but I am the way I am, and I like my life. Having legs might have made things different, and different could well be worse!

"Yes, I am planning to go into that womb and be stuck there for months. But I am doing it only because I can't very well ask anyone else to! Richard has already refused to let me try and regrow his toes. I can't very well go around hoping that someone else will volunteer to let me cut off part of them just so I can try to grow it back!"

Nels took off one of his prosthetic legs and shook his flipper at her. He wiggled his toes and clenched them into a twisted fist. Awkwardly he held it up to her face. "These are my legs. They have always been my legs and I find them useful. I no more want to cut them off than you would want to cut off yours. If this paste does not work, I will be left with stumps. I will truly be handicapped then, but I am willing to risk it. Not for my ego, not in the name of 'normality,' but because if it works for me, it will work for anyone; anyone in this crew, anyone on Earth." He replaced the limb and walked straight and tall out of the lab without waiting to be dismissed.

Jinjur sat for a moment, digesting all he had said. All along she had been looking at Nels through the dark mirror of her own prejudice. He was special not because of his legs, nor despite them. He was just a very special person. Silently she thanked George for seeing what she had missed for so long and his insistence that Nels come with them to the stars. She called up to the *Prometheus*.

"John? I want you to set up that artificial womb in sick bay after all. We'll want for Nels to be able to out of it by the time we reach Gargantua and start preparations for landing on one of the moons, so have it ready for him when we reach the ship."

"Jinjur?" George cut in. "There is word from the landers on Gargantua's moon, Zulu. There is intelligent life there!"

"Explain!"

Suddenly there was not enough time to do anything. With Juno helping, the flouwen had rapidly become adept at flying the *Dragonfly* aeroplane. The nuclear reactor that gave the *Dragonfly* essentially unlimited range had a lifetime of decades, so the flouwen would be able to use the aeroplane either until they crashed it or the next mission came from Earth. With the *Dragonfly* available, the flouwen would be able to ferry the gummies back and forth from Roche to Everwet. They could even fly up to meet an ascent module at the zero-gee point when the human and flouwen explorers on *Prometheus* revisited Rocheworld later in the mission. In the meantime, the flouwen and the gummies would have access to *Prometheus* and the Earth through the laser communication center at Agua Dulce.

Their next landing target, the Gargantuan moon Zulu, was covered with an ocean. It had two known dominant life-forms, one living on the surface and the other in the ocean depths. George and Jinjur agreed that because of the ocean, the flouwen could be of real help in exploring the giant moon, and it was decided to bring along three of them from Eau.

The three flouwen Littles, Little Red, Little White, and Little Purple, would travel on the *Falcon* ascent module in their drysuits for the short trip up to *Prometheus*. There, they would transfer to a special tank on the hydroponics deck that had been filled with an ammonia-water solution and fitted with artificial volcanic vents to make it as much like home as possible for the flouwen and their living food supply. For the trip up to *Prometheus*, Nels filled the water tank in the center of the ascent module with all the Rocheworld plants and animals they had collected.

◎I want to go!◎ Pooh said, as the humans and Littles stood on the beach ready to say their good-byes.

☆We have gone over that,☆ said a revitalized Little Red. ☆You have to stay here. It is dangerous in space and you are just a youngling. Besides, if something happens to one of us Littles, at least there is the rest of us here on the planet. You still concentrate when you go in your suit. If you died, all of you would be gone!☆

Little Red would not miss this chance to explore with his friends. The last taste they brought back from his first adventure had been filled with the love and respect the first Little Red had felt for the humans. Now he was going with them into space.

❒You are young,❒ Little Purple said pacifically. ❒There will be other humans along soon, and if you show yourself worthy maybe you can go to space with them.❒

Pooh was rocking back and forth in anxiety. ❂But what if I am not worthy! I do not fit in with the others. They do not understand me! Who will I sing with?❂

"But, Pooh," Cinnamon said, pushing her way through the humans to hold on to the huge silver baggie with the yellow gumdrop head. "You will always be able to talk to us on the console at Agua Dulce. David and I, we will sing with you anytime you want. Besides, someone has to show the other flouwen how wonderful music is. And what about the gummies? I don't know if they have heard you singing at all. Won't it be fun to teach them?"

Pooh stopped rocking. ❂I can do that,❂ he said hesitantly.

"Of course you can. And you need to pass on pretending into a suit to the others too. You are too important for us to risk taking off planet." She gave the flouwen one last hug. "I love you . . . Make me proud."

With that she hurried back up the ladder of the *Falcon*. The other humans said their good-byes and soon, with as loud a roar as announced their arrival, they lifted off. Behind them they left two alien cultures whose fate had been inexorably altered.

* * *

Three weeks later, Carmen and Reiki were working together quietly. Jinjur had assigned Carmen the task of collecting the reports from the rest of the crew of their findings on Rocheworld. These reports would be put together into a Phase II report that would be a summary of the second planetary mission of the Barnard Star Expedition. Jinjur would normally be in charge of that administrative task, but she felt that doing that important but dull duty would be good therapy to get Carmen back as a functioning part of the crew.

Although Carmen was slowly feeling better, she still didn't have much to do with anyone but John and the anthropologist. Carmen saw a lot of Cinnamon, who was helping with Nels in the sick bay, but when the first sign of leg buds appeared below his hip joints, Nels had been asking for more and more of Cinnamon's time. Carmen suspected there was more going on there than work. The rest of the crew were all too excited at all the new information coming in from Zulu to visit the walking wounded, Carmen told herself, but the truth was, she tried to avoid them.

She worked a little each day and talked a lot to John and James. At their suggestion, she wrote a letter to her uncle. Although he had died long ago, it still helped to confront his ghost with all he had done to her. But James had made one restriction. The letter, no matter what she said in it, must be no longer than one page.

Each day she trimmed off a tiny bit of her litany of complaints. She consolidated and forgave and simplified and forgot. Today she wrote her final draft of that letter, the draft that James had intended she write. It was only two lines. It said: *"You hurt me. I didn't deserve it, but I am strong, and despite you I will be okay."* Then she sent it off to Earth. There was no one to receive it, but she sent it any way. Finally, she was able to stop thinking about it.

They had not really talked about what had happened to her; Carmen saved those details for John and her letter, but Reiki had lent her gentle presence to Carmen, doing most of her work in Carmen's room as Carmen read or watched videos or napped. Somehow Carmen knew that to Reiki she didn't need to explain anything, but there was still the others.

"Reiki?" Carmen asked. "I want to eat in the mess now. I miss seeing the others. But what do I say to them? What if they ask?"

"If they ask, they are being rude. You are under no obligation to explain to anyone. You might feel more comfortable if you apologize to Jinjur about missing work, but with that apology need come no excuses. To any inappropriate questions, you respond with a faint smile and a raised eyebrow. Surely, they couldn't have said anything so boorish. Surely, you must have heard wrong. And you don't hear them until they get it right."

Carmen laughed. It was the first real laugh Reiki had ever heard from her. "You're absolutely right . . . and stop calling me Shirley!"

Technical Report BSE-TR-70-080
July 2070

BARNARD STAR EXPEDITION
PHASE II REPORT

VOLUME I—EXECUTIVE SUMMARY

Submitted by:

Virginia Jones, Major General, GUSSM
Commander, Barnard Star Expedition

INTRODUCTION

This Volume I is the Executive Summary of the information collected to date by the Barnard Star Expedition, especially the more recent information gathered during Phase II of the expedition, which consisted of a second visit to the Barnard double-planet Rocheworld. This Executive Summary is a brief condensation of the extensive amounts of technical material to be found in the companion volume, Volume II—Technical Publications. Volume II, as well as a similar publication that followed Phase I, contains a series of technical papers and reports on various aspects of the mission, each of which runs to hundreds of pages, including tables. Those papers are intended for publication either in archival videojournals or as scientific or technical monovids, and contain many specialized terms that would be understood only by experts in that particular field.

For the benefit of the reader of this volume, who is assumed to be interested only in a brief summary in non-technical language without extensive numerical detail, the more precise specialized words and phrases used in the technical reports and papers have been replaced in this summary with common words, and most of the numerical data have either been eliminated or rounded off to two or three places. In addition, to assist those readers of this Executive Summary who may not have read the previous Phase I summary report, pertinent background material from that report has been included here.

The major topics discussed in this Executive Summary are covered in three sections:

Section 1. The performance of the technical equipment used to carry out the Barnard Star Expedition and the two recent missions to the surface of Rocheworld.

Section 2. The pertinent astronomical data concerning the Barnard star planetary system, with specific emphasis on the unique double-planet Rocheworld.

Section 3. The biology of the aliens discovered on Rocheworld.

SECTION 1
EQUIPMENT PERFORMANCE

Prepared by:
Shirley Everett—Chief Engineer
Anthony Roma, Captain, GUSSF—Chief Lightsail Pilot
Thomas St. Thomas, Captain, GUSAF—Chief Lander Pilot
Arielle Trudeau—Chief Aircraft Pilot

Equipment Configuration At Launch

The expedition sent to the Barnard star system consisted of a crew of twenty persons and their consumables, a habitat for their long journey, and four lander vehicles for visiting the various planets and moons of the Barnard system. This payload, weighing 3000 tons, was carried by a large reflective lightsail 300 kilometers in diameter. The lightsail was of very lightweight construction consisting of a thin film of finely perforated metal stretched over a sparse frame of wires held in tension by the slow rotation of the lightsail about its axis. Although the lightsail averaged only one-tenth of a gram per square meter of area, the total mass of the payload lightsail was over 7000 tons, for a total mass of payload and lightsail of 10,000 tons. Light pressure from photons reflected off the lightsail provided propulsion for the lightsail and its payload. The lightsail used retroreflected coherent laser photons from the solar system to decelerate the payload at the Barnard system, while, for propulsion within the Barnard system, it used incoherent photons from the star Barnard.

At the time of launch from the Solar System, the 300-kilometer payload lightsail was surrounded by a larger retroreflective ring lightsail, 1000 kilometers in diameter, with a hole in the center where the payload lightsail was attached. The ring lightsail had a mass of 72,00 tons, giving a total launch weight of lightsails and payload of over 82,000 tons.

Interstellar Laser Propulsion System

The laser power needed to push the 82,000-ton interstellar vehicle at an acceleration of one percent of Earth gravity was just over 1300 terawatts. This was obtained from an array of 1000 laser generators orbiting around Mercury. Each laser generator used a 30-kilometer-diameter lightweight reflector that collected 6.5 terawatts of sunlight. The reflector was designed to pass most of the solar spectrum and only reflect into its solar-pumped laser the 1.5 terawatts of sunlight that was at the right wavelength for the laser to use. The lasers were quite efficient, so each of the 1000 lasers generated 1.3 terawatts, to produce the total of 1300 terawatts needed to send the expedition on its way.

The transmitter lens for the laser propulsion system consisted of rings of thin plastic film stretched over a spiderweblike circular wire mesh held in tension by slow rotation about the mesh axis. The lens was designed with circular zones of decreasing width that were alternately empty and covered with plastic film whose thickness was chosen to produce a phase delay of one half a wavelength in the laser light. This huge Fresnel zone plate, 100 kilometers in diameter, collimated the laser beam coming from Mercury and sent it off to Barnard with essentially negligible divergence. The relative configuration of the lasers, lens, and lightsails during the launch and deceleration phases can be seen in Figure 1.

The accelerating lasers were left on for eighteen years while the spacecraft continued to gain speed. The lasers were turned off, back in the Solar System, in 2044. The

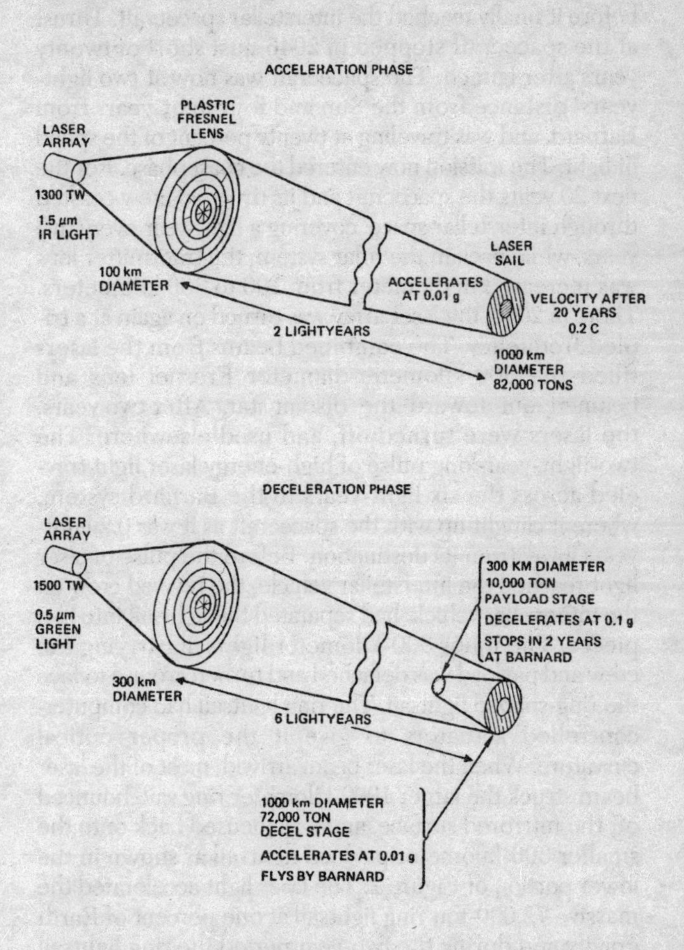

Figure 1—Interstellar laser propulsion system.
[*J. Spacecraft*, Vol. 21, No. 2, pp. 187-195 (1984)]

last of the light from the lasers traveled for two more years before it finally reached the interstellar spacecraft. Thrust at the spacecraft stopped in 2046, just short of twenty years after launch. The spacecraft was now at two light-years' distance from the Sun and four light-years from Barnard, and was traveling at twenty percent of the speed of light. The mission now entered the coast phase. For the next 20 years the spacecraft and its drugged crew coasted through interstellar space, covering a light-year every five years, while back in the solar system, the transmitter lens was increased in diameter from 100 to 300 kilometers. Then, in 2060, the laser array was turned on again at a tripled frequency. The combined beams from the lasers filled the 300-kilometer-diameter Fresnel lens and beamed out toward the distant star. After two years, the lasers were turned off, and used elsewhere. The two-light-year-long pulse of high-energy laser light traveled across the six light-years to the Barnard system, where it caught up with the spacecraft as it was 0.2 light-years away from its destination. Before the pulse of laser light reached the interstellar vehicle, the revived crew on the interstellar vehicle had separated the lightsail into two pieces. The inner 300-kilometer lightsail carrying the crew and payload was detached and turned around to face the ring-shaped lightsail. The ring lightsail had computer-controlled actuators to give it the proper optical curvature. When the laser beam arrived, most of the laser beam struck the larger 1000-kilometer ring sail, bounced off the mirrored surface, and was focused back onto the smaller 300-kilometer payload lightsail as shown in the lower portion of Figure 1. The laser light accelerated the massive 72,000-ton ring lightsail at one percent of Earth gravity and during the two-year period the ring lightsail increased its velocity slightly. The same laser power focused back on the much lighter payload lightsail, however, decelerated the smaller lightsail at nearly ten percent of Earth gravity. In the two years that the laser beam was on, the payload lightsail and its cargo of humans and exploration vehicles slowed from its interstellar velocity of twenty percent of the speed of light to come to rest in the Barnard system. Meanwhile, the ring lightsail continued on into deep space, its function completed.

Prometheus

The interstellar lightsail vehicle that took the exploration crew to the Barnard system was named *Prometheus*, the bringer of light. Its configuration is shown in Figure 2, and consists of a large lightsail supporting a payload containing the crew, their habitat, and their exploration vehicles. A major fraction of the payload volume was taken up by four exploration vehicle units. Each unit consisted of a planetary lander vehicle called the Surface Lander and Ascent Module (SLAM), holding within itself a winged Surface Excursion Module (SEM).

The largest component of *Prometheus* is the lightsail, 1000 kilometers in diameter at launch, and 300 kilometers in diameter during the deceleration and exploration phases of the mission. The frame of the lightsail consists of a hexagonal mesh trusswork made of wires held in tension by a slow rotation of the lightsail around its axis. Attached to the mesh wires are large ultrathin triangular sheets of perforated reflective aluminum film. The perforations in the film are made smaller than a wavelength of light, so they reduce the weight of the film without significantly affecting the reflective properties.

Running all the way through the center of *Prometheus* is a four-meter-diameter, 60-meter-long shaft with an elevator platform that runs up and down the shaft to supply transportation between decks. Capping the top of *Prometheus* on the side toward the direction of travel is a huge double-decked compartmented area that holds the various consumables for use during the 50-year mission, the workshops for the spaceship's computer motile, and an airlock

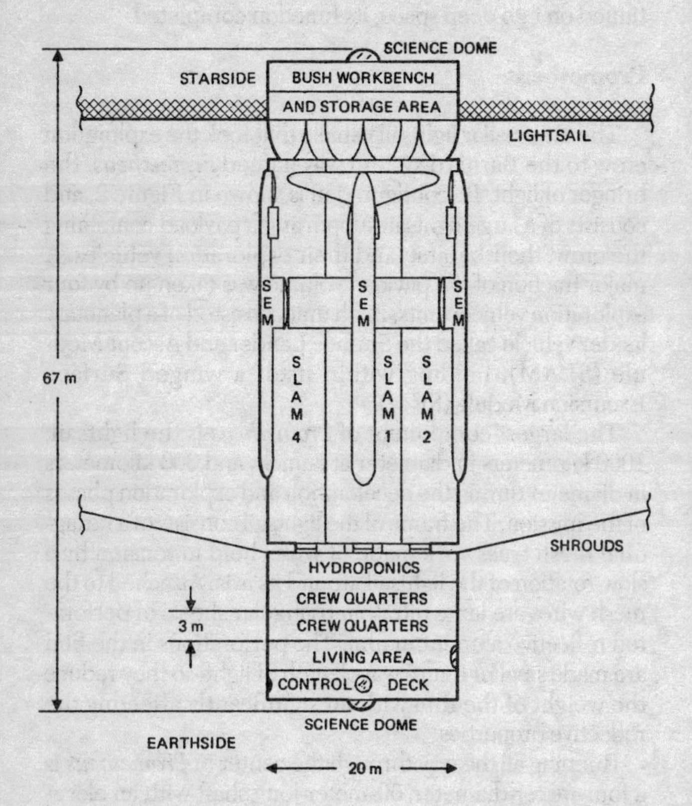

Figure 2—Prometheus

for access to the lightsail. At the very center of the starside deck is the starside science dome, a three-meter-diameter glass hemisphere that was used by the star-science instruments to investigate the Barnard star system as *Prometheus* was moving toward it.

At the base of *Prometheus* are five crew decks. Each deck is a flat cylinder twenty meters in diameter and three meters thick. The control deck at the bottom contains an airlock and the engineering, communication, science, and command consoles to operate the lightcraft and the science instruments. In the center of the control deck is the earthside science dome, a three-meter-diameter hemisphere in the floor, surrounded by a thick circular waist-high wall containing racks of scientific instruments that look out through the dome or directly into the vacuum through holes in the deck. Above the control deck is the living area deck containing the communal dining area, kitchen, exercise room, medical facilities, two small video theaters, and a lounge with a large sofa facing a three-by-four-meter oval view window. The next two decks are the crew quarters decks that are fitted out with individual suites for each of the twenty crew members. Each suite has a private bathroom, sitting area, work area, and a separate bedroom. The wall separating the bedroom from the sitting area is a floor-to-ceiling viewwall that can be seen from either side. There is another viewscreen in the ceiling above the bed.

Above the two crew quarters decks is the hydroponics deck. This contains the hydroponics gardens and the tissue cultures to supply fresh food to the crew. The water in the hydroponics tanks provide additional radiation shielding for the crew quarters below. In the ceilings of four of the corridors running between the hydroponics tanks are airlocks that allow access to the four Surface Lander and Ascent Module (SLAM) spacecraft that are clustered around the central shaft, stacked upside down between the hydroponics deck and the storage deck. Each SLAM is 46 meters long and six meters in diameter.

Surface Lander and Ascent Module

The Surface Lander and Ascent Module (SLAM) is a brute-force chemical rocket that was designed to get the planetary exploration crew and the Surface Excursion Module (SEM) down to the surface of the various worlds in the Barnard system. The upper portion of the SLAM, the Ascent Propulsion Stage (APS), is designed to take the crew off the world and return them back to *Prometheus* at the end of the surface exploration mission. As is shown in Figure 3, the basic shape of the SLAM is a tall cylinder with four descent engines and two main tanks.

The Surface Lander and Ascent Module has a great deal of similarity to the Lunar Excursion Module (LEM) used in the Apollo lunar landings, except that instead of being optimized for a specific airless body, the Surface Lander and Ascent Module had to be general purpose enough to land on planetoids that could be larger than the Moon, as well as have significant atmospheres. The three legs of the Surface Lander and Ascent Module are the minimum for stability, while the weight penalties for any more were felt to be prohibitive.

The Surface Lander and Ascent Module (SLAM) carries within itself the Surface Excursion Module (SEM), an aerospace plane that is almost as large as the lander. Embedded in the side of the SLAM is a long, slim crease that just fits the outer contours of the SEM. The seals on the upper portions were designed to have low gas leakage so that the SLAM crew could transfer to the SEM with minor loss of air.

The upper portion of the SLAM consists of the crew living quarters plus the Ascent Propulsion Stage. The upper deck is a three-meter-high cylinder eight meters in diameter. On its top is a forest of electromagnetic antennas for everything from laser communication directly to Earth to

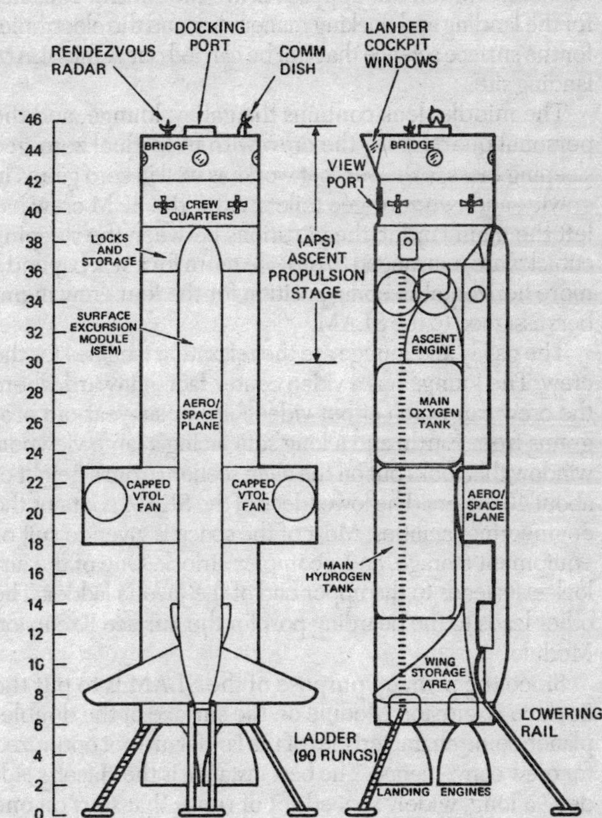

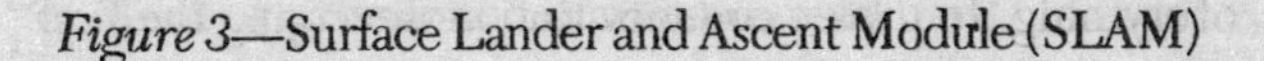
Figure 3—Surface Lander and Ascent Module (SLAM)

omni-antennas that broadcast the position of the ship to the orbiting relay satellites.

The upper deck contains the main docking port at the center. Its exit is upward, into the hydroponics deck of *Prometheus*. Around the upper lock are the control consoles for the landing and docking maneuvers, and the electronics for the surface science that can be carried out at the SLAM landing site.

The middle deck contains the galley, lounge, and the personal quarters for the crew with individual zero-gee sleeping racks, a shower that works as well in zero gee as in gravity, and two zero-gee toilets. After the SEM crew has left the main lander, the partitions between the sleeping cubicles are rearranged to provide room for a sick bay and a more horizontal sleeping position for the four crew members assigned to the SLAM.

The galley and lounge are the relaxation facilities for the crew. The lounge has a video center facing inward where the crew can watch either videochips or six-year-old programs from Earth, and a long sofa facing a large viewport window that looks out on the alien scenery from a height of about 40 meters. The lower deck of the SLAM contains the engineering facilities. Most of the space is given to suit or equipment storage, and a complex airlock. One of the airlock exits leads to the upper end of the Jacob's ladder. The other leads to the boarding port for the Surface Excursion Module.

Since the primary purpose of the SLAM is to put the Surface Excursion Module on the surface of the double-planet, some characteristics of the lander are not optimized for crew convenience. The best instance is the "Jacob's ladder," a long, widely spaced set of rungs that start on one landing leg of the SLAM and work their way up the side of the cylindrical structure to the lower exit-lock door. The "Jacob's ladder" was never meant to be used, since the crew expected to be able to use a powered hoist to reach the top of the ship. In the emergency that arose during the first expedition to Rocheworld, however, the Jacob's ladder proved to be a good, though slow, route up into the ship. The airlock design, however, was found to be faulty. With the lock full of people, the outer door cannot be closed. Other than this flaw, the SLAM performed well on both expeditions to Rocheworld.

One leg of the SLAM is part of the "Jacob's ladder," while another leg acts as the lowering rail for the Surface Excursion Module. The wings of the Surface Excursion Module are chopped off in mid-span just after the VTOL fans. The remainder of each wing is stacked as interleaved sections on either side of the tail section of the Surface Excursion Module. Once the Surface Excursion Module has its wings attached, it is a completely independent vehicle with its own propulsion and life-support system.

Surface Excursion Module

The Surface Excursion Module (SEM) is a specially designed aerospace vehicle capable of flying as a plane in a planetary atmosphere or as a rocket for short hops through empty space. The crew has given the name *Dragonfly* to the SEM because of its long wings, eye-like scanner ports at the front, and its ability to hover. An exterior view of the SEM is shown in Figure 4.

For flying long distances in any type of planetary atmosphere, including those which do not have oxygen in them, propulsion for the SEM comes from the heating of the atmosphere with a nuclear reactor powering a jet-bypass turbine. For short hops outside the atmosphere, the engine draws upon a tank of monopropellant, which not only provides reaction mass for the nuclear reactor to work on, but also makes its own contribution to the rocket plenum pressure and temperature.

The SEM proved to be an ideal exploration vehicle for the conditions on Rocheworld. Rocheworld has two large lobes to explore that are equivalent in land area to the

North American continent. Although there are excellent mapping and exploration instruments onboard, these have distance limitations, and two surface expeditions involving many long crisscross journeys over both lobes were needed to fully determine the true nature of the double-planet. The general flexibility of the basic SEM design is attested to by the fact that the flouwen are able to operate the SEM by themselves without human assistance.

A nuclear reactor could be a significant radiation hazard, but the one in the aerospace plane is well designed. Its outer core is covered with a thick layer of thermoelectric generators that turn the heat coming through the casing into the electrical power needed to operate the computers and scientific instruments aboard the plane. A number of metric tons of shielding protect the crew quarters from nuclear radiation generated by the reactor, but the real protection is in the system design that has the entire power and propulsion complex at the rear of the plane, far from the crew quarters. Since the source of the plane's power (and heat) is in the aft end, it is logical to use the horizontal and vertical stabilizer surfaces in the tail section as heat exchangers. Because most of the weight (the reactor, shielding, and fuel) is at the rear of the plane, the center of mass and the placement of the wings on the SEM are back from the wing position on a normal airplane of its size.

Although the SEM can use its rockets to travel through space, and can fly through practically any atmosphere with its nuclear jet at nearly sonic speeds, the components that made it indispensable in the surface exploration work are the large electrically powered vertical take-off and landing (VTOL) fans built into the wings. These fans take over at low speeds from the more efficient jet, and can safely lower the SEM to the surface. The details of the human-inhabited portion of the SEM are shown in Figure 5.

At the front of the aerospace plane is the cockpit, with the radar dome in front of it. Just behind the cockpit is the science instrument section, including port and starboard

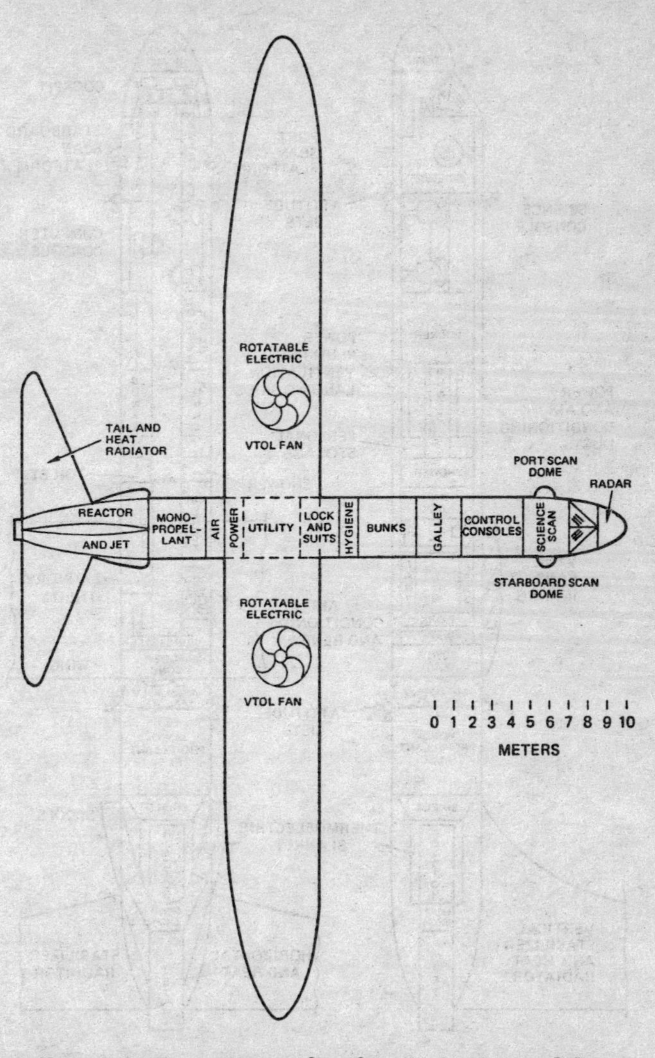

Figure 4—Exterior view of Surface Excursion Module (SEM)

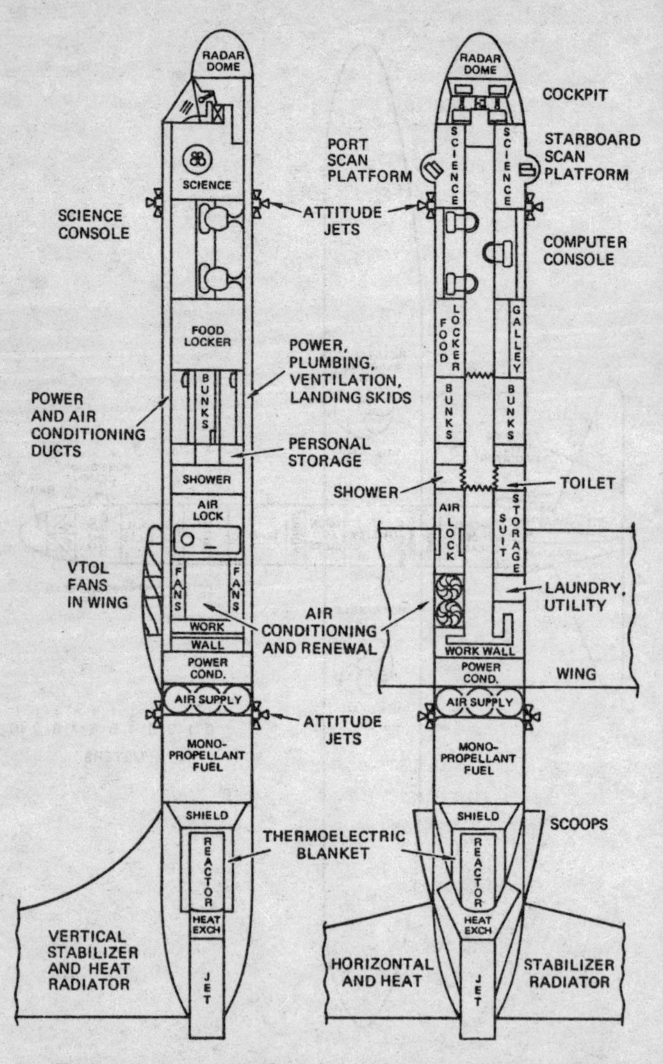

Figure 5—Interior of Surface Excursion Module (SEM)

automatic scanner platforms carrying a number of imaging sensors covering a wide portion of the electromagnetic spectrum. Next are the operating consoles for the science instruments and the computer, where most of the work is done. Farther back are the galley and food storage lockers. This constituted the working quarters where the crew spent most of their waking hours.

The corridor is blocked at this point by a privacy curtain which leads to the crew quarters. Since the crew would be together for long periods, the need for nearly private quarters was imperative, so the SEM was designed so each crew member has a private bunk with a large personal storage volume attached. Aft of the bunks are the shower and toilet, then another privacy curtain.

At the rear of the aerospace plane is the airlock, suit storage, air conditioning equipment, and a "work wall" that is the province of the Christmas Branch, a major subtree of the Christmas Bush that went along with the aerospace plane on its excursions. Not designed for use by a human, the work wall is a compact, floor-to-ceiling rack containing a multitude of housekeeping, analyzing, and synthesizing equipment that the Christmas Branch uses to aid the crew in their research, and to keep the humans and the SEM functioning. Behind the work wall is the power conditioning equipment, the liquefied air supply, and a large tank of monopropellant. All this mass helps the lead shadow shield in front of the nuclear reactor keep the radiation levels down in the inhabited portions of the aerospace plane.

Christmas Bush

The hands and eyes of the near-human computers that ran the various vehicles on the expedition are embodied in a repair and maintenance motile used by the computer, popularly called the "Christmas Bush" because of the twinkling laser lights on the bushy multibranched structure. The bushlike design for the robot has a parallel in the development of life-forms on Earth. The first large form of life on Earth was a worm. The sticklike shape was poorly adapted for manipulation or even locomotion. These sticklike animals then grew smaller sticks, called legs, and the animals could walk, although they were still poor at manipulation. Then the smaller sticks grew yet smaller sticks, and hands with manipulating fingers evolved.

The Christmas Bush is a manifold extension of this concept. The motile has a six-"armed" main body that repeatedly hexfurcates into copies one-third the size of itself, finally ending up with millions of near-microscopic cilia. Each subsegment has a small amount of intelligence, but is mostly motor and communication system. The segments communicate with each other and transmit power down through the structure by means of light-emitting and light-collecting semiconductor diodes. Blue laser beams are used to closely monitor any human beings near the motile, while red and yellow beams are used monitor the rest of the room. The green beams are used to transmit power and information from one portion of the Christmas Bush to another, giving the metallic surface of the multi-branched structure a deep green internal glow. It is the red, yellow, and blue lasers sparkling from the various branches of the greenly glowing Christmas Bush that give the motile the appearance of a Christmas tree. The central computer in the spacecraft is the primary controller of the motile, communicating with the various portions of the Christmas Bush through color-coded laser beams. It takes a great deal of computational power to operate the many limbs of the Christmas Bush, but the built-in "reflex" intelligence in the various levels of segmentation lessen the load on the main computer.

The Christmas Bush shown in Figure 6 is in its "one gee" form. Three of the "trunks" form "legs," one the "head," and two the "arms." The head portions are "bushed" out to give the detector diodes in the subbranches a three-dimensional view of the space around it. One arm ends

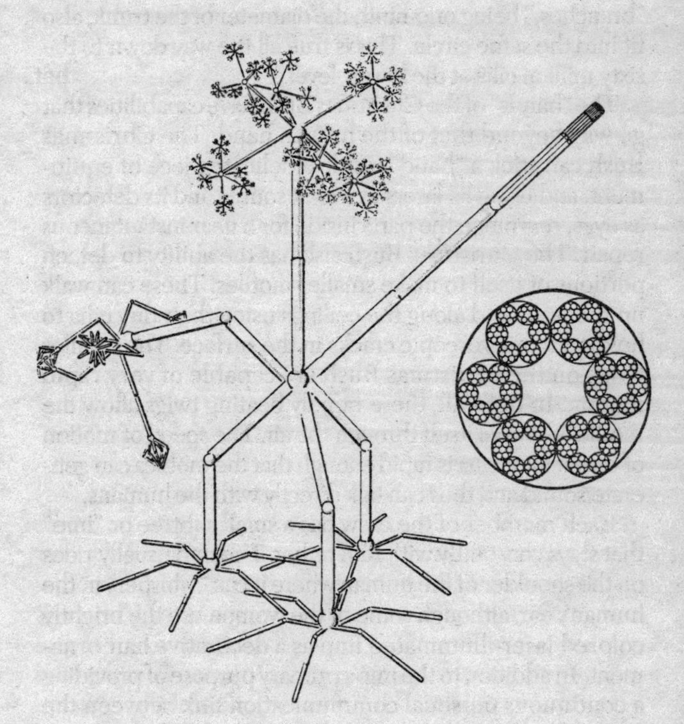

Figure 6—The Christmas Bush

with six "hands," demonstrating the manipulating capability of the Christmas Bush and its subportions. The other arm is in its maximally collapsed form. The six "limbs," being one-third the diameter of the trunk, can fit into a circle with the same diameter as the trunk, while the thirty-six "branches," being one-ninth the diameter of the trunk, also fit into the same circle. This is true all the way down to the sixty million cilia at the lowest level.

The "hands" of the Christmas Bush have capabilities that go way beyond that of the human hand. The Christmas Bush can stick a "hand" inside a delicate piece of equipment, and using its lasers as a light source and its detectors as eyes, rearrange the parts inside for a near instantaneous repair. The Christmas Bush also has the ability to detach portions of itself to make smaller motiles. These can walk up the walls and along the ceilings using their tiny cilia to hold on to microscopic cracks in the surface. The smaller twigs on the Christmas Bush are capable of very rapid motion. In free-fall, these rapidly beating twigs allow the motile to propel itself through the air. The speed of motion of the smaller cilia is rapid enough that the motiles can generate sound and thus can talk directly with the humans.

Each member of the crew has a small subtree or "imp" that stays constantly with him or her. The imp usually rides on the shoulder of the human where it can "whisper" in the human's ear, although some of the women use the brightly colored laser-illuminated imp as a decorative hair ornament. In addition to the imp's primary purpose of providing a continuous personal communication link between the crew member and the central computer, it also acts as a health monitor and personal servant for the human. The imps go with the humans inside their space-suits, and more than one human life has been saved by an imp detecting and repairing a suit failure or patching a leak. The imps can also exit the space-suit, if desired, by worming their way out through the air supply valves.

SECTION 2
BARNARD SYSTEM ASTRONOMICAL DATA

Prepared by:
Linda Regan—Astrophysics
Thomas St. Thomas, Captain, GUSAF—Astrodynamics

Barnard Planetary System

As shown in Figure 7, the Barnard planetary system consists of the red dwarf star Barnard, the huge gas giant planet Gargantua and its large retinue of moons, and an unusual corotating double-planet, Rocheworld. Gargantua is in a standard near-circular planetary orbit around Barnard, while Rocheworld is in a highly elliptical orbit that takes it in very close to Barnard once every orbit, and very close to Gargantua once every three orbits. During its close passage, Rocheworld comes within six gigameters of Gargantua, just outside the orbit of Zeus, the outermost moon of Gargantua. It has been suggested that one lobe of Rocheworld was once an outer large moon of Gargantua, while the other lobe was stray planetoid that interacted with the outer Gargantuan moon to form Rocheworld in its present orbit. Further information about Barnard, Gargantua, and Rocheworld follows.

Barnard

Barnard is a red dwarf star that is the second closest star to the Solar System after the three-star Alpha Centauri system. Barnard was known only by the star catalog number of +4° 3561 until 1916, when the American astronomer Edward E. Barnard measured its proper motion and found it was moving at the high rate of 10.3 seconds of arc per year, or more than half the diameter of the Moon in a century. Parallax measurements soon revealed that the star was the second closest star system. Barnard's Star (or Barnard

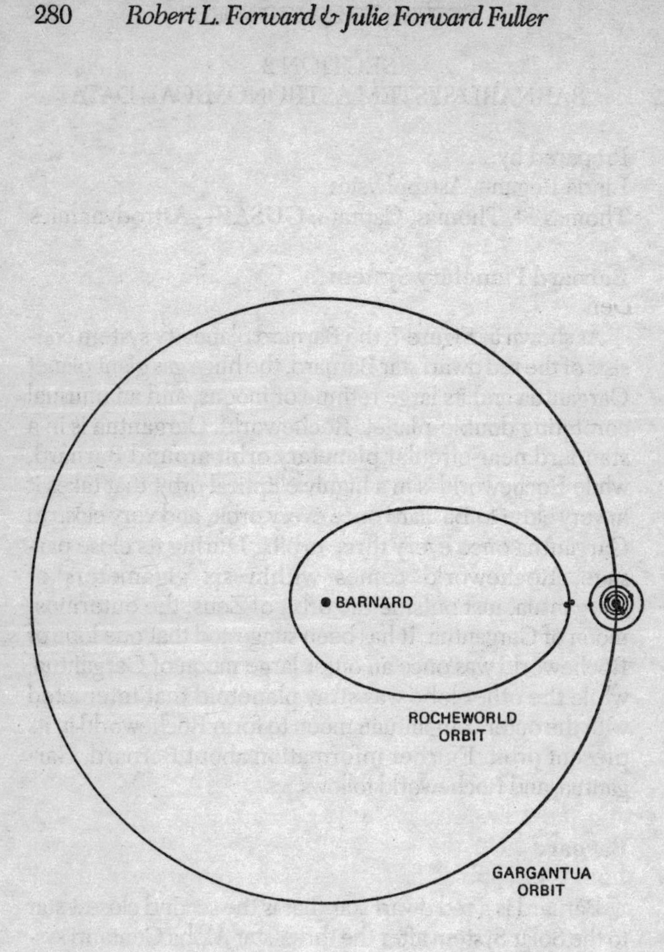

Figure 7—Barnard Planetary System

as it is called now) can be found in the southern skies of Earth, but it is so dim it requires a telescope to see it. The data concerning Barnard follows:

Distance from Earth = 5.6×10^{16} m (5.9 light-years)
Type = M5 Dwarf
Mass = 3.0×10^{29} kg (15% solar mass)
Radius = 8.4×10^{7} m = 84 Mm (12% solar radius)
Density = 121 g/cc (86 times solar density)
Effective Temperature = 3330 K (58% solar temperature)
Luminosity = 0.05% solar (visual); 0.37% solar (thermal)

The illumination from Barnard is not only weak because of the small size of the star, but reddish because of the low temperature. The illumination from the star is not much different in intensity and color than that from a fireplace of glowing coals at midnight. Fortunately, the human eye adjusts to accommodate for both the intensity and color of the local illumination source, and unless there is artificial white-light illumination to provide contrast, most colors (except for dark blue—which looks black) look quite normal under the weak, red light from the star.

Note the high density of the star compared to our Sun. This is typical of a red dwarf star. Because of this high density, the star Barnard is actually slightly smaller in diameter than the gas giant planet Gargantua, even though the star is forty times more massive than the planet.

Gargantua

Gargantua is a huge gas giant like Jupiter, but four times more massive. If Gargantua had been slightly more massive, it would have turned into a star itself, and the Barnard system would have been a binary star system. The pertinent astronomical data about Gargantua follows:

Mass = 7.6×10^{27} kg (4 times Jupiter mass)
Radius = 9.8×10^{7} m = 98 Mm
Density = 1.92 g/cc
Orbital Radius = 3.8×10^{10} m = 38 Gm
Orbital Period = 120.4 Earth days = 3 times Rocheworld period
Rotation Period = 162 h

The radius of Gargantua's orbit is less than that of Mercury. This closeness to Barnard helps compensate for the low luminosity of the star, leading to moderate temperatures on Gargantua and its moons. Gargantua seems to have swept up most of the original stellar nebula that was not used in making the star, for there are no other large planets in the system.

Rocheworld

Most of the planetary data gathered to date by the Barnard Star Expedition is on the unique corotating dumbbell-shaped double-planet Rocheworld. As shown in Figure 8, Rocheworld consists of two moon-sized rocky bodies that whirl about each other with a rotation period of six hours. The data concerning Rocheworld follows:

Type: Co-rotating double planet
Masses:
  Eau Lobe: 4.8×10^{22} kg
  Roche Lobe: 5.2×10^{22} kg
Diameters:
  Eau Lobe: 2900 x 3410 km
  Roche Lobe: 3000 x 3560 km
Separation:
  Centers of Mass: 4,000 km
  Inner Surfaces: 80 km (nominal)
Corotation Period = 6.015 h
Eccentricity = 0.78

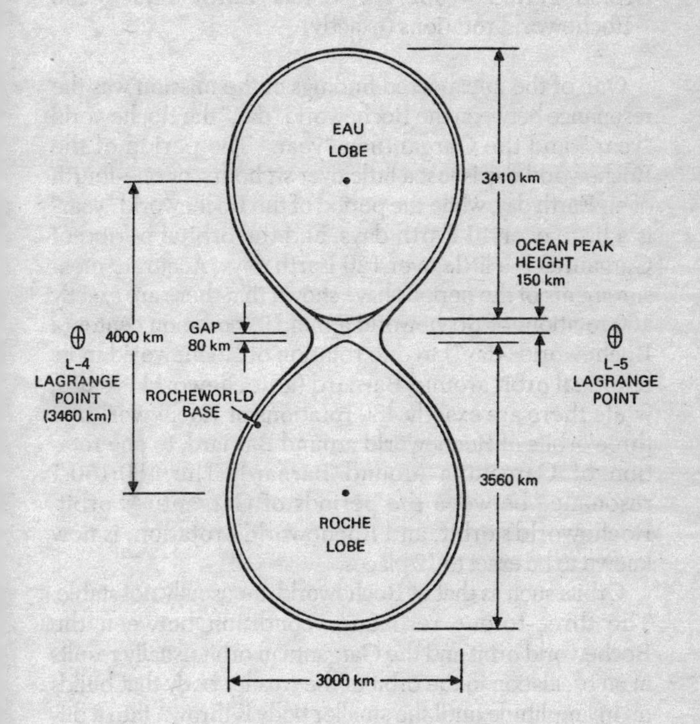

Figure 8—Rocheworld

Orbital Semimajor Axis = 18 Gm
Periapsis = 4 Gm
Apoapsis = 32 Gm
Orbital Period = 962.4 h = 40.1 Earth days = 160 Rocheworld rotations (exactly)

One of the unexpected findings of the mission was the resonance between the Rocheworld "day," the Rocheworld "year," and the Gargantuan "year." The period of the Rocheworld day is just a little over six hours, or one-fourth of an Earth day, while the period of the Rocheworld "year" is a little over 40 Earth days, and the orbital period of Gargantua is a little over 120 Earth days. Accurate measurements of the periods have shown that there are exactly 160 rotations of Rocheworld around its common center (a Rocheworld "day") to one rotation of Rocheworld in its elliptical orbit around Barnard (a Rocheworld "year"), while there are exactly 480 rotations of Rocheworld, or three orbits of Rocheworld around Barnard, to one rotation of Gargantua around Barnard. The 480:160:1 resonance between the periods of Gargantua's orbit, Rocheworld's orbit, and Rocheworld's rotation, is now known to be exact to 12 places.

Orbits such as that of Rocheworld are usually not stable. The three-to-one resonance condition between the Rocheworld orbit and the Gargantuan orbit usually results in an oscillation in the orbit of the smaller body that builds up in amplitude until the smaller body is thrown into a different orbit, or a collision occurs. Due to Rocheworld's close approach to Barnard, however, the tides from Barnard cause a significant amount of dissipation, which stabilizes the Rocheworld orbit. This close approach also supplies a great deal of tidal heating, which keeps Rocheworld warmer than it would normally be if the heat were due to radiation from the star alone.

This locking of Rocheworld's rotation period and orbital period to the orbital period of Gargantua also provides the mechanism for keeping the double-planet rotating and moving in its highly elliptical orbit. The energy input needed to compensate for energy losses due to tidal dissipation comes from the gravitational tug of Gargantua on Rocheworld during their close passage every third orbit.

The two planetoids or lobes of Rocheworld are so close that they are almost touching, but their spin speed is high enough that they maintain a separation of about eighty kilometers. If each were not distorted by the other's gravity, the two planets would have been spheres about the size of our Moon. Since their gravitational tides act upon one another, the two bodies have been stretched out until they are elongated egg-shapes, roughly 3,500 kilometers in the long dimension and 3,000 kilometers in cross section.

Although the two planets do not touch each other, they do share a common atmosphere. The resulting figure-eight configuration is called a Roche-lobe pattern after E. A. Roche, a French mathematician of the later 1880s, who calculated the effects of gravity tides on stars, planets, and moons. The word "roche" also means "rock" in French, so the rocky lobe of the pair of planetoids has been given the name Roche, while the water-covered lobe was named Eau after the French word for water.

The average gravity at the surface of these planetoids is about ten percent of Earth gravity, slightly less than that of Earth's Moon because of their lower density. This average value varies considerably depending upon your position on the surface of the elongated lobes. The gravity at one of the outward facing poles is eight percent of Earth gravity, rising to eleven percent in a belt that includes the north and south spin poles of each lobe; increases slightly to a maximum of eleven and a half percent at a region some thirty degrees inward; then drops precipitously to a half percent at the inner-pole surface. (A detailed gravity map of both lobes may be found in the paper by S. Houston in Volume II.) This lowest gravity point at the inner surfaces is some forty kilometers below the zero gravity point between the two planetoids, where the gravity from the mass of the two lobes cancels out.

On each side of the double planet are the Lagrange L-4 and L-5 points, where there is a minimum in the combined gravitational and centrifugal forces of the system. A satellite placed at either of these two points will stay there, rotating synchronously with the two planets, without consumption of fuel. For the Earth-Moon system, where the Earth is much more massive than the Moon, those stable points are in the orbit of the Moon at plus and minus sixty degrees from the Moon. In the Rocheworld system, where the two bodies are the same mass, the stable points are at plus and minus ninety degrees. The exploration crew established communication satellites at these two points to give continuous coverage of each side of both lobes.

The Roche lobe is slightly less dense than the Eau lobe and thus is larger in diameter. It has a number of ancient craters upon its surface, especially in the outer-facing hemisphere. Although the Eau lobe masses almost as much as the Roche lobe, it has a core that is denser. Since its highest point is some twenty kilometers lower in the combined gravitational well, it is the "lowlands" while the Roche lobe is the "highlands." Eau gets most of the rain that falls from the common atmosphere and thus has captured nearly all of the liquids of the double planet to form one large ocean. The ocean is primarily ammonia water, with trace amounts of hydrogen sulfide and cyanide gas.

The Roche Lobe is dry and rocky, with traces of quiescent volcano vents near its pointed pole. The Eau lobe has a pointed section like the Roche lobe, but the point is not made of rock. The point is a mountain of ammonia water a hundred and fifty kilometers high with sixty degree slopes! One would think that the water would "seek its own level" and flow out until the surface of the ocean became spherical, but because of the unusual configuration of the gravity fields of the double planet, the basic mountain shape is stable—except at periapsis.

Interplanetary Dynamics

Because of the highly elliptical orbit of Rocheworld, which takes it close to both Gargantua and Barnard, the dynamics of the planetary system are quite complicated. When Rocheworld is at its farthest distance from Barnard, the two lobes whirl about each other with a constant separation, and the gravity from the star cause modest tides in the ocean on Eau. As Rocheworld moves around in its orbit, however, it experiences stronger tides as it approaches Gargantua and especially Barnard. During close approach, the variations in tides from one rotation to the next causes large surges in the ocean. The low gravity accentuates these surges into large waves that reach kilometers in height, breaking at the low gravity pole between the two planetoids.

As Rocheworld begins to approach Barnard in its elliptical orbit, the effect of the tides from the star starts to become very large. The peak of the water mountain begins to rise and fall a number of kilometers, with the pattern repeated each half-rotation. Observations show that when Barnard is on one side of Rocheworld, the two lobes separate. This separation then causes the mountain of water on Eau to drop. This behavior is not what would be predicted by a naive model of the gravity forces. Normally, with Barnard off to the side, the gravity tidal forces from Barnard would be expected to draw the lobes closer together, not farther apart. A naive model would also predict that the change in the height of the mountain of water would be about the same as the change in the separation distance between the two lobes. Detailed computer studies that take into account the coupling of the angular rotation and the orbital motion with the planetary dynamics, however, predict a significantly different behavior, which is what is observed.

As is shown in Figure 9, during the first quarter-rotation, with the tide-inducing star Barnard off to one side, the

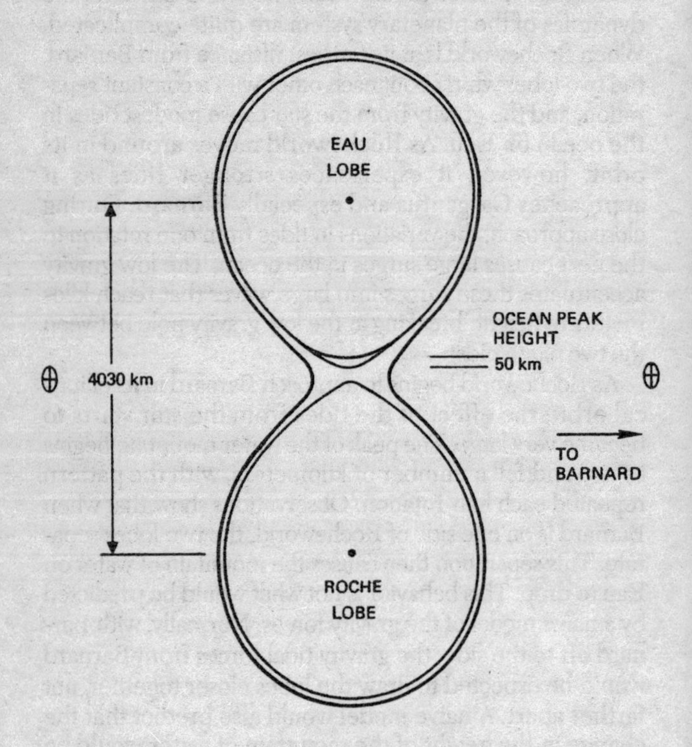

Figure 9—Periapsis tides during first quarter-rotation.

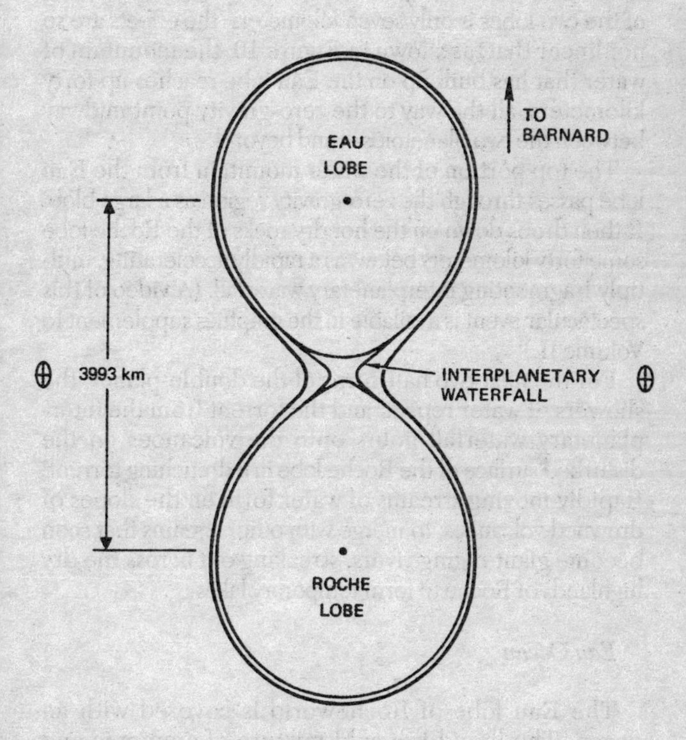

Figure 10—Periapsis tides during second quarter-rotation.

planets separate by thirty kilometers and the water mountain drops one hundred kilometers. Then, just a quarter-rotation later, with the star Barnard now along the line joining the centers of the two planetoids, the tidal forces go the other way. Although the decrease in spacing of the two lobes is only seven kilometers, the effects are so nonlinear that, as shown in Figure 10, the mountain of water that has built up on the Eau lobe reaches up forty kilometers, all the way to the zero-gravity point midway between the two planetoids—and beyond.

The top portion of the water mountain from the Eau lobe passes through the zero-gravity region as a large blob. It then drops down on the hot dry rocks of the Roche lobe some forty kilometers below, as a rapidly accelerating, multiply fragmenting interplanetary waterfall. (A video of this spectacular event is available in the graphics supplement to Volume II.)

For the next two half-turns of the double-planet, the showers of water repeat, and the torrent from the interplanetary waterfall pours onto the volcanoes on the disturbed surface of the Roche lobe in a drenching torrent. Rapidly moving streams of water form on the slopes of drowned volcanoes, to merge with other streams that soon become giant raging rivers, streaking out across the dry highlands of Roche to form temporary lakes.

Eau Ocean

The Eau lobe of Rocheworld is covered with an ocean. The liquid is a cold mixture of ammonia and water similar to what was found inside Jupiter's icy moon Europa. There are no land areas of any size on the Eau lobe, so the climate is determined by the heating patterns from Barnard as modified by the shadowing effects of the Roche lobe. There is a warm "crescent" that is centered on the outer pole and reaches around the equator. This crescent receives the most sunlight and the

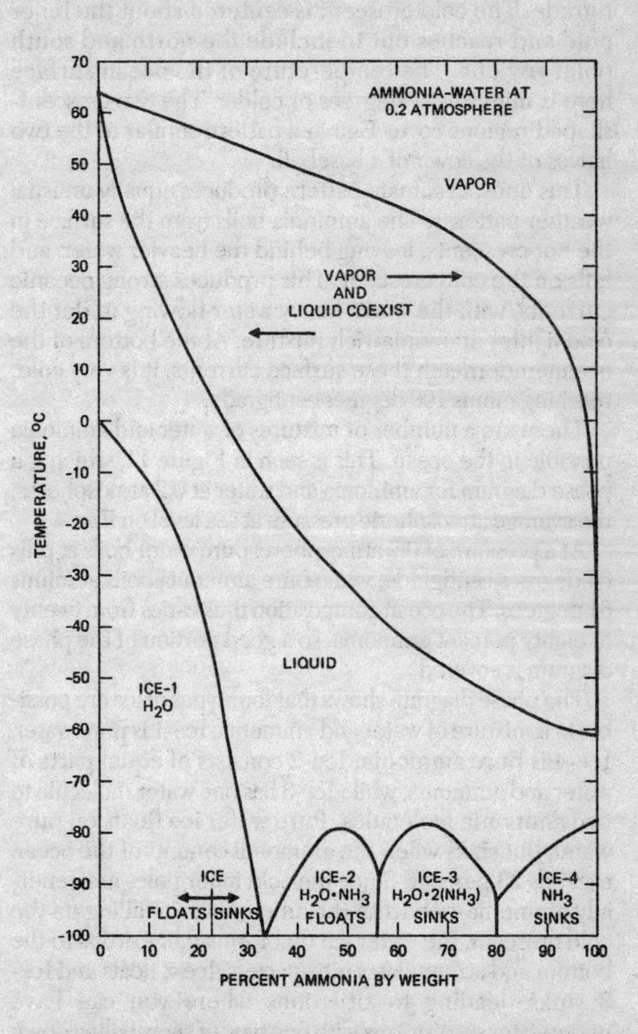

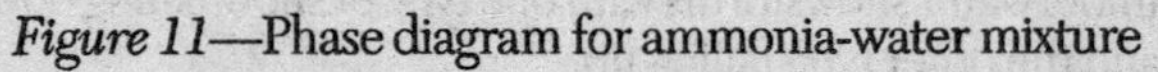
Figure 11—Phase diagram for ammonia-water mixture

surface temperature reaches minus twenty degrees centigrade. The cold crescent is centered about the inner pole and reaches out to include the north and south polar regions. The temperature of the ocean surface here is minus forty degrees or colder. The two crescent-shaped regions cover Eau in a pattern similar to the two halves of the cover of a baseball.

This unusual climate pattern produces equally unusual weather patterns. The ammonia boils from the surface in the hot crescents, leaving behind the heavier water, and falls on the cold crescent. This produces strong oceanic currents, with the warm heavy water flowing under the cold lighter ammonia-rich mixture. At the bottom of the ocean underneath these surface currents, it is very cold, reaching minus 100 degrees centigrade.

There are a number of mixtures of water and ammonia possible in the ocean. This is seen in Figure 11, which is a phase diagram for ammonia and water at 0.2 atmospheres, the average atmospheric pressure at sea level on Eau.

At a pressure of 0.2 atmosphere, pure water boils at plus 64 degrees centigrade, while pure ammonia boils at minus 61 degrees. The ocean composition thus varies from twenty to eighty percent ammonia, so a good portion of the phase diagram is covered.

The phase diagram shows that four types of ice are possible in a mixture of water and ammonia. Ice-1 is pure water, Ice-4 is pure ammonia, Ice-2 consists of equal parts of water and ammonia, while Ice-3 has one water molecule to two ammonia molecules. Pure water ice floats on pure water, but sinks when the ammonia content of the ocean exceeds 23 percent. Since the cold inner poles are generally ammonia-rich from the ammonia rain falling on the cold crescent, the water ice that forms there drops to the bottom and accumulates into glaciers. Ice-2 floats and Ice-3 sinks, leading to situations where you can have underwater snowstorms with one type of snow falling down and the other type falling up.

SECTION 3
ROCHEWORLD BIOLOGY

Prepared by:
Cinnamon Byrd—Zoology
Katrina Kauffmann—Biology
John Kennedy—Physiology
Nels Larson—Botany and Genetics

Introduction

Alien life-forms have been found on both the Eau lobe and the Roche lobe of the double-planet Rocheworld. The biology on each lobe will be described separately.

Eau Lobe Biology

The biology on the Eau lobe of Rocheworld is dominated by the fact that the Eau lobe is nearly completely covered with a deep, cold ocean made of a mixture of water and ammonia. Thus, nearly all the animals and plants are designed for life underwater.

Flouwen

The dominant species on Eau has been given the common name of "flouwen" (singular "flouwen," taken from the Old High German root word for flow). The flouwen are formless, eyeless, flowing blobs of brightly colored jelly massing many tons. They normally stay in a formless, cloudlike shape, moving with and through the water. When they are in their mobile, cloudlike form, the clouds in the water range from ten to thirty meters in diameter and many meters thick. At times, the flouwen will extrude water from their bodies and concentrate the material in their cloud into a dense rock formation a few meters in diameter. They seem to do this when they are thinking, and it is supposed that the denser form allows for faster and more concentrated cogitation.

The flouwen are very intelligent—but non-technological—like the dolphins and whales on Earth. They have a highly developed system of philosophy, and extremely advanced abstract mathematical capability. There is no question that they are centuries ahead of us in mathematics, and further communication with them could lead to great strides in human capabilities in this area.

The flouwen use chemical senses for short-range information gathering, and sound ranging, or sonar, for long-range information gathering. Since sonar penetrates to the interior of an object, especially living objects such as flouwen and their prey, sonar provides "three-dimensional sight" to the flouwen and is their preferred method of "seeing." The bodies of the flouwen are sensitive to light, but, lacking eyes, they normally cannot look at things using light like humans do. In general, sight is a secondary sense, about as important to them as taste is to humans. One of the flouwen learned, however, to deliberately form an imaging lens out of the gel-like material in its body, which it used to study the stars and planets in their stellar system. Called White Whistler by the humans, this individual was one of the more technologically knowledgeable of the flouwen. White Whistler has since taught the eye-making technique to the rest of the flouwen.

In genetic makeup, complexity level, and internal organization, the flouwen have a number of similarities to slime molds here on Earth, as well as to a colony of ants. The flouwen bodies are made up of tiny, nearly featureless, dumbbell-shaped units, something like large cells. Each is the size and shape of the body of the tiny red ants found on Earth. The units are arranged in loosely interlocking layers, with four bulbous ends around each necked-down waist portion, two going in one direction and two going in the other, so that the body of the flouwen is a three-dimensionally interlocked whole.

The interior of each unit is made of a living gel-like material with many of the bonds hydrated. The gel is practically crystalline in its order, although quite flexible because of the high water content. Between the gel-like units is a complex liquid containing two different compounds in three layers. The central layer is a thin film of molecules made up of twelve basic carbohydrate ring molecules that repeat in semi-random patterns. The ring molecules are arranged in large plates held between outer layers of a liquid crystal compound.

The gel material seems to be the equivalent of "bones" for the flouwen, in that it determines the basic structure, while the thin films covering the "skeleton" act as both the nerve tissue and the genetic coding mechanism. The primary functions of the liquid crystal compound are to provide communication between the units through the ionic conduction of nerve impulses, to generate and maintain a short-term memory as circulating nerve impulses, and to keep the ring molecules ordered into sheets. A secondary function is to give the flouwen bodies their bright and differing colors. The medium term memory is carried in the two-dimensional ordering of the twelve ring molecules. The molecules containing this medium term memory can be transferred from one flouwen to another, allowing one flouwen to "taste" the "thoughts" of another—something like a form of "chemical telepathy."

The outer surfaces of the gel dumbbells have ring patterns impressed on them that match the twelve basic compounds. The patterns normally act as a template for ordering the ring molecules, but the patterns, in turn, can be modified by the patterns in the inner layer of ring molecules. The impressed patterns on the units thus provide for the long-term storage of the genetic code and a long-term memory that is nearly permanent, so the flouwen never forget. Since the production of offspring involves the wholesale transfer of a large number of units from the parents, the memories stored on the units can be transferred to the offspring, providing a "racial" memory that is separate from, but related to, the genetic code. The memories are obviously stored in a "holographic" sense and are constantly being refreshed, since the individual units have a finite lifetime and are constantly being replaced.

The units grow in size by absorbing water and simple organic materials through the walls of their body as does any typical single cell on Earth. The units replicate themselves by bifurcation. A unit, after reaching a large enough size, will reduce its waist portion to zero, producing two spheres. The resulting spheres then neck down to form two new dumbbell-shaped units. A damaged or slow-growing unit stops replicating and lyses. The organic material released is absorbed as food by the neighboring units. The average lifetime of a unit is only a few weeks. The units are replaced either by internal replication or by the absorption and "conversion" of units from the lower animals.

When a flouwen eats a plant, the enzymes in the inner liquid layer "digest" the plant by dissolving the plant cells into basic molecules. These basic molecules are then absorbed through the walls of the flouwen units and used by the living gel-like material inside to make more units. When a flouwen "eats" a lower animal, however, it does not break down the animal units into basic molecules by "digestion." The units in an animal are identical to the units in a flouwen, except the patterns on the surface of the animal units have the genetic code and memories of the animal. The flouwen enzymes do not attack the units, but instead attack and dissolve the inner and outer liquid layers surrounding the units. The enzymes then "convert" the animal units to flouwen units by replacing the animal genetic pattern with the flouwen genetic pattern.

Each of the dumbbell units can survive for a while on its own, but has minimal intelligence. A small collection of units can survive as a coherent cloud with enough intelligence to hunt smaller prey and look for plants to eat. These small "animals" are the major form of prey for the flouwen.

Larger collections of units form into more complex "animals." When the collection of units finally becomes large enough, it becomes an intelligent being. Yet, if that being is torn into thousands of pieces, each piece can survive. If the pieces can get back together again, the individual is restored, only a little worse for its experience. As a result, a flouwen never dies, unless it is badly damaged in a natural accident (boiled by a volcanic eruption or stranded on dry land a long distance from water). Most of the flouwen known by the humans are many hundreds of years old. There are flouwen that are much older, most of them rocked up into their maximal thinking form. They can be found in the shallows along the beaches of the small chain of islands on the outer pole of Eau. The effects of the seasonal tides are minimal there, so they don't have to move with the seasons. There are many other colored boulders there, each one some elder thinking through some complex problem in mathematics or logic. Some have not shifted since any flouwen can remember. They are probably still thinking, but they could be dead for all anyone could tell. They slowly waste away over time due to energy expenditure, surface losses, and nibblings of rogues and fauna. From a reproduction point of view, the evolution of the elder flouwen into this thinking form is equivalent to dying, so the flouwen species does conform to the Solem Senescence Pronouncement.

Reproduction for the flouwen is a multiple-individual experience. The flouwen do not seem to have sexes, and it seems that any number from two flouwen on up can produce a new individual. The usual grouping for reproduction is thought to be three or four. The creating of a new flouwen seems to be more of a lark or a creative exercise like music or theater than a physically driven emotional experience. The explorers on the first expedition to Rocheworld witnessed one such coupling put on for their benefit. In this case it involved four flouwen: Loud Red, White Whistler, Green Fizzer, and Yellow Hummer. They each extended a long tendril that contained a substantial portion of their mass, estimated to be one-tenth of the mass of each parent. These tendrils, each a different color, met at the middle and intertwined with a swirling motion like colored paints being stirred together. There was a long pause as each tendril began to lose its distinctive color, indicating that the liquid layers between the units were being withdrawn, leaving only the units.

Then finally the tendrils were snapped off from the adult flouwen bodies, leaving a colorless cloud of gel-like units floating by itself, about forty percent of the size of the adults that created it. After a few minutes, the mass of cells formed themselves into a new individual, who took on a color that was different than any of its progenitors. The adults then take it upon themselves to train the new youngster. The adults and youngsters stay together for hunting and protection, the group again being very much like a pod of whales or porpoises.

The flouwen have a complex art-form similar to acting, which involves carrying out simulations of real or imaginary happenings by forming a replica of the scene with their bodies. They also have developed a language art very similar to poetry. Amazingly enough, despite their inherent ability to make sounds for "seeing" and talking, the flouwen had no knowledge of the acoustic art-form called music. Once introduced to music, however, they rapidly learned the new art. Considering their genius level of mathematical ability, and the close correlation of musical and mathematical ability in humans, perhaps this is not surprising. After a short period of study and experimentation, the flouwen were soon producing complex music compositions that nearly all listeners judge to be superior to those generated by human composers.

Since a small portion of a flouwen can function like a full-sized individual, except for decreased physical and mental capabilities, it was found that a portion weighing only a fifth of a ton (200 kilograms or 440 pounds) can bud off from the multi-ton main flouwen body, get into a specially built space-suit, and ride in human space vehicles in order to take part in joint expeditions with the humans. These sub-flouwen are somewhat more intelligent than humans, and have already proved to be valuable participants in visits to the Roche lobe. In the future, it is planned to take them on expeditions to other worlds in the Barnard planetary and moon system, especially those worlds containing oceans.

Eau Fauna

There are both flora and fauna on Rocheworld. The minor fauna are all in the ocean and similar in chemistry, genetics, and cellular structure to the intelligent flouwen.

The major prey of flouwen are small animals that are formless, eyeless, flowing blobs of brightly colored jelly that to the human eye are indistinguishable from flouwen except for a smaller size. Yet, even the largest of these animals are not very intelligent compared to a human, while the smallest flouwen child is much more intelligent than an adult human. These animals roam wild in the ocean, eating the plants growing around the underwater volcanic vents, and each other.

The flouwen hunt and "eat" the smaller of these wild animals whole by absorbing them into the interior of their bodies, using their enzymes to neutralize and digest the enzymes of the animal, then converting the resulting animal units into flouwen units. Larger animals are torn apart into smaller chunks before ingestion. The flouwen have made "pets" of some of these animals, and use them as "hunting dogs" to round up and drive the wild animals. The human equivalent of this situation would be if humans kept tame chimpanzees that were trained to help the humans hunt down and eat wild apes. There is no indication that the flouwen have attempted to domesticate these food animals in order to rise beyond the hunter-gatherer stage. Considering their dominance, there is probably no need for them to do so.

Another type of fauna is a huge gray rock that stays quiescent for long periods of time, only to suddenly explode, stunning all within a hundred meters and capturing them in their sticky thread nets. After absorbing its prey, it re-forms into multiple rocks that slowly convert the captured food into copies of itself.

Still another type of fauna is a bird-like creature that seems to do little except float around, perfume the water, and make twittering sonic vibrations. The flouwen seem to tolerate them as pets, although they do eat them on occasion.

A fourth type of fauna is a light-brown shapeless vegetarian that feeds on the plants that grow around the underwater volcanic jets. These little animals have proved to be fast growing and easy to breed in captivity as they simply subdivide to reproduce. Called "gingersnaps" by the humans, they served as the main stable for the flouwen that joined the humans on the *Prometheus*. Also collected to live in the Eau tank aboard the *Prometheus* was a vicious little predator that seems to be the same shapeless blob as many of the other fauna—but these "sharp soggies" also have six sharp triangular teeth that fit together in a circular sphincter. These teeth can be used to sever small pieces from larger animals, even those as large as flouwen, which the sharp soggy then carries off to absorb in safety.

Eau Flora

The major flora on the Eau lobe of Rocheworld are gray and brown plants that look like sedentary rocks with controlled thick clouds about them. They send out streamers and form new bud rocks at the ends. The plants do not use photosynthesis, since the red light from Barnard is too weak. Instead, the whole food chain is based on the energy and minerals emitted by volcanic vents. We have similar isolated colonies of plants and animals around underwater vents in our own ocean depths. All life on Eau is concentrated at these few oases, and the rest of the ocean is barren, without significant numbers of bacteria or other microscopic life-forms. Because of this, the exploration crew for the first landing on Rocheworld was unaware there was anything living on the planet until one of the flouwen made contact with them.

Roche Lobe Biology

The biology on the rocklike Roche lobe of Rocheworld is dominated by the fact that the Roche lobe is a desiccated desert during most of the Rocheworld "year." Since the surface of Roche extends many kilometers higher than the surface of Eau, and the two lobes share a common atmosphere, all of the rain released by the atmosphere falls onto the lowlands of Eau. There is no rain at all on the Roche lobe "high desert." As a result, water only flows on the surface of the Roche lobe during the interplanetary waterfalls from the Eau lobe to the Roche lobe that happen during the close passage of Rocheworld to Barnard during periapsis. The waterfalls only occur during three out of the 160 cycles that make up the Rocheworld "year."

The amount of water transferred from Eau is not large and soaks quickly into the ground, so the rivers and lakes left by waterfalls dry up in less than 12 cycles (three Earth days), producing a very short "wet" season. As a result, the life-forms, both flora and fauna, stay in a long underground hibernation state for most of the year, then revive for a short spurt of growth and reproduction during the short wet season.

Gummies

The "gummies" are the dominant life-forms on the Eau lobe of Rocheworld. These are large, starfish-shaped creatures that have viscous, gumlike bodies with five thick appendages that can be used either as arms or legs. The gummies seem to be distant genetic relatives of the more liquid and formless flouwen, since the two species can eat each other's food without being poisoned. It is suspected that the gummies evolved from an early species of flouwen-like creatures who somehow survived being transported from Eau to Roche during one of the interplanetary waterfalls.

During the dry season, the gummies stay buried deep underground, their skin hardened to an impervious rock-like exterior. Reaching out from their body are long "roots" that search through the surrounding soil for whatever water can be found in the soil. Safe in a marsupial pouch of the gummie is a large child. During the long dry season, the gummie supplies the child with small amounts of water and nourishment, but both primarily live on nutrients stored in their bodies at the start of the hibernation. Instead of sleeping, the gummie spends the hibernation time educating the child, preparing it for the ordeal it faces during the short wet season. This knowledge is primarily transferred to the child by the means of memory juices, followed up by questions and discussions of hypothetical examples of problems the child will face.

At the time of the first of the three floods, water begins to seep down through the soil, softening the stone-like exterior of the gummie. The gummie pulls in its roots, and digs its way out of the damp soil with its five strong legs. Around it other gummies are arising from the soil. Their hibernation sites were picked so they would be along the shore of a temporary lake that forms during the first flood. The lake is already teeming with fast-growing plant life and smaller animals that have been hibernating in the lake bottom. The gummies stomp to the shore, and eject the young gummies out of their pouches into the water.

The young gummies then immediately swim out like young five-legged squid after the multitudinous prey, which in turn is feeding as fast as it can on the rapidly growing plant life.

Smaller scavenger animals built like toothed snakes and badgers come out of hiding, and using their sense of smell, burrow down to gnaw on gummies that didn't make it through the drought. The living gummies prey in turn on these animals, enveloping them in their five arms like a starfish attacking a clam. The basic rule is that the larger animal wins the absorption battle, although the vermin have sharp crystalline teeth with which they can run up to a gummie from behind, rip off a piece of a leg, and run away to devour it.

After eating all the vermin visible, and digging up and devouring the dead gummies that are left, the gummies follow their offspring into the water, where they swell and form an efficient five-legged squidlike swimming shape and join in the frenzied feeding. Everyone eats as fast as they can, for within a few days, the lake will have dried up. Young gummies have to be careful not to get too close to a hungry older gummie.

Some time after the third flood has passed, the waters of the lake start soaking into the ground and evaporating away. The gummies, now much larger, come on shore. They squeeze excess water from their bodies until the central portion and five stumpy, elephant-like legs have a gumlike consistency that is strong enough to allow the gummie to hold itself upright in the low gravity. The gummies then engage in primitive, animal-like dominance rituals preparatory to sex.

The starfishlike creatures lift up on three stumpy wide-footed gumlike rubbery legs and challenge each other with the two other legs, which elongate, like an elephant's trunk. The two largest gummies, after sizing everyone else up, finally find each other. Then, instead of fighting, they mate. As with the flouwen, each gummie contributes a portion of his body mass to form the child. In this case they each contribute one "arm." (The arm later regrows.) Again, as with the flouwen, the colored liquid in the arm is extracted back into the main body of the gummie before the arm of now-clear jelly pinches off. The two arms' worth of material join into a single clear blob, held in the arms of its two parents. It then bifurcates into two equal-sized blobs—infant gummies. Each gummie takes one child, and the two separate and go their own ways. Each gummie holds its child lovingly until the child has developed its own color and starts talking. The gummies then put the child in a large marsupial pouch, where it will stay, grow, and be educated by the parent during the long, upcoming drought. This sexual act has been observed by both humans and flouwen many times. It is always completely symmetric, and does not have one partner playing a different role from the other. Like the flouwen, it seems that the gummies do not have different sexes, although they do practice the sexual act of crossmixing genetic pools, so important to the survival of the species.

With the two largest gummies busy, the next largest gummies find each other and mate, then others follow their example. The objective is to make sure that you and your child have enough mass and water to make it through the long dry period. The youngest gummies often go through their first few mating seasons without producing young. They thus retain more mass than those that produce children, increasing their chances of survival through the dominance games and the dry season ahead.

The gummies, most now large with child, then stake out and defend territorial claims. The ideal piece of territory seems to be a shallow bowl-shaped depression, where water will drain down to nourish the gummie buried under the soil at the bottom. Each gummie tries to keep its neighboring gummies and its water-seeking roots at a distance. The bigger a gummie is, the better it is at dominance games. When the dominance tactic fails, there is a fight. Hampered by their massive children, the gummies are not good fighters. They are too equal in size for one to easily absorb the other, but sometimes one is able to rip a child from another's pouch and absorb that. That consequence is so drastic that fights are infrequent.

After a cycle or two of territorial fights, the territorial boundaries have been set, and marked off with stones. The gummies now take trips to the receding lake, eat what little they can find left in the lake , and soak up as much water as possible into their bodies. They stomp back to their territory on watery legs, and expel the water at the center of their territory, where it soaks into the ground for them to gather later with their roots. Then, they go around the perimeter of their territories, bellowing at neighbors to keep their distance, and moving boundary stones back that have been moved during their absence. When they come to a territory boundary that is temporarily undefended, since the occupant is off soaking in the lake, they often move a string of boundary stones outward so as to claim more territory.

The young gummies are named by their parent during their stay in the birthing pouch over the dry season. The parents, knowing that the future life of their child will be nothing but a series of battles for water, territory, and food, give the child impressive-sounding names that hopefully will intimidate future opponents.

Roche Flora

At the time of the annual flooding of Roche, there is a rapid development of plant life around and in the temporary rivers and lakes formed by the floodwaters. The plants do not seem to use photosynthesis, but instead obtain nourishment from the air full of volcanic gases from the Roche lobe volcanoes, and the water from Eau loaded with ammonia and hydrogen sulfide.

The underwater flora are mostly spongelike, with a large effective surface area to better extract the nourishing dissolved gases and particles out of the water. The land flora grow long strands or ribbons that stream out in the strong winds accompanying the floods.

Roche Fauna

Most of the smaller animals on Roche are formless, eyeless, blobs of colored jelly that live in the temporary lakes during the wet season, and burrow under the ground at the lake bottom in order to survive the dry season. These animals are not much different than the smaller animals the flouwen hunt on Eau. The flouwen have eaten them and report they taste much like the animals at home, but have a distinctly different "flavor." This would seem to indicate that these animals are genetically related to those on Eau through common ancestors that were transferred from the Eau lobe to the Roche lobe during some long-ago interplanetary waterfall. Since the flouwen have the ability to form a rocklike exterior, it is not surprising that the Roche animals and gummies use the same technique in order to hibernate through the dry season.

Out on the shores of the temporary rivers and lakes can be found not only the gummies, but a spectrum of smaller animals designed to prey on the gummies and each other. One species, built like a toothed snake, is legless. Another, which has the size, ferocity, digging ability, and protection of an armor-plated badger, has four legs. A third species is a very fast poisonous razor-toothed giant centipede with 1,028 legs and a scorpionlike stinger in its tail. The snakes and badgers primarily prey on dead or weak gummies that have not survived the dry season in good shape. The centipede will attack a gummie from behind, usually while the gummie is distracted by the challenge of another gummie, rip off a piece of a leg, and run away to devour it, counting on its speed and poisonous stinger to discourage pursuit. All of the animals hibernate underground in the lake beds or along the boundaries between gummie territories.

FALLEN ANGELS

Two refugees from one of the last remaining orbital space stations are trapped on the North American icecap, and only science fiction fans can rescue them! Here's an excerpt from *Fallen Angels*, the bestselling new novel by Larry Niven, Jerry Pournelle, and Michael Flynn.

* * *

She opened the door on the first knock and stood out of the way. The wind was whipping the ground snow in swirling circles. Some of it blew in the door as Bob entered. She slammed the door behind him. The snow on the floor decided to wait a while before melting. "Okay. You're here," she snapped. "There's no fire and no place to sit. The bed's the only warm place and you know it. I didn't know you were this hard up. And, by the way, I don't have any company, thanks for asking." If Bob couldn't figure out from that speech that she was pissed, he'd never win the prize as Mr. Perception.

"I am that hard up," he said, moving closer. "Let's get it on."

"Say what?" Bob had never been one for subtle technique, but this was pushing it. She tried to step back but his hands gripped her arms. They were cold as ice, even through the housecoat. "Bob!" He pulled her to him and buried his face in her hair.

"It's not what you think," he whispered. "We don't have time for this, worse luck."

"Bob!"

"No, just bear with me. Let's go to your bedroom. I don't want you to freeze."

He led her to the back of the house and she slid under the covers without inviting him in. He lay on top, still wearing his thick leather coat. Whatever he had in mind, she realized, it wasn't sex. Not with her housecoat, the comforter and his greatcoat playing chaperone.

He kissed her hard and was whispering hoarsely in her ear before she had a chance to react. "Angels down. A scoopship. It crashed."

"Angels?" Was he crazy?

He kissed her neck. "Not so loud. I don't think the 'danes are listening, but why take chances? Angels. Spacemen. *Peace* and *Freedom*."

She'd been away too long. She'd never heard spacemen called *Angels*. And— "Crashed?" She kept it to a whisper. "Where?"

"Just over the border in North Dakota. Near Mapleton."

"Great Ghu, Bob. That's on the Ice!"

He whispered, "Yeah. But they're not too far in."

"How do you know about it?"

He snuggled closer and kissed her on the neck again. Maybe sex made a great cover for his visit, but she didn't think he had to lay it on so thick. "We know."

"We?"

"The Worldcon's in Minneapolis-St. Paul this year—"

The World Science Fiction Convention. "I got the invitation, but I didn't dare go. If anyone saw me—"

"—And it was just getting started when the call came down from *Freedom*. Sherrine, they couldn't have picked a better time or place to crash their scoopship. That's why I came to you. Your grandparents live near the crash site."

She wondered if there was a good time for crashing scoopships. "So?"

"We're going to rescue them."

"We? Who's we?"

"The Con Committee, some of the fans—"

"But why tell me, Bob? I'm fafiated. It's been years since I've dared associate with fen."

Too many years, she thought. She had discovered science fiction in childhood, at her neighborhood branch library. She still remembered that first book: *Star Man's Son*, by Andre Norton. Fors had been persecuted because he was different; but he nurtured a secret, a mutant power. Just the sort of hero to appeal to an ugly-duckling little girl who would not act like other little girls.

SF had opened a whole new world to her. A galaxy, a

universe of new worlds. While the other little girls had played with Barbie dolls, Sherrine played with Lummox and Poddy and Arkady and Susan Calvin. While they went to the malls, she went to Trantor and the Witch World. While they wondered what Look was In, she wondered about resource depletion and nuclear war and genetic engineering. Escape literature, they called it. She missed it terribly.

"There is always one moment in childhood," Graham Greene had written in *The Power and the Glory*, "when the door opens and lets the future in." For some people, that door never closed. She thought that Peter Pan had had the right idea all along.

"Why tell *you*? Sherrine, we want you with us. Your grandparents live near the crash site. They've got all sorts of gear we can borrow for the rescue."

"Me?" A tiny trickle of electric current ran up her spine. But . . . *Nah.* "Bob, I don't dare. If my bosses thought I was associating with fen, I'd lose my job."

He grinned. "Yeah. Me, too." And she saw that he had never considered that she might not go.

'Tis a Proud and Lonely Thing to Be a Fan, they used to say, laughing. It had become a *very* lonely thing. The Establishment had always been hard on science fiction. The government-funded Arts Councils would pass out tax money to write obscure poetry for "little" magazines, but not to write speculative fiction. "Sci-fi isn't literature." *That* wasn't censorship.

Perversely, people went on buying science fiction without grants. Writers even got rich without government funding. *They couldn't kill us that way!*

Then the Luddites and the Greens had come to power. She had watched science fiction books slowly disappear from the library shelves, beginning with the children's departments. (That wasn't censorship either. Libraries couldn't buy *every* book, now could they? So they bought "realistic" children's books funded by the National Endowment for the Arts, books about death and divorce, and really important things like being overweight or fitting in with the right school crowd.)

Then came paper shortages, and paper allocations. The science fiction sections in the chain stores grew smaller. ("You can't expect us to stock books that aren't selling." And they can't sell if you don't stock them.)

Fantasy wasn't hurt so bad. Fantasy was about wizards

and elves, and being kind to the Earth, and harmony with nature, all things the Greens loved. But science fiction was about science.

Science fiction wasn't exactly outlawed. There was still Freedom of Speech; still a Bill of Rights, even if it wasn't taught much in the schools—even if most kids graduated unable to read well enough to understand it. But a person could get into a lot of unofficial trouble for reading SF or for associating with known fen. She could lose her job, say. Not through government persecution—of course not—but because of "reduction in work force" or "poor job performance" or "uncooperative attitude" or "politically incorrect" or a hundred other phrases. And if the neighbors shunned her, and tradesmen wouldn't deal with her, and stores wouldn't give her credit, who could blame them? Science fiction involved science; and science was a conspiracy to pollute the environment, "to bring back technology."

Damn right! she thought savagely. We do conspire to bring back technology. Some of us are crazy enough to think that there are alternatives to freezing in the dark. *And some of us are even crazy enough to try to rescue marooned spacemen before they freeze, or disappear into protective custody.*

Which could be dangerous. The government might declare you mentally ill, and help you.

She shuddered at that thought. She pushed and rolled Bob aside. She sat up and pulled the comforter up tight around herself. "Do you know what it was that attracted me to science fiction?"

He raised himself on one elbow, blinked at her change of subject, and looked quickly around the room, as if suspecting bugs. "No, what?"

"Not Fandom. I was reading the true quill long before I knew about Fandom and cons and such. No, it was the feeling of hope."

"Hope?"

"Even in the most depressing dystopia, there's still the notion that the future is something we build. It doesn't just happen. You can't predict the future, but you can invent it. Build it. That is a hopeful idea, even when the building collapses."

Bob was silent for a moment. Then he nodded. "Yeah. Nobody's building the future anymore. 'We live in an Age of Limited Choices.' " He quoted the government line without cracking a smile. "Hell, you don't *take* choices off a list. You *make* choices and *add* them to the list. Speaking of which, have you made your choice?"

That electric tickle . . . "Are they even alive?"

"So far. I understand it was some kind of miracle that they landed at all. They're unconscious, but not hurt bad. They're hooked up to some sort of magical medical widgets and the Angels overhead are monitoring. But if we don't get them out soon, they'll freeze to death."

She bit her lip. "And you think we can reach them in time?"

Bob shrugged.

"You want me to risk my life on the Ice, defy the government and probably lose my job in a crazy, amateur effort to rescue two spacemen who might easily be dead by the time we reach them."

He scratched his beard. "Is that quixotic, or what?"

"Quixotic. Give me four minutes."

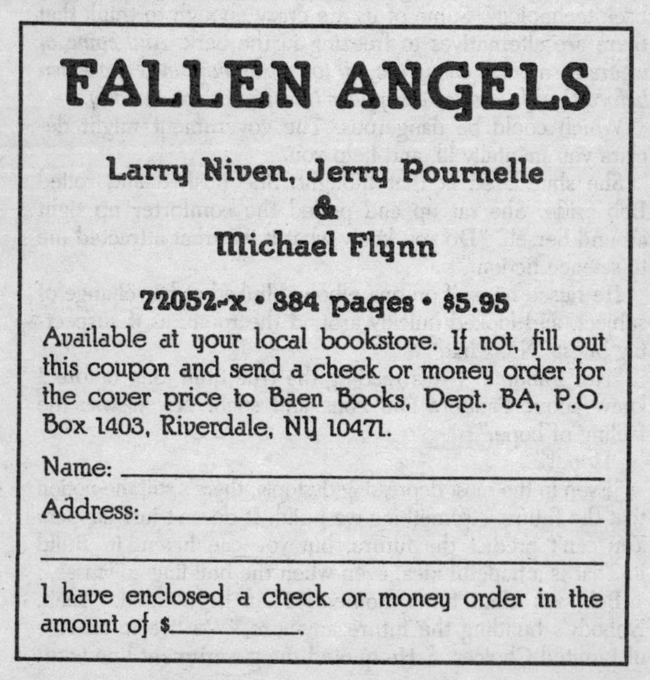